FORGET-ME-NOT BRIDE

Recent Titles by Margaret Pemberton

AN EMBARRASSMENT OF RICHES
MOONFLOWER MADNESS*
A MULTITUDE OF SINS
PIONEER GIRL
TAPESTRY OF FEAR*
WHITE CHRISTMAS IN SAIGON
ZADRUGA

* available from Severn House

FORGET-ME-NOT BRIDE

Margaret Pemberton

This first world edition published in Great Britain 1994 by
SEVERN HOUSE PUBLISHERS LTD of
9–15 High Street, Sutton, Surrey SM1 1DF.
First published in the USA 1995 by
SEVERN HOUSE PUBLISHERS INC., of
425 Park Avenue, New York, NY 10022.

British Library Cataloguing in Publication Data
Pemberton, Margaret
  Forget-me-not Bride
  I. Title
  823.914 [F]

  ISBN 0-7278-4703-1

Typeset by Hewer Text Composition Services, Edinburgh.
Printed and bound in Great Britain by
Hartnolls Ltd, Bodmin, Cornwall.

For MOLLY RUMBELOW

Chapter One

It was the first day of June 1900 but there was no June-like mood in Herbert Mosley's household, high on one of the hills overlooking San Francisco Bay.

'That girl should be whipped!' he thundered as spilt milk ran in rivulets across the damask tablecloth and dribbled on to a hideously patterned Turkish carpet.

'I'm sorry,' Lottie Stullen said contritely, looking not at her enraged uncle but towards her eighteen-year-old sister. 'I didn't mean to do it, Lilli. I just caught the glass with the edge of my hand and . . .'

'It's all right, Lottie,' Lilli said, already mopping the milk up with her napkin. 'No great harm has been done . . .'

'No great harm has been done? *No great harm has been done?*' Her uncle pushed his chair abruptly away from the breakfast table his heavy-jowled face choleric. 'No child of mine would have ever made such a remark! That you have done so is typical of your regrettable upbringing and Irish blood!'

Lilli's face whitened. Since she and her ten-year-old sister and six-year-old brother had, of necessity, moved into her mother's sister's childless home, she had become accustomed to joylessness and petty tyranny. What she had not become accustomed to, and had no intention of becoming accustomed to, were derogatory remarks about her dead father.

'Lottie has made an apology and that should suffice,' she said tightly, pushing her chair away from the table and rising to her feet with an abruptness equal to his own. 'Your remarks about my upbringing and Irishness are totally unwarranted.'

1

Her Aunt Gussie gave a cry of apprehension.

Her little brother, Leo, began to cry.

Lottie clasped her hands tightly in her pinafored lap, hating herself for her clumsiness and hating her English Uncle Herbert even more.

'Your father was a reckless nincompoop who made no provision for his motherless children,' Herbert roared, his hands splayed on the table as he stood, resting his weight on them, leaning bullishly towards her.

Lilli didn't flinch but her forget-me-not-blue eyes flashed fire. 'My father was a gentleman, as any other gentleman would have been well aware!'

Herbert sucked in his breath, hardly able to believe his ears. 'Into my study!' he hissed, ugly splodges of white mottling his flushed colour. 'No-one talks to me like that in my own house! Especially not a slip of a girl who, if it wasn't for my charity, would be on the streets, begging!'

Only responsibility for Leo and Lottie prevented Lilli from retorting that begging would be far preferable to living with him in his tomb of a house. She had, she knew, already gone too far. If he wanted he could turn her out of his hateful house and then what would happen to Leo and Lottie? Her uncle would never allow her to take them with her. Childless himself, she had overheard him discussing with her aunt the possibility of changing Leo's surname from Stullen to Mosley. It was an action she had vowed he would take only over her dead body, but it had served to show the direction of his thoughts and it was a direction that filled her with dark foreboding.

As she followed him out of the room she wondered for the hundredth time how the three of them were ever going to escape him.

At eighteen she was old enough and capable enough to make her own way in the world, but to do so would mean relinquishing Leo and Lottie totally to her aunt and uncle's care. If only her Aunt Gussie were a little more forceful the dilemma might not be so great, but her mother's sister was anything but forceful. Whatever her husband said, she bided by. And she was hungry for children of her own.

2

As she crossed the hallway towards her uncle's study, Lilli was aware that in refusing to be brow-beaten by him she wasn't, in fact, behaving very sensibly. Such behaviour would merely provide him with the ideal excuse to disclaim responsibility for her and he would then have complete guardianship over Leo and Lottie. Hateful though the prospect was, she was going to have to apologise to him. And then she was going to have to think of a way in which she could care for Leo and Lottie without being beholden to her aunt and uncle in any way. '

'Shut the door!' he ordered as she walked into the room after him.

With her head high, her jawline tense, she did as he bid.

He was seated at a large desk that fronted a window through which could be seen a cloud-flecked sky and a corner of the fifty mile expanse of water that was the Bay. He breathed in deeply and then said unequivocally, 'I demand an apology.'

Everything about him was tense: his voice; the set of his shoulders; the way his hands were clasped together in front of him, the knuckles white. With a tightening of her stomach muscles she realised that he anticipated her refusing to do any such thing, and that he then intended ordering her from the house.

'I apologise,' she said, forcing the words through lips that felt frozen, her only solace the bitter disappointment that flared though his eyes.

'The devil you do!' Once again, like a malevolent Jack-in-the-Box, he sprang to his feet. 'You're being insolent, young lady, and don't think I don't know it!'

'You demanded an apology and I gave it,' she retorted icily, keeping her temper well-curbed, knowing how fatal it might be if she were to lose it. Down in the distant Bay the sun sparkled on the white of furled sails. With a pang she remembered the leap of excitement she had felt when her father's lawyer had told her that San Francisco was to be her new home. Compared to the small Kansan town in which her widowed father had died, it had seemed to promise so much . . .

3

''49ers,' Leo had said, his eyes rounding. 'Don't you remember the stories Pa told us about the Gold Rush? That was San Francisco! Do you think there's still gold to be found there, Lilli? Do you think *we* might find gold?'

Leo's thick thatch of hair was nearly as dark as her own and she had laughed and ruffled his curls. 'The San Francisco Gold Rush took place long ago, in 1849,' she had said lovingly. 'That was why the gold prospectors called themselves '49ers.'

Lottie had said, a catch in her voice, 'If Pa hadn't been ill, I know he would have taken us to Alaska looking for gold, because he told me so.'

Neither Leo or Lilli had doubted her. Going to Alaska, panning for gold, was exactly the sort of adventure to have fired their father's imagination. And if he had lived long enough to have embarked upon it he would most certainly have taken them with him, for he took them everywhere with him.

They had all fallen silent, thinking of the father they had loved so much. An immigrant to America, he had been an incurable optimist, always certain that things were 'going to look up' and that good fortune lay 'just around the corner'.

Sometimes his optimism had been well-founded. There had been a time, when their mother had been alive, when home had been an exceedingly comfortable ranch-hand's cabin in Wyoming. Like nearly all Irishmen, Connor Stullen had had magic in his hands when it came to horse-flesh, and it had been when he was working with horses that he had been happiest.

His brother-in-law, an immigrant of a very different stamp, had had no time for a man who earned his living in such a gypsyish fashion. Herbert liked to think of himself as being a businessman, though exactly what his business was remained a family mystery . . .

Nearly as tall as he was, her eyes holding his, Lillie faced Herbert across the solidly built surface of his leather-topped desk. From the moment she had stepped across his threshold, holding Leo and Lottie by the hand, she

4

had known that she was not welcome. The knowledge had shocked her, but it had been a shock her resilient nature had quickly come to terms with.

What she had not been able to come to terms with was the growing realisation that though she was definitely not wanted, and Lottie was only tolerated under sufferance, Leo was wanted very much indeed.

At first she had thought the favouritism shown towards her little brother was simply the favouritism often shown towards the youngest of a family, especially if the youngest were a boy. Then, as she became more attuned to the tense atmosphere in the childless household and to a better understanding of her uncle's character, the ugly truth dawned. Herbert believed Leo was young enough to be moulded by him; young enough to have all traces of Irish accent eradicated from his speech; young enough to be reared as his son and for the world to be duped into believing that he *was* his son.

'You're an insolent chit and you've sponged on my generosity long enough,' her *bête noir* said now, with savage vehemence, spittle forming at the corners of his thin-lipped mouth. 'If your father's boasting about how talented and educated you are were true, you'd be able to find employment quick enough, though as he alone was responsible for that education I don't imagine it amounts to much!'

Lilli, steeped in an upbringing that had embraced her father's idiosyncratic view of world history, the very best in Irish literature, a detailed knowledge of Greek mythology, a wide understanding of botany and the medicinal use of herbs, the ability to play both an accordion and a fiddle and the ability to care for and cure sick horses, remained silent. She also knew her Bible and she had no intention of casting her pearls before swine.

Her refusal to retaliate to his goading enraged Herbert to near apoplexy. 'I want you out of this house today!' he shouted, slamming his fist down hard on the top of his desk. 'I've no legal obligation towards you, and your insolent behaviour has ensured I have no moral obligation either!'

The very idea of Herbert Mosley feeling bound by moral obligations of any sort was so farcical that under other circumstances, Lilli would have hooted with laughter. Instead, knowing how difficult he would make it for her to return for Lottie and Leo if she once left without them, she said tautly, 'It's unreasonable to expect me to leave the house when I have no employment and nowhere to go.'

Satisfaction flared across Herbert's face. 'So you've realized your predicament at last, have you? You should have thought of it much earlier, young lady!'

Lilli's stomach lurched sickeningly. Dear Lord, how low was she going to have to sink in order to gain herself time? Time to find employment; time to find a home for herself and Lottie and Leo; time to think of a way of achieving both without Herbert being able to trace them.

With her hands behind her back, her fingers crossed so the deceit wouldn't stain her soul she said, struggling to sound suitably contrite, 'I've already apologised once for what you perceived as my insolence and I apologise again.'

Her uncle wasn't fooled for a moment.

'You can apologise until the Second Coming!' he snapped viciously. 'And while you're doing so, you can search *The Examiner*'s "Domestics Wanted" column for a suitable situation.'

Striding from around his desk he snatched a copy of the local newspaper from its surface and thrust it into her unwilling hands. 'I want you out of here by the time I return home this evening. Is that understood?'

He was so near to her that she could smell his tobacco-tainted breath. It was clear now, that her uncle had made up his mind as to what the outcome of their interview was going to be and she was wasting her time trying to placate him. Abandoning pretence she held his eyes unflinchingly, letting all her contempt for him show.

'And you needn't think you can take Charlotte and Leopold with you,' he said, falling back a step beneath the force of her gaze. 'No-one will employ you as a live-in maid if you have two brats in tow.'

'What makes you so sure I'll be looking for employment in the "Domestics Wanted" column?' she retorted tartly. She was rewarded by seeing a flash of doubt flare through her uncle's eyes. It disappeared almost immediately.

He gave a bark of laughter. 'How stupid of me! I'd forgotten about your grandiose education. You'll no doubt get employment as a school-mistress or a book-keeper. I only hope your superior salary will be enough to enable you to rent a house and provide a nurse for Leopold,' and, chuckling to himself, he turned on his heel and walked out of the room.

Lilli remained, standing a foot or so before his desk. His amusement was quite justified. Any chance of her finding employment other than that of domestic work was extremely unlikely and, even if she were lucky enough to do so, who would then care for Lottie and Leo?

Dimly, from the direction of the breakfast room, she could hear Aunt Gussie's voice raised in protest. No doubt her husband was informing her of the action he had just taken. Her aunt would be devastated, but it would be a devastation that would count for very little.

She hugged her arms, trying to fight down her rising sense of panic. What on earth was she going to do? She couldn't possibly leave Lottie and Leo in Herbert Mosley's care, yet neither could she see a way in which she could take them with her. And even if she could take them with her, where was she to go?

No more vain protests could be heard coming from the direction of the breakfast room. Instead, there came the sound of muffled weeping. Lilli drew in a deep, steadying breath. In the few months she had been living in the house, there had been many occasions when her aunt had turned to her for comfort, but with the best will in the world she felt no inclination to offer it now.

There came the sound of the front door slamming, and a feeling of palpable relief settled over the house. Herbert was gone, attending to his many business affairs, hopefully until early evening.

'*Lilli! Lilli!*' Lottie shouted, hurtling out of the breakfast room, and running across the hall towards the study. '*Lilli, are you all right?*'

She rocketed into the room, tears streaming down her face. 'You're not going to leave us, are you, Lilli?' she demanded, flinging her arms around Lilli's waist. 'Tell me Uncle Herbert didn't mean it when he said you were to leave the house! Tell me he was only being bullying and beastly and trying to frighten us!'

Lilli's arms folded around her. 'I'm not going to leave you, sweetheart,' she promised, her eyes burning with fierce resolve.

Lottie's hiccupping sobs began to ease but she made no attempt to let go of her big sister. Instead, still hugging her, she said passionately, 'I *hate* Uncle Herbert. He doesn't like you or me. He only likes Leo and I don't think he truly likes Leo, because if he did he wouldn't upset him by telling him he'd told you to leave the house.'

'He was telling Leo the truth,' Lilli said wryly, stroking the top of Lottie's neatly braided hair. 'But I'm going to find a way for us *all* to leave this loveless heap of stones. Pa would never have wanted us to stay here, not if he'd known what it was like, and he never legally gave any of us into Uncle Herbert's and Aunt Gussie's guardianship. Pa's lawyer only sent us here because Aunt Gussie is our next of kin and it never occurred to him that we might not be wanted.'

'Leave?' Lottie turned her face to Lilli's, her eyes widening, hope shining so strong that Lilli's heart tightened. 'Oh, Lilli! Can we? Can we really? Will Uncle Herbert allow it?'

Lilli's face was grim. 'Uncle Herbert is going to have no say in the matter. From now on we're going to make our own decisions.'

As Lottie sighed in ecstasy Lilli looked around the study. Normally it was a sacred sanctum that no-one entered unless commanded to do so. That her uncle had walked out of it leaving her behind him, alone in it, was evidence of how intently his mind had been focussed on the prospect of ridding himself of her.

8

'I'm going to have to visit lots of employment agencies,' she said to Lottie, taking hold of one of the hands clasped tightly around her waist. 'I want you to look after Leo and to collect all your clothes and belongings together. I don't know where Aunt Gussie has put the bags we brought with us. They're probably in an attic somewhere.'

'Do you want me to look for them?' Lottie's voice was eager. 'I've always wanted to go into the attics and . . .'

'No.' With one hand holding the newspaper and the other hand still clasping Lottie's, Lilli began to walk out of the room. 'Goodness only knows how many attics this house has. You could be days looking for them. I'm simply going to tell Aunt Gussie that I'm taking the two of you with me and that I need our travel-bags.'

'She won't like it,' Lottie said prophetically. 'She likes our being here. It stops her from being lonely.'

As they began to walk across the hall and back into the breaskfast room Lilli felt a stab of guilt. What Lottie said was true. Their aunt *did* like them being there. Ineffectual though she was, her affection for all three of them was sincere, and when Herbert discovered he had been robbed of Leo it would be her aunt who would suffer the consequences. For the merest fraction of a second Lilli's resolve faltered. Then she remembered her uncle's intention of changing Leo's name from Stullen to Mosley. With steely determination she entered the breakfast room.

Her aunt was still seated at the table, one arm comfortingly around a bewildered Leo, the other clutching a tear-damp handkerchief.

'Oh, my dear Lilli!' she said in distress, rising clumsily to her feet. 'What on earth are we to do? Once your uncle makes up his mind about something nothing will change it! Oh, if only you hadn't antagonised him so!'

Lilli suppressed a surge of exasperation. Her antagonising her uncle had had very little to do with his decision to order her from the house. It had merely served as an excuse for an action he had long wanted to take, and it was typical of her aunt that she should fail to see that. The large hand on the grandfather-clock in the corner of the room was coming up to half-past-nine, and she was acutely aware of how much she had to accomplish, in such little time, if Leo and Lottie, as well as herself, were to be out of the house by the time her uncle returned to it. She certainly had no time to waste in comforting her aunt.

'If you could ask one of the maids to hunt down our travel-bags I'd be very grateful, Aunt Gussie,' she said practically.

It wasn't the reaction her aunt had anticipated and her eyes flew wide. 'But where will you go?' she protested. 'What will you do?'

There were times when Lilli found it near impossible to believe that her much-loved dead mother had been her Aunt Gussie's younger sister. Her mother hadn't possessed an impractical bone in her body. It had been her Irish husband who had been the day-dreamer and the incurable romantic. Only physical resemblance had borne witness to the blood relationship between the two sisters. Even now, in her late forties, Gussie Mosley was still a stunningly pretty woman. Her blue eyes were wide-set and thick-lashed, her heart-shaped face delicately boned. It was bone structure Lottie and Lilli had also inherited, but where their aunt's finely modelled chin betrayed weakness, their chins bore more than a trace of Irish pugnaciousness.

'I don't know,' Lilli answered truthfully. 'But wherever I go and whatever I do I shall take . . .'

It was Lottie who squeezed her hand, silencing her in mid-sentence.

Their aunt still had one arm protectively around Leo.

Lilli sucked in her breath sharply. Because of her aunt's basic good nature and kindness she had forgotten that she, too, was as eager as her husband to rear Leo as her own son. So eager, that if she knew Leo was about to be taken away it was possible she would send a message to Herbert demanding that he return to the house to deal with the situation. Certainly there was more than mere protectiveness in the way she was holding Leo so closely against her. There was flagrant ownership.

'. . . all my belongings,' she finished adroitly.

'*You're not to go! You're not to go!*' Leo burst out, anguished. Twisting himself away from his aunt's hold, he flung himself into Lilli's arms. 'Pa's ghost will haunt you and haunt you if you leave us!'

Lilli's heart tightened in her chest as she gently took hold of his hands and removed them from around her waist. 'I'm not going to do anything that isn't for the best for all us,' she said gently, offering him as much comfort as she could without awakening her aunt's suspicions.

Lottie's eyes met hers in complicit understanding. 'Don't be such a baby, Leo,' she said in mock exasperation. 'Let's begin packing Lilli's clothes for her. And do stop blubbing. You're only making a rotten situation even worse.'

Thirty minutes later, with a short navy box-coat over her striped pink shirtwaist and cream serge skirt and with her thick cloud of smoke-dark hair piled high in a loose twist on top of her head, Lilli boarded a cable car en route for the commercial heart of the city. It was not a part of the city she was familiar with. The Mosley home, high on Nob Hill, was situated in a superior residential enclave far removed from the rumbustiousness of the areas adjacent to the waterfront.

'Curve!' the cable car conductor yelled. 'Hang on tight!'

Lilli, a novice where cable car riding was concerned, took his advice as the cable car turned a steeply sloping corner almost at a right-angle.

Unnerving though the journey was, it was also exhilarating. She could see Telegraph Hill, its slopes thick with the low, balconied houses of Mexican immigrants, while to the right, Russian Hill towered even higher. Far below, in front of her, lay the glorious spread of the Bay, the early summer sunshine glinting on hundreds of masts and sheening the water to a glittering sapphire.

With a surge of wanderlust she wondered where the many great ships at anchor had sailed from. No doubt many of them had struggled around the roaring hell of Cape Horn while others had probably crossed the Pacific, heavy with spices from the Orient. There were gaunt whaling ships and

11

gaily painted Neapolitan fishing-boats and an armada of private yachts. A smile touched the corners of her mouth. Her father would have loved San Francisco. It possessed a raw edge of excitement that would have deeply appealed to his adventurous spirit.

As the cable car swooped and dipped over other cable car lines, creaking nearer and nearer to the city's harbour adjacent heart, she removed the newspaper from beneath her arm and shook it open at its front page.

There was a report from Kroonstad, South Africa, on the progress of the war taking place between Great Britain and the Boers. Nearer to home there was a report of a speech President McKinley had made to a Republican gathering in New York. On the first inside page there was a photograph of a bride and groom under the headline, *'Bride who shopped for a groom returns to City'*.

Mildly interested, Lilli read on.

'Thirty-year-old spinster, Harriet Dutton, transformed her life a year ago when, via the Peabody Marriage Bureau, she answered gold-miner, Daniel Berton's, advertisement for a wife. Six months ago Mr Berton struck gold in Nome, Alaska and the couple have now returned to the city where Mr Berton intends investing his new-found riches in San Franciscan real estate.'

The groom, heavily moustached and looking awkward in an ill-fitting frock-coat, was smiling sheepishly, one of the bride's net-gloved hands tucked shyly into the crook of his arm. He had the face of an upright, honourable man and Lilli hoped he and his wife would continue to be happy together. There was nothing else of interest on the page and she turned to the Classified Advertisement column. All the employment agencies in the city were listed. All seemed to be clustered south of Market Street, between Eighth Street and the waterfront.

'City Hall!' the conductor yelled as the cable car approached the junction of Market and Larkin Street. 'City Hall!'

Hastily folding the *Examiner* and tucking it once more under her arm, Lilli stepped off the cable car into the busy street. Heads turned in her direction as she did so. Her Celtic colouring of smoke-dark hair, pale creamy skin and deep blue, thick-lashed eyes was a stunning combination and she attracted many appreciative male stares as she walked at a brisk pace towards the nearest of the employment agencies listed in the *Examiner*.

'All the book-keepers we place are required to have previous experience and references,' a thin-lipped, bespectacled woman said to her primly. 'As for a position as a school-mistress . . .' Her rimless spectacles slid down her bony nose. 'No-one under the age of twenty-five is ever considered, no matter how impressive their qualifications. And your qualifications, Miss Stullen, are non-existent.'

She met with a similar response at the next, and then the next, employment agency she visited. Gritting her teeth she then tried her luck at an agency that dealt only with domestic and catering staff.

'And where were you last employed as a chamber-maid, Miss Stullen?' a whey-faced young man inquired.

'I've never been previously employed, but I'm intelligent, quick to learn, hard-working, honest . . .'

The young man looked at her with condescending pity. 'This is a very *selective* employment agency, Miss Stullen. Applicants for positions are required to have experience and . . .'

'I'm looking for a placement as a chamber-maid, not a chef!' Lilli protested frustratedly.

A shutter came down over the young man's palely freckled face. 'Whatever the placement you are looking for, you won't find a placement via *this* agency,' he said, distaste in his voice. 'Domestic staff are required to be polite and respectful, to be seen but not heard . . .'

Lilli didn't wait for him to finish. With her skirt swirling around her ankles she headed for the door, allowing it to swing noisily shut behind her.

Once out in the street she fought down the panic

bubbling in her throat. It was way past lunch-time and she had achieved absolutely nothing. Not only that, she now knew with stomach-churning certainty that her chances of ever achieving the kind of employment she needed, were practically nil. Sick at heart she paused at the street corner, shaking the *Examiner* open yet again, studying the general classified advertisements in the hope that there might be something there:

YOUNG lady, good figure, wants to pose for artist; references exchanged; positively no triflers . . .

ANY person knowing of impending business failures or having any other valuable information can make big money by communicating with smart lawyer . . .

A GENTLEMAN would like to make the acquaintance of a young lady bicyclist matrimonially inclined . . .

CRAFTSMAN desires suitable employment. Urgent . . .

Whoever the last advertiser was, Lilli sympathised with him. She, too, desired suitable employment urgently. The day had become hot and muggy and her head ached. Wryly she wondered what kind of a response she would meet with if she placed an advertisement of her own in the *Examiner*, perhaps,

Young woman (18), penniless, quick-tempered, often accused of being impolite, two young siblings to care for, seeks kind-hearted husband and home . . .

The very ridiculousness of the idea marginally restored her sense of humour. Stuffing the *Examiner* once more beneath her arm she squared her shoulders. She had known before she had set out that her task wasn't going

14

to be easy. Becoming dejected before she had exhausted every possibility was pointless. There were department stores to approach, for department stores were bound to be constantly employing young lady sales assistants. There were other options, too, she hadn't yet explored, such as laundries, hospitals, factories. With renewed resolution she stepped off the sidewalk, intent on crossing the busy street in order to head in the general direction of the great shopping emporiums.

The horse, in the shafts of a hackney cab, skittered as it veered out of her way. Lilli screamed, standing absolutely motionless, unable to believe she hadn't been trampled to the ground.

'*Of all the stupid, idiotic, senseless . . .*' she could hear a male voice expostulating furiously.

Lilli pressed a hand to her palpitating heart. Dear Lord! Another inch and she would have been beneath the horse's hooves! Trembling violently she stepped back upon the sidewalk. The horse, thank heaven, hadn't run amok or injured himself. Though he was still whinnying and tossing his head his driver had regained control of him and had reined him in.

As the fear that had flooded through her ebbed, a feeling of foolishness replaced it. How on earth could she have been so stupid as to have stepped off the sidewalk without looking to see what was approaching? Even more baffling, how could she have been so deep in thought that she hadn't even heard the trotting hooves?

She was aware that the gentleman being conveyed in the carriage had jumped down from it and was striding thunderously towards her. He was perhaps ten years her senior and flamboyantly dressed in a dove-grey lounge suit with pearl-grey facings. There was no customary gold watch-chain looped across his matching chamois vest but his high-collared white linen shirt was worn open at the throat and was as frilled as a woman's.

There was nothing, however, effeminate about the man. He was above average height and as broad-shouldered as a prize fighter. Beneath his Homburg hat his hair

15

was dark blond, cut long and swept back to curl at the collar of his jacket. As he came to a halt, a foot or so away from her, she saw that his eyes were brown and, though she couldn't be absolutely sure, she was almost certain they were gold-flecked. Tanned by the sun and the wind, smelling ever so faintly of lemon cologne, and with a thick, neat moustache, a shade darker than his hair, he was the handsomest man she had ever laid eyes on.

'Are you both blind and deaf?' he demanded, winged eyebrows drawn together satanically.

Under the circumstances, Lilli felt it was a reasonable enough enquiry.

'I'm sorry,' she said, trying to collect her scattered wits. 'I was thinking about something and . . .'

'The only thing you should have been employed thinking about was whether the street was safe to cross!'

He hadn't bothered to lift his hat, and his rudeness and use of the word 'employed' grated on Lilli's already fraught nerves. It was because she had been pondering where next to seek employment that she had been so careless in the first place. Aware that he couldn't know that she checked the tart reply that had risen to her lips and said instead, 'I'm sorry if I frightened the horse.'

The unexpectedness of her response checked his anger, as did the realization that she had eyes so true a blue they were almost azure, and a mouth tantalizingly full and soft. A flicker of amusement, and something else, entered his eyes. 'Don't worry about the horse. Such incidents are all in a day's work for a hackney. He didn't make contact with you, did he? You're not hurt?'

It was a rather belated enquiry and she said stiffly, 'No. I merely gave myself a bad scare.'

'You gave *me* a bad scare.' he said wryly, his mouth tugging into a smile.

Lilli felt her stomach somersault. If he had been handsome before, when angry, he looked like a Greek god now that he was smiling.

'Hey mister!' the hackney cab driver shouted across to him. 'Do you still want taking to the Barbary Coast?'

16

The Greek god signalled assent and then, manners showing for the first time, inclined his head slightly towards her. 'Goodbye, ma'am,' he said, the amusement and admiration in his eyes now naked, 'and take a little more care crossing city streets. San Francisco isn't the Emerald Isle, you know.'

Lilli sucked in her breath, colour rushing to her cheeks. Thanks to her father, her speech occasionally betrayed a slight Irish lilt, but as her mother had been English, and she had been born in England, she never thought of herself as being Irish, and she certainly never thought of herself as having just stepped off a boat from Cork!

'I've never even been to Ireland . . .' she began indignantly, but she was wasting her breath. He had already turned away from her.

Dazedly she watched as he strode back across the busy street and sprang agilely into the hackney. Had that been a small gold earring she had glimpsed when he had bent his head slightly and bidden her goodbye? And was he really going to the notoriously lawless waterfront area known as the Barbary Coast?

She remained standing on the corner of the street, watching until the hackney was swallowed up in a maelstrom of other carriages and carts. An earring! Did that indicate that despite his superbly tailored attire, he was a sailor? His skin had been sun and wind-tanned enough. Or was he perhaps one of the Barbary Coast's many saloon-keepers? She had never met a saloon-keeper but she found it hard to imagine that they dressed so elegantly.

Someone squeezing past on the crowded sidewalk behind her, jarred her, nearly sending her once more precipitately into the street. She tucked her copy of the *Examiner* more securely beneath her arm. She had far more important things to do than stand staring after a man whose name she didn't know, and whom she was unlikely ever to see again. Somehow she had to secure herself a sales position in one of the city's department stores, and, at a salary that would enable her to rent somewhere for herself, and Leo and Lottie, to live.

* * *

17

As the hours crept by and the sun began to creep further and further westwards, it became increasingly obvious that she hadn't a hope of ever doing so. Sales positions were offered to her, but always the salary was totally inadequate for her needs.

'How much rent do you say you can afford?' landlords and landladies asked jeeringly. 'Do me a favour, lady. You couldn't rent a parrot's perch for that!'

Hot, hungry and exhausted she trailed up and down street after street, trawling the city from Howard Street in the south to Lombard Street in the north, from Montgomery Street in the east to Alamo Square in the west. Nor was money, or the lack of it, her only problem.

'Two children and no husband?' she was asked, eyes quickly flying to Lilli's ringless left hand. 'I can imagine your profession, lady. And it ain't wanted round here!'

Door after door was closed in Lilli's face.

By the time she heard a distant clock striking five, tears of desperation were burning the backs of her eyes. What, in God's name, was she going to do? She couldn't, *couldn't*, leave the house on Nob Hill without taking Lottie and Leo with her. She had given Lottie her most solemn promise that she wouldn't do so, and if she didn't keep that promise she would never be able to live with herself.

Wearily she began to climb yet another of San Francisco's interminable hills. The employment agency she was seeking wasn't one advertised in the *Examiner*, but was one that had been suggested to her by another employment agency manager. It was her last hope. Time was fast running out for, once her uncle returned home, her chances of leaving the house with Leo would be nil. The very thought of her uncle, and his intentions where Leo was concerned, sent shivers down her spine. She would not allow Leo to be brought up and to be known as Herbert Mosley's child.

'I will *not*,' she said tautly, beneath her breath.

A middle-aged woman walking a few feet behind her eyed her uneasily.

Lilli's hands clenched into fists. 'I will not, I will not!' she vowed with increasing passion.

Preferring to be safe, rather than sorry, the woman hastily crossed the street.

'The Golden Gate Hotel is looking for chamber-maids,' the greasy-haired middle-aged man at the agency said to her uninterestedly, not bothering to remove a cheroot from his mouth. 'Other than that we have laundry-work, bar-work, domestic cleaning . . .'

'At what kinds of salary?' Lilli asked, tucking a stray strand of hair into the loose knot on top of her head, not caring what the work was if only it would pay her enough to be able to provide for Leo and Lottie.

The man rolled his cheroot to the other side of his mouth and told her. For the first time in her life Lilli felt hysteria bubble up in her throat. No wonder her uncle had laughed when she had intimated she could find an adequately paid job. He had known how impossible it would be. He had known she would never be able to remove Leo and Lottie from his care.

Sick at heart she walked out of the office wondering how other women managed to earn a reasonable and respectable living when employers paid female workers a pittance, and when the choice of work available to them was so limited. She remembered some of the advertisements in the classified column of the *Examiner* and her mouth tightened. The answer was, of course, that the vast majority of women, through no fault of their own, never did manage to fend for themselves; instead they turned to the only alternative there was. Marriage.

She stood on the sidewalk engulfed in despair, not knowing which direction to take next, knowing only that she had let down the two people she loved most in the world; the two people who trusted her implicitly.

On the far side of the street a brass name-plaque gleamed dully in the late afternoon sunshine. The name engraved on it was clearly visible. It was The Peabody Marriage Bureau.

*   *   *

Lilli stared at it, remembering the article she had read in the *Examiner*. As the letters danced before her eyes her heart began to beat in slow, slamming strokes.

She remembered how happy the bride had looked; she remembered Lottie saying how, if he hadn't been ill, their father would have taken them to Alaska, panning for gold; she remembered how excited Leo had been at the very mention of the word 'gold-miner'; she remembered how far Alaska was from California and how Herbert Mosley would never be able to trace them if they went there.

The blood drummed in her ears. A husband would provide a home, and if he provided a home for her, why should he not also provide one for Leo and Lottie? It was common knowledge that men living far from female company, desperate for wives, often married widows. If widows with small children were eligible in these particular marriage stakes, why not not a young woman with a dependent young brother and sister?

The sidewalk seemed to tilt beneath her tired feet. It was a preposterous idea; totally ludicrous. Yet it was the only idea she was left with and, if she jettisoned it, what would happen to the two vulnerable little people she loved best in all the world?

She knew what would happen and she knew it was something she could never allow. Her heart began to beat faster. It would mean abandoning hope of one day falling in love and marrying the man of her dreams. An image of an Americanized Greek God in a dove-grey lounge-suit, a Homburg at a rakish angle, sprang unbidden to her mind. She banished it. Her own happiness was not important. It was Leo and Lottie's happiness that was at stake.

She prided herself on having inherited her mother's practical nature and in the present circumstances practicality decreed only one course of action. Taking a deep breath, her heart racing, she crossed the street and knocked purposefully on the half frosted glass door of The Peabody Marriage Bureau.

Chapter Two

'Alaska?' Amy Peabody, motherly and the wrong side of fifty, was unsurprised by the request. Ever since the *Examiner* had run the story of Mr Daniel Berton's strike at Nome and of how the now fabulously rich gold-prospector had returned to San Francisco with his wife, a wife he had been introduced to via the Peabody Marriage Bureau, the bureau had been inundated with enquiries from young women eager to emulate the lucky Mrs Berton. What she *was* surprised at, however, was the present enquirer's striking good looks and confident bearing. Most young women seeking the help of the Peabody tended to be plain. They also tended to be shyly hesitant. The young woman before her was neither.

'Alaska,' Lilli repeated, 'There are gold-miners in Alaska looking for wives, aren't there?'

Amy nodded. There were, but whether they were the kind of gentlemen this particular young woman was looking for was extremely dubious. She said cautiously, 'You seem a little young, Miss Stullen . . .'

'I'm twenty,' Lilli lied. The clock behind Mrs Peabody's head showed five-forty-five. At any minute Herbert Mosley would be returning home. She crossed her fingers, praying to God that one of his business meetings would delay him. 'If I agree to marry one of the men on your books, they will pay my fare to Alaska, won't they?' she asked, anxious to have her most important query answered.

'When a young lady's photograph has been despatched to the gentleman of her choice, that is the arrangement.' She lifted a heavy album onto her desk. 'It is, of course,

21

a reasonably lengthy process. Perhaps you would like to browse through these photographs . . .'

'Lengthy?' Lilli's voice was thick with anxiety. 'How lengthy?'

Amy opened the album and slid it towards her. 'That depends on the time of year, Miss Stullen. In winter, when no boats can reach or leave the Klondike, it can be as much as five months. In summer, of course, matters can be arranged within five or six weeks. Now these gentleman at the beginning of the album are all . . .'

Lilli didn't even look down at the photographs spread in front of her. 'I can't wait five or six weeks,' she said tautly. 'I can't even wait five or six days. I need to leave for Alaska now. Immediately.'

Amy leaned back in her chair, resting her elbows on the arms, steepling her fingers together. She had known the instant Lilli Stullen had entered her office that she wasn't a typical bride-to-be. And now she knew why. Miss Stullen was running away.

Lilli saw the expression in Amy Peabody's eyes and read her thoughts with crystal-clear clarity. Fresh tension knifed through her. If Mrs Peabody believed her to be running away from criminal charges she wouldn't even consider her as a prospective bride-to-be.

She clasped her hands tightly in her lap. 'I'm not wanted by the police,' she said, her eyes burning with truth. 'I have to get away because of . . . because of a family difficulty.'

Amy Peabody prided herself on recognising the truth when she heard it, and she knew she was hearing it now. She sighed, despairing of the male sex, believing she knew the nature of Lilli Stullen's family difficulty. A father, perhaps. Or a brother. It was a story as old as time; a story she had heard all too often.

She said with genuine regret, 'If you had come to me a few hours earlier I might have been able to arrange something. Though the majority of my lady clients prefer photographs to be exchanged and to know something about the gentleman they will be marrying, we do also run a slightly less exclusive system of intro-ductions.'

She paused, waiting for any questions Lilli might have. Lilli had none. She only wanted to know what the 'less exclusive' system entailed.

'The Alaskan Klondike is a very rough and ready part of the world, Miss Stullen. Communications are poor and gold-hungry men are not known for staying long in one place. The minute there is a rumour of a big strike, they are off to seek it out. Consequently there have been times when lady clients have arrived in Dawson City to find no prospective husbands waiting for them.'

The expression in her voice was clear evidence of her poor opinion of the prospective husbands in question.

'And?' Lilli prompted impatiently.

'And to avoid this kind of catastrophe groups of young ladies travel together and introductions are made by a Peabody Marriage Bureau representative in Dawson *after* their arrival, not before.'

Lilli stared at her. It didn't sound any less exclusive a method of finding a husband than leafing through a dog-eared photograph album, in fact it sounded a lot more civilised.

'And fares are still paid?' she asked, focussing on the most important part of the arrangements.

Amy nodded. 'All fares are paid and then, when a gentleman is happy with the lady of his choice, he reimburses the Peabody representative in Dawson for all expenses she has incurred.'

'I want to go,' Lilli said flatly, 'But I don't want to wait until the next group of brides goes to Dawson, I want to go now, on the very next boat.'

Amy shook her head regretfully. 'But that's just the shame of it, my dear. If you had come in here a few hours earlier you could have done so. The *S.S. Senator* sails tonight with six Peabody young ladies aboard her . . .'

Lilli erupted from her chair, hardly able to believe that her luck had changed so dramatically. 'But why didn't you say!' she demanded feverishly. 'What time? What wharf?'

'Dear heavens, Miss Stullen! You can't leave tonight! You won't even have time to pack!'

'*What time?*'

Amy looked into Lilli's blazing blue eyes and knew she was going to be able to accommodate seven male clients in Dawson City, not six. 'Eight-thirty, Wharf 18,' she said succinctly.

Lilli turned swiftly on her heel, saying as she headed for the door, 'Then if you can make the arrangements for me, I shall be aboard.'

'I can certainly obtain a last minute sailing ticket for you.' Amy rose to her feet, knowing that she was going to have to move nearly as fast as her determined young client. 'The name of the Peabody representative in Dawson is Mr Josh Nelson . . .'

'Three tickets,' Lilli said suddenly, one hand on the door-knob.

'*Three?*' Beneath crêpey lids Amy's eyes flew wide.

'One for me and one each for my young brother and sister.' Lilli yanked the door open. 'And don't worry about the cost, Mrs Peabody. My husband-to-be will reimburse Mr Nelson.'

Before a stunned Amy could draw breath to protest, the door slammed shut. Weakly Amy gripped on to the corner of her desk with a steadying hand. What an extremely *forceful* young woman. She could only hope Josh Nelson would be able to cope with the situation when Miss Stullen arrived in Dawson and for the sake of the reputation of her marriage bureau she hoped the husband-to-be would be able to cope also!

'Please don't let Uncle Herbert be in the house,' Lilli muttered like a mantra as the cable car eased its way up Nob Hill with agonising slowness.

The instant it halted and she stepped onto the sidewalk she broke into an unladylike run. 'Please let Lottie have packed everything!' she prayed, sprinting towards the Mosley mansion as if all the hounds of hell were at her heels. 'Please let nothing go wrong now! Please let the three of us be aboard the *S.S. Senator* when she sails!'

'Where on earth have you been, Lilli?' her aunt asked flusteredly, hurrying into the hall as Lilli rushed into the house. 'I've been so worried about you! I really don't think your uncle can possibly have meant the things he said to you this morning. I shall tell him how much it will distress me if he turns you out of the house and . . .'

Lilli sucked in her breath. Much as she wanted to be gentle with her aunt, she couldn't possibly be so. She simply didn't have the time. It had gone six-o-clock when she had left the Peabody Marriage Bureau and it was after seven-o-clock now. She had an hour and a half. An hour and a half in which to collect Leo and Lottie and their travel-bags and leave the house; to travel down-town to the harbour area; to find Wharf 18 and board the boat.

'Uncle Herbert meant every word he said to me this morning,' she said, her breathing still ragged from running; her chest still hurting. 'I'm truly sorry for the distress this is going to cause you Aunt Gussie, but I'm leaving the house and I'm taking Leo and Lottie with me.'

Even as she was speaking she was heading towards the stairs.

'No!' her aunt's cry of protest was anguished. 'No, you can't do that, Lilli!' She began to hurry in Lilli's wake. 'Your uncle didn't mean for you to take the children with you!'

'I know that, Aunt Gussie,' Lilli said dryly. 'But I shall never be separated from them while they are still so young. They've lost Ma and Pa. They're not going to lose me as well.'

As she turned left at the head of the stairs a bedroom door was flung open and Lottie burst out into the corridor. She was dressed for travel in an oatmeal box-coat, toffee-coloured serge skirt, long black-ribbed stockings and high-buttoned shoes. On the back of her head she wore her Sunday-best sailor-hat, held on by elastic beneath her chin, a long blue ribbon hanging down from the back of it.

'I've done everything you asked me to!' she announced jubilantly, her eyes shining, her face radiant. 'I told the maid we needed all three travel-bags and I've squeezed everything possible into them.'

Lilli's relief was vast. She had no idea what the temperature was in Alaska in June but she knew that come the autumn they would need every single article of warm clothing they possessed. 'Get your coats,' she said as Leo tumbled out of the room, 'and all your winter scarves and gloves.'

'*No*!' With one hand pressed to the base of her lace-covered throat, their aunt tried desperately to put an end to the nightmare that had erupted around her. 'Please, Lilli! Please don't take Leo!'

Lilli entered the bedroom and removed a black felt wallet from the back of her wardrobe shelf. It contained money her father had left to them. Money she had guarded carefully. She buried the wallet deep into one of the travel-bags and then turned to face her aunt, saying starkly, 'I'm sorry, Aunt Gussie, but Ma wouldn't have wanted the three of us to be separated, you know that.'

Her aunt opened her mouth to protest yet again and Lilli said with quiet finality, 'And neither would she want Leo's name to be changed from Stullen to Mosley.'

It was a truth her aunt couldn't deny and her face crumpled, tears streaming down her cheeks.

With her own heart hurting Lilli put the bags down and put her arms around her. 'We all care for you, Aunt Gussie,' she said thickly. 'But Uncle Herbert just isn't . . . reasonable about things.'

Her aunt clung to her, not denying it, knowing she had lost the battle, as she lost every battle.

From downstairs there came the sound of the front door opening and someone entering the hall. All four of them froze.

'It's Uncle Herbert!' Lottie whispered, her pupils dilating.

It was then, as Lilli's mind raced to think of a way of escape, that her aunt came into her moment of glory.

'Leave the house by the servants' stairs,' she said swiftly as, for the first time in her life, she took charge of a situation. 'I'll tell your uncle that you have already left the house and that Leo and Lottie are upset and have gone to bed early. Go now, my dear! Quickly!'

Lilli needed no urging. Seizing hold of the bags she kissed her aunt on the cheek and with a heavily laden Lottie at her side and Leo trotting hard on her heels, she hurried swiftly towards the servants' staircase.

'*Where are we going?*' Leo whispered as they bundled their way downstairs.

'Alaska.'

'*Alaska!*' Leo lost his footing and toppled down the last two steps. '*Alas . . .*'

Lottie clapped her free hand over his mouth. '*Sssh!*' she hissed, almost as stunned as he was. 'Lilli will tell us all about it when we get out of the house. Now *be quiet*, Leo, or Uncle Herbert will hear us and neither of us will be going anywhere!'

At this time of an evening the domestic staff were all in the kitchens or dining-room. Making a way through the laundry-room and sewing-room they left the house by a rear side-door.

'We've very little time,' Lilli said the instant they were clear of the ornate garden. 'We've certainly no time for questions and explanations. I know the bag you're carrying is heavy, Lottie, but you're going to have to run with it. And despite having little legs, you, Leo, are going to have to keep up with us. Is that understood?'

Leo nodded, his eyes like saucers, barely able to believe the enormity of the adventure they were embarking upon.

'All right.' Lilli's heart pounded as she thought of how little time there was before the *S.S. Senator* sailed, 'Are you both ready? Then let's run!'

Though Lottie and Leo were still unclear as to where they were running to, or why there was so much urgency, they broke into a run that would have done credit to professional athletes.

*   *   *

27

Once aboard the cable car Lilli's breathing began to steady. They had an hour in hand. It was enough. Or it would be as long as they found Wharf 18 without difficulty.

'*Now* can you tell us where we're going?' Lottie asked, panting for breath, her arms wrapped around her cumbersome carpet-bag.

'She's already told us.' Leo's voice was thick with exasperation. 'We're going to *Alaska*! We're going to be part of the Gold Rush! We're going to pan for gold and become millionaires!'

Lottie ignored him. 'Are we really going to Alaska?' she asked, her brows puckering in concern. 'Isn't it terribly far? How are we going to get there? How can we afford it? What will . . .'

'Later, Lottie,' Lilli said, not wanting to think about the whys and wherefores, her entire concentration focussed on one thing and one thing only. Being aboard the *S.S. Senator* when she sailed.

Lottie fell silent, wondering if she had been fatally rash in mentioning to Lilli that their father had had dreams of trekking to Alaska and striking gold. The trouble with Lilli was that, like their father, she was totally unrealistic. A dream seized hold of them and in their enthusiasm to pursue it, everyday commonsense deserted them.

'Which is why your Pa needs me, and your big sister will need you, my pet,' their mother had once confided to her when she was little more than a toddler. 'But never forget that it is our secret for it would hurt their feelings terribly if they knew it was us who looked after them, not the other way around.'

As the cable car eased its way down into the harbour area Lottie couldn't help wondering if Lilli had decided on Alaska as an answer to their problems merely because their father, too, had thought Alaska would be lucky for them. The frown puckering her eyebrows deepened. What on earth would they do there? They couldn't mine for gold themselves. The work would be too hard. And, even if it were not, surely all the prime stakes would have been taken? It was three years now since gold nuggets had been found in the Klondike and the initial great stampede north was largely over. She chewed the corner of her lip, wishing to goodness she knew what it was Lilli had in mind, wishing she were a little older so that Lilli would confide in her a little more.

'We're going to have to hire a hackney now,' Lilli said as they trooped off the cable car into the hurly-burly of a part of the city they were totally unfamiliar with. 'A hackney driver will know where Wharf 18 is and get us there much faster than we'd get there on foot.'

Lottie stumbled, nearly falling over the heavy bag she was carrying. 'You mean we're sailing to Alaska *tonight?*'

Lilli stared at her in astonishment. 'Well of course we are. How else did you think we were going to get there?'

Lottie's long braids had fallen over her shoulders and with her free hand she flicked them back, saying with remarkable restraint, 'All you've told us so far, Lilli, is that we're going to Alaska and that you haven't time for questions and explanations. You never said exactly *when* we were going. Or how.'

'Then I'll tell you now.' Lilli looked around for a hackney. 'We're going by boat and the boat sails in less than an hour. Hackney! *Hackney!*'

The accosted hackney driver nudged his horse in their direction.

'Wharf 18 please,' Lilli said, bundling Leo up into the carriage. 'And take us there as fast as you can!'

The driver, well used to such requests, urged his horse into a brisk trot.

'Is this the Barbary Coast?' Leo asked in awe, staring out into the gathering darkness at cobbled streets crammed with roistering sailors.

A group of heavily rouged women burst out of a noisy saloon, a drunken posse of men at their heels. None of the men was elegantly dressed. None looked as if they had ever, in their lives, worn a Homburg.

'I don't know,' Lilli answered, relieved that her Greek God of the afternoon was not among their midst and yet disappointed at not catching a second glimpse of him. 'Whichever part of the water-front it is, it's certainly exotic.'

She wasn't exaggerating. Turbanned Hindus jostled on the narrow sidewalks with brown-skinned Samoans. Africans loitered in groups on the street corners. Chinese scurried hither and thither. It was a part of San Francisco they had all heard about but never imagined they would see; a part of San Francisco worlds removed from the claustrophobic grandeur of the Mosely mansion on Nob Hill.

'Are you intendin' sailin' on the *Senator*, ma'am?' the hackney driver asked as he left the narrow streets behind and the carriage began to clatter over the even rougher cobbles of the docks.

'Yes. Do you know her?' There was a dizzying array of masts and funnels on their left-hand side. 'Is she a sailing ship or a steamship?'

The driver hooted with laughter. 'You're sailin' on her and you don't known whether she's sail or steam?' He turned his head, looking at her curiously, his amusement fading. 'You do know where the *Senator's* bound, ma'am, don't you?' he asked, an edge of concern entering his eyes.

'Alaska,' Lilli said, Leo's hand tightening on hers.

The driver shrugged. If she knew where she was going then he could be of no further assistance to her. He could, however, give her the benefit of his opinion. 'The gold-fields are no place for youngsters,' he said as he reined his horse in at the foot of the *S.S. Senator's* gangplank. 'And no place for women either, unless they're bar-room floosies.'

Lilli disregarded him. The *S.S. Senator* was a steamer and from the smoke belching from her funnels she was about to set sail at any moment. There was no time to be lost if they were to be aboard when she eased her way out into the Bay. Not a second. With the blood drumming in her ears she jumped down from the carriage. 'Pass me the bags, Lottie! Quickly!' she said, lifting Leo down to the ground after her, not waiting for the driver to come to her assistance.

With difficulty Lottie heaved the heavy carpet-bags down over the side of the carriage. 'There are sailors doing things with ropes at the top of the gangplank,' she panted as she did so.

'What are floosies?' Leo asked, tugging on Lilli's skirt.

'If you intend sailing on that boat you'd better look sharp,' the hackney driver said, taking the last of the bags from Lottie and swinging it to the ground.

'Run to the gangplank, Lottie!' Lilli ordered feverishly, scrambling in her purse for money to pay him. 'They can't pull it up if there's someone on it!'

'What are floosies, Lilli?' Leo asked again as, braids flying, Lottie hurtled over the cobbles and launched herself onto the foot of the gangplank.

'Later, darling. Later.' Lilli hoisted one bag beneath her arm and picked up the other two.

'Good luck, ma'am!' the driver called out as she turned hastily away from him and then, beneath his breath as he urged his horse into movement again, 'You sure as hell are going to need it!'

With her heart beating as if it was going to burst Lilli hurried after Lottie. This was it. This was the moment of truth. Either their names had been added to the passenger list or they hadn't. And if they hadn't . . . She daren't think about what would happen if they hadn't.

'Miss Stullen?' a young seaman asked as he strode down the gangplank to meet her. 'You've left it a little late ma'am, if I may say so.'

'I'm sorry.' Relief was flooding over her in such great, glorious waves she had to fight the temptation to drop the bags and throw her arms around him. They'd done it! They were on the passenger list! In another few minutes they would be *en route* to Alaska and Leo would be out of the clutches of their Uncle Herbert forever.

31

'You're in a cabin with another Peabody lady,' the seaman said, taking two of her bags from her.

Lilli's elation soared even higher. She was going to be travelling with young women of her own age; she would be able to make friends; friends who would remain her friends when they had reached their destination.

As Leo and Lottie took hold of her now freed hands and they followed the young man up onto the deck, Lilli became aware of how many passengers were crowding the rails. There wasn't a woman among them and she assumed they were either prospectors journeying to the gold fields for the first time or prospectors returning to the Klondike after sitting out the winter in California.

The ship's hawsers had begun to be creakingly hauled in and then, as Lilli stepped on to the deck, a sailor shouted, 'Hold the gangplank! We've another late arrival!'

Lilli was too intent on following their luggage to take any interest in what was happening at the dock-side. Until now all her thoughts had been directed towards one end and one end only: being aboard the *S.S. Senator* when she sailed. Now that she *was* aboard, other thoughts crowded her brain. How was she going to tell Lottie and Leo that they were only travelling to Alaska on the understanding that when they arrived there she would marry a woman-starved gold-prospector? Until now she hadn't given that part of the arrangement a thought. Now, for the first time, it occurred to her that perhaps she should have done so.

It was a realisation too drastic to allow for people-watching over the deck rail. While other passengers watched with interest as a tall, lithe, elegantly suited figure strode up the gangplank, a Homburg on his dark-gold hair, an ermine-caped lady companion clinging to his arm, Lilli was following the seaman down a narrow companionway, earnestly wishing she had troubled to look at the Peabody Marriage Bureau's photographic album.

'I'm not sharing with kids,' a rough-edged female voice

32

said categorically as the officer deposited Lilli's bags in the cramped doorway.

'This cabin has four berths.' The seaman lifted Leo over the bags, depositing him in the minuscule space between two sets of bunks. 'And three of them are allocated to Miss Stullen.' He turned to Lilli, taking the bag she was carrying and heaving it on to one of the top bunks. 'If you have any problems ma'am, just seek me out.'

'I won't have any problems.' Lilli was appreciative of his attention but needed no-one to fight her battles for her.

The seaman, with no further excuse to stay and pressing duties elsewhere, regretfully took his leave. His courtesy in showing her to her cabin and carrying her bags had not been standard practice. On board the *Senator*, passengers found their own way around and carried their own bags. He didn't, however, regret for one moment the impulse that had prompted him to hurry down the gangplank to assist her. Girls who carried themselves with the grace of a princess were rare aboard the *Senator* and this particular princess had such a thick abundance of upswept, glossy, night-black hair it was a marvel her slender neck could bear the weight. He wanted to get to know Miss Stullen better. And he had a good four days in which to do so.

'I meant what I said,' the sulky-faced girl sitting on the edge of one of the bottom bunks said as Lilli stepped over the two bulging carpet-bags into the cabin, 'I'm not sharing with kids.'

Lilli took hold of one of the bags and swung it onto the opposite bunk, making way for Lottie to squeeze into the cabin beside her. 'Then you'd better find yourself another cabin,' she said pleasantly, 'because we aren't going to.'

The girl's eyes narrowed. Leo put his thumb in his mouth apprehensively. Lottie held her breath. Lilli remained unconcerned.

The girl, taking Lilli's measure, decided it might be wisest to back down a little. 'Maybe I will, and maybe I won't,' she said truculently, her face half-hidden by dishwater-blonde hair; neither it or her dress too clean. 'Who are the kids? They're too old to be yours.'

'They're my brother and sister,' Lilli said, swinging the second bag high on to a top bunk. 'I'm Lilli Stullen. My sister's name is Lottie and my brother is Leo.'

The girl snorted, saying in a voice heavy with sarcasm. 'Didn't your ma and pa know there was any letter in the alphabet other than L?'

Before Lilli could answer, Lottie flicked her braids back over her shoulders and said tartly, 'Those aren't our real names. They're diminutives.'

The girl's mouth dropped open. 'And what in the name of all that's wonderful,' she asked when she had recovered her power of speech, 'is a diminu whatever-you-call-it?'

Lilli, well aware that Lottie could fend for herself, stepped across to the port-hole. Indistinctly she could see the lights of San Francisco glimmering and glittering. Somewhere, high on Nob Hill, her uncle was still blissfully unaware that Leo and Lottie were no longer under his roof. He wouldn't know they were gone until morning. And in the morning they would be somewhere off the coast of California, steaming northwards.

'A diminutive is when you shorten a name,' Lottie was saying, sitting down next to the girl. 'Lilli's name is really Elizabeth, only no-one ever calls her Elizabeth. My name is Charlotte and Leo's is Leopold.'

'"S'truth," the girl said, impressed. 'Is that a fact? And what about my name? What's the diminu whatever-you-call-it of Lettie?'

Lottie regarded her gravely. 'Lettie already is a diminutive,' she said, politely keeping any hint of superiority out of her voice. 'It's either the diminutive of Lettice or Letitia.'

'Well, I don't think much of Lettice,' the girl said flatly. 'Letitia's nice though. It sounds like an actress's name.'

'It's Latin,' Lilli said, turning away from the porthole as the *Senator* began to ease out into the Bay. 'And it means gladness.' It was singularly inapt and a smile quirked the corners of her mouth.

Lettie's sulky face registered astonishment. 'Do you two read books for breakfast?' she asked, her voice no longer unpleasant but genuinely curious.

'Sometimes.' Lilli was rarely put out of good temper for long and she said now, her amusement deepening, 'And you do realize, don't you, that your name begins with an L, just like ours?'

Something fought on Lettie's face. It was as if she were frightened of abandoning unpleasantness. As if she were unfamiliar with any emotion that might replace it.

'It's rather nice, isn't it?' Lottie said ingenuously, still sitting companionably next to her. 'It's as if we were all meant to share a cabin and be friends.'

'If we're all friends,' Leo said, speaking up for the first time, 'Can we all go on deck together and watch San Francisco disappear?' He turned his attention towards Lettie. 'And as Lilli can't tell me what a floosie is, can you?'

'You're crazy! The whole lot of you are crazy?' Lettie rose to her feet, staring round at them as if they were escaped lunatics.

Lilli grinned. 'You could just be right,' she said, thinking of the confession she still had to make to Leo and Lottie, 'but we'd hardly be going to Alaska if we weren't, would we? And I don't suppose you would, either.'

Lettie blinked, clearly disconcerted by such blatant friendliness in the face of her own hostility. Then, slowly, a hint of a smile touched the corners of her mouth. 'No,' she said wryly. 'No, I don't suppose I would.'

Lilli had at first judged their cabin companion to be in her early twenties. Now she revised her estimate. Without a sulky mouth and a heavy scowl Lettie looked to be no older than she was herself and was possibly even a little younger.

'Come on then,' she said to her, more than happy to see an end to all hostilities. 'Let's do as Leo suggests and go up on deck.'

It was just as thronged as it had been earlier. Men of

every age, size and shape massed the rails, leaning over them to watch as, against the dark hills, San Francisco's myriad gaslights flickered and shimmered and grew ever smaller.

'You didn't say, but I presume you're a Peabody girl as well,' Lilli said to Lettie as, with Leo and Lottie in front of them they tried to squeeze a way through to the rails.

'For my sins,' Lettie said with unexpected humour. 'There's another five somewhere. Miss Salway, Miss Bumby, Miss Hobson, Miss Rivere and Miss Nettlesham. The first four are sharing the cabin next to ours. Miss *Nettlesham*,' she added, placing heavy sarcastic emphasis on the name, 'should have been sharing with us but she said she would *die* if she had to share a cabin, and she must have come to a private financial agreement with the captain because she now has a cabin to herself. She's already had a postal introduction to the fella she's to marry and thinks she's a cut above the rest of us.'

'What are Peabody girls?' Lottie asked Lettie curiously as two bear-like figures at the rails obligingly shifted apart a little in order to let Leo squeeze in front of them. 'And what do you mean by saying one of them has already had a postal introduction to the man she's going to marry?'

The gap at the rails widened and Lettie pushed Lottie forward. 'Peabody girls are gold-rush brides,' she said as she squeezed into the gap after her. 'But when we get to Dawson, Miss Nettlesham isn't going to have to marry whatever fella picks her out, like me and your sister will have to do. She already knows who she's going to marry and what he looks like.'

Lottie stared up at her, goggle-eyed. 'You mean Lilli's going to Alaska to *marry*?' she asked in stupefied disbelief.

''Course she is.' Lettie shivered as the night sea breeze seared through her threadbare coat. 'Why else would she be going there?'

Lottie didn't know. She'd thought it had been because Lilli was trying to vicariously fulfil one of their father's many day-dreams. Now she realised that, even for Lilli, such a romantic notion would not be reason enough.

As the *Senator* began to roll in the Pacific swell and as the lights on shore became ever more indistinct, many of the men at the rails turned away from them, heading below deck.

Lottie turned away also, stumbling towards Lilli, her face ashen. 'Is it true?' she demanded hoarsely, grabbing hold of her hand. 'Are we really going to Alaska so that you can marry a man you've never met?'

Lilli didn't answer her. Incredibly, she didn't even seem to hear her. She was staring across the deck to where, several yards away, a gentleman was standing looking shorewards, an astrakhan-collared greatcoat around his shoulders, a Homburg pulled low over his brow.

Chapter Three

'It was the only solution,' Lilli said half an hour later. Lettie had taken Leo into the next cabin to meet their travelling companions and she had no excuse not to answer Lottie's urgent questions.

Lottie stared at her aghast. '*Marriage*?' she said, wondering why Lilli so fondly thought she took after their mother when, in reality, she so spectacularly took after their father, acting first and thinking later. 'But you can't marry someone you don't know, Lilli!'

'Why not?' Lilli said with a lightness she was far from feeling. 'Lettie is. And so are Miss Bumby and Miss Nettlesham and Miss Rivere and Miss Hobson and Miss Salway.'

'I've seen Miss Bumby and she doesn't look as if she'd ever get a husband any other way,' Lottie said starkly, 'And Lettie says Miss Hobson isn't quite right in the head and that Miss Rivere is fast and would marry anyone.'

Lilli's sleek eyebrows rose nearly into her hair. 'You're only ten years old, Lottie,' she chided, genuinely shocked. 'You shouldn't be using words like fast – and you certainly shouldn't be using them in the right context!'

Lottie hadn't known that she had done so. She did know, however, that nothing could be done to alter the situation until they reached their destination and that it was pointless discussing it further, especially when it was obvious Lilli was far more alarmed by it than she was allowing to show.

She leaned her head against Lilli's shoulder, knowing full well why she had taken the crazy step of becoming a Peabody bride. It was because she had been desperate to

38

remove Leo from their Uncle Herbert's care; because she loved her and Leo so much she would do anything, anything at all, if she thought it was in their best interests.

'I love you, Lilli,' she said huskily, forgiving her elder sister her rashness, knowing it had been prompted by the very best of intentions. 'You're the best big sister anyone could ever have.'

'And I love you, pet-lamb,' Lilli said, her arm tightening around Lottie's slender shoulders, her eyes overly bright, her voice unnaturally thick. 'And loving each other, and Leo, is all that truly matters.'

'A nice lady gave me a stick of liquorice' Leo said minutes later as he and Lettie squeezed back into the cabin. He clutched his bounty with glee. 'And another lady says there are gamblers and guns-slingers aboard!'

'I don't care if Billy the Kid is aboard.' Wearily Lettie sat down on the edge of her bunk. 'I'm ready for a little bit of shut-eye.'

So was Lilli. It had been a long, long day. The longest she could ever remember. 'Bed-time,' she said to Leo, beginning to ease his arms out of his jacket sleeves.

'Is Leo going to have the bottom bunk?' Lottie asked, taking off her sailor-hat and standing on tip-toe to lay it carefully at the foot of the top bunk she had already decided was hers.

'Yes.' Lilli ignored Leo's tired yowl of protest. 'That way if it gets rough he'll have less distance to fall.'

'What do you mean "*if* it gets rough"?' Lettie asked darkly, already ensconced, fully dressed, beneath an inadequate-looking blanket. 'It's rough already, or hadn't you noticed?'

Lilli had had too much on her mind to pay attention to the *Senator's* increasing pitch and roll. Now that her attention had been drawn to it, however, she began to feel just the slightest bit queasy. 'The sooner we're all asleep, the better,' she said, tucking Leo into his bunk as securely as possible and laying her box-coat on top of his blanket for extra warmth.

'It's going to feel funny saying my prayers when we're moving,' Leo observed sleepily. 'Do you think God will mind? Do you think He'll think it disres . . . disres . . . not good manners?'

'Not at all, my love,' Lilli said tenderly, brushing a lock of hair from his eyes. 'We decided long ago that He doesn't think it's disrespectful for you to say your prayers in bed when its freezing cold, didn't we? And there isn't room to kneel in this cabin. There's scarcely room to stand.'

Reassured Leo closed his eyes. 'Now I lay me down to sleep,' he began, the familiar words muffled with tiredness. 'I pray the Lord my soul to keep . . .'

'If I die before I wake, I pray the Lord my soul to take,' Lilli finished for him softly as his breathing changed and he fell into almost instant sleep.

Seconds later, as Lilli climbed into her own bunk, there came the sound of Lottie quietly saying her prayers, her feet curled up to her chest so that she wouldn't crush her precious sailor-hat. 'And God Bless Leo and Lilli and Aunt Gussie and Lettie,' she finished, 'And may we all reach Alaska safely.'

In the now thick darkness there came a suspicious sound from Lettie's bunk. It was almost like a stifled sob. Lilli leaned over the edge of her bunk and looked down but Lettie was laying on her side, facing the cabin wall, and all she could see was the shadowy outline of her back. She lay down again, succumbing to exhaustion. It probably hadn't been a sob. It had probably only been a stifled sneeze. She closed her eyes, trying to acclimatise herself to the movement of the boat, every muscle in her body aching. How many miles had she walked since getting out of bed that morning? It must have been well over twelve for she had visited every single employment agency listed in the *Examiner* and more houses with rooms to rent than she cared to remember.

Image after image burned the backs of her eyelids. The spilt milk running in rivulets onto the Turkish carpet; her uncle demanding that she be out of the house, for good, before he returned to it; the abortive hunt for a suitable job and a room; her aunt's anguished face when she had told her she was leaving and taking Leo and Lottie with her; the frantic dash for the cable car and the even more fraught hackney carriage ride. There hadn't been time to think. From the moment she had entered the Peabody Marriage Bureau she had acted on instinct and instinct alone.

There was a gentle snore from the direction of Lettie's bunk. Leo murmured in his sleep. Lottie's rhythmic breathing indicated that she, too, was deep in dreamland. With her every nerve and muscle longing for sleep Lilli remained awake. Had she behaved with crass rashness? And if she had, was the situation she had plunged herself into one from she would be able to extricate herself?

Of all the images that burned against her eyelids, one, grey-suited and Homburg-hatted, predominated. Was he a gold-rich miner returning to his strike? Was he, perhaps, one of the men who had approached the Peabody Marriage Bureau in the hope that the bureau could find him a wife willing to endure the rigours of the pioneer north? Lilli's tummy muscles tightened with fierce, desperate hope.

She remembered the way he had looked at her when he had cautioned her to take more care crossing city streets. There had been amusement in his amber-brown eyes and there had been something more; an expression of open admiration. Merely remembering it sent the blood racing heatedly along her veins. No-one had ever looked at her in such a way before and even if they had, she was certain they wouldn't have aroused such an extraordinary response in her.

When she had seen him on deck she had felt as if Fate had directly intervened in her life. What other explanation could there be for the bizarre events of the last fifteen hours? Destiny had ensured she walked into the Peabody Marriage Bureau and destiny was responsible for their travelling on the same ship. Tomorrow he would see her as she leaned against the deck rails, watching the coast of northern California slide by; tomorrow he would speak to her and introduce himself to her; tomorrow would be the most momentous, most memorable day of her life. Happy anticipation replaced tension and Lilli fell into a deep, but not a dreamless, sleep.

She woke to stark reality. 'I'm going to be sick!' Leo announced as morning light streamed through the porthole into the close confines of the cabin.

Lilli swung her legs over the edge of her bunk and dropped to the floor. 'Not yet!' she said peremptorily. 'Wait till I've got some clothes on!'

Minutes later she was up on deck and Leo was leaning over a brass deck rail, retching up a vile black substance.

'It serves you right,' she said crossly as he moaned piteously for comfort. 'You shouldn't have eaten your liquorice in the middle of the night.'

Across the heaving grey-green waves, hills and mountains could be seen, misty and insubstantial in the early morning heat haze. She had no idea how fast they were travelling and no idea if the land she could see was still California or if it was the State of Oregon or even, perhaps, the State of Washington.

She leaned against the deck rail, trying to create a map of north-west America and Canada in her mind's eye. She couldn't think of any other large, coastal city between San Francisco and the Canadian border. In America there was Seattle, of course, and in Canada, Vancouver. She wondered if the *Senator* would in stop off at either city for more passengers and for the first time wondered how long the voyage to Alaska would take and where they would eventually disembark.

She didn't know much about their eventual destination, which was Dawson City, apart from the fact that it was situated high on the Yukon River, perhaps too high for sea-going vessels to be able to reach it. If that were the case, presumably they would travel by train to Dawson from wherever they disembarked. That is, if there were a train line. Not for the first time she realized how criminally ignorant she was of

42

where she was going and what she would find when she arrived.

'I'm cold, Lilli' Leo said plaintively, interrupting her thoughts. He was still dressed only in his undergarments and the sea breeze had reduced him to goose-pimples.

Reluctantly Lilli turned away from the view. The early morning, before the bulk of the world was awake, was her favourite part of the day and she would have liked to have remained where she was, staring out across the ocean, watching the distant coastline sliding by. She was certainly determined to spend as much time as possible on deck because only on deck was the Greek god likely to see her and renew his acquaintance with her.

'You're now going to have the pleasure of meeting Misses Bumby, Salway, Hobson and Rivere,' Lettie said darkly as, an hour later, they made their way towards the dining saloon for breakfast.

'And Miss Nettlesham,' Lilli reminded her as they squeezed along dark narrow gangways.

Lettie shook her untidy mane of hair. 'I doubt we'll see Miss Nettlesham in the public dining-saloon. She's the kind to have breakfast in her cabin.'

Lilli felt a flash of anxiety. Would the Greek god also be spending most of the voyage in his cabin? The *Senator* was a large boat and there were easily two or three hundred men aboard her. What if she never saw him again? Even worse, what if he wasn't going to Dawson after all but was only travelling as far as Seattle or Vancouver?

'Does the *Senator* stop off anywhere for more passengers?' she asked Lettie as she followed her into the crowded dining-saloon. The noise level was so high that Lettie didn't hear her. Unable to see anything but a mass of bearded faces and nearly overcome by the smell of human sweat and bacon grease she ploughed on in Lettie's wake, Leo clinging to her skirts; Lottie close behind her.

In a far corner of the saloon a table flanked by benches had been set aside for the use of ladies. As Lettie

43

unceremoniously slid onto the end of one of the benches the young women sitting around the table shuffled closer together to make room for her, and for Lilli and Leo and Lottie.

'So you're the late arrival,' one of the young women said to Lilli in a husky voice thick with amusement. 'When we heard you were bringing two kids with you we thought you must be in your dotage. What were you? A child-bride?' The speaker had an odd, almost monkey-like face that couldn't, in a million years, have been described as beautiful. The eyes were too big, the nose too short, the mouth too wide. These deficiencies had, however, been spectacularly overcome. Unnatural-looking fox-red hair was piled high, tumbling forward in a frizz of curls over her forehead. The lemur-like eyes danced with laughter. The wide, dazzlingly smiling mouth was painted as garishly as a chorus-girl's.

'No,' Lilli said with an answering grin. 'Lottie and Leo are my brother and sister.'

'I don't think anyone will choose you as a bride when they know you have a family in tow,' a heavy-featured girl with an unfortunate dark line of hair on her upper lip, said doubtfully.

Lilli sat down and hoisted Leo onto the bench beside her. 'I'm the one that's going to be doing the choosing,' she corrected, keeping her voice friendly.

'I'm afraid that's not quite how it . . .' the girl began, a slight frown drawing thick eyebrows together.

'For goodness sake, we should be making introductions, not getting pickety.' It was the husky-voiced girl. She stretched her hand across the table towards Lilli. 'My name is Marietta Rivere and I'm very pleased to meet you.' It was a small hand, almost paw-like.

'I'm pleased to meet you, too,' Lilli said warmly.

Leo had been gazing at Marietta in almost mesmerized fascination. Now he said admiringly, 'I like that coloured stuff on your mouth. Does it taste nice?'

There was a snort from a pale-looking girl sitting on Marietta's left-hand side. Marietta ignored it. 'I think it must do,' she said, a chuckle in her voice, 'Because I've never had any comp . . .'

'I think you should remember Leo's age,' an auburn-haired girl sitting at the top of the table said quickly, her voice gently reproving. She turned her attention to Lilli. 'I'm Miss Salway. Kate Salway.'

'Lilli Stullen,' Lilli said as the moustached girl next to her passed her three enamel plates.

There was a large dish of crisp bacon rashers in the centre of the table and as Lilli began to fork rashers onto the plates the girl said bluntly. 'Bumby.'

'I beg your pardon?' Lilli said, startled.

'Bumby,' the girl said again. 'Miss Susan Bumby.'

'And I'm Miss Nettlesham,' the almost albino-looking girl sitting on Marietta's left-hand side said, not proferring her christian name, her intonation indicating that she regarded herself as being of far more consequence than Miss Bumby or Miss Salway and certainly of far more consequence than the *outré* Miss Rivere.

'I'm pleased to meet you,' Lilli said politely, hiding her amusement, understanding all too well why Lettie had taken such a dislike to her.

'Edie hasn't introduced herself,' Marietta said as she poured a mug of milk for Leo.

The young woman in question, sitting on Marietta's right-hand side, blushed and bit her bottom lip in an agony of shyness.

Marietta handed Leo the mug of milk and then said, 'Edie's full name is Edith Hobson. She's only sixteen and is the baby amongst us. Or she's the baby gold-rush bride-to-be amongst us, because I don't suppose Lottie is looking for a husband yet and I'm not including young gents, like Leo here, in my reckoning.'

Even though the very expression 'gold-rush bride-to-be' filled Lottie with panic on Lilli's behalf, Marietta's fizzing effervescence was so contagious that Lottie found herself giggling. Leo, highly flattered at being referred to as a 'young gent' positively preened himself.

'If Edie's the youngest, I must be the oldest,' Miss

45

Bumby said gruffly, a gleam of bacon fat trickling down her chin. 'I'm twenty-eight,' she added, so that there would be no need for speculation.

'And I'm twenty-six,' Miss Salway said, doing her bit to break the ice between them all.

It was Lottie who truly broke the ice. 'Why are you all going to Alaska to marry men you've never met?' she asked ingenuously.

There was a sharp, shocked intake of breath from Miss Nettlesham. A peal of husky, unchained laughter from Marietta. Susan Bumby had flushed scarlet. Kate Salway looked discomfited. Edie looked bewildered.

'You're forgetting your manners, Lottie,' Lilli whispered to her with unusual sharpness, aware of the embarrassment that had been caused.

'No, she isn't.' The speaker was Kate Salway and everyone looked towards her. From the moment she had introduced herself to Lilli, Lilli had been aware of the auburn-haired young woman's inner calmness and quiet authority, an authority even Marietta seemed to pay heed to. 'It's a very reasonable question,' Kate said, looking around at them all, 'and I don't mind trying to answer it, though I'm afraid it won't be easy for me.'

'Well, *I* have no intention of baring my soul to a child, or to the rest of you,' Miss Nettlesham said chillily, rising to her feet. 'Nor do I think I shall be joining you for meals in future.'

'Who are you goin' to sit with instead?' Marietta asked intrigued, 'a nice respectable gun-slinger or a decent, hard-working card-sharper?'

Lettie hooted with laughter and even Miss Bumby's mouth twitched.

'If Mrs Peabody had had the slightest inkling of your true character she would never have countenanced your travelling with us!' Furious spots of colour burned Miss Nettlesham's pale cheeks. 'You're not a respectable young woman at all! You're a . . . you're a *floosy*!' She flounced on her heel and marched away, leaving Leo gazing at Marietta with even more avid interest than previously.

46

'Miss Nettlesham's going to have to lose her high and mighty airs when we reach the Klondike,' Susan Bumby said knowledgeably. 'I've lived there and I know.'

'Are you a gold-prospector?' Leo asked, his eyes rounding. 'I didn't know ladies could be gold-prospectors . . .'

'I'm a kindergarten-teacher. In another few weeks I might even be *your* kindergarten-teacher.'

'And you've lived in the Klondike?' There were so many questions Lilli wanted to ask Susan Bumby she didn't know where to start. 'You've lived in Dawson City?'

Susan nodded. 'I most certainly have and if you have any questions you want to ask about Dawson, I'd be happy to oblige.'

Before Lilli could inundate her Marietta said, puzzled, 'If you've lived in Dawson, why'd you travel to 'Frisco to ask Mrs Peabody to fix you up with a husband? Why didn't you find a rich stampeder while you were livin' there?'

Susan Bumby's almost masculine face coloured. 'No-one ever asked me,' she said with brutal honesty. 'I thought this way someone might.'

There was an embarrassed silence and then Kate Salway said warmly, 'I'm sure they will. Everyone has something special to offer in a married relationship and nothing is more important than kindness. Look how you won Leo's heart when you gave him a stick of liquorice. Please tell us a little about what we can expect when we reach Dawson. Is the weather freezing cold? Is the town full of saloons and dance-hall girls in big hats and pretty dresses? And if it is, why is there such a demand for marriage bureau brides?'

Breakfast over, men had begun to push back benches and rise to their feet, eager to take a little air on deck. As they left the dining saloon and the noise level fell, the Peabody girls gathered closer around their table, eager to hear whatever Susan Bumby might tell them.

Susan was unused to being the centre of attention and her downy cheeks were still stained an embarrassed red as she said, answering Kate's first question, 'It isn't freezing

47

cold in the summer. In the summer the Klondike is beautiful.' Her gruff voice softened noticeably and it became patently obvious to them all that she was returning to a land she had fallen in love with. 'First of all there are the forget-me-nots. I don't believe there are forget-me-nots anywhere in the world as blue as Alaskan forget-me-nots. There are white anemones, too. And yellow buttercups. Then, in high summer, the hills are covered with low-bush cranberries and blueberries and kinnikinnik . . .'

'What in the world is kinnikinnik?' Kate Salway asked, relieved that there was, at least, some summer warmth to look forward to.

'Kinnikinnik is a green, red-berried creeper sometimes called Yukon holly. There's lots of wild life, too. Caribou and bear and . . .'

'Bears!' Edie had begun to look distinctly apprehensive. 'I don't think I'd like bears. I think bears would frighten me.'

'Don't worry, honey,' Marietta's paw-like hand patted Edie's comfortingly, 'I don't expect the bears come into town. They'll stay in the woods and . . .'

'Woods?' There was a tremor in Edie's voice and she looked to be fast approaching tears. 'I don't like woods, Marietta. Once, on an outing from the orphanage, I got lost in a wood and when I was found I was beaten.'

There was an appalled silence and then Marietta said thickly, squeezing Edie's hand in hers, 'No-one's going to beat you again, honey. Not while I'm lookin' out for you.'

'If you don't like woods and things, why do you want to live in the wilderness?' Lottie asked with ten-year-old frankness.

It was a question Lilli was also wondering and she couldn't quite understand why everyone suddenly looked so uncomfortable. Everyone, that is, except for Edie. Edie simply looked blank.

It was Kate Salway who answered for her, her eyes, as they met Lilli's above Lottie's head, conveying far more than her words.

'It wasn't really Edie's choice to sail to Alaska, Lottie. Edie has spent all her life in an orphanage and now that she's too old to stay there, the orphanage authorities thought she might like to have a husband and a family and live somewhere pretty, like Alaska.'

A cold chill ran down Lilli's spine. Was Kate saying that the orphanage authorities had simply shipped Edie off as a Peabody bride in order to be rid of her? And was she also saying that Edie had little understanding of where she was going or what would be expected of her when she arrived? As she gazed around the table she saw by the expression in her companions' eyes that the answer to her unspoken question was 'yes.'

'Many people are frightened of woods, Edie,' Susan Bumby said in an attempt to be reassuring. 'It's a very old fear going back to the days of primitive man.'

'And anyone in their right senses is frightened of bears,' Lettie said. It was the first time she had opened her mouth and everyone's head swivelled in her direction. Lettie ignored them, lapsing into uncommunicative silence again and it occurred to Lilli that, though she and Lottie and Leo had established friendly relations with her, so far no-one else had yet done so.

Susan broke the silence. 'Though men love the Klondike, not many women do. They don't like having to battle against nature for eight months out of twelve and they don't like the sheer vastness of the terrain.'

From the alarmed expression on Marietta's face it was obvious that she, too, didn't relish the thought of battling with nature and even Kate Salway had begun to look perturbed.

'Is that why there's such a demand for mail-order brides?' she asked, wondering if it might have been better if Susan had left them all in happy ignorance.

Susan nodded. 'I guess so. The dance-hall girls rarely marry. They're too busy having a good time, pocketing gold nuggets from men who've struck it rich.'

'There's a dance-hall girl aboard the boat,' Edie said in awestruck tones. 'Miss Nettlesham told me. And she's with a man born to be hanged. Miss Nettlesham says he's a professional gambler and as handsome as the devil.'

'Then I'll look out for him,' Marietta said with great feeling. She grinned suddenly, 'I wonder how it is Miss High and Mighty Nettlesham knows so much about him? Do you think she's a dance-hall girl herself?'

The rather sombre mood Susan had occasioned was immediately dispelled. Amid gales of laughter they put forward ridiculous theories as to why Miss Nettlesham should be so well informed about a dance-hall girl and a gambler and by the time they all filed from the dining-saloon it was as if they had known each other for months, not hours.

'I'm actually a sourdough,' Susan said proudly as they surged from the top of the companionway and set about finding somewhere comfortable to sit in the breezy sunshine.

There were more helpless giggles and even Lettie's sulky mouth twitched into a grin of amusement.

'A sourdough?' Kate's grey-green eyes danced with laughter. 'What on earth is a sourdough?'

Scores of male eyes swivelled in their direction as they appropriated seats on the starboard side of the boat. Marietta's upswept and tightly curled fox-red hair would have drawn attention anywhere and Lilli's height and slenderness and natural grace was an automatic head-turner. By contrast, Susan's heavy features and clumsy gait were even more noticeable and there were many cruel male remarks; remarks Susan fortunately did not hear.

'You'll hear the term 'a sourdough' a lot in the Klondike,' she said in her school-marmish manner, hardly able to believe her good fortune in making so many new friends so quickly. 'It's a term used to describe someone who has sat out a Klondike winter. If you've watched the Yukon freeze up in the fall and then break to pieces with a roar in the spring, you're a sourdough.'

'I've heard another definition,' Marietta said, a chuckle in her husky voice, 'It's that no man can be a sourdough until he's shot a bear and slept with a squaw . . .'

50

'And that after he's achieved that, he'd wish he'd shot the squaw and slept with the bear!' Susan finished for her daringly, the spots of colour in her cheeks deepening to crimson.

Helpless laughter convulsed them all. Edie, who hadn't understood the joke but who had laughed all the same said, when their laughter had subsided to giggles, 'This is the nicest morning I can ever remember. It's so nice, I don't ever want it to end.'

'All things come to an end, Edie,' Kate said gently, concern in her eyes.

Lilli was well aware of its cause. Edie's mental age was that of a nine or a ten-year-old and it was possible she would be taken terrible advantage of when they reached Dawson City. Lilli tried to remember exactly what Mrs Peabody had told her about the arrangements they would meet with there. Hadn't it been that introductions between Peabody brides-to-be and men looking for brides would be made by Mr Josh Nelson, a Peabody Marriage Bureau representative? She knew that at the time it had all seemed quite civilised.

At the thought of the faceless, nameless men awaiting them in Dawson City, it suddenly seemed civilised no longer. Her anxiety began to deepen. What was it Susan Bumby had said to her when she, Lilli, had airily announced that when it came to fulfilling her contract and marrying, *she* would do the choosing? Hadn't it been something about that not being the way of it? With mounting anxiety she wondered exactly what Susan had meant. 'Susan . . .' she began urgently, but she was seconds too late.

'Miss Bumby's going to show me round the boat,' Leo said, his face alight with anticipation. 'She's travelled on the *Senator* before and she's going to introduce me to the captain and show me the wheelhouse!'

'And I'm going to lay down,' Kate said, beginning to look queasy even though the Senator's pitch and roll was much less pronounced than it had been the previous evening.

51

'Me too.' Though the sulky expression had long since disappeared from Lettie's mouth it was obvious to Lilli that Lettie was unused to such long stretches of sociability and needed to be on her own for a little while.

'And Edie and I are going in search of dance-hall girls,' Marietta announced gaily. 'Do you want to join us?'

'No, I don't think . . .'

'Can *I* go, Lilli?' Lottie interrupted. 'Please!'

Lilli nodded. Like Lettie, she, too, needed to be on her own for a little while. It would give her time to think and put her chaotic thoughts in order. And, if she were on her own she would be much more likely to be seen and recognised by the Greek god . . .

The mid-morning sun was so warm she had no need of her box-coat and was able to sit in just her shirtwaist and skirt. In front of her and on either side of her the deck was scattered with groups of men, some in cane chairs, others either squatting or sitting with their arms loosely circling their knees, all deep in conversation.

'The place to be is the Third Beach Line,' she heard a grizzled-haired man to her left saying to his companions. 'They figure it's the biggest dam' strike ever hit in Alaska! Why, there's nuggets the size of boulders . . .'

On her right, a young man in a cloth cap, fisherman's jersey and baggy corduroy trousers was saying, 'I hear they've just hit gold near the head of Anvil Creek . . .'

Gold. It seemed to be the only thing her fellow passengers were interested in. When she had asked Lettie why she was travelling to Dawson as a gold-rush bride Lettie had said quite flatly, 'To marry a man who's struck it rich and have him set me up for life.'

A red-haired man, as tall and broad-shouldered as a prize-fighter, walked past her strolling across to the deck-rail. As he leaned against it, looking out towards the coastline, the young man in the fisherman's jersey said in a low voice, but not too low that Lilli couldn't hear him, 'Isn't that one of the paroled convicts?'

'So they say,' one of his companions said. 'There's another two on board somewhere. Been let off the rest of their sentences so long as they go as far north as possible and behave themselves while they're about it.'

Lilli looked across at the ex-convict with interest. With his shock of red hair he was vividly noticeable and she knew she would have no difficulty in recognising him again, resolving to give him a wide berth.

On her left, the conversation was still about gold. 'The damn' stuff's right there under the grass-roots,' an Englishman with a deer-stalker hat on his head was saying, 'All we've got to do is get a grubstake together and stake a claim . . .'

Lilli tapped a neatly booted foot impatiently. She wasn't interested in grubstakes, whatever grubstakes were, or claims, and she certainly wasn't interested in grizzled-haired men or men in baggy trousers or ridiculous English deer-stalkers. She was interested in a slick, suave, grey-suited man with a touch of the gypsy about him, for surely only a man with a touch of the gypsy about him would wear a gold earring?

'What the devil,' his brandy-dark voice said from behind her, disbelief in its tones, '. . . are you doing aboard the *Senator*?'

Her head whirled round. He was standing looking down at her, not with amusement and admiration, but with a frown. A frown very similar to that with which he had first greeted her.

'I . . .' She could hardly tell him she was travelling as a Peabody bride. He would assume she was spoken for; that she had a fiancé waiting for her in Dawson. 'I'm going to the Klondike,' she finished lamely, her heart racing.

He was still wearing dove-grey, but somehow she thought it wasn't the same suit as the one he had been wearing yesterday. And this time there was a watch-chain across his chamois vest; a watch-chain made of very small gold nuggets. 'I hardly thought you were *en route* for Florida.' His sarcasm pierced her dizzy pleasure at his having recognised her and spoken to her.

'I don't like heat,' she snapped, stung into a ridiculous reply. 'And I don't like oranges.'

53

He walked around to the front of her seat and stared down at her, too perturbed to be amused. 'Do you have family in the Klondike, Miss . . .?'

'Stullen.'

'A father perhaps? A brother?'

Despite the devastating effect his physical presence had on her, Lilli was beginning to feel more than a little annoyed. Her reasons for travelling to the Klondike were really none of his business. And his so bluntly asking if she had family there was impertinent. 'I have friends there,' she said, not feeling it was truly a lie because when she arrived she *would* have friends there. She would have Lettie and Edie and Marietta and Kate and Susan.

He had removed his Homburg and his hair glinted wheatgold in the strong sunshine. 'I hope they're the right kind of friends, Miss Stullen.' He was still frowning, hoping to God she wasn't referring to girls who were his employees, wondering even as he did so why it should matter. 'The Klondike is no place for a respectable young woman . . .'

'Really?' Lilli wasn't accustomed to being patronised. Not even by a Greek god. She said spiritedly, 'It may interest you to learn that one of the very respectable female friends I am travelling with is both a kindergarten teacher and a sourdough, Mr . . . Mr . . .?'

'Coolidge,' he said, amusement tugging at him again just as it had when she had so disarmingly apologised for frightening the horse. 'Jack Coolidge.'

'And a sourdough, Mr Coolidge, is a person who has . . .'

'I'm well aware of the definition of a sourdough, Miss Stullen.' Now that he was more or less convinced she wasn't travelling to Dawson to work as a dance-hall floosie he could allow the amusement she aroused in him to surface. 'Dawson City is my home.'

Her relief was so vast she was sure that if she hadn't already been seated her knees would have given way.

'How . . . nice.'

'That's just the problem,' he said dryly. 'Dawson isn't

54

"nice". It's a man's town.' He thought of the saloons and gambling places and raucous red-light district. It was no place for a young woman as beautiful and pure-looking as a Raphael Madonna. 'I wouldn't advise staying there too long.'

'I . . . er . . . I'd thought of making it my home,' she said, realising that she was going to have to tell him she was a Peabody bride. Unless she did so, how could he possibly realise that Fate had singled him out as her future husband-to-be? 'I'm travelling to Dawson with six other young ladies. We're all . . .'

'Lilli! Lilli! Look what I've got!' It was Leo and he was racing towards her, something gold and glittering clutched in his hand. 'It's a nugget, Lilli! A real gold nugget!'

As he barrelled breathlessly into her Lilli slid her arm lovingly around his shoulders. 'I'd like you to meet a gentleman who lives in Dawson City. Leo, Mr Coolidge. Mr Coolidge, my little brother, Leo.'

'Pleased to meet you, young man,' the Greek God said, shaking Leo's free hand with solemnity.

Leo simply stared at him, his eyes like saucers. 'Gosh!' he said, when he found his voice. 'Gosh! Are you *really* Mr Coolidge? 'Lucky' Jack Coolidge? The man Miss Nettlesham says was born to be hanged?'

Chapter Four

Lilli wanted to die with mortification but the Greek god merely chuckled. 'You obviously get around, young man, picking up that kind of information about your fellow passengers on your first day at sea. Is Miss Nettlesham the kindergarten-teacher your sister was telling me about?'

'I don't know,' Leo said truthfully, gazing at him starry-eyed, hardly able to believe he was in conversation with a man he had heard described as being a living legend. 'Miss Bumby is a teacher. She isn't very pretty but she's very kind.' He fumbled in his pocket and withdrew a crumpled paperbag. 'She gave me these humbugs. Would you like one?'

'Leo, I don't think . . .' Lilli began in an agony of embarrassment.

'I'd love one,' Jack Coolidge said, easing a sticky offering free and popping it into his mouth with commendable disregard for the flecks of paper still clinging to it.

'Miss Nettlesham says you own nearly every gambling saloon in Dawson,' Leo said with hero-worshipping wonder. 'Is it true? And is it true there are gun-slingers in Dawson, just like in the old Wild West?'

Not for the first time it occurred to Lilli that both Leo and Lottie were fast gaining the kind of education they could well do without. It had been bad enough Lottie saying that Marietta was fast, without Leo chatting familiarly about gambling saloons and gun-slingers.

'There is an occasional fracas,' Jack said, taking care not to disillusion Leo totally, 'but in the main, Dawson is remarkably law-abiding.'

Lilli was pleased to hear it. How she felt about the

discovery that Jack Coolidge was *Lucky* Jack Coolidge, a professional gambler, she didn't yet know. There simply hadn't been time to assimilate the information and besides, even though Miss Nettlesham had described him as a professional gambler, she could easily have been misinformed. Just because Jack Coolidge had admitted to owning gambling saloons didn't necessarily mean that he . . .

'Would you like me to teach you a couple of card tricks?' He was speaking to Leo and Lilli snapped out of her reverie instantly.

'No!' she said with a vehemence that sent Jack Coolidge's eyebrows towards his wheat-gold hair and plunged Leo into bitter disappointment.

'My apologies if I've offended.' Jack Coolidge didn't look remotely apologetic. 'But if you've a taking against gambling, Miss Stullen, you're going to find life in Dawson pretty hard.'

'I don't have a taking against gambling,' Lilli said indignantly. 'My father was Irish. I've been brought up with race-horse gambling. I just don't think children should be *encouraged* to gamble, that's all.'

'I wasn't encouraging him to gamble.' There was a pained expression in the dark, rich voice. 'I was merely offering to teach him a couple of card tricks.'

Lilli was well aware that under normal circumstances she would now have excused herself, removing Leo firmly from Mr Coolidge's company. The circumstances, however, were not normal. If her instincts of the previous evening were correct — and the way her heart had begun to slam and was continuing to slam indicated that they were — then Jack Coolidge was going to play a very large and important part in Leo's life. All that was necessary was that he be made to appreciate that six-year-old boys were dangerously impressionable and couldn't be spoken to as if they were adults. 'Perhaps you could tell Leo about stampeders, Mr Coolidge,' she said, aware that the necessary conversation couldn't take place now, while Leo was present.

'Stampeders?' He looked bemused as if, despite his nugget watch-chain, gold prospecting was something alien to him.

'Are *you* a stampeder, Mr Coolidge?' Leo asked eagerly. 'My Pa wanted to be a stampeder. He wanted to take the Chilkoot Trail with the first rush of gold-prospectors four years ago, but he was too sick.'

'Pa died six months ago,' Lilli said quietly, before Jack Coolidge could ask after their father's present welfare.

'I'm sorry.' The honey-dark voice was sincere. He hesitated for a moment, frowning slightly, and then he squatted down on his haunches so that he and Leo were eye to eye. 'You want to know about stampeders, do you, young man?' he asked, tipping his Homburg to the back of his head. 'Well, first of all I can tell you that I'm not a stampeder and never have been. Stampeders are far bigger gamblers than card-sharpers. Even when they're on to a sure thing, they'll leave it to follow a rumour. When news came through of the big beach-strike at Nome, way over in the west on the edge of the Bering Sea, men taking bucketfuls of gold from mines around Dawson abandoned them, staking all their new-found riches on the hope of even bigger strikes.'

'But why would they do that, Mr Coolidge?' Leo asked, puzzled. 'They might not be as lucky in Nome as they were in Dawson.'

'I doubt if many of them have been,' Jack Coolidge said wryly, 'but what you've got to understand, young Leo, is that stampeders are not sane men. It's not the gold itself that gets into their blood and bones, it's the *looking* for it that obsesses them. They are all convinced that somewhere, over the next mountain and across the next river, there are nuggets far bigger than the ones they already have in their hands. And so, no matter what the hardships, they hit the trail, abandoning certainties for dreams.'

It was now Lilli's turn to frown. If all gold-prospectors were so feckless they would make alarmingly bad husbands. She thought of her fellow Peabody brides. They deserved far better husband material than Jack Coolidge was describing. Then she remembered Daniel Berton, the gold-prospector photographed in the *Examiner*. Mr Berton hadn't behaved in such a heedless fashion. When he had struck it rich he hadn't squandered his new-found wealth looking for more. He had returned to San Francisco in order to sensibly invest it.

'And so the moral is, don't emulate stampeders,' Jack Coolidge was saying to Leo. 'They are men wasting their lives seeking for something that even when it's found will never content them.'

It was advice Lilli couldn't quarrel with. Happy that Jack Coolidge was proving to be a far more responsible person than he had at first seemed, she said, as he stood up straight once more, 'Thank you for talking to Leo so sensibly about stampeders, Mr Coolidge. I've heard so much talk of gold aboard the *Senator* I was beginning to think everyone was gold-mad.'

He grinned down at her and in the sunlight his earring glistened and his flamboyant watch-chain glittered. 'No point filling young heads with dreams likely to lead to disaster,' he said, enjoying the comedy of sounding like a pontificating schoolmaster. He was just about to return to the subject of exactly why she was travelling to Dawson and what she intended doing when she arrived there when he became aware of a young seaman hovering nearby, trying to catch his eye. 'Yes?' he queried.

'The Captain would like a word, Mr Coolidge. He's on the bridge, sir.'

Jack suppressed his impatience. He had been enjoying his conversation with the delightfully naive Miss Stullen. It had made a welcome change from the bantering, worldly conversations he usually enjoyed with the opposite sex. It was, however, only their first day at sea. He would have plenty of opportunity to talk to her again. 'Excuse me,' he said to her with genuine regret. 'Perhaps next time we meet on deck you'll allow me to tell you a little about Dawson.'

'I'd like that, Mr Coolidge,' Lilli said demurely, her

eyes sparkling, fit to beat the lustre of his watch-chain. 'Goodbye.' She stood holding Leo's hand as Jack Coolidge strode off in the direction of the bridge. Groups of men both seated and standing paused in their conversation as he passed by them, renewing it with vigour the instant he was out of earshot. They were quite obviously talking about him and Lilli wondered what they were saying.

Before she could walk by them herself, and perhaps overhear, the young seaman said, an odd note in his voice, 'I hadn't realised you were a friend of Mr Coolidge's, Miss Stullen.'

Lilli turned to face him. He may have been gallantly helpful when she had boarded the *Senator*, but that gave him no right to engage her in conversation as if she were a familiar acquaintance. 'There's no reason why you should have,' she said coolly. Over his shoulder she could see Marietta approaching. She wondered where Edie and Lottie were and hoped Marietta hadn't carelessly left them in the company of one of the dance-hall girls they had gone in search of.

'I'm surprised, that's all,' the seaman said, standing his ground. 'I thought you were one of Mrs Peabody's girls not a dance-hall floo . . .'

Lilli wasn't listening to him. She was walking towards Marietta, saying anxiously, 'Where are Edie and Lottie? You haven't lost them, have you?'

'No.' Marietta eyed the young seaman with interest, well aware that he was severely disgruntled by her arrival and had clearly been hoping for a much longer tête-à-tête with Lilli. 'They're playing quoits near the stern.'

The seaman, knowing full well he had lost an ideal chance of deepening his acquaintance with Lilli, gave her a long burning look and then reluctantly turned on his heel.

'I think you've made a conquest,' Marietta said, bemused that a virile male had ignored her own presence so spectacularly.

For a second Lilli wondered if Marietta had seen her with Lucky Jack Coolidge and then Marietta said, 'Was that a snake tattoed on your beau's arm?'

There was a slight flush on Lilli's cheeks as, still thinking of Jack Coolidge's promise to seek her out again, she said, 'I don't know, Marietta. Probably. Don't all sailors have snake tattoos?'

Marietta's smile was so wide it nearly split her gamine like face in half. 'Of course they do,' she said agreeably, certain Lilli's faint blush indicated a *tendresse* for the muscular young sailor. She tucked her hand familiarly into the crook of Lilli's arm, for all the world as if they had been friends since childhood. 'Now tell me why you're going to Dawson as a Peabody bride when a girl with your looks could have snared a rich husband in 'Frisco without even trying.'

There was something about Marietta's fizzing ebullience that encouraged confidences and as they strolled down the deck, skirting the many groups of men in close conversation, Lilli said starkly, 'My mother died two years ago and my father passed away six months ago. My mother's sister and her husband gave Leo and Lottie and me a home, but because of my uncle's bad temper and rigidity it was a hateful home. No-one was happy in it, not even my aunt.' She paused, aware that she felt not the slightest twinge of regret for having swept Leo and Lottie so unceremoniously from beneath her uncle's roof.

'And?' Marietta prompted, enthralled.

Lilli checked that Leo was not within hearing distance and then, seeing that he was completely immersed in an imaginary world, pretending to be a steam train, she said simply, 'My uncle and aunt have no children of their own and I overheard my uncle saying he intended changing Leo's surname to his and rearing him as his own child. He would have known I would never have allowed him to carry out his plans and yesterday morning he created an excuse to turn me from the house.' Her vibrant blue eyes had darkened to near-black. 'He would never have allowed me to return. If I hadn't removed Leo and Lottie from the house immediately I might never have got another chance to do so.'

'And from 'Frisco as well?'

'I didn't *intend* leaving San Francisco. I intended getting a job, renting an apartment. I found it impossible to do either and then I walked into the Peabody Marriage Bureau . . .'

'And up the gangplank of the *Senator*!'

Lilli laughed. 'Yes. And so far I don't regret it.'

Marietta looked across at her. 'You might,' she said shrewdly, 'when we arrive.'

Ahead of them, near the stern, Lilli could see Lottie and Edie playing quoits. Lottie's sailor-hat was perched on the back of her head, its blue ribbon flying in the breeze. Edie, short and dumpy, was laughing uproariously, all shyness gone as, childlike, she happily played with someone her own mental age.

Lilli steered Marietta in the direction of the deckrail. The conversation they were having was one that would have to come to an abrupt end the minute they came within Lottie's hearing and she didn't want it to come to an end, not just yet.

'You mean marrying one of the men waiting for Peabody brides?' she asked, her eyebrows drawing together in a slight frown of apprehension.

Marietta nodded, a frizz of fox-red hair tumbling low over her forehead. 'Yes. The gents in question are rather a fly in the ointment, don't you think?'

Lilli didn't quite know how to answer. They certainly would be a fly in the ointment if she thought she was going to have to marry one of them, but she no longer did think she was going to have to marry one of them. She had never regarded herself as being fey but ever since the previous evening she had been convinced she had had a glimpse of the future. It was too much of a coincidence for the man of her dreams to be sailing to Dawson when her own footsteps had been led so extraordinarily to the same destination. Their accidental meeting in the street and the fact that they were now both aboard the *Senator* had to be Fate. Destiny.

She wondered how much she could tell Marietta. She couldn't tell her she had already met the Peabody client

62

she wished to marry because it had become obvious to her the second she had laid eyes on Jack Coolidge again that he would never in a million years be a Peabody client. Such a mere detail wouldn't stand in the way of Fate though. She remembered the heat at the back of his laughing eyes when he had promised to seek her out again and tell her all about Dawson. When she told him she was travelling there as a Peabody bride she just knew what his response was going to be. She just *knew*. 'I'm not sure I'll be fulfilling my contract when we arrive in Dawson,' she said, sensing she could trust Marietta not to divulge her secret. 'I think I might very well be marrying elsewhere.'

Marietta's slightly bulging eyes widened until she looked like a marmoset. They hadn't been aboard the *Senator* twenty-four hours! Miss Lilli Stullen was either the fastest worker she had ever known or else she and her sailor had met elsewhere, some time ago. 'Why, you dark horse! You look so prim and proper I would never have guessed!' Even as she said the words she realised they weren't true. Her new-found friend's generously curved mouth indicated hidden fires and from the moment they had first spoken to each other in the dining-saloon she had been aware of the look of daring in Lilli's black-lashed eyes; a recklessness she had instantly identified with and been drawn towards. She began to giggle. 'I suppose I should make my confession now. Like you, I haven't the slightest intention of marrying an unshaven, grizzle-haired, woman-hungry gold-prospector. The minute I set foot in Dawson I'm heading for the nearest dance-hall.'

Lilli wasn't sure what appalled her more. The image Marietta had conjured up of the kind of men awaiting their arrival, or her declaration that she was going to seek out the first dance-hall she came to. 'But why?' she asked, horribly afraid that she knew the answer but hoping she might be wrong.

'To become a dance-hall girl, of course,' Marietta said, her voice full of sweet reason. 'Dance-hall girls have to be the only sensible women in the Klondike. Do you remember what Susan Bumby said about them? They rarely marry because they're too busy having a good time, pocketing gold nuggets from men who've struck it rich? Well, having a good time and pocketing gold nuggets is going to suit me just fine.'

Looking at her, Lilli didn't doubt it for a moment. Whereas Kate Salway, Susan Bumby and Miss Nettlesham all dressed respectably in neat shirtwaists and formal skirts and even Lettie's and Edie's shabby dresses were properly sombre and plain, Marietta's clothes were vulgarly eye-catching. Yesterday she had been wearing raspberry-pink, a colour that had clashed searingly with her fiery hair. Today she was dressed in a heavily flounced mauve blouse, a deeply frilled turquoise skirt skimming beige high-button boots. 'But if you become a dance-hall girl none of us will be able to even acknowledge you,' she protested, stating the indisputable.

'The likes of Miss Nettlesham will never speak to me,' Marietta agreed, not remotely disconcerted, 'but that won't cause me any grief. And I doubt if, when it comes to it, you will stop speaking to me. Edie certainly won't stop speaking to me and though Susan Bumby might, I'd be surprised if Kate Salway cut me. Or Lettie.'

In one of the *Senator's* most luxurious cabins a handsomely mature woman with hair far redder than Marietta's, and naturally so, was saying to Lucky Jack Coolidge, 'I'd like to befriend Miss Stullen and give her some tips on how to handle life in Dawson but if I did, everyone would assume she was going to be working at the *Gold Nugget* or the *Mother Lode* and by the time we hit town her reputation would be in shreds.'

Jack exhaled a ring of fragrant blue cigar smoke. He was lolling in a comfortably padded cane chair, his legs crossed at the ankle, his booted feet resting on a pink, satin-topped dressing-table stool.

'I suppose you're right, Kitty, but it's a damned shame. I've a feeling Miss Lilli Stullen could do with a bit of straight feminine advice. She's obviously never been in a pioneer town before, much less a mining camp.'

'She'll get used to it,' Kitty said dryly. 'She might even have a protector waiting for her. Captain Stoddart says there are half a dozen Peabody brides aboard.'

Jack shook his head. 'She ain't one of 'em. She has a younger brother in tow. And the girl-friend she's travelling with is a kindergarten-teacher at Dawson public school.'

'Then maybe Miss Stullen's a teacher, too,' Kitty said, shuddering at the thought of such boring respectability. 'Do you think you could exert yourself, dear heart, and unhook me out of this corset? I don't see why I should be pinched damned near in half when I'm not on public view.'

'So what do you think of 'em?' Lettie asked morosely as Lilli sat down thankfully on one of the bottom bunks.

'Who?' Lilli began to unlace her boots. The nervous strain of the previous day was at last catching up with her and she knew she would only have to lie down to be asleep within seconds.

'The others. Miss High and Mighty Nettlesham and that masculine-looking Bumby girl and the racy Miss Rivere.'

Lilli eased her feet out of her boots. 'I liked them,' she said, swinging her legs up onto the bunk. 'Though perhaps not Miss Nettlesham,' she added quickly as Lettie's sullen features transformed themselves into an expression of stunned incredulity.

Lettie pushed a tangle of hair away from her eyes. 'They've all got high opinions of themselves, haven't they?' she said sourly, plucking at the cheap material of her dress.

There was a world of misery in her voice and Lilli abandoned the prospect of a nap. Different though Kate Salway and Susan Bumby and Marietta and Edie were from each other, friendly relations had been established between them all, almost immediately. Only Lettie had remained stubbornly unfriendly, taking no part in the

65

morning's conversation apart from her one comforting remark to Edie.

She looked searchingly across at Lettie, noticing for the first time the bruised look about her eyes and her pathetic thinness. Beneath her well-worn, bilberry-coloured dress her collar-bones were bonily prominent, her wrists and ankles almost stick-like. Her life before she had boarded the *Senator* had obviously been one of deprivation and, with sudden understanding, Lilli realised that Lettie was sullen because she had never had much love in her life and felt the world was against her.

'No,' she said gently, taking care to keep all censure from her voice. 'You haven't read them right, Lettie. None of them have high opinions of themselves. Kate Salway is more nervous than she's showing. Susan Bumby is painfully conscious that she isn't as pretty as you or Kate or Marietta. And Marietta has no false illusions about herself at all. She's simply herself.'

Lettie stopped plucking at her dress. 'They make me feel uncomfortable,' she said with stark frankness. 'Kate Salway talks like a Sunday School teacher and Susan Bumby thinks she knows everything there is to know.'

'Kate Salway probably *is* a Sunday School teacher, but that doesn't mean she has a high opinion of herself. And as Susan is a teacher, it's only to be expected she has a school-marmish manner.'

'I suppose so.' Lettie's voice was grudging. 'But they're both so prissy I can't see either of them standing up to be auctioned off to the highest bidder, can you?'

Lilli's eyes nearly popped out of her head. '*Auctioned?*' she said, leaning her weight on her elbow as she stared across at Lettie. '*Auctioned?* What in the world do you mean, Lettie? No-one's going to be auctioned! They will be introduced by a representative of the marriage bureau, a Mr Nelson, to the gentlemen who have applied to the bureau for wives.'

Lettie regarded her pityingly. 'You don't really think that's going to be the way of it, do you? Didn't you listen to what Susan Bumby said to you at breakfast? She said she didn't think anyone would *choose* you as a bride, not as you had two children in tow.'

'Being chosen is a lot different to being auctioned! And Susan Bumby certainly wouldn't allow herself to be auctioned. It would be far too dangerous for her. What if no-one made a bid?' She shuddered at the very thought. 'Susan certainly wouldn't expose herself to that kind of humiliation. She's far too intelligent.'

'Oh, yeah?' Lettie swung her legs off her bunk and sat on the edge of it, her hands clasped between her knees. 'There are thousands of men roaming the Klondike hoping to strike it rich. Like men everywhere a lot of them would like the home comforts a wife provides, but north of British Columbia respectable woman are as rare as penguins in the Sahara. Which is why the Peabody Marriage Bureau is doing such a roaring trade supplying them with respectable women who can't afford to be choosy. And when we arrive in Dawson it's going to be the *men* who take their pick. Not us.'

Lilli pushed herself up into a sitting position. 'What do you mean by "women who can't afford to be choosy"?' she demanded indignantly. '*I* don't fall in that category! Marietta couldn't possibly fall into that category and neither could Kate . . .'

'Oh yeah?' Lettie said again. 'You don't have to look like the back of a tram to be so desperate you become a Peabody bride. I bet *you* didn't have much choice, did you? Little Edie certainly didn't. I doubt if racy Miss Rivere even *intends* marrying anyone. Kate Salway never did tell us why she was going to Dawson to marry but you can bet your sweet life the alternatives must have been pretty horrendous. I know mine were.'

There was thick bitterness in her voice and Lilli wanted to ask her just what those alternatives had been. Lettie gave her no opportunity.

'And so when we get to Dawson Mr Nelson is going to be able to dispose of us as he thinks fit,' she said savagely, 'and that's going to be in a way which is to his employer's best financial advantage.'

'It isn't going to be with an auction.' Lilli's voice was firm. Even though she had already made up her mind that, like Marietta, she would not be marrying any of Mrs Peabody's clients, it was horrific beyond belief to think that her new-found friends might be treated in such an undignified, abominable manner. And she didn't believe it. Not for a minute.

'Wait and see,' Lilli said darkly. 'We're just cattle to market. Mrs Peabody is nothing but a white slave trader under a different guise.'

Lilli abandoned trying to argue with her. Lettie would find out differently when they arrived. She closed her eyes. She had been up since the crack of dawn and she needed to sleep, if only for thirty minutes.

Jack Coolidge's image fizzed against the backs of her eyelids. He had been wonderfully kind to Leo. Not many men would have taken the time to talk to a six year old boy the way he had done. She was glad he wasn't a gold-prospector, especially if they were all as unshaven and grizzle-haired as Marietta said they were. Initially she had been rather shocked to discover he was a professional gambler but remembering her father's love of gambling had helped her to quickly come to terms with the discovery, especially as her father had never allowed his gambling to harm his family in any way.

She smiled happily and then, just as sleep was about to claim her, another thought tugged at her muzzy brain. Hadn't Marietta, or perhaps it had been Edie or Kate, mentioned a dance-hall girl in the same breath they had spoken of Jack? What was it they had said exactly? She couldn't remember.

'I don't know how you endure it,' Miss Nettlesham said to her that evening as she waylaid her near the stairs on the hurricane-deck. 'Sharing a cabin with that Rivere creature or the retarded overgrown child she seems to have taken under her wing would be bad enough, but sharing it with a low-class, unclean . . .'

68

Assuming rightly that Miss Nettlesham was referring to Lettie, Lilli said sharply, 'Lettie is shabby, not unclean.'

Miss Nettlesham adjusted the chiffon scarf securing her hat with a kid-gloved hand. 'You must have very bad eye-sight, Miss Stullen, if you believe unwashed hair can be described as *shabby*.'

It was a point difficult to argue and Lilli didn't attempt to. She had left Leo and Lottie playing Halma with Susan Bumby and had been strolling the decks in the hope of accidentally-on-purpose meeting Lucky Jack Coolidge again. If she did so in Miss Nettlesham's company the encounter would be a complete waste of time and she was eager for Miss Nettlesham to take her leave of her.

'As for that Rivere woman!' Miss Nettlesham shuddered and Lilli knew it wasn't from cold, even though the evening breeze was decidedly chilly. 'Being seen in the company of a woman like that is enough to damn all our reputations. Do you know that she actually engaged Kitty Dufresne in conversation this morning? And in *public!*'

Lilli pulled the collar of her box-coat closer around her throat. There was no sign of a tall, broad-shouldered, Homburg-hatted figure, and good manners demanded Miss Nettlesham be endured. 'Who is Kitty Dufresne?' she asked politely, wondering how on earth Miss Nettlesham was going to accommodate herself to the hardship of life in a mining camp.

Miss Nettlesham's camel-like nostrils quivered. 'In her day Kitty Dufresne was the most notorious dance-hall girl in Dawson. Now, on behalf of her paramour, she employs dance-hall girls for the *Gold Nugget* and all the other disreputable dance-halls and saloons and 'gaming hells' he owns.'

At the word 'gaming' Lilli's attention was caught. Although she had not the slightest doubt that Jack Coolidge's gambling saloons would not be 'hells' but would be exceedingly well run establishments, it was quite possible that the owner of the *Gold Nugget* was a business rival of his. 'How come you know so much about the

69

personalities of Dawson, Miss Nettlesham?' she asked, intrigued. 'And who is this person who owns so many "gaming hells?"'

Across the silk-grey Pacific the coastline of British Columbia was violet against the twilit sky. Miss Nettlesham made an abrupt about-turn, obliging Lilli to forego the sight and face the open ocean. 'Really, Miss Stullen! I'm surprised you need to ask when he's aboard ship! You must walk around with your eyes closed and your ears shut! He's Lucky Jack Coolidge, of course. Though what's lucky about a man no respectable person would pass the time of day with, I can't begin to imagine!'

Chapter Five

Giddily, Lilli looked out beyond the hurricane-deck over the vast, velvet-dark expanse of the Pacific. Was Miss Nettlesham telling her the gospel truth or was she simply repeating malicious and untrue rumour and gossip? After all, Jack Coolidge had freely admitted to her that he was a professional gambler and that he owned many gambling saloons in Dawson. It was a fact she had already come to terms with and Miss Nettlesham's describing them as 'hells' was utterly meaningless. She was the kind of stiff and starchy young woman who would describe *any* gambling saloon as being a gambling 'hell'. It was the coupling of his name with a woman's, a woman apparently aboard the *Senator*, that made it feel as if the deck was tipping at her feet.

'Did you say Miss Dufresne employs dance-hall girls for Mr Coolidge's establishments?,' she asked, trying to keep her voice cool and disinterested.

'*Procuring* would be a better description,' Miss Nettlesham retorted tartly. 'No doubt she struck gold when she engaged Miss Rivere in conversation. I knew the instant I set eyes on that young woman she was destined for Klondike City.'

'Then Miss Dufresne is an *employee*, of Mr Coolidge's?' Lilli persisted, the deck beginning to steady. 'And where is Klondike City? I've never heard of it. Is it near Dawson?'

The hurricane-deck was small and they had again been obliged to turn-about. In the pale Northern twilight Miss Nettlesham's albino fairness gave her a look of almost ghostly transparency. She raised a gloved hand to her

71

mouth, coughed discreetly behind it and said, 'You won't have heard of Klondike City, Miss Stullen, because under normal circumstances it would *never* be mentioned in polite conversation. Klondike City is the . . .' she lowered her voice almost to a whisper, 'the *red-light* district of Dawson.'

Lilli's eyes widened. Miss Nettlesham's claims seemed to be growing wilder and wilder. She had obviously never set foot inside a gambling saloon and yet authoritively described Jack Coolidge's gambling saloons as 'hells'; she had assumed, on no other evidence apart from Miss Kitty Dufresne being employed by Lucky Jack, that Miss Dufresne was Jack's 'paramour'. And now, without ever having set foot in Dawson, she was quite categorically stating that part of it, known as Klondike City, was an area of ill repute.

'But how can you possibly *know*?' she demanded, putting her thoughts into words. 'You've never *been* to Dawson. You . . .'

'My brother is practically *mayor* of Dawson,' Miss Nettlesham said loftily. 'The gentleman I am to marry is a close friend of his. Dawson may have been a rough pioneer town three years ago but believe me, Miss Stullen, there is an *aristocracy* there now.'

Lilli didn't bother to ask if Miss Nettlesham's brother was a leading light of Dawson's so-called 'aristocracy'. She knew what the answer would be. She knew also that she was wasting her time in hoping to have a moonlit encounter with Jack Coolidge. From beneath their feet, in the saloon, came raucous laughter as around crowded tables men played poker and rummy. No doubt Lucky Jack was also playing cards or shooting dice. It was time for her to abandon hope and go to bed. In the morning she would ask Susan Bumby what she knew about Jack Coolidge and his business enterprises. Susan would be a far more reliable source of information than Miss Nettlesham. Susan *lived* in Dawson. She was a sourdough.

'Goodnight,' she said crisply, knowing that sourdoughs were the true aristocrats of Dawson and doubting if

Miss know-all Nettlesham was even familiar with the term.

When she slipped quietly into the cabin it was to find everyone, even Lettie, fast asleep. Gently she removed Leo's thumb from his mouth and tucked Lottie's blanket higher around her shoulders. Then she undressed, pulled a cambric nightdress over her head and climbed into the bunk above Lettie's.

Perhaps because of her nap earlier in the day, sleep refused to come. She wondered what was happening in the Mosely household. Her uncle would now be very well aware she had taken Leo and Lottie from the house. What would he have done? Employed someone to search for them? Reported them to the police as being missing? Engaged a lawyer in order to issue some kind of legal court order demanding their return? Knowing her uncle, he had probably taken all three courses of action. He would certainly have made it legally impossible for her to return to San Francisco and keep Leo and Lottie in her care.

She turned on her side, queasily trying to ignore the *Senator's* increasing pitch and roll. And what about Miss Nettlesham's allegation that Kitty Dufresne was Lucky Jack's paramour? What if it were correct? What if Kitty Dufresne weren't simply a business associate or employee? She fisted her pillow, trying to break up its uncomfortable bulk. If all her intuitive feelings about Fate and Destiny were wrong, where would that leave her? The answer came with sickening certainty. It would leave her having to fulfil her obligation to the Peabody Marriage Bureau; marrying a man she did not know and would probably never want to know.

She slept restlessly and by the time Leo woke her, demanding to be taken up on deck, she still hadn't arrived at a solution to her dilemma. She could hardly follow Marietta's example and renege on her obligation to the marriage bureau to become a dance-hall girl. And she couldn't emulate Susan Bumby and apply for a position as a kindergarten-teacher. Teaching staff for Dawson's small school were appointed by the superintendent of education for the Yukon. And the superintendent would hardly appoint someone as unqualified as herself.

'Come *on*,' Leo demanded impatiently, tugging at her hand. 'It's stuffy down here. I want to talk to Lucky Jack again. I want him to teach me some card-tricks. Please say you've changed your mind, Lilli, and that he can teach me some card-tricks!'

At the thought of running into Jack Coolidge taking an early morning stroll Lilli began to fish through her carpet-bag for a clean shirtwaist. The one she retrieved was caramel-coloured with a high mandarin neck and long, full sleeves, cinched tightly at the wrist.

'Come *on*,' Leo demanded again in an agony of impatience as she tucked the blouse into her cream serge skirt. She ignored him, lacing up her meticulously polished brown boots, thinking with longing of Marietta's beige boots. Beige was just the shade to tone with caramel and cream.

'We might be able to go ashore today,' Leo was saying, both hands tight around the cabin's door-knob. 'Miss Bumby says the *Senator* will be calling in at Seattle for more passengers and fuel. If we can go ashore, can I go ashore with Miss Bumby? She always has candy in her pockets and she tells wonderful stories of *cheechakos* and mushers and sourdoughs.'

Lilli had no idea what a *cheechako* or a musher was. She brushed her thick, blue-black hair, anchoring it in a neat twist on top of her head with tortoiseshell pins. Ignoring his request that she allow Jack Coolidge to teach him card-tricks, she said instead, 'Tell me what a *cheechako* is? Is it an Alaskan bird? An Alaskan Indian?'

Leo giggled. 'Silly,' he said, as they left the cabin together and began to walk to the nearest companion-way. 'A *cheechako* is a tenderfoot. Someone who's never been to Alaska before. And a musher is an old hand who hasn't yet struck it rich.'

On deck the morning air was fresh and balmy, with already an undertone of summer heat.

'That will be British Columbia,' Leo said knowledgeably, pointing to the green, ragged coastline. 'I know, 'cos Miss Bumby told me we'd be sailing off the coast of British Columbia today. And soon we'll be in the waters of the Inside Passage and in the *real* North! Miss Bumby says we'll see Indian settlements and forts and . . .'

Lilli stopped listening. She was glad Leo had formed an attachment to someone who was so educationally helpful to him, but she had more important things on her mind than scenery and sights. She needed to find out if she had been school-girlishly foolish in believing that Lucky Jack was her Destiny. And the only way she could do that was by telling him she was a Peabody bride. His reaction would either be all that her intuition assured her it would be, or it would be indifference. And if it were indifference . . . If it were indifference then she would have a lot of very hard thinking to do.

'You can jaw on the deck all day, honey,' Kitty Dufresne said, laying back against a mass of pillows far different in quality from the pillows Lilli and her friends endured. 'I'm not moving from here until we reach Skagway. Ships and me have never seen eye to eye. They're too damned unpredictable.'

Jack grinned. He was sitting on the edge of Kitty's bed wearing only his pants. As he reached for silk socks and London-made bespoke boots, the well-toned muscles in his shoulders rippled.

Kitty gave a deep, contented sigh. She was glad to be going back to Dawson, for Dawson had become home, but their trip to London, Paris and Rome had been an eye-opener. The castles and chateaux and palazzi they had seen had been the real thing, some of them built three or even four hundred years ago; not imitations erected in a few crazy, goldrich weeks.

As Jack began to pull on a snowy white shirt, the cuffs and front trimmed in hand-made lace, she reflected that, apart from a few minor incidents, Jack had behaved very well in Europe. They had had a minor fracas over the unladylike persistence of a true-blue lady in England. Why some women couldn't just take 'no' for an answer, Kitty had never been able to understand. As it was, twenty year old Lady Sarah Dunwoody had followed them from London to Paris, so certain of being lovingly welcomed by Jack it had really been quite pathetic. Remembering the incident, Kitty shook her head in disbelief. Maternally she had comforted the distraught girl, given her the kind of straight advice her mother should have given her, and sent her on her way a sadder but wiser young woman; as she had done for so many other girls so often before and would no doubt do many times again.

'I was accosted by a girl wanting dance-hall work yesterday,' she said, dismissing Lady Sarah Dunwoody from her thoughts and adjusting the fall of her ivory-silk negligée so that it set her creamy-fleshed, magnificent bosom off to even greater advantage. 'Her name is Marietta Rivere and she's very sparky. Quite classy too. The only snag is she's travelling as a Peabody girl and so if I take her on you'll have to pay off Josh Nelson.' She pulled a face as she said Nelson's name, giving a theatrical shudder. The negligée, slipping even further, revealed a perky rose-red nipple.

Jack slipped his gold watch into his vest pocket as he looked across at her and grinned. For a woman of thirty-five Kitty was in magnificent shape. If she was thinking of engaging the Rivere girl for the *Gold Nugget*, the Rivere girl would have to be in good shape too. 'I'll be happy to save a female from Nelson's greedy claws,' he said, shrugging an exquisitely tailored jacket on, his shirt still open at his throat. 'What does she look like? If I see her and recognise her I'll be able to give you my opinion.'

'Petite. A rather odd face, but attractively odd. Jungle-green eyes. Wide mouth. Foxy hair piled in an *outré* pompadour. Yesterday her blouse was mauve and her skirt turquoise. If she's half the girl I think she is she'll

76

be dressed in something different today, equally cheap but equally sizzling.'

'She doesn't sound quite the usual Peabody bride,' Jack said, amused by the description. 'I wonder what Amy Peabody was thinking of? She should have known such an exotic bird would fly her coop.'

Kitty shrugged. 'She's still going to get her dough, isn't she?' she said practically as he began to head for the state-room door.

He turned, a hand on the doorhandle. 'Only if I think the goods are worth the outlay.'

'Pah!' A smile dimpled the corner of her mouth. Where girls for the *Gold Nugget* were concerned she made the decisions and they both knew it. 'Don't break any hearts,' she admonished as he opened the door and blew her a kiss.

'I shall behave like a choirboy. My only vice today is going to be in teaching little Leo Stullen how to hold his own at poker.'

A lock of sun-gold hair had fallen low across his brow and Kitty reflected that it would be easy to imagine him as a choirboy. Easy but not very realistic. 'I thought you said his sister had hit the roof when you had suggested teaching the kid card-tricks?' The rose-red nipple wobbled teasingly as she pushed herself into a more comfortable position against the pillows.

Jack's grin deepened. Was she knowingly trying to lure him into staying with her a little longer? If so, she wasn't going to succeed. No matter how great the temptation, he wanted a little fresh sea air. And he wanted to be entertained by Lilli Stullen's refreshing naivety. 'Those were simply tricks. This time I'm going to teach him a life-skill.'

Kitty hooted with laughter and threw a pillow at the closing door. A life-skill indeed! He was more likely going to be put the kid on the road to ruin. She adjusted her negligée, covering the peeping nipple. Just as long as he didn't ruin the sister. She didn't want to be comforting any more sobbing females for a while. She picked a

77

coffee-cream out of a box of Belgian chocolates lying by her side. All that really mattered was that he didn't break *her* heart. And after the length of time they had been together, and all they had gone through together, she was as sure as god made little green apples that he never would.

When Lilli took Leo and Lottie into the crowded dining-saloon for breakfast there was no sign of Miss Nettlesham.

'She obviously meant it when she said she wasn't going to be seen in public with us again,' Kate Salway said wryly, pouring Leo a beaker of milk.

'She talked to Lilli last night,' Edie offered, eager to be helpful. 'I know because they were on the hurricane-deck and I was sitting beneath the stairs.'

Lilli's eyes widened fractionally at the disclosure. Thank goodness she hadn't been enjoying a rendezvous with her Greek god!

'A nice man told me yesterday that we were all very lucky,' Edie confided, making up for her silence of the previous morning. 'We're going to be some of the first people ever to ride the new railway. He said there's nothing to be scared of but I *am* scared. I've never been on a train and he said it goes ever so fast.'

'I'll hold your hand, honey,' Marietta said, buttering a great slab of bread. Her blouse today was a vibrant yellow, her skirt a searing orange.

It occurred to Lilli that now would be a good time to clarify exactly what their travel arrangements were. She still didn't even know where their voyage came to an end. 'What railway?' she asked, forking crisp bacon on to Lottie's plate. 'Where does it go from? Where does it go to?'

'It goes to Dawson, silly,' Edie said, giggling. 'Even *I* know that!'

'We disembark at Skagway,' Marietta said, hoping she would have the chance of another conversation with Kitty Dufresne before Skagway was reached. Kitty had intimated that she *might* be suitable as a dance-hall girl

78

but hadn't yet actually offered her a job. 'From there we go by train, over the White Pass, to Whitehorse.'

'Whitehorse is at the head of the navigational waters of the Yukon,' Susan Bumby added, ever the schoolmistress.

'And from there we sail down the Yukon to Dawson.' Marietta's eyes sparkled naughtily, 'Just like Cleopatra and her handmaidens sailing down the Nile,' she said, causing Edie to giggle yet again and Susan Bumby to blush scarlet.

It was Lottie who first noticed Lilli had become the object of a fellow passenger's attention. She squeezed hold of Lilli's hand. 'Someone is looking at you,' she whispered. 'A man at the next table with hair nearly the colour of Marietta's.'

Even though commonsense told her the description couldn't possibly apply to Lucky Jack Coolidge, Lilli's heart practically leapt into her throat. Eagerly she looked across to the next table, but the eyes that met hers were not teasing and gold-flecked. They were sombre and, at a guess, dark green or grey. They belonged to the red-haired man who had been pointed out to her as being a recently released convict. Swiftly she looked back down again at her plate, disappointment surging through her.

'He's still looking at you,' Lottie said again. 'Do you think he think he knows you?'

'I think he's thinking he'd *like* to get to know her,' Marietta said mischievously. 'I don't think *I'd* object if he wanted to get to know *me* a little better! Have you seen the width of his shoulders? He's the nearest thing to a real live Hercules I've ever seen.'

'He's a criminal,' Lilli said tartly. 'He's a man who's been paroled only on the understanding that he makes a new life for himself in the far north.'

As every head on the ladies-only table turned in his direction the object of their interest returned his attention to his breakfast, a pulse throbbing at the corner of his well-shaped jaw.

'Do you think he's a bank robber?' Edie whispered, wide-eyed. 'Do you think he's a *murderer*?'

'I think we should stop talking about him in case he overhears us,' Kate said wisely. 'Does anyone know if we'll be able to make a detour to see the Whitehorse Rapids when we reach Whitehorse? And if we can, would anyone like to come with me?'

'I'm going to play deck quoits with Edie,' Lottie said the instant breakfast was over.

'And I'm going to play deck quoits, too,' Leo said, aware he was being left out of something and not liking it.

Lottie opened her mouth to protest and then changed her mind. She'd always taken a fair share of responsibility where Leo was concerned and there was no reason, just because they were aboard a boat, that she shouldn't be doing so now.

'Can I come as well?' Lettie said, startling everyone who had become accustomed to her sullen silences.

''Course you can.' Lottie knew Lettie better than anyone else at the table apart, perhaps, from Lilli, and she knew Lettie's unsociability was only a form of shyness.

Lilli gave her little sister's hand a squeeze of gratitude. With Lottie and Leo and Lettie playing quoits she would be able to stroll the deck unaccompanied and again fall into conversation with Lucky Jack Coolidge. And this time she would make quite sure she told him she was a Peabody bride. And then, God willing, he would put all her doubts to rest and fulfil all her fevered expectations.

The minute she stepped out onto the crowded deck relief swamped her. He was standing bare-headed exactly on the spot where they had talked together the previous day. No-one else was with him. With his wheat-gold hair gleaming in the morning sunlight, his hands nonchalantly in his pockets, he was quite obviously waiting for someone. And with singing elation she knew that the someone was herself.

80

'Good morning, Mr Coolidge,' she said demurely as she neared him.

He had been looking out to sea and he turned his head instantly, flashing her his easy, down-slanting smile. 'Good morning, Miss Stullen,' he said, removing his hands from his pockets and inclining his head courteously. 'Have we to take a turn around the deck while I tell you about Dawson?'

'That would be nice.' She could hardly keep the jubilation from her voice. It was going to be all right. She just knew it was. 'I've heard so many confusing things, Mr Coolidge. Have you lived in Dawson long?'

'No-one has lived in Dawson for long, Miss Stullen.' Amusement was once again thick in his voice. 'Until four years ago it didn't exist.'

He began to walk at strolling pace and she fell into step beside him. 'But I guess I've lived there as long as most,' he continued as they skirted past a group of prospectors, one of them neatly kitted out in khaki, another wearing elegant riding-breeches. 'I was in 'Frisco when the *Excelsior* docked in July '97. The prospectors who first struck gold in the Klondike were aboard her. They had brought so much gold out of Bonanza Creek they staggered beneath its weight when they disembarked. Even before the news hit the papers I'd booked a berth on the next ship going north.'

She looked across at him curiously, 'But you told Leo you weren't a prospector,' she said as her stomach somersaulted at the sheer handsomeness of his neatly trimmed moustache and chiselled mouth, his slightly aquiline nose and suntanned-skin. 'That you'd never been a prospector.'

The breeze had blown a lock of hair low across his brow and he brushed it back. 'I was telling him the truth,' he said, a grin in his voice. 'There's more ways of making a fortune than digging it out of the earth.'

She looked puzzled.

'It's easier to take it from a miner's pockets in a saloon than standing knee-deep in water in a creek, don't you think?'

Her mouth curved in a smile. 'Yes. Of course. I wasn't thinking. And so you built and opened up a saloon?'

'Saloons,' he corrected. 'And hotels. By the end of '97 there were more millionaires per square inch in Dawson than any other place in the world and nearly all of 'em were living in shacks not fit for dogs. Until I built the Palace. And then the Majestic.'

The relief she had initially felt when seeing him waiting for her, deepened. He was far more than merely a professional gambler. The 'gambling hells' Miss Nettlesham had spoken off were nothing but a lurid flight of her imagination. Jack Coolidge was a businessman, and businessmen were *respectable*.

Some yards away, his elbows resting on the deck-rail, Ringan Cameron watched them, a slight frown creasing his brows. Although he had kept himself to himself since boarding ship he had heard enough drifts of conversation to know the identity of the man. He was Lucky Jack Coolidge, a professional gambler, who owned more than his fair share of Dawson. He didn't know the young woman's name. What he did know, though, was that she didn't look the kind of young woman who habitually associated with men of such raffish reputation.

As he watched them Coolidge obviously said something amusing because the young woman laughed. It was warm, husky laughter. There was nothing affected or raucous about it. He felt a stab of longing. It had been a long time since he had heard a woman laugh. Christ, until boarding the *Senator* it had been a long time since he had *seen* a woman. Before he could stop himself, before he could protect himself, his thoughts turned to Patti and the stab of longing became a scream of pain.

Patti. Patti was dead and he had served his time and now he was free. Free to do what, though? Though he had leapt at the chance of parole and the Klondike he couldn't honestly see himself grubbing for gold in creeks and gullies. Avarice had never been one of his vices. What he wanted to do was what he had always wanted

82

to do; what he was trained to do. He wanted to practise medicine.

A stiff breeze tugged at his hair and sent a chill knifing through his green plaid shirt. Who the hell would patronise a doctor who had served a prison sentence for murder? Surely not even tough-as-old-boots prospectors would put their lives in the hands of a man who had taken a life. 'Even if they knew the circumstances?' a small inner voice queried. Beneath his thick auburn moustache his lips tightened. The circumstances hadn't hampered the judge from finding him guilty and though other people might regard his ten-year sentence as having been light and his early parole as being generous, he didn't. Why should he? He had decked the man who had destroyed his kid sister's life; the man who had demanded she visit an abortionist; the man who had not even called for a doctor as she lay bleeding to death.

His jaw tightened. When he had driven his fist into Tad Rowntree's jaw he hadn't meant to kill him. But he'd felt no remorse when he had discovered he had done so. And he felt no remorse now. Rowntree had been scum. The lowest of the low. But if he felt no remorse for having taken Rowntree's life, what sort of creature did that make him? Certainly not a very moral one. And doctors were moral men. Or at least the doctors he had had always sought to emulate were moral men.

He could feel the black dog of depression beginning to gnaw at him and with immense mental effort he freed himself from its clutches. He would be damned if, now he was free, he would succumb to the despair that had darkened his days in jail. Not when the breeze was tugging at his hair and there was the tang of salt-spray on his lips and the heat of sunshine on his face. He was a free man, thank God, and he was never going to live in an enclosed space ever again.

Lucky Jack Coolidge and his companion, having completed one circuit of the deck, were now embarking on other. He heard Coolidge chuckle; heard again the young woman's husky warm laughter. There was something

83

delightfully unchained about it. It reminded him of the natural laughter of a child. And then he saw the children running towards her.

He eased himself into a more comfortable position against the deck-rails. It was her easy joyful manner with the children that had first caught his attention. The boy looked a little imp. Full of life and intelligence. And the girl, with her sailor-hat perched jauntily on the back of her braided hair and her black stockings wrinkling slightly about her ankles, radiated well-being and a sense of responsibility beyond her years.

Lucky Jack Coolidge squatted down on his haunches to talk face to face to the the little boy, and as the girl took hold of the young woman's hand, another young woman, who had obviously had temporary care of the children, tentatively approached. She was dark and ungainly and obviously deeply embarrassed at being put in a situation where she had little choice but to acknowledge the disreputable Mr Coolidge.

As he watched the little scene he wondered again what the relationship was between the young woman who was so friendly with Jack Coolidge, and the children in her care. She couldn't possibly be their mother. The little girl was ten or eleven and the young woman looked to be no more than eighteen. His throat tightened. Patti had been eighteen. Eighteen and sweet and loving and very, very foolish.

With steely determination he forced his thoughts away from Patti and back to the young woman who had caught his attention when she had boarded the *Senator* in such haste, almost as the gangplank was being raised.

If she wasn't the children's mother, was she then their sister? It seemed a logical assumption. Her manner with them was too free and easy for her to be their nanny or governess. He liked the way the children's faces lit up whenever they ran to greet her. He liked the way she lovingly ruffled the little boy's hair, always lovingly took hold of the little girl's hand, always seemed as pleased to be with them as they were to be with her.

Coolidge was now standing tall again. The ungainly young woman was looking as though she wished the deck would open and swallow her up. The little boy was tugging at Coolidge's hand, obviously asking him something.

The breeze changed direction and he heard Coolidge say, 'If you want to meet a genuine musher, young Leo, I can sure introduce you to one.'

Leo. It was a nice name. He wondered if it was short for Leonard or Leopold. He wondered what the young woman's name was.

Coolidge took his leave of the young women, strolling off in the direction of the upper-deck companionway, Leo happily at his side.

Ringan adjusted his stance against the rail so that it didn't dig as deeply into the small of his back. However notorious Lucky Jack Coolidge's reputation, he was obviously a man with redeeming qualities. Not many men would have had the sensitivity to realise that if they squatted down on their haunches when speaking to a child they would seem less intimidating.

The two young women were now talking and the little girl turned, looking for diversion. Her eyes met his, just as they had done a little earlier at the breakfast-table. He saw her stiffen and look almost of alarm cross her face. Realizing that it was beginning to look as if he were taking a far from healthy interest in her older sister, if it *was* her older sister, he broke eye contact immediately, pushing himself away from the rail, beginning to stride towards the stern.

'Gambling saloons are gambling saloons,' Susan Bumby said, deeply troubled. 'None of them are respectable.'

'But they're not *hells*, are they?' Lilli persisted. 'Miss Nettlesham made them sound as if they were pits of unimaginable iniquity.'

'Some of them are. Some of them are little better than brothels. And though you weren't to know, and though I must admit Mr Coolidge is very charming, it really wouldn't do for people in Dawson to be under the impression that you were on friendly terms with him. They would think you were fast and . . .'

'But Mr Coolidge is a businessman! He not only owns gambling saloons he owns hotels as well. Hotel owners aren't disreputable. Think of Mr Astor!'

Susan Bumby's gruff voice was troubled. 'Mr Waldorf Astor is worlds removed from Lucky Jack Coolidge. I quite appreciate that you want to see him in the best possible light, Lilli, but please take my word for it, he is *not* a gentleman a respectable young woman should have dealings with. Some of his gambling saloons are very dubious indeed.'

Lilli clenched her jaw mutinously. She didn't believe it. She *couldn't* believe it. From the moment she had realized Jack Coolidge was aboard the *Senator* she had been utterly certain he was her Fate. She still was utterly certain. Life couldn't be so cruel as to have thrown her across the path of the handsomest, most charming man in the world, and then thrown them together again, aboard the *Senator*, both bound for a one-street town thousands of miles from civilization, and *not* destined them for each other. Not when her circumstances were what they were.

'I really don't think . . .' she began and then Lottie, who had been amusing herself playing a makeshift game of hopscotch, suddenly looked up to the deck above them and gave a horrified cry.

'*Lilli! Quick! Look at Leo! He's going to fall!*'

Lilli and Susan looked immediately in the direction Lottie was pointing.

On the deck above them, twenty yards or so nearer to the stern than where they were standing, Leo was swinging on the davits of a lifeboat. It was secured so that it hung in space and each time Leo swung round on the davit he did so with nothing between his feet and a perilous drop to the ocean.

'Dear God in heaven!' Lilli gasped, beginning to run for the companionway. 'Can't he see? Doesn't he realise?'

Susan was hard on her heels. Lottie already ahead of her. Their agitation had alerted their fellow passengers to the awareness that something was amiss and as other eyes flew to the lifeboat and Leo's small figure swinging on the davits there were shouts of, '*Hoist that kid to safety for Christ's sake!*'

All the shouts came seconds too late. As Leo kicked himself off from the lifeboat for another dizzying swing his foot slipped and, in consternation, he let go of the davit.

There was a scream of terror. Shouts of alarm.

Lilli saw Leo's body plunge down over the side of the boat and into the ocean and then she was running, running to the deck-rails.

There were cries of '*Throw a rope! Lower a lifeboat! Bring the boat around!*'

Lilli was heedless of them all. The *Senator's* undertow would suck Leo down. He wouldn't be able to surface. And even if he did so he was far too small to catch a rope even if one were thrown to him.

Before she could reach the rail and throw herself into the ocean, someone else did so. Only he didn't throw himself in. He dived, straight and clean.

As Lilli hurled herself against the rail several pairs of masculine arms steadied and held her.

'No use you takin' a swim as well, lady,' someone said, their grip on her arm tightening. 'The Scottie's got him. And with shoulder muscles like his he'll be able to keep afloat for as long as it takes to get a rope or a lifeboat to the pair of 'em.'

Lilli felt as if her heart was going to burst. Far below and now far behind them in the heaving waves, the red-haired ex-prisoner was treading water, a terrified Leo held tightly in one arm while he helped keep the pair of them afloat with the other.

Through all the shouting and activity around her Lilli was aware only that Leo and his rescuer were growing smaller and smaller by the second as they were left further and further behind in the *Senator's* wake. Then the lifeboat crashed into the water to the accompaniment of rousing cheers. One of the sailors manning it was the sailor who had carried her bags for her when she had boarded, but the fact barely impinged on her consciousness.

'Please God let them stay afloat until it reaches them!' she prayed aloud against her clenched knuckle. 'Please God don't let Leo drown! Please God! Please! *Please*!'

'It's nearly there,' Susan said unsteadily. 'It's going to be all right, Lilli. Leo's safe.'

Not until she saw Leo being hauled aboard the lifeboat like a little drowned rat did Lilli give herself up to relief. With tears streaming down her face she saw the Scotsman heave himself aboard and the sailors begin to pull on the oars.

Leo was safe. It was over. But if it hadn't been for the Scotsman it would have been over in a very different way. Leo would have been drowned. Even if she had thrown herself in after him, she wouldn't have had the strength to have swum against the *Senator's* undertow and nor, she suspected, would anyone else. Ex-prisoner or not, he was a hero. And she would never, in a million years, be able to thank him enough.

Chapter Six

A rope ladder was thrown over the side. The young seaman who had shown such an interest in her when she had first boarded climbed nimbly up it, a white-faced Leo tucked under his arm.

'Oh God!' Lilli's voice broke in a sob. 'Oh, Leo! *Leo!*'

As the seaman set Leo down on the deck and Leo wobbled unsteadily on very shaky legs her arms flew round him, hugging him so tight he was again in danger of dying, this time by suffocation.

'Thank Christ!' A familiar male voice said with heartfelt relief. 'One minute he was with me, the next . . .' Lucky Jack's sun-tanned face was drained of colour.

Little Leo Stullen had come within a hair's breadth of drowning and if he had drowned, he would have been responsible.

'It's all right.' Lilli didn't need excuses or explanations. At least not now. Now all that mattered was that Leo was safe and sound.

'I was being a trapeze artiste,' Leo said, his head pressed close against her shoulder, his voice as wobbly as his legs. 'Like the trapeze artistes in Wild Bill Hickock's Wild West Show.'

Another sailor climbed the rope-ladder and heaved himself on to the deck and then a resounding cheer went up as he was followed by the Scotsman. He was still breathing heavily. His thick mass of curly hair, so dark with water it was no longer a fiery red but a rich mahogany, hung in dripping rats' tails. Water streamed from his eyebrows and his heavy moustache.

His sodden plaid shirt and his britches clung to him like a second skin.

Gently Lilli released her hold of Leo and faced his rescuer. He had kicked off his boots before diving into the ocean and even without them he towered above her. If she hadn't raised her head, her eyes would have been facing the centre of his chest.

'I'm Miss Lilli Stullen. I don't know how to thank you,' she said unsteadily, tears of relief still glittering on her long, dark eyelashes. 'If it hadn't been for you . . .'

'It was nothing,' he said with embarrassed dismissiveness. 'I was simply the first to react. If I hadna dived in, a dozen others would have.'

Though he didn't speak with a heavy Scots accent, there was an attractive burr in his voice. His eyes were grey. A warm, deep grey. Beneath his rust-coloured, water-logged moustache she could see that his mouth was well-shaped, as was his strong-looking, straight nose and the blunt line of his jaw. He looked acutely discomfited.

'It was a very brave thing to do,' Lilli said simply, aware of the scores of listening ears and not wishing to embarrass him any further.

It was Lottie who did that. 'You were a hero!' she declared and, as even standing on tip-toe she couldn't reach his cheek to give him a kiss, she seized hold of his wet hand and pressed a heartfelt kiss on the back of it.

There was another surge of whooping and cheering from the crowd of spectators.

'There's a swig of whiskey waiting for you here, Scottie,' someone called out. Someone else called out, 'If you're as quick off the mark at finding gold we'll all be right behind you!'

'You'd better get the wee laddie dry and rested,' Ringan said to Lilli, eager to get dry and rested himself and more than eager to escape from the unwelcome attention.

'Yes.' There were goose-bumps on his strongly muscled arms. She wondered what his profession had been before he had been imprisoned. A blacksmith perhaps, or a professional wrestler. 'Before I do as you suggest Mr . . .'

90

A flush of colour touched her cheeks. He had saved Leo's life and she didn't even know his name!

'Cameron. Ringan Cameron.'

'Mr Cameron, Leo would like to thank you himself.'

'I don't know what to say,' Leo said truthfully as she took his hand and gently positioned him in front of her. 'No-one's ever saved my life before.' His teeth began to chatter as the breeze knifed through his sodden clothes and a pool of water began to collect at his feet. 'Does it mean we'll be special friends from now on?' he asked, uncaring of the cold. 'And if we're special friends will you teach me to dive and swim and to swim underwater?'

Despite his acute discomfiture and his longing to escape to his cabin and change into dry duds Ringan felt a smile nudge his mouth. It changed his appearance drastically. No longer did he look broodingly forbidding. Instead he looked remarkably attractive.

'I'd regard it an honour to be friends,' he said, a far from manly lump in his throat. 'But the swimming lessons will have to wait a wee while. The Pacific's a mite too deep for swimming lessons.'

Over the top of Leo's head Lilli smiled at him. Whatever he had been imprisoned for it couldn't have been a serious offence. A hardened criminal would never have behaved in such a gallant way.

'Goodbye, Mr Cameron,' she said, aware that she was beginning to suffer from delayed shock and that she was in dire need of a mug of sweet tea. 'Come along, Leo. Let's get you dry and warm.'

As they turned away from Mr Cameron, heading towards the stairs leading down to the cabins, Jack Coolidge swung Leo high up onto his shoulders, uncaring of the sea-water that immediately began seeping into his elegant suit. Lilli and Susan followed, Lottie holding Lilli's hand.

'I suppose really you should give Leo a spanking,' she said sensibly to Lilli. 'Pa would have. What if he had drowned? What if Mr Cameron had drowned trying to save him?'

Lilli shuddered, refusing to dwell on such horrors. 'I'm not going to spank him,' she said categorically as they reached the companionway. 'I couldn't. I haven't the strength. I feel as weak as a kitten. I'm simply going to make him stay in his bunk for the rest of the day.'

'*Lilli! Lilli*! We saw what happened! Was it the ex-convict who saved Leo?'

Like a flock of noisy starlings Marietta, Lettie, Edie and Kate surged towards them.

Jack slowed his pace. Miss Lilli Stullen certainly wasn't backward when it came to making friends. And though the friend she had already introduced him to was dauntingly unfeminine, one of the girls now milling around them was passably attractive and another, all eyes and mouth and fox-red hair, was definitely eye-catching.

He grinned suddenly, recognising Kitty's description of Miss Marietta Rivere. Marietta, as instantly aware of his identity as he was of hers, flashed him a dazzling smile. Jack felt a rising in his crotch. Miss Rivere was definitely *Gold Nugget* material. How Amy Peabody had imagined that in Miss Rivere she had a docile Peabody bride on her hands he couldn't possibly imagine.

'You certainly know how to attract attention, little Leo,' Marietta said merrily. 'There's not a soul on board ship won't know who you are now.'

'And next time you go up on deck they'll all be plying you with candy,' Kate said, blushing rosily as she realised that the gentleman carrying Leo was quite outrageously handsome.

'Leo needs drying and putting to bed,' Susan said gruffly, terrified that at any moment Lilli was going to begin introducing everyone to Lucky Jack Coolidge and that all their reputations would then be jeopardised.

Leo sneezed, emphasising his need of towels, and the procession continued on its way. When they reached the section devoted to ladies only cabins, Jack swung Leo down from his shoulders.

'You've given us all a very eventful morning,' he said, his equilibrium fully recovered. 'If I'd known a little earlier what you were going to do I'd have sold tickets for it.'

Marietta and Edie giggled. Kate and Lilli laughed. Only Lettie and Susan remained visibly unamused.

Aware that he'd got off lightly, without anyone demanding to know why he hadn't kept a closer eye on young Leo, Jack made his way to the state-room he shared with Kitty. Kids! Thank Christ he wasn't married with kids of his own! How could anyone keep an eye on them? They were like eels. Here, there and everywhere.

'What in heck happened to you?' Kitty asked, her eyes widening at the sight of the damp-stains on the shoulders of his jacket. 'Have you had a dolphin on your back or have you been standing under a leaky faucet?'

'So that was Lucky Jack Coolidge?' Marietta was saying zestfully. 'My, oh my, but isn't he handsome?'

'And kind,' Kate said as she and Marietta and Lilli and Lottie squashed up on her bottom bunk and Edie and Susan and Lettie squeezed onto the opposite bunk. 'Kind enough to carry an exhausted and dripping-wet child. It just goes to prove that you should never judge a book by its cover.'

Susan Bumby made a rude, snorting sound, tempted to disclose that Leo had been in Jack Coolidge's care when he had begun swinging on the davits. To do that, however, would be to disclose that Lilli had struck up an acquaintanceship with Jack Coolidge and, in her opinion, the fewer people who knew of that acquaintanceship, the better.

With Leo safely tucked up in his bunk in the next cabin and with her hands cupping a hot mug of tea, Lilli felt at peace with the entire world. The next time she spoke with Jack Coolidge he would no doubt tell her what the circumstances had been that had resulted in his not knowing where Leo was playing. Wryly she wondered if his dove-grey jacket would dry out satisfactorily. Even more wryly, she reflected that she still hadn't told him she was a Peabody bride.

*　　*　　*

That evening, when she went for a solitary stroll on the deck, she didn't do so with the express intention of again meeting with him. She did so because she wanted to be on her own for a little while. The friendship that had already been healthily burgeoning between all the Peabody brides, bar Miss Nettlesham, had been very firmly cemented after the drama of Leo's near escape with death and, though she enjoyed the female cama-raderie now surrounding her, she was unaccustomed to being with people of her own age for such long periods and needed a brief respite.

The *Senator* was no longer sailing on the open ocean but up the Inside Passage, an island-sheltered waterway close to the coast of Canada. Small shanty-like fishing villages clustered round pale slivers of beach and from each and every one came the pungent aroma of halibut and herring.

'It's fish-canning country,' a by now dearly familiar voice said, strolling up to her from behind. 'Pioneer country as well. Out there,' he gave a nod towards the ragged coastline, 'the frontier is being literally pushed back mile by mile, day by day.'

She turned towards him, one hand resting on the burnished deck-rail. 'It's exciting, isn't it? You can almost *feel* the excitement in the air. My father was a pioneer at heart. He was certainly an adventurer. If he hadn't already been ill in '97 he would have taken to the Chilkoot Trail with the other stampeders. And he would have taken us with him. He never left us behind. We went everywhere with him. Montana. Wyoming. Kansas.'

'He wouldn't have been able to take you on the Chilkoot Trail with him,' Jack said, standing very close to her as he looked out to sea. 'The Chilkoot was a nightmare. I know because I was one of the first to take it. A solid line of men, bent nearly double under the burden of their supplies, forming a human chain across the snow and ice of the face of the mountains. God only knows how so many of us made it. The final slope was so steep no animal could cross it.'

She looked at him, deeply intrigued. Lean and lithe though he was, he didn't look like a man who would relish hardship. He looked too citified. Too sophisticated.

He turned his head towards her and saw the look in her eyes. Interpreting it correctly he shot her a flashing, down-slanting smile. 'It was worth it. I knew exactly what I was going to do when I reached Dawson, and it wasn't to grub-stake. All I had to do was build saloons and rake in gold that way.'

'And was there no other way of reaching Dawson in '97?' she asked, realising how deeply grateful she should be for the railway that now linked the coast of Alaska with the interior.

'There was the White Pass, another narrow funnel through the mountains and equally treacherous and there was a way by sea and river, via the Bering Sea and the Yukon.'

She turned slightly, resting both her folded arms on the deck rail, completely at ease with him, feeling as if she had found a friend as well as a soon-to-be husband.

'Surely the sea route would have been by far the easiest and most comfortable?'

He, too, leaned his weight on his arms as he rested them on the rails, his hands loosely clasped. 'At that particular point in time it would have taken too long. By the time the Bering Sea had been crossed the Yukon would have been frozen up until the spring. And by the spring Dawson would have been established and I wouldn't have had a monopoly on the saloon and dance-hall trade.'

It was a logical explanation. A businessman's explanation. She said, not looking at him but staring out across the silk-dark water, 'The friend I introduced you to, the friend who teaches in Dawson, told me that I shouldn't be seen in conversation with you. She said Dawson saloons and dance halls were little better than . . . than . . .' She couldn't bring herself to say the word brothel. Well brought up young ladies weren't supposed to know brothels existed.

'I can quite well imagine the word your friend used,'

he said dryly, amused by her as always. 'All I can say in defence is that not all saloons and dance-halls fall into the same category. The *Gold Nugget* is the slickest dance-hall in Dawson but it doesn't have upstairs rooms. At least not of the kind Miss Bumby was thinking of.' He was speaking the truth. It was the *Mother Lode* that had the monopoly on upstairs rooms.

Relief surged through her. He was being totally frank with her, making no apologies for the way he earned his living, because there was no need for such apologies.

She turned her head so that her eyes met his. 'I have another friend,' she said, hoping he would again set her mind at rest, 'and Marietta isn't very . . . conventional. She's set her heart on becoming a dance-hall girl and naturally, after what Susan told me . . .'

'You're worried?'

She nodded.

In the Northern evening light her creamy skin was as pale as ivory and her blue-black hair had the sheen of satin. He wondered what it would be like unpinned. How long it would be. How thick. With an effort he forced his mind to the matter in hand. How the devil had she become friends, in such short a time, with the racy Miss Rivere? And what had her long-term friend, the ultra-respectable Miss Bumby, been thinking of to have allowed it to happen?

'Dance-hall girls are a breed apart,' he said at last, not wanting to damn them all as prostitutes, for he knew very well that many of them were not. 'Once a girl enters a saloon or dance-hall she leaves her good name at the door. As I'm sure your friend Miss Bumby has already told you.'

'Yes, but if a dance-hall girl isn't also a lady of the . . . of the . . .'

'Night,' he finished for her helpfully.

'. . . why should she be ostracised?'

It was a good question and one he would have liked to be able to answer. The fact that they were having such a conversation at all was bizarre enough. Despite

96

all the sensuality of Lilli Stullen's slender, deliciously curved figure and of her wide-spaced, thick-lashed eyes and full-lipped mouth, respectability oozed from her every pore. And he wasn't in the habit of amusing himself with girls so respectable, not when they were vulnerably young and innocent into the bargain.

'How come you've got to know Miss Rivere so well?' he asked, intrigued. 'She's aboard the *Senator* as a Peabody bride and Peabody brides are . . .'

She was relieved that the conversation had come so easily and naturally around to the subject of Peabody brides that the fact of his knowing Marietta's surname and circumstances slid right by her.

'I know what Peabody brides are, Mr Coolidge.' Her eyes held his. This was it. This was the crucial all or nothing moment. Her heart was pounding so fiercely she was sure he must be able to hear it. With her voice betraying her inner emotions only by the faintest tremor she said quietly, 'You see, I'm a Peabody bride as well.'

If she had said she was Calamity Jane he couldn't have looked more astounded.

'*You*? How can you be? You have your kid brother and sister with you and you're going to Dawson to stay with Miss Bumby!'

She shook her head. Neither of them were looking out at the ocean now. Though she was still holding onto the deck-rail with one hand he had now turned completely towards her, so near to her that she could smell his cologne and the linen-freshness of his shirt.

'No,' she said, feeling as breathless as if she were in a race, a race far from finished and a race she had to win. 'I only met Susan Bumby the evening I boarded the boat. Susan is a Peabody bride too.'

Lilli, Marietta and Susan Bumby. They made such a disparate trio that it took all his self-control not to blaspheme with incredulity. Instead he said, 'I don't wish to be ungallant but I can understand Miss Bumby resorting to the help of a marriage bureau. As for your friend Marietta, we both know she's only using the bureau to pay for her passage north and that the instant she reaches Dawson she's going to renege on her agreement. But what about yourself? Miss Bumby may be plain as a pikestaff and unable to get a husband by any other method, but her reasons hardly apply to you!'

She was devoutly glad he didn't think they did. She also knew that her fate was still hanging precariously in the balance. He was incredulous at what she had told him, which was all to the good. But she needed him to be far more than incredulous. She needed him to be outraged.

'And have you any idea of the way Peabody brides are disposed of when they reach Dawson?' he asked, outraged. 'Josh Nelson has reduced the process to something akin to a Turkish slave market!'

Lilli looked suitably aghast. It would never do for him to realise she already knew a Peabody bride's fate and to believe she was apparently resigned to meeting it.

'What on earth possessed you?' he continued angrily, the moonlight emphasising the Greek god perfection of his cheekbones and jaw. 'Only women desperate for the security of marriage become mail-order brides! Though what security there can possibly be in marrying selfish and shiftless stampeders beats me!'

His anger was genuine. Josh Nelson was a snake. Before Nelson had begun acting on the Peabody Marriage Bureau's behalf, girls the bureau sent north had been matched up with husbands in a reasonably decorous manner; a generous statuary fee being paid to the bureau by the men availing themselves of its services. Nelson had put an end to all such decorum. Seizing advantage of the huge disparity in numbers between men wanting Peabody brides and girls willing to become Peabody brides, Nelson had set up a system whereby the girls went to men willing to pay the most for them. The Marriage Bureau still received its standard, statuary fee. The difference went into Josh Nelson's greasy palm.

'I didn't see that I had a choice,' Lilli said, her heart still hammering, knowing that though she was now in her stride the sprint to the finish still lay before her. 'My widowed father died six months ago and . . .'

'Judas priest!' It was the kind of story Jack had heard countless times before and it never failed to infuriate him. When a young single woman lost her home and family the results were nearly always catastrophic. Except for the fortunate few, work opportunities were limited to lowly paid drudgery. Which was why so many homeless girls flocked into saloon and dance-hall work.

'Don't say a word more!' he commanded tightly. 'And don't go fretting yourself an instant longer about marrying a loutish miner because I'm not going to allow it to happen.'

Too damned right he wasn't! She was too naive, too sparky, too goddamned *nice* to be subjected to Josh Nelson's crude auctioneering techniques. Nelson would have to be paid off, of course, but that was no problem. And Miss Lilli Stullen would have to be found respectable, adequate-paying work, and for a man with his contacts that wouldn't be too much of a problem either.

Lilli was gripping hold of the deck-rail so tightly her knuckles were white. The race was over! And she'd won! His reaction had been all she had prayed it would be. He wasn't going to stand by and watch her marry another man. Which had to mean he was going to marry her himself. Joy flooded through her. Bemused and radiant her eyes held his. Everything was going to be all right. Everything was going to be absolutely perfect.

As he saw the dizzying relief in her eyes Jack knew he wasn't going to be strong enough to refrain from taking physical advantage of it. Until now he had behaved towards the delightful Miss Stullen with faultless propriety, enjoying nothing more than her quirky conversation. Now, however, he had come to her aid in the most magnaminous way, saving her, in Gothic novel terms, from a fate worse than death. A kiss, or maybe two or three kisses, would be very small payment in reward. As he reached out an arm towards her waist, drawing her indecently close to him, he felt her quiver.

'Mr Coolidge, I . . .'

Her voice was low and husky and not for the first time he wondered what her singing voice would be like.

'Jack,' he said, his lips brushing her silky-soft hair. 'We're friends, aren't we? And friends should always be on christian name terms.'

Heat beat through her. Friends. They would always be friends. And soon they would be betrothed.

'Trust me,' he said softly, 'I'm going to make everything all right, not only for you but for little Leo and for Lottie as well.'

She melted against the strength of his body like wax. His arms circled her waist. With her heart racing against his he lowered his head to hers.

All time seemed to have stopped for Lilli. He was going to kiss her. It would be a kiss she would remember for all time. The first kiss of a lifetime of kisses.

His mouth was hot and demanding, his tongue touching and teasing hers. Shock rippled through her. It was her first adult kiss and she hadn't known that tongues, as well as lips, were involved. It was a startling sensation. Startling but exciting. As his mouth continued to plunder hers, her confidence grew. Her hands, which had been pressed close against his chest, now slid up and around his neck. Every nerve in her body was tingling. She felt scorched. Ablaze.

Her artlessly passionate response nearly unhinged him. He had intended a few moments of pleasant relaxation instead of which she was awakening in him fierce, raw need. With his heart racing nearly as chaotically as hers he slid one hand from her waist and cupped a voluptuously full, pert breast.

She gasped, stiffening in his arms with shock. Whether, when the moment of shock had passed, she would have sweetly surrendered to his caresses, he never found out. Two men were approaching. Inwardly cursing their presence Jack reluctantly released his hold of Lilli.

'I wouldn't mind a partner with your kind of guts,' one man's deep guttural voice said to his companion. 'Trust

100

is what is important between men out in the wilds and I reckon I could trust a man who'd risk his life for a kid he didn't know.'

'I havna decided on quite what I'm going to do when I reach Dawson.'

There was no mistaking the deep, soft burr. Lilli felt her cheeks flush scarlet. What if he had seen the liberties Jack had been taking with her person? Not that they really were liberties, considering the circumstances, but Mr Cameron was not to know the circumstances and the thought of him leaping to a grossly wrong conclusion mortified her. She kept her head well down, allowing Jack's body to shield her from view.

Instead of walking on past them, the two men came to a halt beside the deck-rail, only feet away from them.

'What in heck do y'mean, you haven't figgered out what you're goin' to do when we arrive?' the guttural voice said incredulously. 'What else would a man do in the Klondike but mine for gold?'

Jack, too, had recognised Ringan Cameron's Scots burr. He also realised that as Cameron and his companion seemed settled in for a long discussion he had no alternative but to escort Lilli away as discreetly as possible.

Taking hold of her arm by the elbow he turned with her away from the deck-rail, keeping between her and the two men.

'My reason for being aboard the Senator isna quite as uncomplicated as most people's reasons,' Ringan was saying dryly.

Lilli knew that he was referring to the circumstances of his parole and instinctively, without thinking, she raised her head, looking across at him.

Having recognised Lucky Jack Cameron's distinctive thatch of sun-bleached hair Ringan had been idly curious as to the identity of his lady-friend.

When Lilli suddenly turned, looking across at him, he sucked in his breath sharply. Dear God in heaven! He'd known Miss Stullen was on friendly speaking terms with Coolidge but he'd never suspected she was on terms of intimacy with him! Even now, though he had seen the proof before his very eyes, he could hardly credit it. Coolidge was, after all, a man whose name was freely linked with that of the most notorious madam north of San Francisco, and Miss Lilli Stullen was a young woman who radiated purity and innocence.

'I don't give a hang for your reason for being aboard the *Senator*,' his companion was saying to him. 'I seen what I seen and I know I ain't ridin' the wrong trail. You'll make a good partner . . .'

Lilli didn't hear any more. With her cheeks burning she allowed Jack to walk her down the deck.

When they had gone so far that Mr Cameron and his companion were swallowed up in the blue-spangled dusk Jack came to a halt, hoping to recommence from the point where they had been so annoyingly interrupted.

As his arms slid once more around her waist Lilli said, her voice sounding oddly strangled in her throat, 'No. I must get back to Leo and Lottie. They'll be worrying about me.'

Jack curbed a surge of exasperation. The trouble with respectable women was that when they made such remarks there was every chance they meant them. 'Tomorrow then,' he said obligingly, reflecting that he could now enjoy a few hands of stud poker. 'And when we get to Whitehorse, I'd like to show you the rapids.'

'I'd like that.' Her voice was thick with love. They would take Leo and Lottie and it would be almost as though they were a family.

For a moment she regretted her decision to leave him when he so obviously wanted her to stay, but she had been speaking the truth when she had said Leo and Lottie would be wondering where she was and even if she hadn't been, the deck was getting quite crowded with strolling groups of men. Too crowded for them to be able to continue kissing and caressing.

He raised her hand to his mouth, kissing the tips of her fingers. She forgot all about the mortification she had felt when Ringan Cameron's shocked eyes had met hers. She was in love. Truly in love. Just as her parents had been. Just as she had always dreamed of being.

Later that night, as she lay in her uncomfortably narrow bunk, she tried to hold his image against her closed eyelids. Frustratingly though it was Ringan Cameron who loomed large in her mind's eye and as she recalled the disbelief that had flared through his eyes, followed so swiftly by shock, the emotion that accompanied her into sleep wasn't joy, but deep, deep discomfort. A discomfort so deep it was almost regret.

Chapter Seven

'So I'm going to be paying Nelson off for *two* Peabody brides, not just one,' Jack said wryly as he partially unbuttoned his shirt and dragged it over his head.

It was the early hours of the morning and he had just returned to the state-room after a highly successful game of poker.

'Why the sudden altruistic concern?' Kitty asked, bemused. 'You're not about to suddenly start saving girls from ruin instead of leading them to it, are you? Because if you are, you're going to have one mighty big job on your hands!'

He chuckled, easing off his boots. 'Nope. I reckon I prefer my women to be happily on the road to ruin rather than respectability, but Lilli Stullen would never be happy ruined, it shows in her eyes.'

And Lilli Stullen's happiness matters?' Kitty asked queryingly, wondering if, just for once, she should start to worry a little.

Jack unbuckled his belt and dropped his pants. 'I owe her,' he said simply, no longer grinning. 'If her kid brother had drowned this afternoon it would have been my fault. Hell, *I* was the one supposed to be looking after him.'

His hair was ruffled where he had dragged his shirt over his head and he looked far younger than his twenty-eight years.

'She should have known better,' Kitty said dryly, wondering how old she would have to be before the seven years difference in their ages began to be chronically noticeable. 'I wouldn't give you a dog to look after. Not if I valued it.'

He hooted with laughter, striding towards the bed magnificently naked. 'Is that so?' he asked, smacking her on her negligéed rump. 'Then maybe I should teach you to think differently and have a little more respect.'

Kitty slithered voluptuously down against her pillows, chuckling throatily. 'I don't think there's much you or anyone else can teach me, but you're sure welcome to try. Especially if all the trying is going to take place between the sheets!'

'You're a wicked woman, Kitty Dufresne,' he said, rolling his hard muscled weight on top of her. 'And what the hell I'd do without you I can't begin to imagine.'

'I'm not being patronising!' Kate protested next morning to Lettie. 'This dress really is too small for me and it really would fit you perfectly!'

'I don't like charity,' Lettie persisted mulishly, making no move to take the dress from her.

Lilli swung her legs over the edge of her top bunk. 'If Lettie's going to be idiotic about it, I'll have it. I've never owned a raspberry-pink day-dress. It looks heaven.'

'You're the same curvy shape as Kate so it would be too small for you,' Lottie said, knowing that Lilli hadn't meant her statement seriously but was simply trying to provoke Lettie into being sensible.

She turned her attention towards their sulky cabin-mate. 'Come on, Lettie. At least try it on. If you don't, Kate will cut it up into dish-rags.'

Lettie looked at the dress, longing in her eyes. It wasn't in the least worn out and even if it had been, it's cut and colour were far superior to the drab dress she was wearing or any dress she had ever worn.

'Come on,' Lottie said again persuasively, 'You can wear it when we reach Whitehorse and visit the rapids.'

The temptation and combined coercion were too much for Lettie. 'All right,' she said, trying not to sound desperately eager, 'if you're really sure it isn't charity.'

'Lord, if you say that word again I think I'll scream,' Kate said, exchanging a triumphant wink with Lilli as

Lettie began to unbutton the monstrosity she had been wearing day and night since boarding the boat. 'And I've a nightdress I've replaced too. You may as well have that as well. It will be less for me to carry when we disembark.'

A few minutes later Lettie stood before them in the cramped confines of the cabin, arrayed in her new finery. It was obvious to both Lilli and Lottie that Kate had been fibbing when she had said the dress was too small for her, for the waist was a good two inches or so slack.

'I'll just tighten that up while you're wearing it, Lettie,' Kate said, a needle and thread already in her hand. 'And then if you don't mind, I'd like to have a shot at putting your hair in a French knot.'

By the time they left the cabin for breakfast Lettie was a young woman transformed. Her dull looking dark-blonde hair had been brushed to an almost metallic sheen and pinned in a neat, sophisticated knot high on the top of her head. The raspberry-red dress fit her like a glove, the colour draining the sallowness out of her complexion and imparting instead a rosy glow.

'You look *beautiful*, Lettie,' Leo said when he saw her. 'Almost like a princess!'

Lettie blushed and told him not to be ridiculous, but she was pleased and her pleasure showed.

'Did you know Susan has a beau?' Kate said companionably to Lilli as Lettie and Leo walked hand in hand ahead of them. 'I was going to tell you last night but I couldn't find you anywhere.'

'Susan?' Lilli couldn't help the surprise in her voice. Susan had admitted that she had *never* had a beau and she couldn't quite imagine Susan being courted by any of the *Senator's* rough and ready prospectors. 'Are you serious?' she asked, wondering if Kate was teasing her.

'Absolutely. You may have seen him. He's a clergyman. A Methodist minister.'

Lilli's eyes widened. If what Kate was saying was true, Susan's life might just be about to be transformed. A

Methodist minister would be an ideal beau for her and if he were to propose marriage . . .'

She began to giggle. If he proposed marriage and paid Josh Nelson off it would leave only four Peabody brides available out of a total of seven.

Immediately she entered the crowded, smoky dining-saloon she glimpsed red-gold hair and green plaid. He raised his head, his eyes meeting hers. Discomfort swept through her. He thought her fast. He had seen her embrace with Jack the previous night and he had leapt to quite erroneous conclusions. As he gave her a brief, acknowledging nod she wished fiercely she had an engagement ring on her finger. *Then* he wouldn't think her fast.

Answering his nod with a polite, brittle smile she sat down beside Lettie. Life was exceedingly infuriating at times. She was, after all, engaged in an unofficial kind of way to Lucky Jack. And she would have been an odd sort of woman if, after the man she had fallen in love with had declared he would never stand by and watch her marry another man, she hadn't responded with a display of physical affection. Logically she knew she had no reason to feel as if she had behaved in a shameless manner. Illogically, the disbelief and then the shock she had seen in Ringan Cameron's eyes made her feel as if she had done so.

'Mr Jenkinson has never been north before,' Susan said, eager to impart every last bit of knowledge about the man who had begun to show an interest in her. 'He is replacing the incumbent minister and hopes to be remaining in Dawson for a considerable length of time. He is a lepidopterist and . . .'

Pleased as she was for Susan, Lilli's attention wandered. She wondered where and when Lucky Jack breakfasted. The woman Marietta had said was his business partner never appeared in the dining-saloon, or anywhere else for that matter, and she couldn't help wondering if they took breakfast together. A frown creased her forehead. Breakfast was an odd meal to share *tête-à-tête* with someone of the opposite sex, even if that someone was a professional colleague.

107

'Mr Jenkinson is over there,' Kate hissed to Lilli, wondering again where Lilli had been the previous evening when Susan had revealed her burgeoning romantic friendship.

Dutifully Lilli looked across a sea of male heads to where the clerically dressed Mr Jenkinson was helping himself to bacon. He was older than she had expected, in late middle age, and had a moon-face and an earnest manner.

'Does he know Susan's circumstances?' Lilli asked doubtfully, keeping her voice low so that Susan shouldn't hear her. 'Does he know that she's a Peabody bride?'

'Not yet. He knows that she's a kindergarten-teacher though. And that she's a resident of Dawson.'

The chatter at the other end of the table had lessened and it was impossible to continue their conversation without being overheard.

As Lilli continued with her breakfast she reflected that it was a miracle any Peabody bride ever arrived in Dawson without already being spoken for. There were so many men heading north, men who knew what a dearth of women awaited them, that any single young woman could have her pick of beaus.

Certainly she could have done so. From the moment she had stepped aboard the *Senator's* gangplank she had been aware of the droves of men eyeing her with unabashed interest. And she wasn't the only one. According to Kate, Marietta had nearly caused a stampede when she had played quoits with Lottie and Leo. Kate herself hadn't been neglected. The young man Lilli had overheard telling his friends about nuggets as big as rocks persistently tried to engage her in conversation and his khaki-dressed companion, who proved to be an Englishman with a cut-glass accent, also blatantly followed her about the boat.

'I wonder if we should make another attempt at befriending Miss Nettlesham,' Kate said ruminatively. 'I didn't see her all day yesterday and it can't be much fun for her, cooped up in a cabin all day.'

Marietta raised her eyes to heaven.

108

Susan said dryly: 'If she is cooped up she has only herself to blame.'

Edie said, 'I don't like her. She frightens me.'

'You've got to learn not to be frightened,' Lettie said bluntly. 'You're frightened of too many things, Edie. Woods, the sea, Miss Nettlesham . . .'

'And men,' Edie added tentatively. 'I'm frightened of men, Lettie.'

She was wearing a a dress with a sailor-collar. It was too tight across her plump bosom and bizarrely childish in style and looked as if it might have been regulation orphanage wear.

Once again the entire table stared at her, appalled.

'I don't like their beards,' Edie said defensively, knowing something was wrong but not knowing what. 'And their deep voices. They always sound angry and I get frightened when people are angry with me.'

'Sweet Jesus,' Kate said softly beneath her breath. It wasn't a blasphemy but a prayer of supplication.

'If I could get my hands on those orphanage authorities I'd murder every last one of them!' Marietta said, her green eyes feral.

Lilli chewed the corner of her lip meditatively. Josh Nelson was going to be paid off for both herself and, presumably, Marietta. If Susan's romance with her clergyman flourished then he might even by paid off a third time. Why shouldn't he also be paid off for Edie? Between the five of them they would surely be able to offer her a home and she could perhaps find work as a maid or a waitress. She wondered what kind of amount Josh Nelson would find acceptable. It would have to cover the cost of the voyage of course and a little more to compensate the marriage bureau, but if they all clubbed together, especially if people like Lucky Jack and the Reverend Mr Jenkinson also chipped in, it might just be possible.

Later, as she sat with Kate on a seat looking out over the stern, she said, 'Do you think if we all put together we might be able to pay the marriage bureau off where

Edie is concerned? She doesn't have a clue as to what is to happen to her when we reach Dawson and she's not mentally or emotionally fitted for marriage. Especially marriage to a stranger.'

Kate's kind, sensible face was sombre. 'I think the kind of amount bridegrooms pay to the Peabody would be completely beyond us. Don't forget we're talking about men who use gold for currency. In an auctioneering situation the amount bid could either be embarrassingly low or astronomically high and I imagine Mr Nelson would prefer to gamble on the chance that it might be astronomically high.'

They fell into an unhappy silence. Everyone else who had signed up with the Peabody Marriage Bureau had known exactly what they were letting themselves in for. But Edie hadn't signed with the Peabody voluntarily. Edie was a victim.

As usual the deck was crowded and as Lilli looked out over the array of men sitting and standing in close-knit groups or lounging against the deck-rail, she knew Edie's chances of being partnered with a gentle, understanding man were virtually nil. Gentle men didn't choose to prospect for gold in the harsh climate of the Klondike. Although some looked respectable and well-bred the vast majority looked to be hooligans.

A man sitting on an upturned water-can a few yards in front of them was typical. He had the features and neckless build of a bulldog. His hair needed cutting, his nails needed trimming and his neck needed scrubbing. Even from a distance he smelled of dried sweat and he had a twist of chewing tobacco in his hand. She watched him gnaw off a piece, her stomach heaving in revulsion. Dear Lord, what if Lucky Jack hadn't come to her rescue! What if she had found herself legally shackled to a man like that!

There were a few, very few, exceptions to the rule. The Englishman in his superbly cut riding breeches. The Easterner in khaki. The Reverend Mr Jenkinson. Ringan Cameron.

Even as his name came into her mind she saw him. He was standing, as always, alone. His green plaid shirt was open at the throat, his britches snug on his hips. He was a fine figure of a man, honed, hard and, though red-headed men were most definitely not to her own taste, handsome.

And he thought her a trollop. She clasped her hands together a little tighter in her lap. He had totally misunderstood the situation and why she was allowing it to so trouble her she didn't know. It wasn't as if he was a friend whose good opinion she valued. He had saved Leo's life and for that she was deeply grateful and always would be. But what he thought of her morals was neither here nor there and feeling so uncomfortable just because he obviously thought badly of her was downright ridiculous.

Ridiculous or not, when he turned his head in her direction she turned her own head swiftly away, not wanting him to catch her staring at him, not wanting to have to live with the expression she knew she would see in his eyes.

Ringan frowned. Yesterday, when he had deposited her kid brother streaming with sea water at her feet, her warmth and gratitude had been overpowering. He hadn't wanted her gratitude of course. It had deeply embarrassed him. But it had pleased him to realise that he hadn't been wrong in surmising she had a loving, generous nature. Her character had shone in her eyes. Eyes the blue of forget-me-nots.

He knew, of course, the reason for her change of attitude towards him. Being seen walking the decks with Lucky Jack Coolidge during daylight hours was one thing. Being caught in a passionate embrace with him in the moonlight was quite another.

He dug his hands deep in his britches pockets. God damn it to hell! What was a young woman who looked so absolutely untarnished doing in an indecently close clinch with a worldly ne'er-do-well like Lucky Jack Coolidge?

He shrugged his massive shoulders. What she was

111

doing with Coolidge was really none of his business. The affair was a pity though. She deserved better than to be hoodwinked by a professional rogue and her bright-faced brother and sister deserved better than to be towed along in such a dubious wake.

There was no point in remaining within her view and he turned on his heel, strolling aimlessly in the direction of the prow.

Sensing his departure Lilli looked covertly after him. Why was he always so determinedly alone? The other men aboard boat were always deep in conversation with each other, those venturing north for the first time eager to glean tips from those returning. She wondered if it was because it had become public knowledge he was a paroled criminal, but dismissed the thought as ludicrous. The hardened men travelling north in the hope of wresting a fortune in gold from Arctic creeks would hardly be chary of consorting with a man with a prison record. Looking around at her fellow passengers, Lilli felt sure that a very high proportion of them probably had a similar history.

As she watched his receding back she saw heads turn admiringly. The focus of their attention was a young woman. And the young woman was Lettie.

'Kate!' she said urgently, 'Turn round and look at this!'

Kate swivelled round, resting an arm on the back of their bench seat. 'My, oh my,' she said in satisfaction when she saw Lettie, 'isn't that just a sight for sore eyes?'

Lettie was no longer slouching, nor was her face a sullen mask. The deep raspberry-pink of her dress set her apart from the drably dressed men like an exotic flower amidst a field of rank weeds. Though there was still a certain petulance about her mouth it had the effect of making her look sultry, not bad-tempered, and with her dark-blonde hair burnished to a gleaming sheen and swirled into an elegant knot she looked every inch a lady.

'Leo and Lottie are with Edie,' she said as she approached them. 'And Susan is walking with her Reverend and Marietta is scouting for a Mrs Dufresne.'

112

'Are you sure she said *Mrs* Dufresne?' Lilli asked with interest. 'Not Miss?'

'Mrs, Miss, what difference does it make?' Lettie asked, sitting down beside them. 'You know Marietta has no intention of honouring her agreement with the marriage bureau when she reaches Dawson, don't you? Do you think it's an actionable offence? I mean, do you think she could have the law set on her and be sent to jail?'

Suppressing her frustration at not having the question of Kitty Dufresne's marital status settled, Lilli said, 'I imagine all that Mrs Peabody is really interested in is recouping her expenses. If the bureau is adequately paid off I don't think she'll be bothered what Marietta does.'

All the time they were talking she was keeping a sharp eye out for Lucky Jack. Immediately after breakfast she had hurried to the part of the deck she now thought of as their private meeting place but he hadn't been waiting for her there and though it was now nearly lunch-time there was still no sign of him strolling the decks, looking for her.

'I think I might take a little walk,' she said, hoping neither Lettie or Kate would suggest accompanying her.

From beneath sandy lashes Lettie shot her such a knowing look that Lilli realised she wasn't keeping any secrets from Lettie at all. Lettie had guessed what was going on and she certainly wasn't going to suggest walking with her when it was so obvious she was hoping to accidentally-on-purpose meet with a gentleman.

She walked off in the direction Ringan Cameron had taken. Alone, she was even more acutely aware of the interest she was arousing than she normally was. There were men everywhere. Tall men, short men, pasty men, ruddy men. Men in mackinaws, men in stetsons and fringed jackets. The only thing they seemed to have in common was that, whether broad-shouldered and muscular, or skinny and wiry, they were all undeniably fit. And they were all young or in their prime.

With a shock she realised that what she was seeing was a microcosm of the society she would meet with when she

113

arrived in Dawson. A male-dominated society. A society with only one over-riding interest. The finding of gold.

'*Lilli! Lilli!*' It was Leo. He was running towards her, Lottie following him at a more ladylike pace. 'Can we stay with Mr Cameron for a while?' he gasped as he ran up to her. 'We were with Edie but she's talking to a funny man and Mr Cameron is in the prow and he knows the names of all the different sea-birds and . . .'

'What funny man?' Lilli asked apprehensively, knowing that Leo didn't mean funny as in amusing, but funny as in funny peculiar.

'Just a man going to Dawson. I thought I'd better ask permission to be with Mr Cameron, just so that you know where I am and don't begin worrying about me.'

'I think Edie might need rescuing,' Lottie said as she walked towards them, confirming all Lilli's worst fears. 'There's a man talking to her and I don't think she likes it and I don't think she knows how to get away from him.'

'So I'm going to be with Mr Cameron for the rest of the morning,' Leo said, impatient to be on his way.

'I think we should go and rescue Edie *now*,' Lottie said, the ribbons of her sailor hat streaming in the breeze.

Lilli thought they should as well. 'You can stay with Mr Cameron just as long you don't misbehave and you're not to run off or to play suicidal games like acrobats,' she said sternly to Leo. 'And you're not to talk to anyone you don't know or . . .'

'Come *on*, Lilli,' Lottie said, tugging at her hand. 'I really do think Edie's in need of you.'

Walking so fast she was almost running Lilli hurried with Lottie to where Lottie had left Edie. She wasn't there.

'What was the man like?' she asked Lottie, standing and staring around her.

'Not very tall, very broad, very strong-looking . . .'

All around them men were milling, smoking and talking and laughing. Then, beneath a stair-well, she saw a man built like an ox. He had his back towards her with one arm resting on the frame of the stairs, barring the way of the person he was talking to. Beneath his muscular, tattooed arm Lilli saw the distinctive navy and white flash of a sailor collar. A sailor collar that belonged to a girl's dress, not to a sailor's uniform.

Lilli broke into a run, pushing her way past a group of startled men, hurtling up to the broad, menacing male back.

Edie was pressed against the rear of the stair-well, her eyes wide and bewildered. And frightened. Over the muscular arm she saw Lilli's hurricane-like approach and her relief was so obvious and vast that Lilli felt as if her heart had been physically squeezed. 'My friend would like to come with me,' she said crisply, reaching beneath the iron-like arm to grasp hold of Edie's hand.

The arm didn't move. Neither did his body. Only his head turned. 'Git,' he said, his eye boring into hers balefully. 'This is a private conversation and you ain't wanted.'

'My friend doesn't want to be in conversation with you,' she snapped tautly, knowing she hadn't a hope in hell of physically forcing him to allow Edie to leave the stair-well and knowing that an appeal to good nature would be useless in a situation where good nature didn't exist.

'Git,' he said again, turning his head away from her and once more fixing Edie with his lecherous stare.

Edie was breathing fast and light, her plump breasts straining against the tightness of her too-small dress. 'Please, Mister. I want to go,' she said quaveringly. 'I don't like it beneath these stairs. It's dark and I don't like the dark. I want to go with my friend.'

Lilli didn't know just when Lottie vanished. She only realised she had gone when she looked around for supportive help and found none. Kate and Lettie were presumably still sitting companiably together in the stern. There was no sign of Susan and the Reverend Mr Jenkinson. No sign of Marietta.

'If you don't release my friend this minute I shall go for the captain.'

The man didn't turn again to face her. Still pinning

Edie with his gaze he gave a bark of laughter. 'By the time you find him and he finds us you'll be too late to stop whatever it is you're trying to stop.'

His crudity was the last straw. Lilli looked towards the nearest knot of men and sensed that unless there was a real ruckus she would receive no help from them. She was on her own. Turning again to the sweat-stale body she released her hold of Edie's hand and sank her teeth deep into the hairy tattooed arm.

As he yelled in surprise and rage and pain, swinging round towards her to retaliate, she clenched her fist and drove it with all the strength she possessed straight into his crotch.

The pandemonium was immediate. As he curled over, bellowing with pain and as the knot of men immediately became aware of the fracas, some of them merely calling out to know what the hell was going on, other striding towards the scene, Lilli seized hold of Edie's hand and dragged her out of the shadow of the stair-well. The urge to run was nearly overpowering but she knew that if she did so the man would only seek Edie out on another occasion when she was on her own. Thrusting Edie protectively behind her, she said so loudly that men as far as twenty yards away heard her, 'This lecher has been forcing his attentions on my friend and frightening her!'

'Bitch!' A hand like iron had hold of her shoulder. '*Bitch!*' he spat at her again, raising his other hand in order to strike her across the face.

'*What in heck . . .*' one of their, by now, many spectators shouted, leaping towards him, seizing hold of his arm.

'There's no hittin' wimmen on this boat!' someone else shouted as Lilli and Edie were suddenly surrounded by a swarm of protective prospectors.

The raging bull at the centre of the ruckus shook off the man trying to restrain him as if he were nothing more than an annoying blue-bottle. 'I'll do for you, you whore!' he spat and this time no-one was quick enough to deflect the blow he aimed at Lilli.

It was like being slammed into a solid steel wall at

116

the speed of light. Her knees buckled and a blood-red curtain flooded her vision. Dimly she was aware of Edie screaming, of men blaspheming, of punches being thrown. The wood of the deck was rough beneath her cheek. Edie was at her side, sobbing hysterically, '*Lilli! Lilli! Please talk to me! Please don't be dead, Lilli!*'

There came the sound of running feet. Voices of authority. The blood-red wash in front of her eyes began to be peppered with a dizzying array of flashing lights.

A Scots voice, no longer imbued with an attractive soft burr but raw with rage, demanded, '*What in God's name is going on?*'

Lilli tried to tell him but her tongue felt as if it were a million times its normal size. She wondered if she had bitten it. She wondered if she would ever speak again.

'He was frightening Edie and Lilli tried to make him stop!' she heard Lottie saying in a voice thick with tears and terror. 'Is Lilli going to be all right, Mr Cameron? Is she going to open her eyes soon? Is she . . .'

'Get everyone to stand back and give her some air,' she heard Ringan Cameron command tightly. There was authority in his voice, almost as much authority as in the voice that responded by ordering, 'Clear back please! Right back.'

That was the captain speaking. She was sure of it.

'I'm . . .' she said thickly, trying to say that she was all right and didn't need anyone fussing over her. 'I'm . . .' No other words would come. Her vision was clearing though. Disjointedly she could see colours and shapes. The captain's uniform. An entire array of boots and britches, all at a respectful distance. Lottie's terrified face. But the figure closest to her was that of Ringan Cameron. He was bending over her, his face so near to hers she could see the coppery stubble of his beard.

Taking her jaw very gently between his thumb and forefinger he said, 'Can you move your jaw for me, Miss Stullen? A little to the left? A little to the right?'

Gingerly Lilli did as he asked. Her jaw moved. It felt as though it was broken, but it wasn't.

He leaned even closer to her and for a bizarre moment she thought he was going to kiss her and then she realised that he was looking into each eye with an expertise that seemed almost professional. 'She's safe to be moved,' he said at last, though who to she had no idea.

'I'm . . .' she began again, about to say that, given another few minutes, she would be perfectly capable of moving without assistance.

To her intense annoyance he scooped her up in his arms, saying to Lottie, 'Will ye lead the way to your cabin, Lottie?'

Lottie. Muzzily Lilli wondered just when Mr Cameron and Lottie had become such buddy-buddy friends. Less muzzily she wondered just why he thought *he* was the one to take control of events, to examine her person as if he had a right to such liberties, to carry her through the crowd of spectators without so much as a by-your-leave.

However deep her indignation there was no way she could give expression to it. Though her vision had finally cleared her head felt as if an army was hammering inside it and the ear on the side of her head which had been hit was ringing fit to wake the dead. There was no strength in her legs either. And all as the result of one blow. At the thought of what the result would be of a beating at the hands of such a man she shuddered. It would be permanent disablement or death.

As the men made a passageway for Ringan she saw that there was no sign of the monster who had hit her with such barbaric force. She wondered if the captain had ordered him to be detained somewhere and, if he had, hoped he was in chains.

As Ringan negotiated the narrow companian-way stairs with surprising agility it occurred to her that she was now doubly in his debt. Yesterday he had saved Leo's life. Today he was very visibly offering her his assistance. All it needed was for Lottie to come a cropper and for him to come to her aid and Mr Cameron would have scored a hat-trick where the Stullen family was concerned.

The knowledge was oddly infuriating. She didn't *want*

118

to be in the debt of a man who erroneously thought her a trollop. The gratitude she owed him for Leo's life was one thing and she would never skimp on it, but she was damned if was going to fall over herself being grateful to him for the aid he had just so publicly given her and was still so publicly giving her. After all, if he hadn't so pushily assumed the role of a man with medical expertise any one of a score of other men would have made sure that she still wasn't concussed and that her jaw hadn't been broken.

'We've just heard what happened!' she heard Kate's voice saying anxiously from behind them. 'Our cabin is third down on the left-hand side, Mr Cameron. Would you like me to squeeze past you so I can open the door?'

'I can get past easier,' She heard Leo say, eager to assume a role of importance.' Do you think the captain will keep that man in a locked cabin all the way to Skagway, Ringan? And if he does, do you think the man will break out of it? Do you think he'll go berserk and . . .'

'"Open the door, Leo" Ringan said, an edge of amusement in his voice. "Your sister may look a lightweight but looks can be verrra deceiving."

Lilli's indignation reached almost unmanageable proportions. She hadn't *asked* him to come to her aid. She hadn't *asked* to be carried like a parcel for what had seemed to be the entire length of a deck whilst a sea of prurient eyes feasted on the sight. Lucky Jack hadn't been one of the spectators though. Where was he that news of what had taken place still hadn't reached him? If Lucky Jack had seen what had happened, Ringan Cameron would never have been able to come near her. It would have been Lucky Jack who would have come to her aid. Lucky Jack who would have been carrying her masterfully to her cabin. And Lucky Jack certainly wouldn't have made rude remarks about her weight!

Leo had scampered past them and thrown the cabin door open. 'In here,' he said, enjoying the drama to the full now that he knew Lilli hadn't been seriously hurt. 'Lilli's bunk is the top one. I don't think you'll be able to get her up there, will you, Ringan? Are you going to put her on my bunk? Will I be able to sleep in the top bunk tonight?'

'I don't need anyone man-handling me any further,' Lilli said stiffly, the side of her face where she had been struck feeling as if it would never be mobile again. 'I'm feeling much better and . . .'

'You need a mug of sweet tea and rest,' Ringan Cameron said curtly, carrying her into the cabin and setting her down on Leo's bunk with surprising gentleness.

The cabin was far too small for him. Or Ringan Cameron was far too big for the cabin. Lilli couldn't quite work out which was the problem. The army in her head was still hammering. The bells in her bruised ear were still ringing. All she knew was that Ringan Cameron filled the cabin with his bulk. Despite the resentment she was feeling she had to admit that it wasn't graceless bulk. Unlike many powerfully built men there was nothing clumsy about him, his movements were rather those of a big, lithe cat. And there was no denying his gentleness. When he had held her already swelling jaw between thumb and forefinger she hadn't even winced.

'I'll get the tea,' Kate said from the doorway of the cabin. 'Lottie, you come with me. I think we're *all* going to need tea and I'll need an extra pair of hands to carry another tray. Is Edie still crying? Lettie, can you assure Edie that Lilli is going to be all right? And where on earth are Marietta and Susan? I would have thought news of what had happened would have spread right through the ship by now.'

'You're going to feel a bit fashed for a while,' Ringan Cameron said, looking down at her from what seemed to Lilli to be an impossible height. 'If ye should have any trouble with your speech or the movements of your right hand and arm will ye send someone to come for me?'

Fashed. Whatever fashed meant she felt far worse. But not so bad she couldn't bring the bossily pushy Mr Cameron down peg or two.

'If I should experience any nasty side-effects I shall

120

consult a doctor when we reach Skagway,' she said with as much firmness as was possible when every word she uttered sounded as though it were coated in thick fog.

He looked as though he were about to say something and then changed his mind. Turning away from her he said to Lettie, who had replaced Kate at the doorway. 'Could I just have a wee look at the other lassie?'

Lettie's protective instincts came to the fore. 'Edie's not been physically hurt,' she said as Edie continued to snivel and hiccup behind her. 'And men scare her . . .'

'I'll no scairt her,' Ringan said quietly.

Lettie looked up into his strong-boned face and his auburn-lashed, gray, steady eyes and knew he was speaking the truth.

Silently she stepped aside so that he could speak face to face with Edie.

'Did the man who was bullying ye, touch ye?' he asked gently.

Edie shook her head. 'No,' she said in a voice little more than a whisper. 'But he wouldn't let me out of the stairwell and he scared me . . .'

'Ye needn't be scairt of me,' Ringan said, carrying out a shrewd medical examination of her with his eyes only. 'I think ye should stay with your friends now and have a cup of tea and bite to eat.'

'Is Lilli going to be all right?' Edie asked, wondering how a man so big could be so comforting.

Ringan smiled and, like Lilli before her, Kate noticed how his smile utterly transformed his face. 'She'll be a wee bit the worse for wear for a while, but it's nothing rest won't put right.'

He turned again to Kate. 'Don't let Miss Stullen sleep for a good while and don't let Edie wander about the boat unless she's accompanied by someone a lot older than Lottie.'

Lettie nodded, wondering what the hell they were going to do to protect Edie once they reached Dawson.

Ringan, unaware of the problem, stepped out of the cabin and into the narrow passageway beyond. He had

121

done all that was necessary. With a little luck Lilli Stullen would suffer no after-effects more serious than a bruised jaw and a powerful headache. As he strode back towards the companion-way he wondered why he hadn't admitted to his profession. Was it because he was scared that if he had done so he might be called upon to give medical aid to any passenger that fell sick? That he might once again be publicly regarded as a doctor when he still hadn't determined if he ever wanted to be regarded so ever again?

He took the steep steps of the companion-way two at a time with athletic ease. If he allowed himself to be known as Doctor Cameron he would be setting himself up for the inevitable moment when the nature of the crime he had served time for became public knowledge. And then, as a doctor, he would be ostracised. He would again feel not worthy of the profession that he loved. The profession that was his vocation.

He stood on the deck, his face raised to the refreshing sea breeze. He had other things on his mind, too, apart from the problem of whether he could honourably ever practise medicine again. And those other things were all bound up with Miss Lilli Stullen.

'And so the Scottie carried her off and the captain didn't make the slightest objection,' one of Lucky Jack's cohorts concluded, still breathless from his run down to the stateroom.

Jack laid his hand of cards face down on the table. The three men playing with him did the same.

'Was she hurt bad?' he asked, a frown pulling his winged eyebrows together.

'She went down pretty hard. And she was out of it for a few minutes. I think the Scottie must be a doc. He seemed to know what he was about.

One of Lucky Jack's companions gave a staccato hoot of laughter. 'The Scottie ain't a doc. He's the very opposite.'

'Which is?' Jack asked. If there was anything derogatory

to know about Cameron he wanted to know it. The guy being a big hero once he could accept. Being a knight on a white charger for the second time in two days was too much to stomach, especilly considering the identity of the damsel in distress. He was the one who should have sorted that particular incident. And if there had been any carrying off to do, he was the one who should have done it.

'He's a killer,' his card-playing buddy said laconically. 'A killer who's served time.'

'How'd he kill?' another of the men sitting at the card-table asked with interest.

'A knuckle-fight'

Jack began to grin. Knights in white armour didn't kill with their bare fists. Miss Lilli Stullen was going to be very disillusioned when she learned the truth about Ringan Cameron. Very disillusioned indeed.

Chapter Eight

'A killer?' Lilli stared at Lucky Jack round-eyed. Was killer Klondike terminology for a man of powerful physique as musher was terminology for an old hand who hadn't yet struck it rich, and *cheechako* was terminology for a tenderfoot?

'What do you mean by saying Mr Cameron's a killer?' she asked again, bewildered. 'Do you mean he's a big man? Or a blacksmith? Or a . . .'

They were standing on the part of the deck that had become their regular meeting-place. The air was balmy, the water as smooth as glass as the *Senator* sailed sheltered waters. On one side of them lay a long line of islands and on the other lay a vast shimmering wilderness of virgin forest.

Jack grinned down at her. He would have had to be inhuman not to be enjoying himself immensely. 'No, I don't. I mean a killer as in convicted killer.'

She continued to stare at him, feeling stupid. What did he mean 'as in convicted killer'? Ringan Cameron had saved Leo's life. Though she hadn't particularly wanted him to, he had given her assistance. He had been extraordinarily sensitive and gentle with Edie, telling her she need not be 'scairt' of him. Despite his being an ex-convict, from the moment she had spoken to him face-to-face, she had known he couldn't possibly have been convicted of any violent crime. His eyes had, quite simply, not been the eyes of a violent man. And now her Greek god was telling her that Ringan Cameron was a killer. It was utterly ridiculous. Quite preposterous.

'I don't know where you got your information from,

124

but I'm sure it's wrong,' she said, trying not to sound too schoolmarmish. 'Mr Cameron couldn't possible be . . .'

Lucky Jack did his best to look suitably regretful. Tipping his Homburg to the back of his head he said, 'I'm afraid it's true, Lilli. I had it from a card-sharp aboard ship released from the same prison. Cameron killed a man with his bare hands.'

Lilli blinked away a mental image of a man being torn literally apart limb from limb. That wasn't what Lucky Jack meant. He meant that Ringan Cameron had strangled his victim or beaten him to death. Bile rose in her throat. Were either of those two methods of killing any improvement on tearing a man apart limb from limb? The end result was, after all, exactly the same. A man had died violently and Ringan Cameron had been responsible.

'It just goes to show you can't tell a book by its cover,' Jack said gravely, wondering if he hadn't, perhaps, missed his way in life. It really was ridiculously easy to sound like a sanctimonious preacher. 'I know you're grateful to him for saving Leo's life,' he continued, seeing no reason why he shouldn't put an end utterly to Cameron's aspirations where Lilli was concerned, 'but you've given him your thanks for that and it might be best now to give him a wide berth.'

Lilli tried to remember who else, quite recently, had made a similar remark about not being able to tell a book by its cover. Had it been Kate? And who had she been referring to? She gave herself a mental shake. Whoever had said it and whoever it had been about, it wasn't of the slightest importance. What *was* important was the advice Lucky Jack had just given her. She remembered how she had allowed Leo to spend time alone with Ringan Cameron the previous afternoon and shuddered.

Ringan Cameron may have redeemed himself in the eyes of his Maker by saving Leo's life but a man who had once killed with his bare hands was a man too unstable to have a child in his care. She remembered how he had swept her up in his arms and carried her off to her cabin and waited for another shudder of horror. None came. Even though

125

she now knew the crime he had been imprisoned for she couldn't pretend to herself that she had felt anything but safe and secure in Ringan Cameron's muscular arms.

From across the Strait came the sound of whirring saw-mills and exploding dynamite.

'Pioneers blasting a new town out of the coastal granite,' Jack said knowledgeably, aware that he had achieved his object and that it was now time the subject was changed. 'All the way up this coastline you'll see similar sights.'

Lilli looked shorewards to where a seemingly endless forest shelved down on an irregular collection of log cabins and tents all crowded at the water's edge.

'A little further north of here is an Indian settlement,' Jack continued, remembering how soft and yielding her lips had been the previous evening; remembering the brief, sweet feel of her breasts against the palms of his hands. 'Indian towns aren't remotely like white towns. The pace of life is much more slow-moving.'

Even just thinking about the previous evening gave him a rising in his crotch. He hadn't intended a shipboard dalliance with Lilli Stullen, past experience having taught him that respectable young women were far more trouble than they were worth, but a shipboard dalliance it had turned into and, as it had done so, he saw no reason not to enjoy it to the full.

'I'd like to take you for a walk through an Indian settlement,' he said, a hot flush at the backs of his eyes as he slid an arm around her waist. 'We'll be at Skagway by early afternoon but Skagway isn't Indian and it isn't the prettiest place on earth.'

She felt heat surge into her cheeks. No matter what private understanding there might now be between them she couldn't stand in broad daylight with his arm around her waist! Not when it was common knowledge they were not travelling together and when there was no engagement ring on the fourth finger of her left hand. If people thought she was allowing a near stranger to take liberties with her person it would reflect badly on the other Peabody brides' reputations. And Edie had already

126

had one hideous experience without her own behaviour encouraging another.

'People are looking,' she said huskily, moving away from him slightly so that the contact between them was broken.

He suppressed a surge of exasperation knowing that she was quite right, that people *were* looking. And certainly if once the rumour that she was on intimate terms with him spread, it would be impossible for her to be accepted by polite society in Dawson. And that was, after all, what he wanted for her? Wasn't it?

'Sure you can get her a respectable, well-paying job,' Kitty had said to him when he had told her of his plans to pay off Josh Nelson and make arrangements whereby Lilli could support herself and Leo and Lottie, 'but she'll never be able to fit into her own kind of society in Dawson if gossip has it there's more between the two of you than meets the eye.'

She had looked at him with the kind of directness he had never known any other woman capable of, 'And if there is more between the two of you than meets the eye, I'd like to be the first to hear about it.'

He had grinned, sliding his arms around her waist, holding her close. 'There's been nothing more than a goodnight kiss,' he said, knowing Kitty would take such a revelation in her stride. 'She's a nice kid who has had a raw deal and who I'd like to help, okay?'

Kitty had cocked her head slightly to one side, 'It's okay for now,' she had said, regarding him shrewdly, 'but it won't be okay if you start getting in too deep. Women can't be played with as if they're a deck of cards, Jack. And that goes for me as well as Miss Lilli Stullen.'

It had been a warning and he had taken due note of it. Now, however, again within kissing distance of Lilli Stullen's full-lipped mouth, he couldn't help wondering if it was a warning he was going to ignore. There was something oddly moving about engaging the attentions of a young woman who took the charade so very seriously. He thought back to the previous night and wondered if she

127

had ever been kissed before. Somehow he doubted it. A smile tugged at the corner of his mouth. If his assumption was correct it made the warmth and willingness of her response even more remarkable.

'We'll be able to get away from prying eyes when we reach Whitehorse,' he said, beginning to stroll with her down the deck, enjoying the smell of lemon-blossom that emanated from her hair. He wondered what she rinsed it in; how long it would be unpinned; how heavy and silky it would feel falling across the backs of his hands. 'I'll hire a buggy to take us out to the rapids.'

She was so conscious of his nearness she could barely think of anything else. She hadn't wanted to step away from his arm when it had circled her waist. It had been one of the hardest things she had ever done and she had only done it because she didn't want gossip about herself to adversely affect Susan and Kate and Edie and Lettie.

'That would be lovely,' she said sincerely, 'Leo and Lottie would love a buggy-ride. They haven't been in a buggy since we left Kansas.'

Jack opened his mouth to say he had been envisioning a buggy-ride that would give them an opportunity for a little privacy and then thought better of it. Her innocence was such she hadn't realised how far he had intended their kissing and caressing to go and suddenly the idea of violating such innocence, for no reason other than selfish amusement, didn't seem to be quite such a good one.

'We could take one of your friends as well,' he said, abandoning all thoughts of seduction, 'the more the merrier.' The wryness in his voice was lost on her. She only thought how extraordinarily kind he was.

'Morning, Miss Stullen!' a grizzled-haired, roly-poly figure she had seen before but had never spoken to, said, breezing up to them like an old family friend. 'Morning, Lucky Jack! It's mighty good weather we're havin', ain't it?'

'It sure is, Stan,' Jack said easily and then, knowing that Stan only knew Lilli's name by hearsay and had never been introduced to her, he said, 'Stan, may I introduce you to

128

Miss Lilli Stullen. Lilli, this here is Saskatchewan Stan. He's an old Klondike hand.'

'Sure am, ma'am,' Stan said, eyes as black as currants twinkling with good humour. 'Mushed it over the Chilkoot in the spring of '98 and struck lucky practically straight away. So darn lucky I needn't never go back but I'm just an old shovel-stiff at heart and I can't seem to keep away from those rivers and creeks and bare, blue hills.'

'I'm very pleased to meet you Mr . . . Mr . . .'

'Just call me Stan, ma'am,' Saskatchewan Stan said, coming to her aid. 'Everyone does.'

'I'm very pleased to meet you, Stan,' Lilli said, wondering if he was younger than he looked, for he looked to be at least fifty years old.

'And I'm right pleased to meet you, Miss Stullen. I seed what happened the other day when your kid brother went for a dip in the ocean and I felt real bad about it.'

Jack cleared his throat, certain of what was about to come. 'Stan I don't think . . .' he began, frowning warningly in Stan's direction.

Stan was oblivious. When he got into a conversational roll nothing could stop him and he was on a roll now. 'Why, if me and Blueberry Pete hadn't gotten into a dice game with Lucky Jack, the little nipper might never have wandered off on his own. Kids never do like hangin' around unattended, do they? Never had kids of my own, ma'am, 'cos I've never bin married, but I sure would like to have kids. Kids kind of settle a man, don't they?'

Lilli dutifully agreed that children certainly brought stability. A dice-game! So that was where Jack's attention was when he should have been keeping an eye on Leo! A wave of indignation flooded through her. Leo could easily have drowned and if he had drowned it would have been due to Lucky Jack's negligence. It was a terrible thought and she didn't know how to come to terms with it. She was, after all, in love with Jack. He was her Destiny. Her Fate. And he loved her. The mere memory of the way he had kissed and caressed her the previous evening was proof enough of that.

'. . . and so I've been in Californey for the winter,' Saskatchewan Stan was saying, barely pausing for breath, 'and next winter I might mush down to Arizoney or even Floridy.'

Lilli smiled encouragement, her thoughts far from either Arizona or Florida. She shot Jack a covert look. He was smoothing his neatly clipped blond moustache with his thumb and forefinger, the sun glinting on his rakish earring as he listened to Saskatchewan Stan's ramblings as if they were pronouncements of the greatest relevance.

Her heart felt as if it were turning over within her breast. What other man could look so sophisticated and yet so devil-may-care? And what other man would have the kindness to pay such attention to an amiable windbag such as Saskatchewan Stan? If she felt distressed at the thought of his negligence where Leo was concerned, how much worse must he feel? With great difficulty she stopped herself from slipping her hand into his and giving it a comforting squeeze.

'. . . and my apologies for not bein' more spruced up,' Stan was now saying to her. 'I hadn't expected there to be so many ladies aboard ship. Mighty pretty ladies too.'

'And all looking for husbands,' Jack said roguish-ly.

Saskatchewan Stan flushed beetroot. 'Now don't you go tryin' to pair me off with any pretty lady, Jack. You know how ham-fisted I am around pretty ladies. They make me real jittery.'

'You're not jittery now and Lilli's a pretty lady,' Jack pointed out, causing Stan to flush an even deeper shade of red.

'She sure is. She's a *mighty* pretty lady, but she ain't *on the loose* so to speak.' Stan's consternation was so acute it was all Lilli could to prevent herself from bursting into giggles. 'She's kind of with you and that makes a difference to a man.'

Jack laughed and then, looking beyond Stan, his laughter faded. 'Your friend is approaching,' he said to Lilli, frowning slightly. 'And she's got a clergyman with her.'

130

He made it sound as if Susan was being accompanied by a dread disease.

'The gentleman in question is the Reverend Mr Jenkinson,' Lilli said, unable to keep amusement out of her voice any longer. 'He's travelling to Dawson to replace the incumbent Methodist minister there.'

'Then if that's the case I don't think he should see you with me,' Jack said, mindful of Kitty's warnings on the subject. 'Come on, Stan. Let's take our leave of Lilli. Clerical respectability is in the offing.'

With almost indecent speed they turned on their heels, leaving her strolling alone towards Susan and the Reverend Mr Jenkinson.

With a twitch of her lips Lilli noted that the Reverend Mr Jenkinson was keeping a very proprietal distance away from Susan. So far, that, if she had chosen to, she could have easily walked between the two of them.

'I'd like to introduce you to a friend of mine,' Susan said to him, her large face looking almost pretty she was so happy. 'Lilli, the Reverend Mr Jenkinson. Mr Jenkinson, my friend Miss Stullen.'

'I'm very pleased to meet you, Miss Stullen,' Susan's beau said, his moon-face beaming. 'I understand we will be neighbours in Dawson. I'm hoping to start a small school there for Indian children as I understand from Miss Bumby that at present there are no such facilities. As a work colleague of Miss Bumby's, perhaps you could give me a little advice as to how I should go about organising such a school without offending the orthodox school-board authorities?'

'I'm afraid you are mistaken about my being a colleague of Miss Bumby's,' Lilli said, vastly entertained at having being taken for a school-mistress, especially a school-mistress capable of giving a mature clergyman professional advice.

'Although Miss Stullen doesn't teach, she's very good with children,' Susan said quickly. 'Her younger brother and sister are travelling with her to Dawson. Leo is six years of age and Lottie, ten, and I'm very much looking forward to having Leo in my class next term.'

'Splendid, splendid,' Mr Jenkinson said affably, hiding his perplexity as to what a single young woman with two young siblings was doing en route to the pioneering north.

Lilli, seeing Lettie and Marietta in the distance, politely excused herself and made an escape. It was obvious Susan hadn't yet disclosed to Mr Jenkinson that she was returning to Dawson as a Peabody bride for if she had done so, she would have said that she, Lilli, was a Peabody bride also.

'Where are Lottie and Leo?' she asked when she came within hailing distance of her friends. 'I thought they were with you?'

'They were but we ran into Leo's saviour and they're hanging over the bow with him, eager for a first sighting of Skagway.'

'Oh Lord!' Lilli said, aware that she had a problem on her hands.

Marietta's green cat-eyes widened. 'What's the matter? We didn't think you'd mind. Leo's got a bad case of hero-worship where Mr Cameron is concerned and Lottie obviously thinks he's pretty wonderful as well.'

'Yes, well, I think I'd better go and relieve him of them all the same.'

Both Marietta and Lettie stared at her, mystified. Lilli stared back at them helplessly. She couldn't explain. She owed Ringan Cameron too much to be responsible for spreading the news that his criminal offence had been murder. He had, after all, served time for his crime. Like herself, he was embarking on a new life in Dawson and the fewer people who knew about his past the better his chances of success in that new life would be.

Quickly she began to walk towards the bow, aware for the first time of the sense of expectation amongst her fellow passengers.

'Portal of Romance, that's Skagway,' one old-timer was saying to a party of new-comers. 'You'll see it any minute now, crouched at the foot of the White Pass mountains . . .'

132

'This is the Lynn Canal, Miss Nettlesham,' a senior member of crew was saying as Miss Nettlesham held a pair of binoculars to her eyes. 'It's a long, natural arm of water . . .'

Lilli took a detour behind them so as not to be waylaid. She had a guilty conscience where Miss Nettlesham was concerned feeling she should have made more effort to befriend her. Now, however, was not the time to put her omission to rights.

There was quite a crowd of people in the bow, all of them looking towards the soaring, snow-covered mountains that now seemed almost close enough to touch.

As always, Ringan Cameron's distinctive colouring and build set him apart from the men nearby him. He was standing at the deck-rails, his back towards her, Leo and Lottie at either side of him. As she approached him she couldn't help noting that he had the most beautiful head of hair she'd ever seen on a man. Ranging subtly in hue from mahogany to nutmeg it had enough natural curl in it to spring and twine around a woman's finger.

She gave herself a sharp mental reprimand. What on earth was she thinking of? Ringan Cameron's fiery hair would certainly never curl around *her* finger. Thick, sleek, wheat-gold hair was the only kind of hair that interested her.

She cleared her throat. 'Excuse me, Mr Cameron, but it's time Leo and Lottie started getting ready to disembark.'

He turned round to face her, but not with an easy, dazzling smile as Lucky Jack would have done. Beneath his bushy moustache his well-shaped mouth remained straight and there was an unreadable expression in his dark grey eyes. She remembered the intimate embrace he had witnessed between herself and Jack Coolidge and wondered if he was remembering it also and if that was the reason for his reserve. At the thought that he might be thinking her the kind of woman he didn't want to associate with, indignation flooded through her. He was a *murderer* for goodness sake! How dare he

133

take a holier-than-thou attitude where she was concerned?

'We've another hour, easy, before we dock,' he said,
and against her will she was reminded how pleasant a
Highland burr was in a rich, dark, male voice.

'All the same I'd like them to come with me back to
our cabin,' she said firmly, knowing she sounded like a
bossy school-mistress but not knowing how else to tackle
the situation.

Lottie turned away from the view and looked at her
in astonishment. 'But we haven't anything to pack,' she
pointed out reasonably. 'We've been living out of our
travel-bags ever since we boarded. All we have to do is
pick them up and carry them off the ship with us.'

Lilli came as close to glaring at her as she'd ever
done in her life. If she insisted again that Leo and
Lottie return with her to their cabin, Ringan Cameron
would immediately leap to the right conclusion about the
reason which, under the circumstances, would be deeply
embarrassing. She gritted her teeth. There was only one
alternative. As she obviously couldn't leave Leo and Lottie
alone in the company of a man who had murdered, she
would simply have to stay with them, with him.

'We'll stay on deck for another fifteen minutes and then
we'll have to return to the cabin for our bags,' she said
tightly.

Lottie, aware that something had deeply ruffled Lilli's
feathers but mystified as to what it could have been, said,
'Are you feeling all right, Lilli? You look a bit fraught.'

'I'm feeling fine,' Lilli said, resisting the urge to throt-
tle her.

Even Ringan Cameron had begun to look at her a little
oddly. Only Leo was impervious to the tension. Standing
on the bottom deck-rail, his weight against the top rail,
he hadn't even turned round to her but was staring at the
shimmering mountains in wide-eyed wonder.

Not wanting Ringan Cameron to come to any correct
conclusions she forced a taut smile. 'The scenery is
staggering, isn't it? Is it similar to Scotland?'

A glimmer of a smile touched his straight mouth. 'Not verra. These mountains make Scottish mountains seem like wee hills.' The glimmer of a smile deepened. 'Scottish mountains are more beautiful though.

She smiled in response, unable to stop herself. He was a Celt, like herself. And like herself his homeland would always be more beautiful to him than anywhere else on earth.

'I was born in Ireland, in Wicklow,' she said, moving nearer to the deck-rails and leaning her weight against them. 'The Wicklow Mountains are the most beautiful mountains in the world.'

'I was born in Skye, within shadow of the Cuillins, and I'd have to dispute that last statement.'

She laughed. Of course he would. The whereabouts of the most beautiful mountains in the world were something an Irish girl and a Scotsman would never agree on in a million years.

'Ye havna much of an accent,' he said, glad that her earlier abrupt manner had mellowed into pleasantness. Her curtness had sat oddly on her. She had neither the face nor the voice for it and he doubted it was something she gave vent to very often. Certainly little Lottie had seemed totally perplexed by it.

Lottie said now, tossing her braids back over her shoulders, 'Ma and Pa left Ireland with Lilli when she was my age. After that we lived in America.'

He made an indeterminate sound low in his throat that could be interpreted to mean almost anything and Lilli, caught unexpectedly in a mood of deep nostalgia, said, 'Our Pa was a travelling-man. He worked with horses whenever he could. One time we lived on a ranch in Wyoming for two years. Another time we lived in Colorado . . .'

'And don't forget Montana, Lilli,' Leo said suddenly, 'I liked Montana.'

Ringan chuckled. 'Ye got around a tidy bit. I've been to Montana myself, but only to camp and hike.

'Do you think we'll be able to camp and hike in the

Klondike?' Leo asked, turning his head and looking up at Ringan hopefully. 'I'd like to camp. Especially if there were wolves and grizzlies around!'

'I believe wolves and grizzlies are verra mean-tempered animals,' Ringan said equably, 'and from what I've heard aboard ship, the Klondike is plagued by mosquitos and I wouldna fancy sharing a tent with those wee devils.' His hands were on the brass rail, his arms splayed. The sleeves of his plaid shirt were rolled to the elbows and the strength of his arm muscles was impressively apparent. Lilli felt a tingle run down her spine. For all his apparent equability, it was a strength he had once unleashed with fatal consequences and there was no way on God's earth she could ever allow Leo to go camping and hiking with him.

'We could have a wee stroll together at Whitehorse though,' Ringan was saying to Leo. 'There are rapids there and I believe they're verra bonny.'

'Mr Coolidge is taking us to see the rapids,' Lilli said speedily.

'I'd rather go with Ringan,' Leo said, blissfully oblivious of the signals she was giving him with her eyes.

'Well you can't,' Lilli said with a bluntness that startled even him. 'Mr Coolidge is going to hire a buggy and Lettie is going to come with us and . . .'

As Leo opened his mouth to protest further Ringan Cameron said in his easy-going manner, 'If arrangements have been made it would be verra impolite to renege on them, young Leo.'

Lilli felt a shaft of gratitude towards him. That difficulty, at least, had been surmounted.

'*Skagway*!' a burly individual standing nearby them suddenly shouted. 'I can see it clear as day!'

A great cheer went up and Lilli said in relief, 'We need to get back to our cabin now to collect our bags.'

Ringan merely nodded, but there was an odd expression again in his eyes, one almost of concern. Heartily wishing Ringan Cameron was a more comfortable acquaintance, she herded Leo and Lottie to the nearest companion-way.

136

'No-one else is getting their bags yet,' Leo complained as she shepherded him down the stairs.

'We are.'

Lottie's braids had fallen over her shoulders and she flicked them back again, saying, 'You're being awfully bossy, Lilli. What's the matter? Are you worrying about what's going to happen when we reach Dawson?'

'No.' Lilli steered Leo in front of her as they began to negotiate the long narrow corridor that led to their cabin. 'That's all been sorted out, Lottie. There's no longer anything to worry about.'

'Sorted out?' Lottie hurried after her. 'How do you mean "sorted out?" Do you mean you're no longer going to have to marry anyone?'

Lilli opened the cabin door and Leo tumbled into the minuscule space beyond. She had been waiting for a suitable opportunity to tell Lottie about the understanding that now existed between herself and Lucky Jack but there had never been a suitable opportunity. 'I *am* going to marry someone,' she said, aware that the present moment was far from ideal for such a disclosure. 'But someone I *want* to marry.'

'Oh God,' Lottie said, in a manner far too old for her years. She sat down weakly on Lettie's bunk. 'Oh *dear* God. It's Mr Coolidge isn't it? You're fancying yourself in love with Mr Coolidge.'

Leo had scrambled up into a top bunk out of the way and was now laying on his tummy, his head and shoulders over the bunk's edge, looking down at them and listening to them with wide-eyed incredulity.

'You're ten years old, Lottie!' Lilli said sharply, rifling through her travel-bag for a clean shirtwaist with which to disembark in. 'You shouldn't be taking the Lord's name in vain and accusing me of 'fancying' myself to be in love when I've told you I *am* in love!'

Lottie gripped her hands tightly together in her lap, her face pinched and white. Lilli was being absurdly romantic and impractical again. Mr Coolidge *looked* rather wonderful and so Lilli though he *was* wonderful.

137

But she, Lottie, didn't think he was wonderful. He hadn't kept an eye on Leo when Leo had been in his care and Leo had nearly drowned as a result. Ringan Cameron had saved Leo's life and was far, *far* more wonderful than Mr Coolidge and yet Lilli, at times, was barely civil to him! It was all beyond her understanding.

'You should be very glad for me,' Lilli was saying, unbuttoning her blouse with such vigour a button sprang free of its moorings. 'At least I won't be marrying a stranger!' She began to fight her way into a crisp, clean shirtwaist. 'Mr Coolidge is a man of importance in Dawson. He's a businessman and an hotelier *and* he's handsome!' Her voice was thick with indignation at Lottie's lack of understanding. 'As handsome as a Greek god!'

Lottie raised her eyes to heaven. A Greek god indeed! Still, it did sound as if Lilli was sincerely in love with Mr Coolidge. And if Mr Coolidge had asked her marry him . . .

'If you're going to marry Mr Coolidge does that mean you don't object anymore to his teaching me card-tricks?' Leo asked hopefully.

Lilli tucked her shirtwaist beneath the waistband of her cream serge skirt with unnecessary briskness.

'I find that question extremely tactless and ill-timed.' She thrust her discarded blouse into her travel-bag. 'Why you and Lottie have to be quite so annoying just when everything is going so well, I can't imagine. And everything *is* going well. We'll be in Dawson within another day or so and . . .'

The cabin door burst open and an ashen-faced Marietta stood on the threshold. 'We've got trouble,' she announced tautly. 'The pig who terrorised Edie says that when we get to Dawson he's going to outbid anyone else who fancies marrying her.' Her oddly attractive, feline face was so grim it was scarcely recognisable. 'And he's boasting that he'll then do whatever the hell he wants with her!'

Chapter Nine

'Where is Edie now?' Lilli asked urgently, picking up her heavy travel-bag.

'She's on deck with Kate and Lettie, waiting to disembark.'

'And the pig?' Lilli felt sick. Somehow she had just known something like this was going to happen and she hadn't a clue as to what could be done about it. 'Where is he? And how did you get to know what he's been saying?'

'He's still being forcibly kept to his cabin by the captain and crew,' Marietta said as she gave Leo a hand down from the bunk. 'He's had plenty of friends visiting him though and they've not been shy of announcing his intentions.'

Lilli stared at her, appalled. 'You mean he isn't afraid of what people will say?'

Marietta's wide mouth twisted in an ironic grimace. 'We're in the Klondike now, Lilli. Or as near as makes no difference. As far as our male travelling companions are concerned, respect for women is pretty low on their list of priorities. And Edie is a Peabody bride. She's up for grabs anyway and if the pig wants to do the grabbing . . .'

She didn't finish her sentence. She didn't have to. Lilli felt the sting of bile in her throat. 'Up for grabs.' In those three ugly small words lay the true reality of what it meant to be a Peabody bride. Mrs Amy Peabody's apparent motherliness, the deceiving cosiness of the bulging photograph albums, the false reassurance of the newspaper article about the radiantly happy Peabody bride and her gold-rich husband, were all red herrings designed to lure naive and indigent young women into the Peabody Bureau's clutches.

'What are we going to do, Lilli?' Lottie asked tremulously, her usually happy shining face pinched and pale.

As she looked across at her, Lilli felt crucified by guilt. Lottie was only ten years old. The anxieties and fears she was experiencing on Edie's behalf were anxieties and fears she shouldn't even be conversant with, let alone be burdened with. 'I don't know,' she said thickly, 'but we'll think of something.

Leo held tightly to Marietta's hand, knowing that something was deeply wrong but not understanding just what. 'Why does Edie have to marry anyone?' he asked bewilderedly. 'Why can't she live with us or with Marietta?'

Over his silk-dark mop of hair Marietta and Lilli's eyes met and held, both wondering if it were a possibility.

'I'll speak to Kitty Dufresne,' Marietta said, wondering if Kitty would hire Edie as a maid or a kitchen assistant.

'And I'll speak to Lucky Jack,' Lilli said as she led the way out of the cabin.

'Lucky Jack?' Marietta's eyebrows shot high into her frizz of fiery hair. 'Lucky Jack Coolidge? Land's sakes! He isn't a beau of yours as well, is he?'

'As well as who?' Leo asked interestedly as Lilli, struggling to negotiate the narrow corridor with her bulky carpet-bag, didn't trouble to reply.

Marietta didn't belong to the school of thought that believed certain subjects of conversation should be censored for young ears. 'As well as a very handsome seaman and the very personable Mr Cameron. Thank goodness the voyage is at an end, Leo. If it had continued for much longer there wouldn't have been a man aboard ship not carrying a torch for your sister!'

Leo giggled, because Marietta always made him giggle, and with his hand in hers followed Lilli and Lottie up onto the crowded deck.

The crush was horrendous. Every man seemed to have a ton of equipment with him. Newcomers hoisted bedding-rolls and bags of flour and frying-pans. Men who had already struck it rich and were returning after spending the winter in warmer climes were burdened with gigantic brass-cornered leather suitcases and parcels and crates bearing labels as diverse as London, Paris and Rome.

With a colossal shudder the *Senator's* gangplank was lowered. Lottie's sailor's hat was nearly knocked from her head as the stampede to be amongst the first ashore began.

'Where is Lettie?' Lilli shouted across to Marietta. 'Do you think she's alright?'

'She's with Kate and the others,' Marietta shouted back. 'I'm going to have to leave you now to go and get my own bags. Will you be okay?'

Lilli nodded, certain that at any moment Lucky Jack would be at her side.

'There's Ringan!' Lottie said suddenly as they were buffeted about on all sides. 'Look! Over there! He'll help us!'

'We don't need help!' Lilli said exasperatedly as Lottie began to wave to attract Ringan Cameron's attention. 'And please don't refer to Mr Cameron by his christian name, Lottie. It's not at all polite.'

Vainly she searched the sea of heads in search of one wheat-gold and Homburg-hatted, but the only figure forging his way through the crush to her side was copper-haired and bare-headed.

'Can I be of any assistance?' he asked as he reached her side, his voice as always thick with a Highland burr. There was something else in his voice as well. Something Lilli couldn't quite define. Was it reluctance? The thought sent the blood boiling through her veins.

'No, thank you,' she said crisply.

'Yes, please,' Lottie and Leo chorused.

He frowned slightly, wondering if Lilli Stullen's negative reply was because she didn't want to receive assistance which might arouse Lucky Jack Coolidge's annoyance or if it was something less easy to accept; if it was because she had heard gossip as to his jail-bird past.

The temptation to simply accept her refusal and leave her to struggle with her bag was almost overpowering, but it wasn't only Lilli Stullen who was struggling with a heavy bag. It was little Lottie also.

'If you're waiting for someone, I'll leave you to wait for them,' he said diplomatically, 'but the bag wee Lottie's carrying is too heavy for a child.' He removed it from Lottie's unprotesting hands. 'I'll take care of it for her till she's safely aboard the train.' He hesitated. The arrangements for all passengers bound for Dawson was that they would partake of a late lunch at the Golden North Hotel, Skagway, before boarding the train which would take them on the next stage of their journey. Tables at the Golden North would, however, be limited, and by insisting on struggling with her heavy carpet-bag Lilli Stullen was running the risk of arriving there too late to be fed at all. 'Taking your bag as well wouldna be a problem,' he said as the stampede for the gangplank continued.

Over the sea of heads Lilli could see Miss Nettlesham's tall, thin figure being uncomfortably jostled as she stepped on to the gangplank. A little way ahead of her Susan was being accompanied off the ship by the Reverend Mr Jenkinson. Behind her, Kate and Lettie and Edie could be seen, all of them battling not to be knocked off their feet.

She turned her head slightly looking to see if, coming from the direction of the nearest companion-way, Marietta was also being buffeted in the crush. There was no sign of her distinctive fox-red hair but with vast relief she saw Lucky Jack making his way towards her, two slick-suited men on either side of him.

She turned again to face Ringan Cameron. 'Thank you for the offer,' she said, smiling radiantly, her inner happiness such she would have found it impossible *not* to smile, 'but I can manage.'

Ringan shrugged, gave Leo and Lottie a friendly grin and, slinging the heavy bag over his shoulder and holding it by the thumb as if it weighed no more than a jacket, turned away from her.

Lilli stared after him for a few seconds, the annoyance he so often aroused in her surfacing yet again. His friendly grin hadn't been directed at herself. To herself he was always faultlessly polite but . . . reserved? Was that the word she was looking for? Unbending? Or was he simply dour? A dour Scot who had a naturally easy manner with children and who was uncommonly gentle with frightened, mentally-retarded young women such as Edie?

Shrugging him from her thoughts she heaved the weight of her heavy carpet-bag from one hand to the other and turned to greet Lucky Jack. He wasn't there. Bewildered, she scanned the forest of heads, a forest that was fast beginning to thin. There was no sign of him. Swinging round she looked in the direction of the gangplank.

There was no longer any sign of Ringan Cameron's tall, broad-shouldered figure but three men, all similarly-suited, were just about to step onto the gangplank. As she watched she saw the man on the right-hand side of the Homburg-hatted man in the middle jovially slap his companion's back. The Homburg-hatted man threw back his head, obviously laughing uproariously. Blue cigar smoke rose in a cloud above all three of them.

The word Lilli muttered beneath her breath was not one she was in the habit of using. And it wasn't directed at Lucky Jack. When she had seen him heading in her direction she had simply *assumed* that he had seen her and that he was making his way towards her. And he hadn't seen her. He no doubt thought she was way ahead of him, with Lettie and Kate and Edie.

'I didn't know ladies said words like that,' Leo said naively, as impatient to be off the *Senator* as he had been to board her.

'They don't and I shouldn't have,' Lilli retorted, even crosser with herself than she had been a few moments earlier. 'Come on, pet lamb, if we don't get a move on we're going to be the last passengers to disembark.'

'Where did you learn a word like that?' Lottie asked curiously, grateful she wasn't still lugging a cumbersome travel-bag.

143

Lilli was just about to reprimand her for asking such an improper question when innate good humour and sense of proportion came to her aid. 'From Pa's fellow ranch-hands when we were in Wyoming.' There was the suspicion of a giggle in her voice. 'But *you're* not to start using it, Lottie. And Leo mustn't either!'

She put a hand on the rail flanking the gangplank and, as she stepped onto the gangplank and saw the view in front of her, she sucked in her breath. 'Oh my, Lottie! Look at that. Just look at that!' She wasn't referring to Skagway, which at first glance looked to be rackety and ramshackle, but at its setting. Behind the untidy conglomeration of wooden-built houses, saloons, and stores the mountains rose in dazzling, snow-covered splendour. Mountains they would shortly be crossing.

'How on earth did men traverse them by foot?' Lottie asked, reading Lilli's thoughts.

Lilli shook her head, not knowing the answer, overcome by the knowledge that one of the men who had done so was Lucky Jack. As she thought of his feat of endurance her admiration for him was boundless. There was far more to Lucky Jack Coolidge than some people seemed to think.

'Why didn't you let Ri . . . Mr Cameron carry your bags off the ship for you?' Lottie asked musingly, breaking in on her thoughts.

Lilli stepped off the gangplank and onto dry land. 'I thought Mr Coolidge was on his way over to us.' The air was dazzling in its purity. The brassy-blue bowl of the sky cast a limpid haze on the snow-covered slopes of the White Pass and lower down, on the grass-covered foothills, drifts of lupins and forget-me-nots stretched as far as the eye could see. 'I thought he'd seen us,' she continued as they began to walk on a rickety side-walk towards the Golden North Hotel, 'but I was mistaken.'

Lottie chewed the corner of her lip thoughtfully for a moment and then said, 'It shouldn't have mattered whether he had seen us or not. If he's your beau, he should have sought you out. If Ri . . . If Mr Cameron was your beau *he* would have sought you out.'

'I'm getting tired of hearing about Mr Cameron!' Lilli said sharply, stepping a neatly booted foot onto the first of the steps leading to the Golden North's entrance. 'Mr Cameron isn't quite the Mr Perfect you obviously think he is, though as to *why* he isn't, I can't tell you. On the subject of Mr Cameron you'll just have to trust me. And I'm getting tired of your constant criticism of Lucky Jack! Lucky Jack is being an absolute . . . an absolute . . . *saviour* to us. If it weren't for him I would have to fulfil my obligations to the marriage bureau and marry any Tom, Dick or Harry!'

Lottie bit the corner of her lip even harder. In saying that Ringan wasn't Mr Perfect Lilli was obviously referring to his history as an ex-convict. Not for the first time she wondered just where Lilli had first gleaned that particular piece of incredible information. She, Lottie, didn't believe it was true for a moment and neither did Leo. Ringan Cameron was a hero, not a criminal, anyone with half an eye could see that. As to Lucky Jack Coolidge . . . She sighed heavily and straightened her sailor-hat. If Lilli *was* in love with him and if he loved her in return, then Lilli was right and she, Lottie, would have to stop being so critical of him.

She followed Lilli into the gloomy confines of the hotel wondering what their Pa would have thought of Lucky Jack. In his own way their Pa had been a gambling man and so Lucky Jack's reputation at the tables wouldn't have disconcerted him too much. Even so, she couldn't help thinking that their father would have preferred a brawny Celt as a prospective son-in-law, rather than a suave American.

'Lilli! Lottie! We're over here!' Marietta called out, waving to signal just where she, Kate, Edie, Lettie and Susan, were sitting.

Lilli wove her way between the crowded tables, Leo and Lottie close behind her.

Kate was seated at the head of the table her high-necked,

145

long-sleeved, ankle-length navy-blue dress giving her a matriachal air. 'Where on earth have you been? she asked as Lilli sat down. 'We thought you must have been one of the first to disembark. As it is you must have been one of the last.'

'*I* came ashore with Miss Dufresne,' Marietta said exuberantly before Lilli could reply to Kate. 'And everything is settled. I'm going to work for her at the *Gold Nugget* and Mr Coolidge is going to square everything with Mr Nelson as far as money and the marriage-bureau is concerned. Lord! I can't tell you how relieved I am!'

'Is Kitty Dufresne in the hotel?' Lilli asked, her stomach muscles tightening with nervous tension. 'Is she here, in the dining-room?'

'She's seated at Mr Coolidge's table,' Lettie said, her voice expressionless, 'over near the far window.'

Lilli was too eager to see what Kitty Dufresne looked like in the flesh to trouble to be circumspect. She turned her head swiftly, looking with apprehensive curiosity in the direction Lettie had indicated. Lucky Jack was seated at a table for four. Two of his companions were the slick-suited men who had accompanied him off the *Senator*. His third companion was seated on his left, looking towards him, her back towards the rest of the dining-room. From the rear all that Lilli could see was a glorious pompadour of Titian-red hair crowned by a nonsense of a hat lavishly trimmed with exotic feathers. The hat was emerald and so was Kitty Dufresne's exquisitely-fitted travelling costume. The bolero jacket was trimmed with extravagant curlicues of black astrakhan, as was the hem of the bell-shaped skirt.

'Paris,' she heard Kate say to Susan, 'that outfit was definitely made in Paris, France, not in America.'

Lilli's stomach muscles were so taut she felt physically sick. Miss Nettlesham had said that Kitty Dufresne was Lucky Jack's paramour and certainly from the partial view Lilli had of her, Kitty Dufresne looked the part.

As if to oblige her in order that she could have a clearer view Kitty turned slightly, speaking to the man seated

146

opposite her. With an elbow resting on the table, her chin propped by a suede-gloved hand, she was utterly at ease. In profile Lilli could see that Kitty's eyelashes were long, her nose girlishly retroussé.

Panic seized her. Had she been foolishly naive in clinging to the belief that Miss Nettlesham totally misunderstood the relationship between Kitty and Lucky Jack? Was Kitty far more to Lucky Jack than merely a business partner?

From this new angle Lilli could see Kitty Dufresne's figure in more detail. The elegant travelling-costume was not quite as nip-waisted as she had expected. In fact, it wasn't nip-waisted at all. And though the retroussé nose was deliciously girlish, there was nothing girlish about the line of jaw and throat. Shock, followed by overwhelming relief, roared through her. What on earth had Miss Nettlesham been thinking of, spreading the rumour that Kitty was Lucky Jack's paramour! She was far too old! Why, she was easily in her thirties!

Suddenly, as if sensing she was being stared at, Kitty turned, looking directly across the crowded dining-room, her eyes, behind a saucy froth of veiling, meeting Lilli's before Lilli had a chance of looking away.

Fresh shock sizzled through Lilli. Though they had never been introduced, never even met, there was recognition in Kitty Dufresne's eyes, recognition that could mean only one thing. Lucky Jack had spoken to Kitty about her.

'And Mr Jenkinson has kindly agreed to accompany us to the rapids when we reach Whitehorse,' Susan was saying when Lilli finally returned her attention to her own table. 'He's hoping there will be some rare species of butterfly in the area and . . .'

'And does he know of your situation yet?' Kate interrupted gently. 'Does he know that when you reach Dawson you'll be obliged to marry a Peabody Marriage Bureau client?'

Susan shook her head, her large featured face flushing blotchily. 'No . . . it isn't a subject easy to bring up, is it? I mean, it makes it sound as if I'm desperate for a husband . . . any husband . . . and as if I'm no great

147

prize.' She gave a small, mirthless laugh. 'And all that's true, of course. Or at least, it *was* true.' She plucked at her napkin with carefully buffed nails. 'It's no longer all true because I no longer want to marry just anyone. I want to marry Mr Jenkinson.' She looked up from the napkin, looking around at them, despair in her eyes. 'And I'm sure, if only there was time for our friendship to deepen in a proper manner, he would ask me to marry him. But there isn't *going* to be time . . .'

'Oh, Lord!' Lettie said suddenly, her naturally pale face turning even paler as she looked beyond Susan to the entrance of the dining-room. 'They've let him off the ship!'

It was blatantly obvious she wasn't referring to Mr Jenkinson.

Only Lettie and Marietta were facing the dining-room door.

'Damn!' Marietta said forcefully through her teeth as everyone else turned to look, 'Damn! damn! damn!'

The brute who had terrified Edie and assaulted Lilli swaggered across the room to a table where his cronies were seated.

'Well, we all know he couldn't be kept in unofficial custody for ever,' Kate said practically as Edie slid her hand nervously into Marietta's.

'The best thing to do is to ignore him,' Lilli said crisply, aware that Lottie and Leo were also beginning to look apprehensive. 'Did you speak to Kitty Dufresne about Edie, Marietta?'

Marietta shook her head. 'No . . . there wasn't time. But I will do. And if she can be helpful, I think she will be.'

Lilli thought Marietta was right in her judgement. When Kitty Dufresne's eyes had met hers there had been no prurience or meanness in their sloe-black depths, only kindly curiosity. And if kindness was one of Kitty Dufresne's virtues, there was every reason to hope she would extend that kindness towards Edie.

*   *   *

'Your maiden in distress obviously knows my identity,' Kitty said dryly to Jack. 'And she's far more striking looking than you ever indicated. Why on earth do Irish girls hold all the aces when it comes to night-black hair and magnolia-cream skin? Perhaps next time when we're trawling for working girls we should trawl for them in Dublin or Cork.'

Jack grinned and their two male companions cracked up with laughter. 'With regard to what we were talking about earlier, I think Miss Stullen could manage *The Eldorado* very nicely,' he said, his eyes holding Kitty's. 'We need someone respectable in there as we're aiming for respectable custom . . .'

'Then *The Eldorado's* not a dance-hall or saloon?' one of his companions asked, interrupting him.

Jack shook his head. 'It's a hotel. And a damn good one too. The Reverend over there . . .' he indicated the Reverend Mr Jenkinson. 'He's booked in at *The Eldorado.*'

'I thought Reverends lived in parsonages.'

Jack's grinned widened. 'They do. But the Reverend Mr Jenkinson has had the sense to realise that his new home will likely need quite a bit of work doing on it after weathering a Yukon winter.'

If Ringan could have eaten lunch alone he would have done so. No such luxury was possible, however, with almost the entire passenger list of the *Senator* eager to pitch into moosemeat, macaroni and cheese, hash, baked beans, pickled beets, blueberry pie and canned milk.

For himself, he passed on the pickled beets and wondered if he would ever be able to develop a taste for moosemeat.

'You could pitch in with us, Scottie,' the grizzled-haired prospector sitting on his left-hand side said generously. 'Rumour has it though that the strikes around Dawson are well nigh played-out and that Nome's the place to be.'

'And if that's the case,' the young man on his right-hand side said, scooping baked beans up on his fork,

'We'll be heading on out there just as soon as we're able.'

Ringan made an indeterminate sound in his throat.

Interpreting it as assent, the grizzled-haired man said, 'If we all grub-stake an equal amount we'll all git along just fine.'

'Och, aye,' Ringan said, knowing some kind of response was necessary and not able to think of anything more adequate. Nome? With the men now flanking him? It would be almost as much of an imprisonment as prison had been. What on earth would he talk about with them? What sort of satisfaction would he find doing nothing but grub for gold?'

As the conversation drifted on without him, he looked across the dining-room to where Lilli Stullen was seated, a shaft of light from a nearby window falling full on her. In its rays her smoke-black hair had a satin sheen. She was wearing blue. A misty-blue mandarin-necked blouse and a seven-gored skirt in a deeper tone of the same colour. The colour suited her, but then he hadn't seen her in anything that didn't suit her.

He wondered why, if she was indulging in a love affair with Lucky Jack Coolidge, she wasn't seated at Lucky Jack's table. And he wondered as to the identity of the woman who *was* sitting with Lucky Jack, and as to her relationship with him. They certainly looked to be on the best of terms and though she was no longer in the first flush of youth she was as lushly beautiful as a full-blown rose.

'There's plenty of men with your type of past in the goldfields,' his grizzled-haired companion was saying. 'Skagway's run by 'em. Why, Soapy Smith would shoot a man as soon as look at him and he's boss of Skagway! I remember when . . .'

Ringan's mouth tightened. If his jail-bird past was already such common knowledge what chance did he have of living it down and practising as a doctor again? And if he didn't return to the profession he was trained for, the profession he had a vocation for, what the hell did life hold for him? How was he ever going to make it meaningful again?

As if sensing his inner chaos, a small, sailor-hatted head turned in his direction. Immediately, as their eyes met, his spirits lifted. He shot her an answering grin and a wink. Little Lottie Stullen reminded him an awful lot of Pattie when Pattie had been her age and sometimes merely looking at her brought a lump into his throat. She was a grand wee lassie on every count and her elder sister could be justifiably proud of her.

Lilli *was* proud of Lottie, but she was also often exasperated by her.

'I've told you before, Lottie,' she said as they boarded the narrow-gauged train that was to take them over the White Pass, 'I don't like you spending so much time in Mr Cameron's company.'

Lottie's eyes, so blue they were almost navy, held hers in such a manner that Lilli felt ridiculously uncomfortable. 'Mr Cameron saved Leo's life,' Lottie said steadily, her waist-length braids framing her face. 'I think he's magnificent and I'm proud to be his friend and no-one, not even you, is going to prevent me from being his friend.'

Lilli's discomfort increased. Lottie was shaming her and both of them knew it. 'I've no objection to your being Mr Cameron's friend,' she said stiltedly, knowing she wasn't speaking the absolute truth. 'But I'd still prefer it if you would sit with me and Leo for the journey to Whitehorse.'

'I don't want to.' Lottie's voice was low and resolutely obstinate. 'Mr Cameron doesn't have friends like the rest of the prospectors do. He's different from them, just as Pa was different from the ranch-hands he worked with. If I don't sit with him, he'll sit alone. And I don't want him to sit alone and Pa wouldn't have wanted him to sit alone either.'

As Lilli's jaw sagged Lottie shot her a look both pleading and defiant and then, interpreting Lilli's dumbfounded silence as reluctant acquiescence, she turned and walked

151

away to the rear of the train where she knew she would find her friend.

Lilli opened her mouth to call her back and then closed it again. What could she possibly say to Lottie in explanation? She certainly wasn't going to give her nightmares by telling her that Ringan Cameron had once been convicted of murder.

Wryly it occurred to her as she settled Leo comfortably into a seat next to a window that such a disclosure might not give Lottie nightmares at all. Lottie would most likely dismiss such a revelation as being unbelievable, which it very nearly was. The shock she had felt when Lottie had spoken of Ringan Cameron and their Pa in the same breath was still reverberating through her. Lottie was unnervingly perceptive, but surely this time she was very, very wrong? If anyone resembled Pa it was Lucky Jack, with his adventurous spirit and love of gambling.

Leo broke into her train of thought by saying, 'Marietta and Edie are about to board. Will they know where we're sitting?'

Lilli bent down slightly to look through the window. Marietta was making what looked to be an almost royal procession through a sea of men, Edie protectively in her wake. Lilli grinned. It wouldn't matter where Marietta was, sophisticated city or small town, male heads would turn. Here, in Skagway, her fox-red hair clashing sizzlingly with her shocking-pink shirtwaist and mulberry coloured skirt, she was almost causing a riot.

She waved furiously to attract her attention and indicate whereabouts she and Leo were sitting. Marietta's grin almost split her face as she waved back in acknowledgement.

'Phew,' Lettie said as she sat gratefully into the seat opposite Leo. 'I thought we weren't going to be able to all sit together. Where's Lottie? Have I just stolen her seat?'

Lilli turned away from the window and sat down next to Leo. 'No, she's gone off to chat with Mr Cameron. Where are Kate and Susan?'

Lettie smoothed a stray wisp of hair back into her immaculate chignon. Ever since Kate had shown her how to make the best of herself and had given her a dress she could feel proud to wear she had taken infinite pains with her grooming. 'Susan is being escorted aboard by her parson friend and Kate is being escorted aboard by Lord Lister.'

'By *who*?'

Lilli goggled at her. Lettie, for the first time since Lilli had met her, giggled.

'Lord Lister. You must have noticed him aboard the *Senator*. He was the only man wearing English jodhpurs.'

'And he's a *Lord*?'

Lettie nodded.

'And he's paying his attentions to *Kate*?'

Lettie nodded again.

Marietta breezed into the compartment, saying fizzily, 'Lord knows why any of us girls bothered going to a marriage bureau! Susan looks all set to embark on life as a parson's wife, Kate has collared a member of the British aristocracy and even Edie here has been indulging in a little flirtation.'

'I haven't' Edie protested, flushing rosily.

'His name is Saskatchewan Stan,' Marietta said, adding, to put Lilli and Lettie's minds at rest, 'and having met him I don't think there's any need to worry he'll take advantage where he shouldn't. In fact I'd go so far as to say he's absolutely harmless.'

'He carried my bag for me,' Edie said with childish pleasure, her cheeks still apple-red. 'He didn't ask to carry Marietta's. He asked to carry *mine*. And he didn't frighten me. He was all roly-poly and he made me laugh.'

'Then that leaves only Lilli and me without beaus,' Lettie said, squeezing up a little to make room for Edie as she sat down.

Marietta looked across at Lilli and raised her eyebrows. 'I think it only leaves you, Lettie,' she said, her voice thick with amusement 'Lilli is inundated with beaus. The only

153

thing is, I'm not sure which is the one she's hoping will take her to the altar.'

Lilli felt a little pulse begin to beat fast and light in her throat. There really was no reason why she should keep her relationship with Lucky Jack a secret any longer.

'My beau is Lucky Jack Coolidge,' she said blandly, enjoying the expression of incredulity on her friends' faces. 'And when we get to Dawson he's going to pay off Mr Nelson and marry me.'

Chapter Ten

'So when Pa died we went to live with Uncle Herbert and Aunt Hettie,' Lottie said, standing with Ringan on the tiny open observation platform as the train inched its zig-zagging way up the glittering heights of the White Pass. 'Only Uncle Herbert didn't want Lilli living with him and I don't really think he wanted me, either. The only one of us he wanted was Leo.'

Ringan made the little noise in his throat that Lottie thought of as his 'Scottish' noise.

'And then Uncle Herbert said he was going to change Leo's surname to his own and make-believe that Leo was his son. He told Lilli she was to leave the house and Lilli knew that once she did so he would never let her see us again. And so when she left the house she took us with her,' Lottie finished simply.

'Your sister's a verra feisty young lady,' Ringan said, wondering how any man, given a little family like the Stullens to care for, could have been so crass as to have earned their contempt instead of their affection.

'We had to go quickly,' Lottie continued, raising her face up to the afternoon sun and the dizzying summits of the mountains, 'because Uncle Herbert had told Lilli she had to be out of the house that very day. Lilli went to every employment bureau in San Francisco but no-one would give her a job – or not a job that would pay her enough to keep us all. And so she became a Peabody bride.'

Ringan nearly toppled off the observation platform in shock. 'A *bride*? But I didna ken your sister was married. She doesna wear a ring . . .'

'Oh, she's not married yet. Peabody brides don't marry

155

until they reach Dawson. Then there's a kind of auction and . . .'

'*Auction?*' There wasn't only shock in his voice and on his face, there was disbelief. Then, as understanding dawned as to what just kind of a bride a Peabody bride was, disbelief gave way to rage so white-hot Lottie thought he was going to explode.

'I know. It's medieval, isn't it?' she said, tossing a wayward braid back over her shoulder. 'But you don't have to worry. It isn't going to happen to Lilli. And I don't think it's going to happen to anyone else, unless it's to Lettie. Miss Bumby is being paid attentions by the Reverend Mr Jenkinson. Miss Salway is suddenly being paid attentions by an English lord. Marietta isn't going to marry anyone but is going to be a dance-hall girl and Edie is either going to be a maid somewhere where Marietta can look after her, or she's going to live with us.'

'Live with you where, and with whom?' Ringan demanded, his hand grasping the observation platform rail so tightly the knuckles were white. Another thought occurred to him and he said, his voice raw, 'Your sister isna thinking of becoming a dance-hall girl too, is she?'

Lottie giggled. 'No, silly. Dance-hall girls aren't respectable. Which is a pity, because Marietta says they have a lot of fun.'

Ringan blanched. Dear Lord a-mighty, what kind of a conversation was this to be having with a ten-year-old girl? First of all wee Lottie was chatting about young women being auctioned off to men like so many lumps of meat and then she was talking enviously of dance-hall girls!

Not feeling able to embark on an explanation as to just why she shouldn't be aspiring to such a racy profession he brought the conversation back to a far more pressing subject. 'Just why is there no need for me or anyone else to worry after your sister?' he asked, dimly aware that the thin little footpath flanking the track was that of the original route taken by the pioneers of three and four years ago.

'Mr Coolidge is going to offer for her,' Lottie said, a

156

note of resigned acceptance in her voice. 'Lilli's in love with him so I suppose it will be all right but it doesn't *feel* all right.'

Ringan kept silent. It didn't feel all right to him either. It felt gut-sickeningly wrong.

'The problem is, Mr Coolidge is ever so careless about things that matter,' Lottie continued, troubled, 'When Leo fell overboard it was because Mr Coolidge wasn't keeping an eye on him as he had promised to. And even though it was a terrible crush leaving the ship, he didn't think to look for us and help us.'

'No, well, maybe he had other obligations,' Ringan said, staggered by her perceptiveness and wondering just what her opinion was of himself.

'But if he's in love with Lilli, she should come first, shouldn't she?' Lottie persisted.

'Aye,' Ringan said, wishing he knew just what kind of a story Coolidge had spun to Lilli. It didn't seem likely to him that a man with Lucky Jack's reputation would have fallen irrevocably in love and proposed marriage, all in the space of a few short days aboard ship. On the other hand, what did Lucky Jack have to gain by deceiving her in such a manner? Seduction was the obvious answer, but with Lilli Stullen sharing a cabin with her younger brother and sister and a fellow Peabody bride, seduction would not be very easy to accomplish.

He thought back to the scene in the hotel dining-room. Where sex was concerned, he doubted Coolidge was living in a state of deprivation. If the beautiful, mature red-head who had been seated at his table wasn't his mistress, he would eat his hat.

Lottie gave a deep sigh and, as Ringan seemed unable, or unwilling, to explain Jack Coolidge's behaviour, she changed the subject, saying, 'Is that Dead Horse Gulch down there? Miss Bumby told Leo it was called Dead Horse Gulch because so many pack animals struggling up the trail fell into it and died.'

'And I trod up that trail in the winter of '97,' Saskatchewan

Stan was saying to his spellbound audience. 'Why, the snow blew down the valley in screaming gusts but the trail itself was so hard-packed by tramping feet that no wind could budge it. No, sirree. It just packed down as hard as cement until in some places it was ten feet higher than the loose snow on either side of us.'

'And what happened if anyone fell off the trail?' Lettie asked, trying to imagine the hell it had been before the railway had been built.

Stan grinned. 'Why, if a man and his sled was upset into the drifts the man climbing behind him would take his place and the shovel-stiff in the snow would have to wait till there was a gap in the chain before he could take his place in it again.'

'Did you ever fall off into the snow, Mr Saskatchewan Stan?' Edie asked, her eyes like saucers. 'I hope you didn't. I wouldn't like for you to have fallen off into the snow.'

Beneath his stubbly beard Stan flushed as red as a beetroot. 'I ain't never fallen off nowhere I couldn't get back from Miss,' he said, turning a battered black hat round and round in his hands.

Remembering Stan's confession as to feeling 'jittery' when with pretty ladies, Lilli's mouth twitched at the corners. Until Edie's guileless interruption he had been doing remarkably well. Now, however, he seemed to become acutely aware of the sex of his audience.

'It's been nice speaking with you ladies, real nice,' he said, his composure fast deserting him. 'I wouldn't have troubled you if you hadn't been friends of Miss Stullen's, what with Miss Stullen being a friend of my friend, Lucky Jack, and all.'

The shabby black hat was revolving faster and faster in his gnarled, calloused hands. Lilli could see a gleam of dull green on the edge of the brim and couldn't help wondering if it was mildew.

'So I'll just mush along now,' Stan was saying, backing out of the carriage clumsily. 'I guess Lucky Jack will have a poker game in play. I always did like a game of poker. Not that I'm a gambling man, you

158

understand. No, sirree. I'm just a plain old shovel-stiff . . .'

'He's rather a lamb, isn't he?' Marietta said, amusement thick in her voice as Stan finally blundered on his way. 'It must be quite a strange sensation for men like him, men who crossed the Pass by foot, covering the same trail in the comfort of a train.'

Lilli nodded agreement, but unlike Lettie and Edie she didn't begin chatting about the trail, or the stupendous views, or the grimness of the gulch plunging away on their left-hand side. Her thoughts were elsewhere, centred firmly on Lucky Jack.

A poker-game. Was that what was taking up his attention at the present moment? Was that why he hadn't walked through the train looking for her? The irritation which had been growing ever since she had been obliged to carry her heavy bag off the *Senator* and to the hotel and then on to the train, surged into something disturbingly close to resentment. And if he were playing poker, was he doing so in Kitty Dufresne's company? And if he could play poker in Kitty Dufresne's company, why hadn't he asked her, Lilli, to sit with him and so that he could play poker in *her* company?

She looked over Leo's thick shock of hair to where the International Border Post on the summit could now be seen. The answer was, of course, that she had made no secret of the fact that she disapproved of his displaying his prowess at cards in front of Leo. *That* was why they were not at the present moment seated next to each other.

A Mountie came into sight, his scarlet tunic eye-catchingly exotic. Her resentment ebbed but a flame of irritation remained. It was all right making excuses for his remaining in Kitty Dufresne's company and not hers, but why did he have to play poker at all? Why couldn't he have kept her and Leo and Lottie company, telling them stories of the Trail and Dead Horse Gulch as Saskatchewan Stan had done?

'Look, Marietta! Look! There's a Mountie!' Edie exclaimed excitedly.

'Don't go overboard about him,' Marietta said in affectionate amusement, 'We'll be seeing a whole lot more now we're in Canadian territory.'

Still deep in thoughts of Lucky Jack, Lilli's irritation once again deepened, this time into a sickening niggle of doubt. When the hideous accident with Leo had occurred it had occurred because Lucky Jack's attention had been on a card game and not on Leo. She pursed her lips. There was obviously a thoughtless side to her Greek god but it was, surely, a thoughtlessness he would grow out of when they were all living together as a family.

'That must be Lake Bennett,' Lettie said as a serpentine-green lake came into view, surrounding mountains reflected mirror-like in its glacial depths.

The train chugged on, down the long, thin crescent of the lake and into a patchy forest ablaze with crimson drifts of fireweed.

Lilli continued to stare silently out of the window as Marietta and Lettie and Edie laughed and chatted. The trouble with falling in love so very quickly was that it made some things so hard to imagine. She couldn't, for instance, imagine Lucky Jack in a family situation, which was silly when he was so obviously her soul-mate and when she was going to marry him.

The forest gave way to open country. Rivers gushed down through canyons, rapids threw up spume yards high, lakes shimmered like burnished shields.

Lilli stared at them unseeingly. One fact she could draw comfort from was Lucky Jack's easy-going nature. Her mother had always said that easy-going men made the best husbands. Repressing the unworthy thought that Lucky Jack might just be a little *too* easy-going, Lilli looked down at her clasped hands, wondering what her left hand would look like with a wedding ring gracing it; wondering what the future held for her as Mrs Jack Coolidge.

'And so here we are,' the Reverend Mr Jenkinson said sunnily as they all emerged from the train onto the platform at Whitehorse station, 'on the very brink of the Yukon!'

'Welcome to Whitehorse, ladies!' a top-hatted man called to them as he walked towards them from the direction of a hotel, the name *White Pass* emblazoned above its doorway. 'Are you the mail-order brides? If so, I'm Jess Winthrop, manager of the White Pass Hotel, and there's rooms booked for all of you for tonight.'

Mr Jenkinson's sunny smile vanished. 'Mail-order brides?' he exclaimed indignantly, '*Mail-order brides*? How dare you sir! Miss Bumby is an esteemed resident of Dawson and a member of the teaching profession and her companions are equally respectable young ladies.'

Silence hung in the air.

All the blood drained from Susan's heavy-featured face. Lord Lister was standing only a few feet away from Kate, and Kate looked equally appalled. Marietta looked outraged. Edie looked bewildered. Lettie's face was inscrutable.

'Then if that's the case I've three good rooms I can relet,' Mr Winthrop said dryly, wondering just what sort of a respectable young lady the ginger-haired piece in shocking pink and mulberry was. She certainly wasn't a school-teacher, that was for sure.

'I don't think that will be necessary, Mr Winthrop,' Lilli said pleasantly. 'The Peabody Bureau has, I believe, reserved rooms for those of us travelling to Dawson under its auspices. Is there someone who can carry our bags for us?'

Mr Winthrop grinned at her, revealing yellowing incisors. He should have had the sense to realise that such a classy looking little group wouldn't want a preacher knowing their business. He corrected himself. A classy and peculiar group. One saucy piece, one stunner, two passable looking, one downright ugly, one who looked as if she wasn't altogether right in the head and, just for good measure, two children.

'Leave your bags right where they are ma'am and I'll have 'em carried over to the hotel in two shakes of a cat's tail,' he said obligingly. 'And now, ladies. This way if you please.'

As they walked across the dusty road Lilli saw Lord Lister step a little nearer to Kate and say something to her very quietly. Too quietly for anyone else to hear. Kate's eyes sparkled with happiness, her appalled expression of a few moments ago replaced by one of glowing radiance.

Lilli felt a surge of pleasure. So . . . It really was true that Lord Lister was making romantic approaches to Kate. Well, he could do far worse. Kate was as sweet-natured as she was sweet-looking and she possessed natural grace and dignity. If Lord Lister should ask her to marry him the transition from Peabody bride to Lady Lister was one she would be able to make with remarkable ease.

She shot him a covert look as they mounted the hotel's rickety steps. Not only did Lord Lister have the glamour and prestige of his title to recommend him as a prospective husband, he was also extraordinarily good-looking. His eyes were grey and long-lashed, his mid-brown hair thick and sleek and smooth. There was a faint hollow under his cheek-bones and the line of his nose was aristocratically straight.

'If you would sign your names in the hotel register,' Mr Winthrop urged as they stepped into a large lobby. 'This way, ladies. This way.'

As Susan stepped towards an enormous desk supporting an even more enormous book, Lilli saw that, unlike Kate, Susan had still not recovered from the near disaster of a few moments ago. Her face was pinched and white and the incipient moustache on her upper lip was beaded with sweat. Lilli's heart went out to her. After a lifetime without any beau whatsoever she finally had one and he had made it quite clear that he thought any young woman who became a mail-order bride was a young woman of regrettable morals. What on earth would his reaction be when he learnt that Susan was a mail-order bride? Would he be compassionately understanding or would he be appalled? And even if he were compassionately

162

understanding, would pride prevent him from taking a mail-order bride as his own bride?

'And now ma'am, if you please,' Mr Winthrop was saying to her.

She signed the register, wondering where her own beau was. She hadn't seen him anywhere on the platform when she had stepped off the train, nor had she seen Miss Kitty Dufresne. A quick inspection of the page she had just signed showed that neither of them had, as yet, signed the register.

As she turned away from the desk to allow Lettie to sign the register it occurred to her that perhaps Lucky Jack and Kitty Dufresne weren't staying overnight in the *White Pass Hotel*. If the decor of its lobby was anything to go by it certainly wasn't very elegant or refined. A giant sheet-iron stove, ringed by cracked leather chairs, held pride of place. The chairs were all occupied by disreputable-looking men and between each pair of chairs stood an enamel spittoon.

As one of the spittoons was put to use she suppressed a little shudder. No, Lucky Jack and Kitty Dufresne wouldn't be staying in the *White Pass Hotel*. They would be staying somewhere much more refined.

'Wee Lottie's bag,' a familiar Scottish male voice said, depositing Lottie's travel-bag on the linoleum-covered floor by her feet. In the confines of the lobby he seemed even taller and more wide-shouldered, if that was possible, than he had aboard the *Senator*.

'Thank you, Mr Cameron,' she said stiffly, wrenched from her thoughts of her much more pleasingly proportioned Greek god.

Ringan frowned slightly. He knew from the dismissive tone of her voice that she didn't want him to engage her in further conversation, but now that he knew so much more about her he found it impossible to turn away from her. It was now early evening and, after a days travelling, she looked tired. There was a smudge of soot on her cheek, legacy of their long train ride, and a silky tendril of curling hair had come adrift from her high-piled chignon.

163

Knowing now that without Lucky Jack Coolidge as a beau she would be obliged to marry some gold-grubbing prospector she hadn't even met as yet, he was far more understanding of the scene he had witnessed aboard the *Senator*. If Lilli Stullen believed herself to be in love with Lucky Jack then she certainly had no time to waste in which to capture his heart. Where, however, was Coolidge at the present moment? As Lottie had so tartly pointed out, he hadn't been at Lilli's side when she had disembarked from the *Senator*, and he wasn't at her side now.

If he didn't know where Lucky Jack was, he had a very good idea as to whose company Lucky Jack was in. And the person in question was dressed in the very best that Parisian couturiers could supply. Sure that Lilli Stullen had made a very grave error of judgement where Lucky Jack's intentions towards her were concerned, feeling intense pity for her predicament and boundless admiration for the way she cared so fiercely for Lottie and Leo's welfare, he said impulsively, 'Would you care to have dinner with me tonight?'

The words were out of his mouth before his brain had had chance to realise what it was he was going to say. 'The invitation extends to Leo and wee Lottie too, of course,' he added hurriedly, almost as taken aback as she was.

'I . . .' She raised a hand to her hair and tucked the stray tendril back into her chignon. 'I . . . it's very kind of you to invite me, Mr Cameron, but I don't think . . .'

Lottie and Leo had trooped off up the stairs towards the bedrooms in Marietta and Edie's wake. Susan and Mr Jenkinson were leaving the lobby by its main door, obviously intent on enjoying whatever sights Skagway had to offer. Kate and Lord Lister were deep in conversation, oblivious of their unprepossessing surroundings and the many pairs of male eyes turned pruriently in their direction.

Under normal circumstances, realising her lack of enthusiasm for his suggestion, he wouldn't have pressed her any further. He wasn't a man who had ever had to make an effort where women were concerned, rather the

164

reverse, but this wasn't normal circumstances. Looking at her graceful figure; at the way she held herself tall and with pride, even when tiredness and circumstances were against her; at the heavy mass of her upswept hair, a mass that looked far too heavy for her slender neck to support, he felt his throat constrict.

Self-knowledge roared through his veins like a tidal wave. He had been deluding himself when he had told himself he had asked her to dine with him because he felt pity for her predicament and admiration for her loving care of Leo and Lottie. Pity and admiration were part of the compound of his feelings for her, but they were far from being the whole of it. He was fiercely sexually attracted to her.

His heart jarred against his ribs. Christ! He was *still* fooling himself! It wasn't just sexual attraction he felt for her, it was far, far more. He wanted to protect her; to take the look of anxiety from the backs of her eyes. He wanted to love her, comfort her, honour and keep her in sickness and in health. He wanted her to bear his children; children she would love and cherish just as exquisitely as she loved and cherished Leo and Lottie. He wanted to remain faithful to her for as long as he lived. He wanted to *marry* her. And she needed a husband. She *needed* his love and protection. 'Miss Stullen, I . . .' he began, about to make quite sure that she did, at least, spend time with him that evening.

He was too late. Her eyes were no longer anxious and doubtful and they were no longer on him. No longer even listening to him, her face radiant, she was looking towards the hotel's entrance. Ringan had no need to turn around to know who it was who had just entered the lobby.

'Howdy, Jess,' Lucky Jack said breezily to the *White Pass*'s manager. 'Gossip tells me Dawson's been emptying out whilst I've been away.'

'Sure has,' Jess Winthrop said, striding across the lobby to shake vigorous hold of Jack's hand. 'Dawson's beginning to die. Everyone who hasn't already made a strike is heading out to Nome. I'm tempted to head out in that direction myself. Reports are they're finding nuggets as big as boulders.'

Jack grinned. It was a story he had heard before. Many times.

'We're dining at seven,' he said as he reached Lilli's side. 'I've someone I want you to meet. Her name is Miss Kitty Dufresne and what she can't tell you about Dawson isn't worth knowing.' He glanced across at Ringan. 'Perhaps you'd like to dine with us as well, Mr Cameron?' he asked, wondering just what the hell Cameron had been up to with Lilli. The Scotsman looked like a man who'd lost a hundred dollar bill and found a nickel.

Ringan shook his head. 'No, thanks,' he said shortly. 'Bye, Miss Stullen.' With a brief, polite nod of his head he took his leave of them, walking swiftly towards the foot of the wide staircase.

'I'd love to meet Miss Dufresne,' Lilli said, her face upturned to his, her eyes glowing, Ringan Cameron immediately forgotten.

'Kitty thinks it would be bad for your reputation if you were seen dining with her, but Jess has a private dining-room we can use,' Jack's eyes were still on Ringan as Ringan took the wooden treads two at a time in easy, athletic strides. 'And she's rather looking forward to meeting Leo and Lottie. She's never had much contact with children, which is rather a pity. I have a feeling she'd be pretty good with them.'

More people were now entering the lobby, among them his two card-playing buddies. He touched her elbow lightly. 'I have to go now. I've things to see to. I'll see you at seven.'

As he joined his cronies, disappearing with them into a room marked PRIVATE that led off the far side of the lobby, Lilli cupped the elbow he had touched. It was going to be all right. He had touched her in a way which was openly proprietal. *It was going to be all right.*

If she had hoped Lucky Jack would introduce her to Kitty Dufresne as his fiancée she was disappointed.

'As the two of you are going to be seeing a lot of each other when we get to Dawson I thought tonight would be a chance for you both to get acquainted,' he said when all introductions had been made and they had all seated themselves around a large, round, candle-lit table.

'We won't be seeing a lot of each other publicly,' Kitty said in a voice so fascinatingly throaty Leo stared at her goggle-eyed. 'I think Jack has already explained to you why, Miss Stullen. But under the circumstances, and as I'm Jack's business partner, it won't do any harm for the two of us to be on friendly terms.'

'No, of course not.' Lilli wasn't quite sure how to respond to such a startlingly frank statement. Didn't Kitty Dufresne *mind* that she wasn't socially acceptable? She thought of Marietta. Marietta certainly wouldn't mind. 'I *want* us to be on friendly terms,' she said warmly, aware that Kitty and Marietta had much in common,

'Then let's have some wine and drink to friendship,' Kitty said, touching the rim of her still empty wine-glass.

Lucky Jack obligingly began to pour a ruby-red wine into the wine-glasses, his gold earring gleaming in the candle-light, his fair hair glistening, pale as barley in September.

With difficulty Lilli wrenched her eyes aware from the blazing bravura of his handsomeness. There was Leo and Lottie to think of; proprieties to be observed.

'Can I have some wine?' Leo asked, sensing the evening was like no other evening he had ever experienced and that anything was possible.

'No, of course not,' Lilli chided, praying that Leo wasn't going to behave badly.

'Perhaps Leo could just have a *taste* of wine,' Kitty suggested, 'in water, of course.'

'It's French,' Lucky Jack said, his eyes meeting Lilli's over the candle-flames. 'It's good quality. A dash of it in water won't do any harm.'

'Well . . . just a little dash,' Lilli concurred, wondering if she, too, should mix it with water. She had never drunk wine before and she didn't want it to go to her head.

Leo gave a sigh of pure happiness. He had known the instant he had set eyes on Lucky Jack's friend that she was a magic lady. And not only a magic lady, but a *royal* magic lady, for surely only queens wore lace and satin and diamonds.

Lilli, too, was very well aware of Kitty Dufresne's almost royal raiment. Her dress was of midnight-blue and daringly décolleté. There were diamonds at her ears and in her hair. Lilli had never seen a tiara before and only deeply bred good manners prevented her from staring in wonder at the feast of wealth winking and twinkling in Kitty Dufresne's Titian-red hair.

'To your new life in Dawson,' Jack said, raising his glass towards Lilli and Leo and Lottie. 'May you soon feel at home there.'

'And may you soon come to love it just as much as I do,' Kitty added, smiling at them with such genuine warmth she won Lottie's heart as well as Leo's.

That Kitty really did love Dawson became blatantly apparent when Lucky Jack began to recount the remarks Jess Winthrop had made to him earlier on, in the lobby.

'He says Dawson is beginning to die. That everyone is lighting out for Nome.'

Kitty laid down her fork and looked towards him. 'I'm not going to light for Nome,' she said, an odd undertone to her voice.

Jack poured more wine into his glass. 'It's not only Winthrop's opinion. Everyone's saying the same thing. There's already a tent city on the beach. Men are making fortunes. Buildings are going up. Saloons are opening. It's too late, now, for us to get in early as we did in Dawson, but . . .'

Kitty was very still. The big-hearted smile that had encompassed Lilli and Leo and Lottie like a ray of hot summer sunshine, was now gone. 'I'm not interested, Jack. I've had it with opening new saloons in new towns. The money we've made and invested this last two years will see me through life. And the life I want is in Dawson. I've become *part* of the place, for God's sake. I've never called anywhere home before, but Dawson has become home. And whether it dies or not, I'm not leaving it.'

Lottie's eyes met Lilli's uncomfortably. The conversation had suddenly become embarrassingly serious.

Lucky Jack knew it had become serious too and he didn't like it. 'We'll talk about Nome later,' he said, angry with himself for having broached just a ticklish subject when the Stullens were present. 'How about livening things up and treating young Lottie to an ice-worm cocktail?'

As he leaned back in his chair, pressing the bell on the wall to summon a waiter, Lottie said incredulously. 'A *what*? A *worm* cocktail? I don't believe it!'

'White worms are a prime delicacy in Whitehorse,' Jack said, keeping his face straight with difficulty. 'In fact they're so much of a delicacy I think Leo and Lilli should have an ice-worm cocktail as well.'

When the drinks were set on the table, white worms wriggling at the bottom of each glass, there were shrieks of horror, shrieks which quickly turned to shrieks of laughter when Kitty finally took pity on them and revealed that the 'worms' were small pieces of spaghetti.

As the evening progressed Lilli felt herself becoming pleasantly drowsy. The wine was far nicer than she had anticipated it would be and she understood for the first time why people enjoyed drinking wine so much. Leo, for all he had only had a small amount in water, was asleep at the table, his head resting on his folded hands.

'I think it's time we broke the party up,' Lucky Jack said at last, well aware that until they did so, he couldn't resume his discussion with Kitty. 'Don't try and wake Leo, Lilli. I'll carry him.'

Walking with Lottie along the dimly-lit corridor towards her bedroom, Lucky Jack by their side, Leo in his arms, Lilli felt truly blessed. Even though she and Jack were not yet married it was as if they were already a family.

When they got to the door of their room Lucky Jack opened it and carried Leo over to the nearest bed. 'I'd let him sleep in his clothes tonight,' he said, amusement in his voice. 'It won't harm for one night.'

169

'I think I might sleep in mine,' Lottie said, sinking down on the truckle bed next to Leo's. 'I can't ever remember being so tired and I can't ever remember a nicer evening. Thank you, Lucky Jack. I'll never forget it.' She began to giggle. 'And I'll never forget the ice-worm cocktails!'

Now that Lucky Jack was free of his burden his hand reached out for Lilli's. 'I think we'd better say our goodnights in the corridor,' he said in a low voice.

Her fingers tightened on his, a pulse beginning to beat light and fast in her throat.

Once the bedroom door was closed on Leo and Lottie he took her in his arms. This time there was no Ringan Cameron standing intrusively near to them. With a little gasp of pleasure she raised her face to his, her hands sliding up and around his neck.

'You're a very beautiful young woman Lilli,' he said softly, his mouth skimming the silky smoothness of her hair. 'So beautiful that I think you could change my life.'

A smile touched Lilli's mouth as he bent his head lower, his lips brushing her temple. She *was* going to change his life; just as he was going to change hers.

With expert ease he pressed her back against the walnut panelling of the wall and, holding her close against him with a strong, firm hand, slid his other hand over the primness of her high-necked shirtwaist, cupping the exquisite weight of her breast in his palm.

Lilli gasped, brought almost to insensibility by the combination of wine and the pleasure of his touch.

'You're a very special lady, Lilli,' he said sincerely, his mouth at the corner of hers, 'Very, very special.'

She could feel the hardness of his body through the folds of her skirt and as his mouth closed at last on hers, answering desire shot through her, shocking in its intensity.

It was an ecstasy quickly and rudely shattered.

'It's so dark I can hardly see where I'm going,' Edie's voice said nervously from the direction of the top of the stairs. 'You go first, Marietta. You don't get scared like I do.'

With a softly, but sincerely muttered blasphemy, Lucky Jack released his hold of Lilli, stepping a discreet foot or so away from her.

Lilli sagged against the wall, her heart pounding as if it was going to burst.

'Sorry folks,' Marietta said apologetically, well aware of the kind of scene she and Edie had just interrrupted. 'We're just passing through.'

Edie paused. 'Are you all right, Lilli,' she asked solicitously. 'You look a little out of breath. Would you like a cup of cocoa? Marietta's just going to make one for me and . . .'

'Not tonight, Edie,' Marietta said firmly, tugging on Edie's hand, pulling her after her down the darkened corridor.

Jack suppressed the temptation to take Lilli in his arms again. He needed to continue his discussion with Kitty and make her see the pointlessnss of staying in Dawson, if Dawson was dying. 'We never have much luck with our romantic trysts, do we?' he said, sounding suitably rueful. 'Perhaps we'll be luckier tomorrow, at the rapids. Goodnight, Lilli. Sweet dreams.'

'Goodnight.'

Dizzily she wondered why, with the corridor again deserted, he couldn't again take her in his arms. When she finally summoned the strength to move away from the support of the wall, she knew that whatever his reason, she was grateful for it. She couldn't, absolutely couldn't, remain upright for any longer than it was going to take her to reach her bed.

'Did you sleep in your clothes too?' Lottie asked her eight hours later as morning sunlight flooded into their bedroom.

Lilli opened her eyes cautiously, wondering if her headache would eventually disappear or if she was going to have it for life. 'I must have done. I was so tired. It was such a long day. Skagway. The train journey . . .'

'You drank too much wine,' Lottie said baldly. 'I don't

171

know what people do when they've drunk too much wine, but whatever it is you'd better do it. We're going to the rapids with Lucky Jack this morning.'

With a super-human effort Lilli forced herself up off the bed. There was a pitcher of cold water on the washstand and with an unsteady hand she poured it into its matching porcelain bowl.

'Edie and Marietta are going to the rapids with Susan and the Reverend Mr Jenkinson,' Lottie said informatively. 'Kate is going to see them with Lord Lister.'

'And Lettie is coming with us,' Lilli finished for her. 'It's alright, Lottie. I hadn't forgotten.'

'Then you'd better get a move on,' Lottie said mercilessly. 'We have to be there *and back* by lunch-time, because that's when the steamer leaves for Dawson.'

'Another boat?' Leo asked, sitting up in bed and rubbing the sleep from his eyes. 'Are we going on another boat?'

'Yes, but it won't be as big as the *Senator*.' Lilli divested herself of her crumpled shirtwaist and skirt. 'It will be a riverboat.'

'And will it take us down the Yukon to Dawson?' Leo asked, hoping Lilli wasn't going to expect him to take off the clothes he had slept in. The best thing about sleeping in your clothes was the time it saved getting ready for breakfast next morning.

Lilli took her toffee coloured blouse and cream serge skirt from out of her travel-bag and shook them vigorously to rid them of creases. 'All the way. There's water in the bowl for you to have a wash, Leo. And take those clothes off and put on fresh ones. You can't possibly go down to breakfast like that. You look worse than a shovel-stiff!'

'Bye!' Kate called from the buggy she was sharing with Lord Lister. 'See you at the rapids!'

'Bye!' Marietta and Edie chorused as the carriage they were sharing with Susan and the Reverend Mr Jenkinson bowled away in the buggy's wake.

Lilli, Lottie, Leo and Lettie remained standing in the

dust at the foot of the hotel's steps. There was much to-ing and fro-ing going on all around them. Buggy's arriving. Buggy's leaving. But there was no sign of Lucky Jack.

Fifteen minutes later there was still no sign of him.

'He's forgotten,' Lottie said flatly, her sailor-hat rammed straight on top of her head.

'He's delayed,' Lilli corrected, fiercely hoping she would be proved to be right.

Half an hour later Lettie echoed Lottie. 'He's forgotten,' she said, no surprise in her voice. 'Shall I take Leo and Lottie for a walk somewhere? We won't be able to get as far as the rapids but we could at least have a short walk by the river.'

'But I wanted to see the rapids!' Leo protested, his bottom lip beginning to tremble.

'Don't be a baby, Leo.' Fighting her own disappointment Lottie took hold of his hand. 'We're going to have a nice walk with Lettie. Are you coming as well, Lilli?'

Lilli shook her head. 'No. I want to be here when Lucky Jack arrives to explain what has delayed him. He's bound to be upset.'

Lettie gave her a long, penetrating look. So penetrating that Lilli turned her head away. 'I expect it was business,' she said, her voice full of a confidence she didn't truly feel. 'He had a business meeting with someone yesterday afternoon when we arrived.'

No-one said anything. Leo wiped his nose on the back of his hand. Lilli didn't have the heart to reprimand him. She knew how much he had been looking forward to seeing the rapids and, if only Lucky Jack had been able to get word to them that he was going to be unable to take them, he could have gone with Kate and Lord Lister, or with the Reverend Mr Jenkinson's party. Desultorily he set off with Lottie and Lettie.

Lilli remained standing at the foot of the hotel steps. Lucky Jack would come eventually. And when he came he would apologise and explain.

It was Kitty Dufresne who walked briskly down the hotel steps towards her and who apologised and explained.

173

'I'm sorry, Miss Stullen. If you're waiting for Jack you're wasting your time. He's in no state to go to the rapids.

Lilli stared at her. 'What on earth do you mean? Is he ill?'

'No, drunk,' Kitty said succinctly. She was wearing the emerald-green, astrakhan-trimmed travelling-costume she had worn the previous day. Near to, and in the brutal light of day, the light web of lines around her eyes were clearly visible beneath her face powder.

'*Drunk*? But he wasn't drunk when he said goodnight to me last night! And it's only ten o'clock in the morning!'

Despite her own anger at Jack's behaviour a slight smile tugged at the corner of Kitty's carmine-red mouth. 'You don't know an awful lot about men, Miss Stullen. But, to be fair to Jack, he didn't start on a bender this morning. He started last night.'

'I'm sorry. I don't understand. Could you explain a little more?' Lilli could feel her headache returning. In the distance, in the direction of the river, a tall, broad-shouldered, red-haired figure had stopped to talk to Lettie and Leo and Lottie. Lilli's nails dug deep into her palms. Ringan Cameron would be asking why Leo and Lottie weren't at the rapids. Someone, Leo or Lottie, or even Lettie, would be bound to tell him it was because Lucky Jack had let them down.

'I like you, Miss Stullen,' Kitty said sincerely. 'But you're very young and inexperienced to be dealing with a man like Jack.' She paused, as if making up her mind about something, and then said, 'Last night Jack and I continued our discussion about Nome. I told him that I wouldn't, under any circumstances, uproot myself from Dawson in order to open saloons there. He didn't like my decision and so he did what he always does when things aren't going his way. He kept company with a whiskey bottle all night.'

'I . . . see.' Lilli said unsteadily, not really seeing at all. 'He must have forgotten, before he started drinking, that he had promised Leo he would take him to the rapids this morning.'

Kitty laid a kid-gloved hand lightly on her arm. 'You're deluding yourself, my dear,' she said gently.' Jack's a charmer. But that's all he is. He isn't trustworthy or honourable or, if being kind clashes with his own wants and desires, even kind. He does have one redeeming feature though.'

'What is it?' The pain behind her eyes was blinding. In the distance she could see that Ringan Cameron had said his goodbyes to Leo and Lottie and Lettie and that he was again walking in the direction of the hotel.

'He doesn't kid himself he's anything that he's not. He knows he's a selfish, self-centred bastard. And . . .' she paused slightly, a wry smile again touching her mouth. 'He knows he's a damned handsome devil.'

Lilli didn't say anything. There seemed suddenly to be nothing to say. Ringan Cameron was drawing swiftly nearer and only the realization that he would soon be within eye-contact distance prompted her into speech. 'I have a headache, Miss Dufresne. I think I'd better lay down for a while. Thank you for taking the trouble to come and explain things to me.'

'That's all right,' Kitty shrugged the thanks away. 'Goodbye, Miss Stullen.'

'Goodbye,' Lilli responded, turning towards the steps in order to mount them and be in the lobby before Ringan Cameron reached their foot.

Kitty's eyes darkened. Lucky Jack had done it again, God damn him. He'd captured a heart he had no intention of cherishing. A heart she knew quite well he was already in the process of breaking.

175

Chapter Eleven

Miss Nettlesham was in the hotel lobby. As usual she was alone and, as usual, Lilli felt a spasm of guilt. Where Miss Nettlesham was concerned she really had to make an effort. This morning, however, with Ringan Cameron hard on her heels, was not the time to start.

'Good morning, Miss Nettlesham,' she said, making a bee-line for the stairs. 'Only another day or so and we'll be in Dawson.'

What Miss Nettlesham's response was, Lilli had no idea. Like a bullet from a gun she made straight for the sanctuary of her room. She needed rest and quiet. She needed to be able to think over Kitty Dufresne's disturbing revelations where Lucky Jack was concerned. And when she had thought them over, she needed to come to terms with them.

The room was north facing and gloomy. It wasn't, however, gloomy enough. With the pain behind her eyes now almost unbearable she drew the drapes, plunging the room into Stygian darkness. Then, wearily, she sat down on the edge of her bed and unlaced her high-button boots.

Drunk. She didn't for a moment doubt the truthfulness of what Kitty Dufresne had told her. The problem was, how did she feel about it?

She lay down, her fingers pressed to her throbbing temples. In certain circumstances she was quite sure she wouldn't have minded at all. She hadn't spent large wodges of her childhood living amongst ranch-hands without becoming accustomed to drunkenness. Even her Pa had been riotously drunk at times. It wasn't the drunkenness, then. It was the fact that he had become drunk knowing he would then be unable to keep his promise to take Leo to see the rapids.

Was it so great a crime? She thought of the intensity of Leo's disappointment. It was a crime her father would never have committed, but then fathers fell into a special category. Before she could be comforted by this realization another thought sprang unbidden. Ringan Cameron would never have committed such a crime either.

With a groan she turned over, pummelling her pillow. She would *not* start comparing Lucky Jack with Ringan Cameron. Ringan Cameron was a *murderer*! All Lucky Jack had done was to get drunk in understandable circumstances and neglect to take a small boy to see the rapids. And herself. He had, after all, promised her he would take her to see the rapids as well.

There was an ache somewhere in the region of her heart. For a second she nearly capitulated to it and then commonsense came to her aid. She was being utterly ridiculous and seeing everything totally out of perspective. Kitty Dufresne was Lucky Jack's business partner and if Kitty was adamant that she didn't want to join with him in extending their business operations, then Lucky Jack had a serious problem on his hands. No wonder he had had a few drinks too many! And what were one lot of rapids when they had all the magnificent scenery of the Yukon to look forward to?

And Kitty Dufresne's accusation that Lucky Jack was neither trustworthy or honourable? a small inner voice persisted.

Her eyes flew wide. Kitty Dufresne was *jealous*, for goodness sake! She was in love with Jack herself and so of course she had tried to paint him in a bad light!

Swamped with relief she sprang from the bed and crossed to the wash-stand. She had been making a mountain out of a mole-hill. After all, Lucky Jack wasn't the only person with a hang-over this morning. She had one as well. Another wash in cold water was what she needed. And perhaps a cup of hot, strong, black coffee.

*　　*　　*

'This is a prettier boat than the *Senator*, isn't it?' Leo said as they boarded the steamer *Casca*, a white, three-storeyed river boat with gingerbread fretwork around the cabins, a yellow smokestack and a bright red paddle-wheel at the stern.

'The *Senator* was a ship,' Lilli corrected mildly, 'Boats are smaller than ships.'

'We're going a long way, aren't we?' Edie said naively. 'I never thought we'd be going such a long way.'

'For some of us, it can't be far enough.'

The speaker was Lettie. Edie disregarded the remark, not appreciating the undertone that lay behind it.

'What do you mean?' Lilli asked curiously. None of them had troubled to explain to each other just *why* they had become Peabody brides. Kate had said she would do so and never followed through with her promise. Lettie had never even come close to doing so.

She said now, as Leo skipped on ahead of them and Edie paused to stand on the gangplank, gazing in child-like wonder at the glittering red paddle-wheel, 'I had Pa trouble. My Ma died when I was eight and ever since then Pa treated me as a substitute wife.'

'There's always a lot of housework for a daughter to do when her mother dies,' Lilli said, knowing the fact from her own experience and rather surprised that Lettie should have objected to such a burden. Where Lettie was concerned, she would have vowed she was a hard worker.

'I wasn't talking housework,' Lettie said bleakly, 'I was talking bed.'

Lilli missed her footing as she stepped off the gangplank onto the *Casca's* deck. '*Bed*?' she asked incredulously.

Lettie merely nodded and Lilli didn't ask for any further clarification. One look at the expression on Lettie's face was enough to tell her all she needed to know. She felt sick. No wonder Lettie had been so sullen and reserved and bruised-looking when they had first met her.

'I figured nothing that could happen to me as a Peabody

bride could be any worse than what I had already experienced and that as a wife I would at least have some rights.'

Edie was still hugging the gangplank's rail. Leo was no longer anywhere to be seen.

'Kate's here for the same reason. Though it wasn't her pa who made her life hell. It was her brother.'

Lilli was beyond speech. Lettie and Kate's reasons for fleeing north made her own seem very trivial. It also made Kate's burgeoning romance with Lord Lister seem even more fairytale.

'All I want is to be able to feel clean again,' Lettie said simply. 'And it's easy to feel clean in this country, isn't it? It's so wide-open and pure and fresh.'

Lilli nodded, knowing exactly what Lettie meant. She, too, had fallen in love with the magnificent scenery, scenery she was sure was unlike anything else anywhere in the world. All afternoon she sat in a cane chair on deck, watching it roll by. In the far distance were mountains, their peaks lost amidst plumes of cloud. Nearer were rolling blue hills their colour intensified by drift after drift of forget-me-nots and the deep, drowned-purple of lupins. Occasionally, as the hills melted into valleys, the blue would be pierced by the sharp yellow of arnicas and the piercing white of daisies and anemones. It wasn't only the vegetation that was lush. Birds, too, were in thick profusion.

'Mr Cameron says those are martins,' Lottie said informatively as she sat by Lilli's side watching birds dart from the Yukon's high clay banks. 'and that's a thrush and that's a yellow warbler.'

Lilli made no comment. Since boarding the *Casca* she had managed to avoid Ringan Cameron and she had no particular desire to begin talking about him.

'Mr Cameron knows an awful lot about birds,' Lotti added, wondering what the situation now was between Lilli and Lucky Jack but not liking to ask. 'He's a Highlander and he says parts of the Highlands are very like the Yukon, though on a lot smaller scale of course.

179

Lilli allowed her to chatter on. Lucky Jack still hadn't made an appearance on deck, though discreet enquiries on her part had confirmed that he and Kitty Dufresne were aboard.

'And that's a Redpoll,' Lottie was saying, proud of her new knowledge, 'Can you see him? He's in the willow tree. And that bird singing those three descending notes is the olivesided flycatcher.'

Despite the fact that she was only listening to Lottie with a quarter of her attention, Lilli was impressed. She didn't particularly like Leo and Lottie spending as much time as they did in Ringan Cameron's company but they didn't seem to be coming to much harm by doing so. In fact, where natural history was concerned, they seemed to be gleaning themselves quite an education.

It was late evening, the sky still as light as if it was mid-afternoon, when Lucky Jack finally sought her out. 'Am I in disgrace?' he asked with a rueful grin as he settled himself in the cane chair next to hers, his Homburg at a rakish angle,

'I . . . Yes . . . No . . .' Her confusion took her by surprise. He *wasn't* still in disgrace. If he were, she wouldn't even be speaking to him. She had, however, expected him to be a little more shamefacedly contrite. And the disarming grin indicated that his contrition was marginal and not very shame-faced at all.

He reached for her hand and gave it a squeeze. 'Least said, soonest mended,' he said in his teasing voice, confirming her suspicions, 'or at least that's what my old Ma always used to say.'

Despite her disappointment in him, her lips twitched in unwilling amusement, pleasure at his touch knifing through her. 'Miss Dufresne apologised to me on your behalf,' she said, trying to keep her voice cool in order to signify how very much he had let her, and Leo and Lottie, down. 'And she also explained why it was you weren't able to take us to the rapids.' If she had thought

180

that this revelation would convulse him with shame she was very much disappointed.

'Did she now?' His grin deepened. 'And Kitty usually so loyal too.'

Aware that he was lovingly laughing at her and knowing that nothing she could say or do was going to elicit the kind of response she had been anticipating, she abandoned the subject. 'What will happen when we reach Dawson? Will we be staying there or will we be going on to Nome?'

'Don't worry about Nome,' he said reassuringly, imagining she was worrying that he might have decided to employ her in a new business venture rather than one of his established businesses. 'I shan't be expecting you to trail Leo and Lottie across the Norton Sound to the Seward Peninsula. And cutting across the Sound is, unfortunately, the only sensible way to reach Nome.'

'But if *you're* going there . . .'

Miss Nettlesham hoved into view.

He released hold of her hand. 'I don't know that I am, yet. Everything depends on what I find when we reach Dawson. Whatever I find, though, isn't going to affect you. You're going to have a home on Dawson's main street, Leo and Lottie will be within a hundred yards of the school-house . . .'

'Good evening, Miss Stullen. Our journey has become exceedingly tedious, hasn't it? I . . .' Miss Nettlesham broke off abruptly. 'Oh! I didn't realise I was intruding on a private conversation!'

Lucky Jack cursed beneath his breath and then rose reluctantly to his feet. No wonder he'd never attempted a courtship with a respectable young woman before. Even a few minutes privacy was impossible to achieve. 'Evening, ma'am,' he said through his teeth. 'I was just informing Miss Stullen that we'll be in Dawson in another thirty hours or so.'

'Only if we meet with no mishap,' Miss Nettlesham said, showing no sign of resuming her lonely evening stroll. 'My brother is a resident of Dawson, an *esteemed*

181

resident of Dawson, and he has informed me that delays due to groundings on sand-bars are very likely.'

Lucky Jack didn't doubt it, he also didn't doubt Miss Nettlesham's ability to reduce him, within minutes, to a state of gibbering dementia. He *had* been about to reassure Lilli as to the comfort of the rooms set apart at *The Eldorado* for the housekeeper's own use. Without disclosing to Miss Nettlesham that he was *The Eldorado's* proprietor, a piece of information that, if it became public knowledge, would ensure that *The Eldorado's* reputation for respectability would be immediately compromised, he couldn't very well now do so. 'It's been nice speaking with you, ladies,' he said, aware that yet again Lilli Stullen's virtue had been saved, this time by a guardian angel in a very unlikely guise, 'and now I must wish you both goodnight.'

'Goodnight,' Lilli said frustratedly, understanding his reason for his making a hasty departure and wishing Miss Nettlesham at the bottom of the Yukon.

'How *very* fortunate that I was passing by,' Miss Nettlesham said, seating herself in the cane chair Lucky Jack had just vacated. 'Gentlemen such as Mr Coolidge are *not* to be encouraged, Miss Stullen. Why, if it wasn't for my coming to your rescue as I did, I do believe you would have had to endure the embarrassment of his making a pass at you!'

'And so before I could decently escape I had twenty minutes of hearing all about how *esteemed* her brother is in Dawson and of how equally *esteemed* her husband-to-be is!' Lilli said bitterly as she crawled into the bunk above Lottie's.

'Does Miss Nettlesham know that Kate's beau is a member of the English aristocracy?' Lottie asked interestedly. 'Because if she doesn't, someone should tell her. It might take her down peg or two.'

'Better not tell her,' Leo's muffled voice said from beneath his blankets, 'she might start having breakfast with us again and we don't want that, do we?'

*   *   *

182

'I'm going to tell Mr Jenkinson that I'm a Peabody bride,' a pale-faced Susan said at breakfast next morning. 'We stop off at an Indian camp in an hour or two to pick up cord-wood and I'm going to tell him then, when we go for a short walk together.'

'If he's the man you think he is, he won't think any the less of you,' Lettie said, passing a plate of sourdough hot cakes across to Leo.

'Perhaps not.' Susan's heavy jawline was tense. 'But will he offer to marry me when he knows my circumstances? And even if he does, will he be able to *afford* to marry me? None of us know what sort of amount Mr Nelson will be willing to accept as compensation for our breaking our contract with the marriage bureau. And clergymen aren't overly well paid.'

No-one said anything because no-one could think of anything reassuring to say. The problem of how much compensation Mr Nelson would demand was one that was troubling all of them to a greater or lesser degree. Even more troubling was the worry as to how he might decide on the sum concerned.

'What if he insists on seeing what each of us would fetch at auction and then demanding *that* figure as compensation?' Kate had said the last time the subject had come under discussion. 'How could Lord Lister and the Reverend Mr Jenkinson take part in such a demeaning exercise?'

The answer was, of course, that they couldn't. And though Lucky Jack undoubtedly could, the very thought of him doing so filled Lilli with unspeakable horror. Savagely she reflected that it was no wonder Mrs Peabody had glossed over the actual arrangements for teaming a Peabody bride up with a husband. If she had been more frank, she would never have had a bride on her books.

'We're stopping to take wood on for fuel,' Lilli said to Leo as the *Casca* dropped anchor. 'Do you want to go ashore for a little while? Susan says we're going to be here for an hour or so.'

'Yes,' Leo said unhesitatingly. 'I want to see the Indians.'

So, it seemed, did nearly everyone else who was journeying up the Yukon for the first time.

'Miss Bumby says the Indians wear rings in their noses,' Lottie said as they squeezed into the small, overcrowded boat that was to carry them over the shallows to the river bank. 'I wouldn't want to wear a ring in my nose, would you? It must be very uncomfortable.'

'Lucky Jack wears a ring in his ear,' Leo pointed out, leaning over the edge of the boat and trailing a hand in the swirling grey water, 'Do you think that is uncomfortable as well?'

'Where is Lucky Jack?' Lottie asked ingenuously. 'Doesn't he want to see the Indians?'

'You forget that Indians aren't a novelty to him.' Lilli tried to keep her irritation at Lucky Jack's not taking advantage of an opportunity for them to be together, from showing in her voice. 'He probably even *lived* with Indians when he first travelled the Yukon.'

'Lucky Jack's playing cards,' Leo said, answering the first part of Lottie's question, 'and I don't think he did live with Indians,' he added, commenting on Lilli's last remark as he stared in fascination at the Indians lining the bank, 'or he would have told us, wouldn't he?'

The minute they stepped ashore a clamour of howling erupted. There were dogs everywhere. Snarling, barking, playing, fighting.

'Don't touch them!' Lilli instructed sharply. 'They look to be more wolf than dog!'

'They're certainly fearsome,' Lottie said, edging nearer to her. 'Oh look, Lilli! The Indian ladies are carrying their babies on their backs in beaded bags!'

Tiny faces, with black alert eyes, peeped out from within their snug cradles.

'Indian ladies are called squaws,' Leo said knowledge-ably, wrinkling his nose as a rank smell assailed them. 'And the babies are called papooses. I don't like that smell very much, do you? What do you think it is?'

184

'I think they're preserving fish by smoking it,' Lilli answered, entranced by the bright colours of the squaws' shawls and kerchiefs. 'From the smell of it I think it could be salmon.'

Leo wasn't the only sight-seer to find the smell of smoking fish hard to take. All around them their fellow passengers from the *Casca* were fast dispersing either upriver or downriver, eager for a short, brisk walk and unpolluted air.

Lilli saw Susan and Mr Jenkinson begin to walk downriver together. Tension rippled through her. Susan would be telling Mr Jenkinson she was a Peabody bride and his response to her disclosure would determine her entire future.

Lord Lister was walking quite unconcernedly amid the uproar of half-wild dogs and swarming children, his English jodhpurs and white silk shirt looking very restrained in contrast to the Indians' jaunty buckskin jackets and heavily beaded waistcoats. Kate's eyes weren't on the children or the dogs; they were anxiously following Susan and her companion. Lilli felt for her. The outcome between Susan and Mr Jenkinson was of more than academic interest to Kate. It would either give her the confidence to make a similar confession to Lord Lister or it would terrify her into keeping silent, and the consequences of such a silence were anybody's guess.

'Me liket you,' a little girl of seven or eight was saying beguilingly to Lottie in pidgin English. 'You liket Inchen? You ketchet Inchen shawls?' She was dragging Lottie across to a tepee made of hides, in front of which lay a display of the goods she was trying to sell.

'You'll have to tell her we can't buy, Lottie,' Lilli said regretfully, looking at the exquisite beadwork with longing eyes.

The little girl giggled. 'No wantum money,' she said when Lottie had explained that though they thought the shawls beautiful they had no money with which to buy. 'Wantum gold.'

Now Lottie giggled. 'We haven't any gold,' she said,

vastly entertained that her new-found friend should have thought she had.

The little girl looked longingly at Lottie's sailor-hat. 'Me Nana. Me likum muchee fancy headdress. Me likum muchee dan gold.'

Lilli, aware that a trade-off was about to take place, opened her mouth to protest and then thought better of it. The beadwork was exquisite and the sailor-hat could be easily replaced.

As the dialogue between Lottie and her Indian friend continued there was much to-ing and fro-ing in and out of the tepee and some very disturbing cries coming from within it.

Lottie turned round to Lilli, saying in explanation, 'Nana's mother is having a baby and the baby is a long time coming.'

Lilli's eyes widened. 'Her mother's having a baby *now*? In the tepee?'

Lottie nodded.

'Then tell her that the two of you must do your bartering somewhere else!' Lilli said, appalled at the thought of standing only yards away from a woman who must, surely, want as much privacy as she could get.

Lottie had just embarked on her task when a wizened female hurtled out of the tepee and darted across to them, seizing Lilli by the arm.

'*Quickum! Quickum! Makum white man's medicine!*'

This time Lilli didn't need Lottie to act as interpreter.

'I'm sorry,' she said hastily. 'I'm not a midwife. I don't have any medicine . . .'

'*You comum!*' the century-old-looking crone demanded, tugging fiercely on her arm and pulling her towards the tepee's entrance. '*You comum quickum!*'

With vast relief Lilli saw that Lord Lister and Kate were hurrying to her aid.

'I've been mistaken for a midwife!' she said, still struggling to free herself from the old woman's tenacious grip. 'Lord only knows why! Can you make her understand that I don't know anything about midwifery?'

186

Lord Lister tried his best to prise the demented woman's bony fingers from Lilli's arm, saying firmly, 'We have no knowledge, no medicines.'

From inside the tepee came a scream that froze all of them into immobility.

'Sweet Jesus!' Lord Lister said devoutly, his *savoir-faire* slipping, 'don't these people have their own midwives and doctors?'

Nana began speaking wildly to Lottie, her wheeling and dealing forgotten. With her hand still holding Nana's, Lottie began to translate the frantic pidgin-English. 'Her mother has been in labour since yesterday morning. It's her fifth baby and all the other babies came quickly but this baby refuses to be born. The midwives say the baby is sick. They say only special medicine will make the baby strong enough to be born.'

'You must tell her that we have no such special medicine,' Lord Lister said, still failing in his efforts to free Lilli from the old crone's grasp. 'You must tell her that . . .'

Another scream rent the air.

'We have to at least *try* to help,' Kate said, ashen-faced. 'Where's Lettie? Lettie may have some midwifery experience. And Marietta? Marietta may know what to do.'

As blackened nails dug even deeper into the flesh of her upper arm Lilli looked around the encampment for a glimpse of Lettie or Marietta. Neither of them were anywhere to be seen.

'Where has everyone gone?' she demanded hoarsely. 'I can't see *anyone* from the *Casca*. They can't *all* have gone on walks surely?'

'They did when the rumpus started,' Lord Lister said dryly, wondering if he was going to have to resort to physical violence in order to prevent Lilli being dragged inch by inch into the tepee.

'I know who can help your mother,' Lottie said to Nana, vast relief in her voice. 'My friend will be able to help her!'

Lilli, guessing immediately who Lottie had in mind, struggled even more violently to free herself. 'Lottie! No!'

187

You're being ridiculous! Mr Cameron can't possibly . . . *Lottie!*'

'Where is she going?' Kate asked as Lottie headed off in a run towards the river and the boat, her braids flying in the wind behind her. 'Who is the friend who can help? Is it Lettie?'

'No,' Lilli said, staggering slightly as Lord Lister's efforts finally freed her from the old woman's clutch. 'It's Mr Cameron.' There was a slight edge of hysteria in her voice and neither Kate or Lord Lister blamed her.

'The Scot?' Lord Lister asked disbelievingly, 'But what use will he be in a situation like this? And isn't he a jailbird? I have heard a rumour that he . . .'

'He saved Leo's life,' Kate interrupted swiftly. 'I suppose that's why Lottie thought he could help now. She's only a child and she doesn't realise how different the circumstances are . . .'

A deep, guttural groan came from the tepee. It was the groan of someone only semi-conscious; someone fast losing whatever strength remained to them.

The old woman began shrieking abuse at them. Nana began crying.

Lilli's eyes met Kate's. 'Let's go inside and see what we can do. At least then they'll know that we care.'

Nana's mother hadn't been left unattended. Another wizened female was sat at her side, a bowl of evil-smelling liquid in her hands. She barely looked up as they entered. Muttering to herself she continued sponging her patient's distended body with a filthy-looking rag.

'What should we do?' Kate whispered as Lilli's captor squeezed into the tepee behind them.

'I don't know.' Lilli's voice was raw. The woman groaning in agony only feet away from them was obviously *in extremis* and she couldn't think of one single thing they could do to ease her pain. Never, ever, had she felt so hopelessly inadequate. If the reality of life in the wild was no doctors or skilled midwives or chloroform, she would never again think of it as being romantic.

From outside the tepee came the sound of pounding feet

and Lord Lister's voice saying incredulously, 'Cameron! You've come! But do you know what the situation is? How much did Lottie tell you?'

'Enough,' Ringan said briefly, ducking his head and entering the tepee.

Lilli was aware of Kate's gasp of horror, for Nana's mother was semi-naked. And she was aware of something else. The professional looking battered bag Ringan Cameron had brought into the tepee with him.

He put the bag down on the beaten earth floor, felt the woman's pulse with one hand and laid his other hand on her forehead, saying tersely as he did so, 'I need boiled water and clean linen.'

'But Mr Cameron! That just isn't possible . . .' Kate began, totally disorientated by his presence.

'It is,' Lilli said, realising that Ringan Cameron knew exactly what he was about. 'There'll be a fire in the camp and we can boil whatever water the Indians use for drinking. And we can use our petticoats for the linen.'

'Be verra quick,' Ringan said, his large capable hands gently probing the woman's swollen belly. 'The baby's a breech. If I canna turn it, I'm going to have to perform a Caesarean.'

'*Here?*' Kate pressed a fist to her mouth, gagging.

Lilli, aware that Kate wasn't going to be of much use, said, 'Give me your petticoat. Then ask Lord Lister to take you back to the *Casca*. If he informs Captain Stoddart of the reason we're not all back on board Captain Stoddart might delay sailing indefinitely. I'll see to the water and stay to help Mr Cameron.'

Kate nodded, stepping out of her petticoat and then stumbling with relief out of the tepee and into blessed fresh air.

'Be verra quick,' Ringan said, opening his bag and taking out a stethoscope. 'We havna much time if this lassie's going to give birth to a live bairn.'

Lilli didn't waste time in asking questions. Wondering where on earth she was going to find a container remotely

189

clean enough, she ducked out of the tepee and ran in the direction of the nearest camp fire.

The Indians' drinking water proved to be spring water, mercifully pure. The cleanest container she could find was a skillet smelling strongly of fish.

'It was the best I could do,' she said as she set the skillet of boiled water down on the earth, next to his shabby doctor's bag.

'Have ye ever helped at a birthing before?' he asked, rolling the sleeves of his green plaid shirt high.

She shook her head, her stomach muscles tightening. She knew what he was going to do. She had watched her father do it times without number to mares whose foals were laying awkwardly.

'No, but I've seen my pa manhandle badly positioned foals into a position in which they can be born.'

The woman groaned again, her arms flailing as if trying vainly to push the pain away.

'Then if ye could just ease the lassie's knees high for me . . .'

They were the last word he said to her for a long time. Whenever he spoke again his words, gentle and reassuring, were addressed to the labouring woman.

Lilli knew that Nana's mother wouldn't be able to understand him and she knew that it didn't matter. Her father had always talked in a similar crooning manner when helping distressed mares give birth. It was the tone of voice that mattered. And the reassurance and compassion that lay behind it.

Nana's mother gave a loud, racked cry, her body arching high.

This time when Ringan spoke, it was to Lilli.

'I think we're going to be all right.' Perspiration beaded his brow. 'I think I've done it.'

'But will she be strong enough to push the baby out?' Lilli asked urgently, her own forehead sheened with sweat.

'I dinna know,' Ringan said truthfully. 'But the head is now at the top of the birth canal and . . .'

Despite all her exhaustion a deep contraction trembled Nana's mother's pelvic floor.

In vast relief Ringan positioned himself so that he could steady the baby's head the instant it emerged. To Lilli it seemed an eternity of time before, aided by forceps, it did so. Moments later the baby slithered into Ringan's large, capable hands, it's mouth slack, it's mucus-streaked, wrinkled face completely still. It was a boy.

'Is he dead?' There was a crack in Lilli's voice. 'Oh, sweet heaven, please don't let him be dead!'

Ringan didn't answer her. Very gently, with a saturated piece of Lilli's petticoat, he wiped the baby's face free of mucus. Then he ran his forefinger around the inside of the baby's mouth. The little body trembled, the eyelids fluttering, but still there was no gasp for air, no loud undulating cry.

'Shouldn't you smack him?' Lilli asked urgently as he took string from his pocket and swiftly and deftly tied the umbilical cord in two places, an inch or so apart. 'Shouldn't you smack him to make him cry?'

'What? Smack a tiny wee mite like this?' With a pair of scissors from his bag he severed the cord. 'I'd be damned to hell before I'd commit such a crime.'

'But . . .'

He threw the baby up into the air. There were cries of protest from the two old women. Hazily Lilli wondered how long they had been there. Not once through the birth had she been aware of their presence.

The baby dropped into Ringan's hands, its mouth opening wide in a gasp of shock, its lungs filling. The puny, healthy, enraged cries that followed were the most beautiful sounds Lilli had ever heard.

'Isn't he grand?' Ringan said with a grin, holding the bawling baby high in his hands as if it were a trophy. The best, most magnificent trophy in the world. 'Isn't he just the bonniest little laddie you've ever seen?'

The baby was red, wrinkled, and still streaked in mucus. 'Yes,' she said, laughing through tears of emotion. 'Yes, Ringan. He's the bonniest thing I've ever seen in my life.'

'*Cameron*!' From outside the tepee footsteps approached, Lord Lister's cultured voice carrying clearly, 'Stoddart says he's waited as long as he can and that he can't wait any longer. He's right, y'know. We need to be underway. Either you board now or you'll have to stay here till the next steamer puts in for wood.'

The two old crones were already busily seeing to the after-birth. Nana's mother was again fully conscious, her eyes fixed longingly on her son.

'We'll be right with you!' Ringan called back, laying the squalling baby in its mother's arms.

Lilli picked up his instruments and put them in his bag. Then, as Ringan turned away from mother and child, she retrieved what remained of her and Kate's petticoats.

'You deserve a bloody medal,' Lord Lister said baldly as Ringan stepped out of the tepee. 'I'd as soon face the Boers single-handed as do what you've just done.'

Ringan grinned. 'Then you dinna show very good judgment,' he said, his battered doctor's bag easy in his hand, his sense of well-being euphoric. He had done that which he had thought he would never do again. He had brought a child into the world. A child who, if it hadn't been for him, would very probably have died, taking its mother's life with it. In the most unexpected way possible, the decision that had been tormenting him had been resolved for him. Of *course* he was going to continue practising the profession he had been trained for. And he was going to practise it amongst Indians. He had seen more disease and sickness in his short walk through the camp than he would have seen in a year on the streets of a Canadian or an American city. He knew now, beyond a shadow of a doubt, where his future lay. And the knowledge elated him.

'You'll not find many people curious about what you've been up to,' Lord Lister said as they neared the river-bank. 'Kate thought you wouldn't want people to know what it was that was keeping you in the camp and they think you've merely been powwowing.'

Lilli could see Marietta and Edie standing at the *Casca's*

rails. And Lucky Jack. 'I've something I want to say to you before we board the *Casca*,' she said urgently to Ringan as Lord Lister strode a little ahead of them. 'I want to . . . to apologise.'

He turned his head so that his eyes met hers, his eyebrows rising. 'Apologise? I canna imagine what you have to apologise to me about.' His grey eyes, usually so cool and clear, had darkened in perplexity.

'Someone slandered you to me aboard the *Senator*,' she said, wondering how she could have ever have allowed the slander to affect her behaviour towards him. 'They didn't do it maliciously, they were merely passing on a piece of information they believed to be true. I only half-believed it when I was told it, but I know now there was no truth in it at all. And I'm ashamed that I even half-believed it.'

Lord Lister was already in the small boat waiting to ferry them out to the *Senator*.

Ringan stopped walking, his eyes holding hers. Perspiration still sheened her face. Tendrils of hair had escaped from the twist on top of her head and were curling down to her shoulders. The sleeves of her caramel coloured shirtwaist were pushed high, like a washerwoman's, and there was a smear of blood on her cream serge skirt. She was the most beautiful woman he had ever seen and why the hell she was in love with a rogue like Lucky Jack Coolidge he couldn't begin to imagine. 'If you've been told I'm an ex-prisoner, then I'm verra afraid you were told the truth,' he said slowly, wondering if any other woman in the world had eyes of a such a pure, clear, forget-me-not blue.

'For the Lord's sake, hurry both of you!' Lord Lister shouted impatiently. 'I don't want to be left kicking my heels here for the next few days!'

Both of them ignored him.

'No, it wasn't that.'

The mid-day sun was flaming his hair with gleams of gold and copper and she saw that his long eye-lashes, dark auburn at the tips, were almost blond at the roots.

'I knew about that even before you rescued Leo,' she

said, wondering why she had ever thought red hair on a man, less than attractive.

He stood very still. In a nearby bush two birds wrangled furiously.

'My informant told me you had been imprisoned for murder,' she said simply, 'And I know you couldn't have murdered anyone. I know that if anyone ever died at your hands they would have done so by accident.'

'Come *on*!' Lord Lister exhorted as the *Casca's* whistle shrilled. 'The boat's going to sail, don't y'know!'

Ringan's eyes held her's. He didn't speak. He couldn't. The emotions raging through him were far too shattering to be articulated.

The *Casca's* whistle shrilled again. Tearing her eyes from his, Lilli gave her hand to Lord Lister and, her emotions in tumult, allowed him to help her into the waiting boat.

Chapter Twelve

All through the short boat ride her emotions were in tumult. The time she had spent with Ringan Cameron in the Indian tepee had been the most extraordinary of her life. She had felt utterly in tune with him and with what he was trying to achieve. And together, what they had achieved had been marvellous. She wondered what Nana's mother would call her son. She wondered if she would one day be able to return to the camp and see him.

She looked across to where Ringan was sitting, his doctor's bag between his feet, and her breath came quick in her throat. He was an amazing man. A big man in every sense of the word. She wondered why, when he had tended her after she had been hit by The Pig, he hadn't admitted to her that he was a doctor. Was it because of his jailbird past? Or was it just the natural reserve of a Highlander? There was so much she didn't know about him and wanted to know, but one thing she *did* know was that she liked him. She liked him very much indeed.

'What *have* you all been doing?' Marietta shouted down to them, hanging over the deck rails as the boat rocked against the *Casca's* side. 'We thought you'd at least been eaten by bears!'

Lilli laughed up at her and then Lord Lister was on his feet, steadying her as she stepped from the rocking boat onto the *Casca's* ladder. Before beginning to climb she looked over her shoulder at Ringan. Beneath his thick tumble of curly red hair his eyes met hers. Shock stabbed through her. A few moments ago, when they had walked from the Indian camp to the river-bank, he had been euphoric. Now the skin was taut across his cheekbones and beneath his rusty moustache his mouth was a tight line of pain. He looked like a man on the brink of an abyss; a man faced with a realization totally unacceptable to him.

Deeply disconcerted she climbed the ladder. Was he worried that gossip would spread of how he had left the *Casca* carrying a doctor's bag? And if so, why? Were there legal difficulties which made it impossible for him to openly practise his profession? What if . . .'

'What in blazes have you been doing?' Lucky Jack demanded, his eyes dark with concern as he helped her aboard the *Casca*. 'And if you wanted to get so friendly with the Indians why didn't you ask me to accompany you?'

For once his touch didn't drive every other thought from her brain. She was aware of Lord Lister stepping onto the deck behind her. In another second or so Ringan would be following him.

'You were playing cards,' she said, wondering when she would next have an opportunity to talk in private to Ringan. She wanted to ask him what it was that was so deeply troubling him. They were, after all, friends now. Shared experience had forged a bond of profound camaraderie between them.

'We're dining with Captain Stoddart and Kitty,' Lucky Jack was saying to her as they walked towards the companionway leading down to the cabins. 'Privately, of course. No use in ruining your reputation now when we've so carefully avoided doing so for so long.'

Lilli was barely listening to him. She had too many other things on her mind to worry overmuch about the arrangements for dinner. She now knew what it was she wanted to do when she had settled in Dawson. She wanted to work with the Indians. She wanted to teach bright-eyed intelligent children like Nana to read and write in English so that they could better communicate with the Americans and Canadians and Europeans now living alongside them in the Yukon Valley.

196

'Did you really see bears, Lilli?' Edie was asking round-eyed as she and Marietta accompanied them towards the cabins. 'Mr Saskatchewan Stan says he once flushed a brown bear from giant blueberry bushes and the bear ran and ran it was so scairt of him!'

Lilli frowned slightly. Hadn't Mr Jenkinson said something about starting a school for Indian children in Dawson? Such a school would surely not come under the jurisdiction of the Canadian Education Authority. When it came to teaching staff, Mr Jenkinson would be able to engage whoever he chose.

'Unless you're a Highland Scot the word is scared, Edie. Not scairt,' Marietta said, wondering what on earth Lilli was thinking about to be so totally self-absorbed, she didn't seem to be even aware of the proprietal way Lucky Jack Coolidge was shepherding her towards her cabin. She looked across at him, hoping to catch his eye. He was handsome enough to ruin a nun. Her mouth twitched into a naughty smile. She would be more than happy for him to ruin her, any time or any place. Or she would be if he wasn't Lilli's beau.

'The children are invited to dinner as well,' Lucky Jack said as they reached Lilli's cabin door. 'Stoddart likes children. He has five of his own.'

With great difficulty Lilli dragged her attention away from the dizzying prospect of doing something truly useful with her life. 'Has he? I wonder why he doesn't have them with him aboard the *Casca*? It would be easy for him to, wouldn't it?'

Lucky Jack shot her a down-slanting smile and for the first time since she had re-boarded the *Casca* she registered the reality of his presence at her side. Her heart felt as if it were flipping over within her breast. He had been worried about her. He had been concerned. And he had arranged for them to be able to dine together in near privacy that evening.

She smiled sunnily back at him, loving the gold flecks in his amber-brown eyes; loving the way his wheat-gold hair curled low in the nape of his neck; at the way his

197

gold earring made him look for all the world like a swashbuckling pirate.

It was only later, when she was telling Marietta and Edie what had happened in the Indian camp, that it occurred to her to wonder what Lucky Jack's reaction would be when she told him of her plans. And to wonder what the situation now was between Susan and Mr Jenkinson.

'Terrible,' Marietta said succinctly. 'Susan's in her cabin sobbing her eyes out. Mr Jenkinson is up on deck, looking so traumatized it wouldn't surprise me if he didn't throw himself overboard. Lettie's tried talking to him but she didn't get anywhere. She says he seems too shocked to even speak. She's with Susan now but I don't see what comfort she can give her. The romance is off. Methodist ministers do not, apparently, marry mail-order brides, no matter how suitable as a minster's wife the bride may be.'

Lilli's throat was too tight for speech. Tears glittered on her eyelashes. Poor Susan. She had been so near to happiness and now it was as far beyond her reach as ever.

'Does Kate know?' she asked at last.

Marietta nodded, her usually animated little monkey-face sombre. 'Yes. But what's she's going to do where Lord Lister is concerned she hasn't yet said.'

'I'm not going to tell him,' Kate said an hour later as she joined Marietta and Edie on deck.

'But if you don't tell him, how can he decide whether he's going to pay off Josh Nelson and marry you?' Marietta asked, perplexed.

Kate's high-necked, midnight-blue dress seemed to draw all the colour from her face. 'He can't,' she said brokenly, 'but neither will he be able to reject me as Mr Jenkinson has rejected Susan. And I couldn't bear it if he rejected me. I couldn't live with such pain.'

'But I still don't see . . .' Marietta persisted, more perplexed than ever.

Kate pressed a hand against her throat. I'm going to tell Perry . . .'

'Perry?' Lilli interrupted.

'Peregrine. Lord Lister.' Kate's voice was barely audible. 'I'm going to tell Perry that I'm already affianced and that once we reach Dawson I will no longer be able to continue my . . . my friendship with him. That way I will always be able to pretend to myself that perhaps he *would* have wanted to pay off Mr Nelson and marry me. And for the rest of my life I'll be able to remember these precious days we've spent together with joy. My memories won't be tarnished, as Susan's memories are going to be, by rejection and heartache.'

'But what if you tell him and he *doesn't* reject you?' Marietta demanded explosively. 'Isn't that a possibility worth gambling on? Lord, if it was me, I'd gamble *everything* on it!'

A small, sad smile touched Kate's gentle mouth. 'That's because, like Lucky Jack, you're a gambler by nature, Marietta. I'm not. And this way I can at least keep my dreams.'

Later, as she sat at the dinner table with Captain Stoddart and Kitty Dufresne and Lucky Jack, Leo squeezed between Kitty and the Captain and Lottie seated between herself and Lucky Jack, Lilly found herself wondering what she would do if she were in Kate's position. The answer came almost immediately. Like Marietta, she would risk everything in the fevered hope that by doing so she would win a lifetime of happiness with the man she loved.

She looked across at the man in question, wishing she could talk to him about her amazing experience that afternoon in the Indian encampment, wanting to discuss with him her intention of becoming a schoolmistress in the Reverend Mr Jenkinson's school for Indian children. Because of the company they were in it was impossible for her to do so.

Captain Stoddart was saying quite flatly that in the

199

months Lucky Jack and Kitty had been absent from it, Dawson had peaked. 'Another few months, a year maybe, and it'll be a ghost town,' he said, stabbing a piece of moose-meat with his fork.

Lilli looked across at Kitty, hoping she wasn't going to let the topic of conversation distress her. Her worry was needless. Kitty was leaning towards Leo, whispering something in his ear, and Leo was giggling, his eyes aglow at receiving such attention from his magic lady.

'Help Mr Jenkinson out at his school?'

It was nearly midnight and they were standing on a secluded section of the deck. The sun had set an hour or so previously, but there was still no darkness, only a glorious amber light diffusing the grey Yukon into tones of tawny splendour.

'Yes. He intends setting up a school for Indian children. It would be such a privilege to be able to teach them! Nana was so quick and eager and . . .'

'Hey, steady on a moment.' He looked across at her, wondering if he had misjudged the kind of background she came from. If his trip to Europe had taught him nothing else, it had taught him that upper-class Englishwomen were like no other breed he had ever encountered. With no need to work for a living they undertook volunteer hospital and educational work with ridiculous enthusiasm. Was Lilli's background far more privileged than she had admitted? Going by the classiness of her looks it was certainly a possibility. And she held herself like a member of the English aristocracy; straight and tall and with an air of pride.

He frowned. Lilli wasn't English. Or at least not wholly English. She was half-Irish. Would that preclude her from coming from the kind of background he had in mind? He had no idea. What he did know, though, was that her position as housekeeper at *The Eldorado* wouldn't give her time for the kind of commendable volunteer work she had in mind.

'Time isn't going to be exactly hanging heavy on your

hands in Dawson, you know,' he said reasonably. 'House-keeping is a major job. It needs a lot of time and effort to do it well.'

'I know.' She was touched by his concern, but apprehensive also. She knew how taxing housework could be, especially when there were no conveniences such as piped water, for she had been a housekeeper to her father in just such conditions. It surprised her that Lucky Jack, with his air of careless extravagance, should be expecting her to run their future home without help, but she wasn't afraid of hard work and it wasn't that prospect that was filling her with dark doubts. It was the sudden suspicion that Lucky Jack was raising objections to her plans merely because, like many men, he didn't want his wife to have a life of her own outside the home. 'I know,' she said again, wondering how best to broach such a delicate issue, 'I'm very practised at running a house and caring for Leo and Lottie and I know I can do it in such a way that I'll still have time to help Mr Jenkinson . . .'

'*The Eldorado* isn't a ranch house,' he interrupted gently, 'it's big. Thirty rooms at least. And though the staff are pretty keen, they're also pretty itinerant. Half of them are only in Dawson in the hope of staking a claim on whatever new gold strike is made and it wouldn't surprise me if we returned to find half of them had already left for Nome.'

They were standing close together, as close as propriety allowed. Fifteen yards or so away from them, in the direction of the stern, Saskatchewan Stan was holding court, telling a group of first-timers all about the old days of '97 and '98. In the other direction the unmistakable pink of Marietta's ankle-length skirt sizzled in the copper-gold light. She was leaning against the deck-rails, Edie at her side. There was no sign of Susan or Lettie or Kate.

'I'm glad to know I'll have some help at *The Eldorado*,' she said, relief thick in her voice. 'And as I am going to have help . . .'

She was just about to say that as she was going to have help she could quite easily organise her time so that she could also teach Indian children the rudiments of written English, when she saw The Pig swagger into view. He had two companions with him, both of them as repellent looking as he and they were walking with dreadful intent towards Marietta and Edie. 'Oh God!' she said devoutly. 'Quick, Lucky Jack! We've got to get Edie to a place of safety!'

From where he was standing, in the shadow of the overhang of the upperdeck, Ringan saw her anxiety quite clearly. And he also saw that there was no need for him to help her rescue Edie. Lucky Jack already had everything under control. As Lilli ran to warn Marietta and Edie, Jack was striding purposefully towards the brute intent on terrorising them.

Ringan watched the exchange that followed with grudging respect. Whatever Coolidge's faults, cowardice was obviously not one of them. When the brute looked as if he were going to deck him, Jack stood his ground, verbally threatening the brute, though with what, Ringan was too far away to hear. The threats proved to be startlingly effective. The brute and his companions turned on their heels and, as Lilli had disappeared speedily below deck with Marietta and Edie, Lucky Jack remained where he was, taking a cigar from his vest pocket and lighting it.

Ringan moved out of the shadows but not to join Lucky Jack. What would be the point? He could hardly catechise Coolidge as to whether he intended being a worthy husband to Lilli. On the face of it there was no reason why he shouldn't be. There was no reason why he should be worrying where Leo or Lottie were concerned, either. Coolidge obviously had an easy manner with children and both Leo and Lottie liked him well enough. He remembered Lottie's reservations about Coolidge's suitability as a husband and a glimmer of a smile touched his mouth. Wee Lottie was so perceptive at determining a person's faults she would probably have reservations about anyone her sister considered marrying.

Bleakly he walked towards the stern. Lilli would no

doubt not enjoy coming to terms with Coolidge's often cavalier manner, but he had no reason to suspect that she would lead a miserable existence as Coolidge's wife. And so, if she was in love with him, and from what he had seen he was quite sure she *was* in love with him, he had absolutely no excuse for wanting, with all his heart and soul, to try and break the relationship up. No reason except that he was in love with Lilli Stullen himself. Deeply and irrevocably in love.

When he reached the stern he stood, staring broodingly down into the *Casca's* foaming wake, his massive shoulders hunched, his fisted hands thrust deep into his breeches pockets. God Almighty, but he'd never known what the word jealousy meant until now. Whenever he saw Lilli in Lucky Jack's company he was racked by it. Crucified by it.

Balling his hands into even tighter fists he thought back to the time they had spent together helping the young Indian woman give birth. They had worked together in absolute unison and afterwards, in their shared euphoria, he had felt they were in complete mental accord; that they both wanted exactly the same kind of things in life; that their values and ambitions were identical. And then, confirming everything he felt, she had turned to him and told him that she knew he had served time for murder and she knew it was a crime he was incapable of.

He had known then, absolutely and utterly, that all his instincts about her being the other, missing half of himself, were correct. But she didn't feel the same, God help him. She was in love with Coolidge and according to Lottie, Coolidge had declared his intention of marrying her.

On the far bank of the river a lone moose stood, dramatically silhouetted against the now blood-red sky.

A pulse throbbed at the corner of Ringan's blunt jawline. In comparison to Coolidge, what could he offer Lilli? He was going to be spending his entire time travelling up and down the Yukon Valley treating the various tribes of Indians who lived along its banks. During the summer his home would be a tent. In the winter it would be a log cabin. And even though that log cabin would be as comfortable as human endeavour could make it, it wouldn't remotely reach the standard of comfort Jack Coolidge would be able to provide for her. Coolidge was a man who had made himself as gold-rich as any lucky-strike prospector. And lucky-strike prospectors were able to live like kings.

The moose switched its tail and turned, plodding in stately splendour away from the river through fetlock-deep grass.

Ringan drew in a deep, shuddering breath. All through the years of his imprisonment he had been cooped in claustrophobic proximity to other men, and always he had felt alone. Loneliness was something he had grown accustomed to. A bitter smile twisted the corner of his mouth. It was just as well he had become accustomed to it because he knew now that his loneliness was going to become a permanent condition. Without Lilli by his side, and Leo and Lottie to care for, how could he ever be anything else?

'Susan isn't eating,' Lettie said next morning when they all met for breakfast. 'She knows you all want to sympathise with her and console her, but she says she just can't face seeing anyone.

'Oh God,' Marietta said graphically. 'Oh hell.'

No-one censured her for her language, not even Kate.

Lilli pushed her chair away from the table and stood up. 'I need to talk with Mr Jenkinson about the Indian school he intends opening in Dawson. Perhaps I'll be able to talk to him about Susan as well.'

'I wish you luck,' Lettie said dryly, spreading honey on a sourdough hot-cake. 'He wouldn't say a word to me. I don't think he even knew who I was.'

When Lilli stepped out on deck she was immediately aware of an air of expectancy amongst her fellow-passengers. Dawson was only a few miles away and their long, long journey was finally nearing its end. She had dressed with care for the event, wearing her Sunday-best, white lace, leg o' mutton sleeved shirtwaist, a cameo that had been her mother's pinned to its high, mandarin neck. Her deep blue, seven-gored skirt was carefully brushed. Her high-button boots immaculately polished.

As always, every pair of male eyes in the vicinity swivelled in her direction.

'Morning, Miss Stullen,' a crony of Saskatchewan Stan's called to her.

'Morning, ma'am,' a half dozen others said, eager to be the recipient of a greeting back. 'We'll soon be in Dawson now and we've got a right fine day for it too.'

It was a fine day. The sun was high in the brassy blue bowl of the sky, the air milk-warm, heady with the pungent scent of fir and pine. A herd of caribou were in the river, swimming against the current. On the far bank Indians were drying fish near their cluster of tents.

Mr Jenkinson stood near the stern, looking unseeingly at the scenic glories unfolding before him. Lilli felt her stomach muscles contract in shock. Even though Lettie had warned her that Mr Jenkinson was nearly as distressed as Susan, she hadn't expected to see such a startling physical change in him. All his bouncy perkiness was gone. His moon face was haggard. His shoulders slumped in such a manner that he looked altogether diminished.

'Excuse me, Mr Jenkinson,' she said hesitantly. 'I wonder if I could have a word with you for a few moments?'

He turned towards her, staring at her as if he had never seen her before.

'I'm Miss Stullen. A friend of Miss Bumby's.'

'Ah, yes . . .' His voice was vague, his eyes still dazed. He no longer looked middle-aged. He looked old. Old and vulnerable.

'I . . .' Lilli hesitated. It was quite obvious Mr Jenkinson was in no condition to exchange pleasantries. 'It's about the school you intend opening in Dawson for Indian children,' she said, plunging straight in. 'Would you engage me as a teacher? I want to work with the Indians

205

and though I'm not a registered teacher I've had a very good education. I could certainly teach the children to read and write in English and . . .'

'School?' Mr Jenkinson looked at her in pathetic bewilderment. 'There won't be a school now, Miss Stullen. I won't be staying in Dawson you see. Not now. No, I couldn't possibly. I couldn't begin my ministry knowing that Miss Bumby was . . . was . . . no, absolutely not. It would be impossible. I shall stay aboard the *Casca* and return immediately to Whitehorse and from there I shall return to Seattle.'

'But is that really necessary?' Lilli queried, appalled. 'If you and Miss Bumby are so . . . so well-suited and happy in each other's company, why should the circumstances of her being a Peabody bride ruin your future happiness and hers?'

At the words 'Peabody bride' Mr Jenkinson had shuddered, shooting a hand out to grasp onto the deck-rail for support.

'Mail-order brides . . . Dance-hall girls . . . little better than . . . It seems incredible. Miss Bumby so refined. So educated. I can hardly believe . . .' With his free hand he fumbled for a handkerchief, pressing it against his mouth as if to prevent himself from vomiting.

Despite her sympathy for him Lilli felt a flare of annoyance. 'I don't think your being very sensible about this,' she said in a manner not far removed from Susan's schoolmarmishness. 'Mail-order brides are *not* dance-hall girls.' She thought of Marietta and hoped she would be forgiven. 'Mail-order brides are respectable young women yearning for a husband and a home.'

She thought of Kate and Edie and Lettie and herself. Not one of them had become a Peabody bride because they were yearning for a husband. Apart from Edie, they had all become Peabody brides because they were running away from unbearable domestic situations.

'Susan *is* all the things you thought her. She's refined and educated and honest and kind. She's also very, very shy. And it isn't easy for a shy woman to find a husband,

Mr Jenkinson. Especially when she's over twenty-five and especially when she's not particularly pretty.'

'Not pretty?' Mr Jenkinson looked at her as if she had taken leave of her senses. 'Not pretty? Miss *Bumby*?' He drew in a deep shuddering, incredulous breath. 'I would have you know, young lady, that Miss Bumby is *beautiful*! A veritable pearl among women! A . . . a *Zenobia*!'

Lilli didn't know who Zenobia was, but whoever she was, she was obviously someone Mr Jenkinson held in high esteem.

'Then why not try and understand how deeply unhappy she has been,' she said reasonably. 'For only a very unhappy woman would have resorted to the Peabody marriage bureau. And can't you also try and imagine how she feels now? She doesn't *want* to marry a man she doesn't know. She wants to marry a man who is congenial to her, a man she respects.

'But the scandal . . . the gossip . . .' There was perspiration on his forehead, agony in his eyes. 'I'm a man of the cloth . . . a minister of religion . . .'

'If you don't save Susan from the humiliation of being auctioned in Dawson City like a piece of meat you're a man not worthy of that religion,' Lilli rejoined crisply. 'You would certainly be proving yourself to be not worthy of Susan.'

Deciding it was a parting shot she couldn't improve on she turned her back on him, walking swiftly away, hoping to God she hadn't made a tortuous situation even worse.

'How could it be worse?' Marietta said bleakly, heaving her travel-bag to the door of her cabin ready for disembarkation. 'Susan is still crying as if she's never going to stop. Kate is with Lord Lister and when she's finished telling him her rigmarole about being affianced he's going to think she's nothing but an immoral little flirt. The Pig is still stalking Edie. Lettie is convinced Josh Nelson isn't going to accept any pay-offs. And Lucky Jack has just told me that Dawson is dying and near dead and that all the dance-hall girls are leaving for Nome.' It was a depressing litany.

'I think I'll go and try and find Lucky Jack,' Lilli said, knowing that if anyone could cheer her, he could. 'Where is he?'

'When he left me he was heading in the direction of the lower-deck saloon. Do you think I should try and make myself look monstrously ugly so that Josh Nelson won't even consider putting me up for auction, but will be grateful for whatever pay-off he's given?'

When Lilli peeped into the lower-deck saloon it was to see Lucky Jack deep in a game of cards with Saskatchewan Stan and the two men who had accompanied him when he had disembarked from the *Senator*. She sighed. Where cards were concerned, Lucky Jack was a lost cause.

She strolled across to the deck-rails, looking out at a river bank thick with trees. Across the swirling slate-grey water came the sound of woodpeckers drumming against the bark of spruce and pine. In their shade an enormous bear was fishing. High in the sky chicken hawks wheeled and hovered.

She sighed again. It was beautiful country. The wildest and the most beautiful she had ever seen. She wanted to be out in it, exploring it. She wanted to be able to camp beside gurgling creeks; to stride over hills thick with wild flowers; to learn all about the Indians and their ancient way of life.

Her mouth quirked ruefully. She couldn't imagine Lucky Jack camping beside creeks or striding over hills. In fact the longer she knew him, the harder it was to imagine him anywhere but at a card-table. And she could no longer imagine him enthusing about her desire to learn more about the Indians and to be of some service to them.

Her eyes darkened as the *Casca* steamed around yet another of the Yukon's interminable bends. Without Mr Jenkinson's school there was no obvious way for her to be of service to them. Unless . . .

Across the water came the carrying howl of dogs. Soon she could see a scattering of tents. At the *Casca's* approach a half dozen Indian children rushed down to the river's edge, waving furiously. Her spirits lifting, Lilli waved back.

Unless she opened a school of her own. Elation suffused her. Unless the Reverend Mr Jenkinson came to his senses and married Susan and settled in Dawson, opening the school he had intended to open, she would open her own school. And she wouldn't allow Lucky Jack's lack of enthusiasm to deter her. This was something she had to do for herself. This was something she knew she was *meant* to do.

'We're nearly there,' Lettie's voice said from behind her. 'According to Saskatchewan Stan, Dawson is just around the next bend.

'Where are Marietta and Edie? And Kate? Has she told Lord Lister she's affianced?'

Lettie nodded. 'I don't know how he's taken the news. Kate is perfectly calm. It's not a natural calm though. Marietta says she's retreating into herself as a form of self-protection against her grief. She says we shouldn't leave her on her own in case she . . . in case she . . .'

She didn't have to finish her sentence. Lilli knew very well what it was she unable to say.

Over Lettie's shoulder she saw Marietta and Edie, Kate and Susan, walking towards them. Susan looked dreadful, the dark line of hair on her upper lip starkly noticeable against the pallor of her skin. She was dressed, however, impeccably. Her tailored suit was toffee-brown. Her shirtwaist was cream, its high collar impeccably starched. Her silk tie was burnt umber as was the ribbon on her boater hat.

Kate looked perfectly composed and deathly ill. She was still wearing her midnight-blue, leg o' mutton sleeved dress. Where once it had enhanced her gentle dignity, now it served only to age her, making her look a woman in her thirties, not her twenties.

'So we're nearly there,' Marietta said, a sizzling orange

blouse clashing gloriously with her frizz of ginger hair and vivid pink skirt. 'Come over here, Edie. Next to the rail. Then you'll be able to see.'

A huge rocky bluff masked the next bend in the river.

'And it's the last bend!' they could hear Saskatchewan Stan saying to his acolytes excitedly. 'Lord a-mighty but we're nearly there now! Nearly there!'

The *Casca* began to steam around the bend. Edie slid her hand into Marietta's. Lilli's hands tightened on the deck-rail. Marietta sucked in her breath. Susan clasped her hands so tightly together her nails dug deep into her palms. Only Kate remain oblivious, not caring anymore about anything.

The *Casca* rounded the bluff and there, before them, lay a sight Lilli knew she would remember life-long. Another river, a river she knew to be the Klondike, roared into the Yukon from the right. Beyond the junction of the rivers rose a tapering mountain with the great scar of a land-slide slashed across its face. And at its feet, spilling into the surrounding hills, lay a city of false-faced saloons, frame stores, two-storeyed log hotels, dance-halls and banks. And tucked higgledy-piggledy everywhere, squeezed between saloons, oozing out of alleys onto the water's edge, overflowing up the hillside, were small log cabins and tiny shacks.

'Well, here we are,' Susan said tightly. 'Welcome to Dawson.'

Chapter Thirteen

As the *Casca* passed the foaming mouth of the Klondike and swung in towards Dawson all Lilli could see were men. The dock was black with them. There were men with breeches tucked into high-top boots, broad-brimmed hats shadowing their faces; slick-suited men sporting gold nugget watch-chains and big black Stetons; men wearing high starched collars, diamond pins glittering on their shirt-fronts; men wearing Prince Albert coats and top hats; men wearing mukluks and gaudy mackinaws and thick caps; men wearing hard hats; men wearing ten-gallon hats; men in the blue and gold uniform of police officers; men in the Mountie scarlet of police constables; Indians in beaded skincoats and moccasins.

'But no women,' Lettie said, her face impassive. 'Mrs Peabody wasn't joking when she said there was a dearth of women in the Klondike.'

'I'm scared,' Edie said apprehensively. 'You won't leave me, will you, Marietta? Promise me you won't leave me.'

'I'm going to do my best not to leave you,' Marietta said, a furrow of anxiety creasing her forehead. 'But if I have to, you'll be all right a long as you keep with Lilli or Lettie or . . .'

'There's Mr Nelson,' Susan said bleakly. 'I wonder what arrangements he's made?'

'We'll probably all be boarding together somewhere,' Lilli said, aware that Susan must have lodgings of her own in Dawson. 'Will you be coming with us, Susan?'

Susan nodded. 'Oh yes,' she said, her eyes red from weeping. 'That's the only comfort I have now. That we're in this together and that I'm not alone.'

211

The *Casca* shuddered as the anchor chain rattled out. Seconds later the gangplank crashed down and the stampede to disembark began.

'Let them all go,' Susan said, not moving. 'After all, we're not in a hurry, are we?'

Remaining on deck, they watched as hordes of men they now knew by sight strode down the gangplank and on to dry land. Some of the disembarking men they were on more familiar terms with.

Saskatchewan Stan, so short and roly-poly he seemed to roll off the *Casca*, not walk; Lord Lister, his handsome face white with tension; the Reverend Mr Jenkinson, walking without any sense of purpose, merely letting the crowd carry him along.

Susan's net-gloved hand was pressed tight to her throat, her heavy-featured face so ravaged by heartache Lilli couldn't bear to look at her.

'There goes Miss Nettlesham,' Lettie said, mercifully attracting attention away from Lord Lister and Mr Jenkinson. 'Do you think her beau is waiting to greet her?'

Miss Nettlesham, sensibly attired in a brown broadcloth skirt and double-breasted wool jacket and dutifully escorted by a member of the *Casca's* crew, was walking with barely concealed excitment towards the slick-suited figures at the front of the crowd.

'It's time we were following her,' Marietta said at last. 'Otherwise Mr Nelson will be sending a search party out for us.'

In nervous apprehension, carrying their suitcases and boxes, they walked towards the gangplank.

As Lilli stepped on it she could see Lucky Jack stepping on to the dock. With vast relief she saw him make a bee-line towards Josh Nelson. Hopefully, by the time she introduced herself to Josh Nelson, he and Lucky Jack would have come to a satisfactory financial arrangement and there would be no question of her being subjected to the medievally barbaric humiliation of an auction.

'Oh poor Miss Nettlesham!' Lottie suddenly exclaimed.

'Look, Lilli! She's having an argument with a quite dreadful looking man!'

From her birds-eye view on the gangplank Lilli looked in the direction Lottie was pointing. Miss Nettlesham was indeed having an argument and not only with one man, but with two. One of them obviously thought himself quite a swell. He was wearing a shiny-looking suit with a garish vest and had a cigar clamped firmly in one hand, a hand he was angrily gesticulating with.

The other man reminded Lilli of The Pig. Coarse black hair grew so far down on his forehead it nearly met with his beetling eyebrows. Similar mats covered his immense forearms, exposed by the rolled-up sleeves of a none-too-clean shirt.

'Do you think she needs help?' Lottie asked, perturbed. 'Do you think one of those men is her beau?'

'Very possibly,' Lilli said, aware that if she was going to go to Miss Nettlesham's aid she would have to do so before she introduced herself to Josh Nelson.

As she stepped foot on Dawson soil she said, 'Tell Marietta what's happening, Lottie. Tell her I'll catch you all up in a few minutes time.'

As Lottie scurried to do her bidding, Lilli pushed through the throng towards Miss Nettlesham.

'You told me he was a gentleman!' Miss Nettlesham was protesting in cracked tones to the cigar-smoking swell. 'You said he was a member of Dawson's élite! You said *you* were a member of Dawson's élite! How could you have lied to me so shamefully? How could you have lured me out here, to the back of beyond . . .'

'Aw, come off it Rosalind,' the swell said impatiently. 'This isn't Boston! As far as Dawson is concerned I *am* a member of its élite . . .'

'Not wearing such a cheap, shiny suit you aren't!' Miss Nettlesham had begun to cry. 'And your friend is . . . your friend is . . .' Words failed her and sobs convulsed her.

Lilli touched her arm. 'Miss Nettlesham. Can I be of any assistance?'

Mortification flashed across Miss Nettlesham's patrician

features. Lilli could see her struggling to decide whether to salvage her pride and deny that anything was amiss or to admit that things were very much amiss and to accept whatever help was available.

'Judas priest!' the swell's companion said explosively. 'I ain't here to be insulted! You ain't the only person bin lied to shamefully, ma'am. I wuss told you wuss a fair bit o' flesh. If I'd wanted a dried up prune for a wife I could have git meself one without no help from no-one.'

Bright spots of humiliated colour burned Miss Nettlesham's cheeks. Tears of humiliation glittered on her sandy eyelashes. 'I've been duped, Miss Stullen,' she said unsteadily, looking almost as if she might faint. 'My brother has criminally misled me.'

'Quit the bullshit, Rosalind' her brother said crudely. 'Lou here has paid good money both to me and to the marriage bureau for a wife. Whether he's happy with the goods he's getting or whether you're happy is neither here nor there. You're stuck with each other so you'd better start getting acquainted.'

'I don't mind comin' to terms with a grievous disapointment,' his companion said magnaminously, clearing his throat and spitting.

Miss Nettlesham swayed slightly and Lilli tightened hold of her arm. 'I think your sister needs time to adjust to the shock she's received,' she said to the swell, intent only on preventing Miss Nettlesham from being swept off and married instantly against her will. 'I think she should remain with the other Peabody brides for a little while. This way, Miss Nettlesham. Mr Nelson is waiting for us to introduce ourselves to him.'

Still crying, Miss Nettlesham gratefully allowed Lilli to lead her away. 'I can't believe it!' she gasped between sobs. 'That ghastly man! All hairy and sweaty! I thought he was a *gentleman*. My brother had assured me he was a gentleman! He wasn't even wearing a bow-tie or a cravat, Miss Stullen! He looked like a . . . he looked like a *labourer*!'

As they neared Josh Nelson, Marietta turned around

and saw them. 'Oh Lord,' she said as Miss Nettlesham hiccuped and sobbed and continued to protest that she had been infamously, criminally duped, 'Not another broken heart.'

'I don't know about broken but it's certainly cruelly diappointed,' Lilli said, relieved to see that Lucky Jack was still in animated conversation with Josh Nelson. 'What's happening here? Has Mr Nelson agreed to a pay-off?'

'Don't cry,' Edie was saying to Miss Nettlesham. 'It don't do no good to cry. It only makes you feel ever so ill. Have you a handkerchief? Would you like to borrow mine?'

'Nelson has agreed to one pay-off but not to two,' Marietta said as Edie pulled a mean-looking handkerchief from her dress pocket and thrust it into Miss Nettlesham's kid-gloved hand.

'But that's no good at all! He has to agree to a pay-off for both of us! And for Edie as well!'

Miss Nettlesham was blotting her eyes with Edie's handkerchief. Kate was standing a little apart from everyone else, her eyes dazed and unfocussed. Susan and Lettie were standing to the rear of Josh Nelson, waiting for his conversation with Lucky Jack to come to an end. All around them men were noisily milling about.

Lilli moved forward a step or two so that she could hear what Lucky Jack and Josh Nelson were saying.

'One, yes. Two, no. Lord almighty, Jack! What do you take me for? If you want girls for the *Gold Nugget* and the *Mother Lode*, you find them for yourself! You've just come back from the Outside. You should have been able to find yourself plenty!'

'I'm not arguing this toss out on the dock-side,' Lucky Jack said, aware of the many men around them listening with avid interest. 'We'll discuss it over a bottle of bourbon at the *Gold Nugget*.'

'If it's bourbon you've brought in from Outside I'll be right with you. First, though, I have to get these women over to the *Phoenix*.'

Lucky Jack nodded and then turned towards Lilli.

215

'Don't worry about anything,' he said reassuringly. 'I'll have it all sorted out by tonight.'

'But Lucky Jack, what if . . .'

'This way, ladies,' Josh Nelson boomed. 'You ain't got much time for primping. Your would-be husbands are already in town and by tomorrow you'll all be married ladies! Now this way, follow me.'

'Don't worry,' Lucky Jack said again, his hand cupping her elbow. 'I'll see to it you don't provide the town with free entertainment this evening. The sooner everyone gets to the *Phoenix* and gets settled in, the sooner I can come to an agreement with Josh.'

Leo tugged hard on Lilli's hand. 'What's happening?' he asked, disturbed. 'What did that man mean when he said you would be married by tomorrow? Why was Miss Bumby crying this morning and why is Miss Nettlesham crying now?'

'Will you take Leo with you?' Lilli asked Lucky Jack urgently. 'I don't want him seeing or hearing too much. He's very fond of Susan and Kate and . . .'

There was instant understanding in Lucky Jack's eyes. 'Come with me, young Leo,' he said, unable to keep amusement from his voice. 'Your sister is *asking* that you see the inside of the *Gold Nugget*! Such an occasion is never likely to happen again so we'd best take advantage of it!.'

'I didn't know the auction was going to be *tonight*,' Lettie said to Lilli as they began to walk in Josh Nelson's wake. 'I thought we'd be here for a few days first. Neither Susan or Kate are in any fit condition for such an ordeal.'

They had stepped onto a shaded boardwalk and their heels were playing a tom-tom on the hollow floor. Every other falsefronted building seemed to be a saloon. Doors opened and closed constantly, releasing peals of tinny piano music and laughter. Many men they passed doffed their hats as if they knew them. Others leered. All of them obviously knew exactly why they were in Dawson.

'Perhaps if we tell Mr Nelson that Kate is ill he'll abandon whatever plans he's made,' Lilli said, wondering

216

how on earth they had all been so foolish or desperate to get into such a situation.

In front of them, Edie's hand was securely in Marietta's. Miss Nettlesham was walking hard behind them, still clutching tight hold of Edie's by-now sodden handkerchief. Susan was walking straight and tall and heavy-footedly. Kate still seemed to be in a trance, so totally withdrawn from what was going on around her that Lilli was beginning to seriously fear for her sanity.

Apart from saloons they passed tin shops, hardware shops, grocers' shops, barbers' shops and tobacconists. At last Josh Nelson announced with a flourish, 'Here we are, ladies! The heart of Dawson! The *Phoenix*! Here you can prettify yourselves up ready to meet all the hopeful husbands at seven sharp.'

Even Lettie blanched. 'Lord in heaven,' she said as she stepped into the *Phoenix's* gaudy interior, 'What have we gotten into?'

She wasn't the only one wondering what they had all gotten into. With his kit-bag resting easily on his shoulder Ringan had watched the scene at the dock-side between Josh Nelson and Lilli and her friends with increasing perturbation. His disquiet wasn't on Lilli's account. Lilli, he knew, was not going to have to suffer the indignity of being auctioned off in marriage to the highest bidder. His disquiet was for three of the other girls. The heavy-featured, dark-haired girl who, when they had been aboard the *Senator*, had seemed to be on such agreeable terms with the clergyman; the dignified, pretty girl he had seen in the company of Peregrine Lister; and Edie. The heavy-featured girl was obviously in a state of deep distress. Peregrine Lister's former companion looked physically ill. And Edie looked pathetically bewildered.

When yet another distressed young woman had joined their ranks, shepherded by Lilli, his disquiet had deepened into anxious concern. None of the lassies looked as though they were going willingly with the marriage bureau's representative, and he didn't blame them. With

217

his bulldog expression, carefully oiled and parted hair and dark, curled moustache, the gent in question looked more like a pimp than a respectable employee of a respectable establishment.

Lilli had assured him that Edie wasn't going to be put at the mercy of the brute who had tried to take advantage of her aboard the *Senator*, or of any other oaf; that Lucky Jack's business partner, the lustrous looking Kitty Dufresne, was going to pay off the marriage bureau representative and engage Edie as a maid.

Watching Edie as she trooped trustingly off in the representative's wake, her hand in Marietta's, Ringan hoped to God Kitty Dufresne didn't let Edie down. And if she did? The blunt angle of his jaw tightened. If she did then other arrangements would have to be made. And he would have to make them.

Lucky Jack's jaw was almost as tense as Ringan's. The instant he had begun his walk up Front Street, towards the *Gold Nugget*, he had been aware of the vast change that had taken place in Dawson. The same hodge-podge of banners, pennants, signs and placards, suspended from doors and windows and slung on poles across the street, advertised mining exchanges and gold-dust buyers, but the sense of fevered excitement had gone. Dawson was no longer the centre of the Gold Rush world. That honour was now, quite obviously, Nome's.

By the time he reached the *Gold Nugget's* swing saloon doors, he had determined to head off to Nome at the earliest opportunity. Kitty would either have to see sense and accompany him or she would have to remain in Dawson without him. He thought of the eight hundred mile or so voyage down the Yukon to its mouth. If he were to make the journey in time to be able to cross the Norton Sound to Nome before autumn ice made the Sound unnavigable, then he was going to have to leave immediately. And he was going to have to leave well-supplied.

'I've got a lot of business to attend to, young Leo,' he said apologetically as they stepped into what had

218

been the city's most popular and prosperous saloon. 'I'm going to have to leave you to your own devices for a little while.'

'That's all right.' Leo was gazing around at his surroundings in rapture. A real saloon! There was a long, curving, mahogany bar, a host of green-baized tables, great big posters showing Gentleman Jim Corbett trying to regain his heavy-weight title and Frank Slavin, 'The Sydney Cornstalk', winning the Empire's heavyweight championship. There was also a host of men at the tables and, even though it was only the middle of the afternoon, a piano was being played and lots of pretty ladies in silk and satin were circulating between the tables.

Lucky Jack lifted Leo onto the bar. 'You'll be able to see everything that's going on from here, young Leo. Gerry will see you're alright for lemonade.'

The bar-man gave Leo a wink and then said, 'Takings are down, Mr Coolidge, but then I reckon you've guessed that already.'

'It's nothing to fret about, Gerry,' Lucky Jack said easily, 'We'll do what we always do. Pack up and move on.'

'And Miss Kitty?' Gerry queried, continuing to clean glasses.

'And Kitty too,' Lucky Jack responded, not having time to express his doubts on such a ticklish subject.

Gerry raised an eyebrow slightly but said nothing. Lucky Jack, having ascertained Leo was in safe hands, headed up the stairs, taking them two at a time and acknowledging noisy greetings every step of the way.

'So it's a lemonade, is it?' Gerry said to Leo, wondering what in tarnation Lucky Jack was doing with a youngster in tow. 'You a relative of Lucky Jack's, son?'

Leo shook his head, 'No. But I might be when Lucky Jack marries Lilli.'

A glass dropped from Gerry's hand and shattered on the floor. '*Marries*? Lucky Jack? Now who in tarnation's been feeding you that garbage? And who's Lilli? A new dance-hall girl?'

Leo shook his head. 'No,' he said, watching in fascination as, on a nearby table, chips clicked on green baize. 'She's my sister and she's a Peabody bride. Or she was,' he added, wishing he understood things a little better. 'Because if she's going to marry Lucky Jack, I don't suppose she's a Peabody bride any longer.'

'I wish I'd never heard the word Peabody bride,' Susan was saying bitterly. 'I only thought of becoming one because a friend of mine, Harriet Berton, was a Peabody bride. Like me, she was a kindergarten teacher, and like me she was nearly thirty and had given up all hope of marriage. Then she went to the marriage bureau and married Daniel.'

'And were she and her husband happy?' Lettie asked, sitting close to a window so that she could see the activity in the street below.

'Yes.' The speaker was Lilli and everyone looked at her in astonishment. 'I read about Harriet's marriage in the San Francisco *Examiner*. There was a wedding photograph of them and they were obviously very happy.'

'But why was their photograph in *The Examiner*?' Marietta asked, puzzled.

'Because Daniel Berton went to Nome, struck it rich and had just returned to San Francisco with his bride to invest his new-found wealth in real estate,' Lilli said, remembering the moment in the cable-car when she had read the Bertons' story; remembering how, so soon afterwards, she had met Lucky Jack for the first time.

From the barn of a room beneath them came the sound of loud hurdy-gurdy music and male laughter.

'I don't think I like it here,' Edie said tremulously, looking round the shabbily ornate room they had been cooped up in ever since Josh Nelson had left them to share a bottle of bourbon with Lucky Jack. 'I liked it better on the boat. I liked it better when Mr Saskatchewan Stan told his funny stories and made me laugh.'

There was a heavy silence. All of them had liked it better on the boat. On the boat, for a little while at least, it had seemed as if nearly all their stories were going to have happy endings. Lucky Jack was going to pay off Josh Nelson for Lilli and Marietta and marry Lilli. Kitty Dufresne was going to pay off Josh Nelson for Edie and employ her as a maid. Susan had been hopeful of becoming the Reverend Mrs Jenkinson. Kate had been hopeful of becoming Lady Lister. Rosalind Nettlesham had had dreams of marrying a gentleman. Now, with only an hour to go before the process of marrying them off began, half those hopes lay in ashes and only one pay-off had been achieved.

'It will be all right,' Lilli said, knowing that Edie's problem was in the forefront of all their minds. 'Kitty won't forget her promise. I know she won't.'

'And Rosalind is all right,' Lettie said practically. 'She signed a completely different contract to ours and she has enough money to pay for an immediate passage back to San Francisco.'

'But I don't *want* to go back to San Francisco!' Rosalind Nettlesham wailed. 'I told everyone I was getting married. I told everyone my husband-to-be was practically the *mayor* of Dawson!'

'Then you're going to have to think up another fairy-story to tell them,' Marietta said unsympathetically, 'and while you're doing it, just be grateful that in another few minutes' time you're not going to have to go down to the dance-hall and be sold to the highest bidder like Susan and Kate and Lettie and Lilli.'

Lilli's pupils dilated so wide her blue eyes seemed black. 'Me?' she queried in a voice that seemed to come from a very great distance. 'Don't you mean yourself, Marietta? You said Lucky Jack had made arrangements for my pay off with Josh Nelson and that Josh Nelson wouldn't accept a second pay-off from him. A pay-off for yourself. That's why Lucky Jack asked Josh Nelson to join him for a drink at the *Gold Nugget*, so that he could persuade Josh Nelson to accept a pay off for you as well.'

Marietta shook her head, her pekinese eyes full of pain. 'No,' she said bleakly. 'I said that Nelson would only accept one pay off. I never said who it was for.'

'And it was for you?' Lilli's voice was a croak. Why hadn't she asked? Why hadn't she realised?'

'But Lucky Jack won't let you down,' Edie said comfortingly, not really understanding all the anxious talk about pay-offs, understanding only that her friends were happy no longer and that *their* unhappiness was making *her* feel unhappy.

Lilli thought of Lucky Jack neglecting to keep an eye on Leo on the *Senator*, of his not thinking to help them when they disembarked at Skagway, at his forgetting his promise to take them to the rapids. Her clasped hands tightened together until her knuckles were white. 'Oh sweet heaven!' she prayed inwardly, 'don't let me down this time, Lucky Jack! Please, please, *please*, don't be playing cards now, not when I really need you!'

Lottie, who had been sitting next to Kate giving her what silent comfort she could, was equally appalled. Lucky Jack's intentions were always well-meant, but experience had taught there was often a disastrous gap between his intentions and their fulfilment.

'Something is beginning to happen,' Lettie said suddenly from her viewpoint at the window. 'A crowd's beginning to gather.'

The music from downstairs had also changed in tone. Now there was the sound of a tinkling piano, scraping fiddles and blaring horns.

'Oh, it's all so vulgar!' Rosalind Nettlesham moaned, rocking herself backwards and forwards slightly, her brown tailored jacket still crisply buttoned, her hands still immaculately gloved.

'Open the window, Lettie,' Marietta said, 'Let's hear what's going on.'

Lettie pushed the window open and they were instantly inundated with a cacophony of noise. Dogs were barking, huskies howling, a newsboy was selling papers, crying over and over again 'The *Nugget*! The *Nugget*! The dear little *Nugget*!' A dance hall caller was shouting through a megaphone, 'Come to the *Phoenix*, boys! Come to the *Phoenix*! The brides are here and if it's a wife you're wanting, all you have to do is shout your bid!'

'I cannot believe Harriet Dutton endured such a hell,' Susan said, beads of perspiration gleaming on her incipient moustache. 'I must have been mad to have walked across Mrs Peabody's threshold. Insane.'

'Susan, I . . .' Lettie began and then the door was flung open.

'Well, ladies, have your prettified yourselves?' Josh Nelson demanded, looking round at them and seeing quite clearly that they hadn't. A couple of 'em, of course, didn't need to. The dark-haired girl in the white lace shirtwaist, for instance, and the pale-looking girl in the midnight-blue dress and the saucy ginger-haired piece. He reminded himself that the saucy ginger-haired piece wasn't for auction, having already been expensively purchased by Lucky Jack.

He hooked his thumbs in his vest, surveying his goods, relieved that Lucky Jack had been too busy with his own affairs to carry out his promise to share a bottle of bourbon with him. If Lucky Jack had done, as sure as eggs were eggs, he'd have thought of some way of persuading him to accept a pay off for the other looker and then where would he have been? Looking at Susan he groaned. How the hell was he going to slide any money into his palm where she was concerned? He'd be lucky if he even recouped her fare for Mrs Peabody.

'Come on then, this is the moment you've been waiting for,' he exhorted, beckoning them towards the open doorway, 'But not you,' he nodded his head in the direction of Marietta. 'You can stay here and look after the kiddie. And not you,' his eyes had flicked towards Rosalind Nettlesham. 'You shouldn't be here at all. Your husband-to-be was supposed to meet you off the boat.'

Lettie rose from her seat near the window and crossed the room. Watching her, Lilli realised that out of all of them, she was the only one who had appreciated right from the outset what the realities of being a Peabody bride would be. And she was the only one of them

223

still quite willing to fulfil her contract to the marriage bureau.

Susan rose clumsily to her feet and, taking Kate gently by the arm, began to walk with her towards the door.

Lilli stood up slowly. 'I think you've made a mistake, Mr Nelson,' she said through parched lips. 'You only told Miss Rivere and Miss Nettlesham they were to remain behind. You should have also stipulated Miss Hobson and myself.'

Josh Nelson's eyebrows rose towards his slickly oiled hairline. He knew darn well that one of the remaining girls was under the impression Coolidge was going to pay him off for her, because he'd attempted to do so at the dock and, having failed, had announced his intention of doing so over a bottle of bourbon at the *Gold Nugget*. He hadn't, however, realised that Coolidge intended trying to pay him off for *two* more girls. And looking at the dumpy, blank-faced Miss Hobson he couldn't even begin to believe it.

He opened his mouth to tell the young woman facing him so, and then checked himself. Her eyes had a captivating slant, as did the soft tilt of her brows, but there was nothing soft in her expression. Rather, there was a fierce intelligence that threatened trouble.

'No doubt Lucky Jack is downstairs by now, ma'am. When we get downstairs and see him we can solve all your little problems.'

It was a blatant lie but he told it with practised ease.

'And Edie?' The words were like a whip-lash and they came from the saucy ginger-haired piece.

Presuming correctly that Edie was the dumpy, simple-looking girl he said smoothly, 'If Mr Coolidge was going to come to some arrangement with me about Miss Hobson then no doubt he'll do so at the same time he clarifies Miss Stullen's situation.'

'It isn't Mr Coolidge who wishes to pay you off for Miss Hobson. It's Miss Dufresne.'

Josh Nelson felt a shaft of relief. At least now he didn't have to worry about Lucky Jack's sanity.

'The same thing applies ma'am,' he said soothingly, knowing the sooner he separated the girl he was speaking to from the simple-looking girl, the better. 'Now, ladies. If you'd just come with me . . .'

'I don't believe him,' Marietta said tautly to Lilli. 'I don't believe either Lucky Jack or Kitty are in the building.'

Neither did Lilli. 'Find them,' she said, trying to keep the panic she was feeling out of her voice. 'Find them and bring them here, Marietta. Quickly!'

Marietta turned to Edie, 'Do you remember when I said there might come a time when I wouldn't be able to be with you, Edie? Well, this is it. I want you to go with Susan and Lilli and Lettie and Kate. And there's no need to get frightened. I'm going to come back for you and I'm not going to let anything horrid happen to you. I promise.'

With her little monkey face a mask of determination she pushed her way past Josh Nelson and ignoring his cries of protest, ran fleet-footedly down the stairs.

'Stay with Miss Nettlesham,' Lilli said to Lottie.

Lottie nodded, careful not to verbally make a promise she knew she was going to break.

Susan and Kate were already at the door. Feeling as if she were about to walk into the jaws of hell, Lilli took hold of Edie's hand and crossed the room to join them.

225

Chapter Fourteen

Leo was having the time of his life. Gerry, in starched shirt and apron, a white waistcoat drawing attention to his flamboyant diamond stickpin, kept him regularly supplied with lemonade, introducing him to all and sundry as 'Lucky Jack's new sidekick'.

Gamblers and miners obligingly took him round the tables, educating him in the niceties of faro, poker, dice and roulette.

When his magic lady entered the saloon, escorted by a veritable platoon of men carrying her steamer trunks, a roar of welcome went up so deafening Leo thought it must have been heard in Skagway.

Kitty had dressed up for her return in a glorious hat fairly dripping willow plumes. The plumes tickled Leo's nose as she chucked him under the chin and kissed his cheek.

'It hasn't taken long for you to find where all the action in Dawson takes place,' she said, amusement thick in her voice. 'Is there any champagne in that lemonade and if not, why not? Gerry! A little champagne for my friend here. Not too much but enough to make him feel a part of things.'

'Lucky Jack's upstairs,' Gerry said, topping up Leo's glass with the *Gold Nugget's* sixty dollars a quart best. 'Seems like he's all set to ship out for Nome.'

The radiance drained from Kitty's peaches and cream complexion. 'Is he?' she said, such a queer note in her voice Leo wondered if she was perhaps not feeling very well. 'Well I'm not, Gerry. My days of chasing rainbows are over.'

Abruptly she turned away from the mirror-backed bar

and mounted the stairs, the heavy emerald silk of her travelling dress swirling around her ankles.

Leo was plunged into disappointment, but not for long. A man dressed in fringed buckskin, with black locks hanging to his shoulders, began telling him how, every evening at eight o'clock, he gave a shooting display, his *pièce de résistance* being to shoot glass balls from between the thumb and forefinger of his pretty blonde wife.

Leo was just about to ask him for a demonstration when Lord Lister entered the bar, his handsome face taut and strained. 'A double shot of whiskey,' he said peremptorily to Gerry and then, to Leo, 'You shouldn't be in here, y'know. You should be with your sister.'

Assuming, quite rightly, that Lord Lister was referring to Lilli and not Lottie, Leo said, 'I can't be with her. She's with all the other Peabody brides and Mr Nelson has taken them to the *Phoenix.*'

Lord Lister knocked his whiskey back in two swift gulps. He had entered the *Gold Nugget* intent on becoming drunk in the shortest time possible and he wasn't going to let even Leo stand in his way. Affianced! The words rang in his memory like thunderclaps. The quality that had first attracted him to Kate had been her shining, moral integrity. It had made a welcome change from the worldly sophistication he was accustomed to. And she hadn't been shiningly moral after all. All the time she had been accepting his advances she had been affianced. Somewhere, here in Dawson, was the man she had been faithless to; the man she was still intent on marrying.

'Peabody brides? What the devil are they?' he asked, dragging his attention back to Leo.

Leo hesitated, not quite sure. Seeing his difficulty Gerry said, 'Mail-order brides. Respectable women are in short supply in Dawson and women keen on getting hitched are shipped up here by the Peabody Marriage Bureau. There's usually a fair old scramble when Nelson auctions 'em off.'

Lord Lister set his empty glass down on the bar, too incredulous to ask for it to be refilled. Lilli Stullen a mail order bride! Lilli Stullen, a girl who could have her pick of men, being auctioned off as if she were a slave in a Turkish market-place! 'I don't believe it,' he said flatly. 'Why the devil would a girl like your sister become a mail-order bride?

Leo had listened in to enough conversations to have a very good idea. 'My uncle didn't like her and wouldn't let her live with us anymore and so we ran away,' he said succinctly, 'Kate and Lettie ran away too.'

'*Kate*?' In a swift, disbelieving movement, Lord Lister sent his empty glass skidding across the polished surface of the bar.

Leo nodded. 'Kate didn't run away because of her uncle,' he said, trying to remember all he had overheard and not understood, 'she ran away because of her brother. And it wasn't because he didn't like her. It was because he liked her too much and . . .'

'*Jesus God*!'

Too late Leo remembered that Kate had told Lord Lister she was affianced, though just why she had told him such an untruth he wasn't quite sure. One thing he was sure of, though, was that she hadn't wanted to tell him such a lie. Telling it had made her ill.

'And I suppose she thought you wouldn't like her anymore if you knew and so she fibbed about having a fiancé and . . .'

Lord Lister was no longer listening to him. He was striding out of the saloon with the speed and urgency of a man bent on a life and death mission.

Seconds later, over and above the noisy shouting and laughter at the bar and the tables, voices could be heard in furious argument, one of them a woman's.

'There's trouble afoot,' Gerry said to Leo, his eyes flicking towards the top of the broad, central staircase. 'Kitty's reached the end of the line where moving on is concerned. And Lucky Jack's going to be moving on until the Second Trump.'

At a nearby table a faro player was saying loudly in

disgust, 'Well, that's the way I made it, and that's the way it's gone, so what the hell!'

And then, simultaneously, Marietta hurtled through the *Gold Nugget's* swing doors and Kitty began to storm down the stairs.

'Josh Nelson's intent on auctioning Edie!' Marietta said urgently, panting for breath. 'If you don't come quickly, Miss Dufresne, Edie's going to find herself married to The Pig!'

'Oh no she isn't,' Kitty said grim-faced, not pausing in momentum as she reached the bottom of the stairs and began to walk quickly towards Marietta. 'I've just about had enough of the male sex for one day and The Pig is one member of it who's not going to get things his own way!'

Lottie was almost as out-of-breath as Marietta. Within seconds of Lilli being herded with Kate and Susan and Edie and Lettie downstairs to the *Phoenix's* dance-floor, she had left Miss Nettlesham and run out of the building. She had to find Ringan. Ringan would know what to do. He always knew what to do. The problem was, where to find him?

Front Street was thick with men and the vast majority of them seemed to be heading towards the *Phoenix*. She began to run down the boardwalk in the direction of the river. Ringan would probably have rented a room at one of the hotels. On her way to the *Phoenix* she had seen several, *The Fairview*, *The Palace*, *The Majestic*.

The din from the saloons rattled up and down the thoroughfare. On an open platform two young girls, little older than herself, were singing 'A Bird in a Gilded Cage' to the accompaniment of a wheezing portable organ played by a big beefy woman with a pompadour hairstyle. From a restaurant there came the improbable sound of a string orchestra playing *Cavalleria Rusticana*. Everywhere there was a sea of signs proclaiming, 'Gold! Gold! Gold dust bought and sold . . . Jewelry . . . Fine diamond work . . .

229

Watches . . . Tintypes . . . Cigars . . . Souvenirs and fine native gold . . .'

And then, just as she was about to race inside *The Fairview*, she saw him. He was striding down the board-walk on the opposite side of the wide, busy street, head and shoulders above the mass of men swarming around him, his thick shock of red hair as fiery as a beacon.

'*Ringan*!' she shouted, her voice breaking on a sob of relief as she sprinted across the street towards him, dodging through the crowds, avoiding a horse and trap by inches. '*Ringan*!'

He was heading in the direction she was coming from but the instant he heard her voice he halted, scanning the street for a sight of her.

She burst from the throng on the street and leapt up on to the broadwalk.

'*Oh, Ringan*! Please come quickly! Lucky Jack hasn't paid Mr Nelson off for Lilli and Mr Nelsn is going to auction her as a Peabody bride!'

The dance hall at the *Phoenix* was full of smoke, men, noise and laughter. On a rickety stage five upright chairs were positioned and Josh Nelson led his unwilling flock towards them. A huge roar went up from the male audience as he did so. Lilli flinched. This was worse than anything she had ever imagined. It was unspeakable. Vile beyond description.

Edie's hand gripped hers tightly, 'I want Marietta,' she whimpered. 'I want Mr Saskatchewan Stan.'

Vainly Lilli's eye scanned the sea of faces for a glimpse of Marietta or Kitty or Lucky Jack. Instead she saw The Pig. He was in the forefront of the men standing ten and twelve deep on the sawdust-covered dance-floor. Her heart contracted. What was about to happen was so monstrous she couldn't even begin to imagine how she had ever thought it could possibly be otherwise. And Lucky Jack could have saved her from it. He had promised to save her from it. And he had reneged on his promise. He had let her down in the most gross, unforgivable way possible.

Bitterly she wondered if he had done so because a card game had prior claim on his attention. Whatever the reason, whatever his eventual excuse, she would never again think of him as being her Fate, her Destiny. However scintillating his vivid charm, he had none of the qualities that really mattered. He wasn't dependable. And as Kitty Dufresne had so perceptively pointed out, if being kind clashed with his own needs and pleasures, he wasn't even kind.

'Come on gentlemen! This is it! This is the moment you've been waiting for! Which of these lovely-looking ladies are you going to take to Nome as your bride?'

'Not the one in the middle!' some wit called out coarsely, referring to Susan.

There was a gale of laughter.

Lilli couldn't bear to look across and witness Susan's suffering. Rage was licking through her. Rage so hot she thought it was going to consume her.

'I think this lovely lady should be the first to start the ball rolling,' Josh Nelson announced, stationing himself behind Kate's chair. 'Now, gentlemen! You couldn't ask for a fairer bride than Miss Kate Salway! What about a thousand dollar bid for a start?'

'What about ten thousand dollars?' a clipped, cut-glass English accent suggested tightly.

Uproar broke out as the crowd made way for Lord Lister. In cream silk shirt and khaki flannels, looking as different from the other men in the dance-hall as if he came from another planet, Lord Lister vaulted on to the platform.

'Ten thousand?' Josh Nelson repeated, not knowing whether to be pleased at the unusually high bid or angry that, as it was unlikely to be topped, there was no entertainment mileage in it. 'Gold or cash?'

'Cash,' Lord Lister said tersely.

'Then unless there's a raise on ten thousand I guess we're one down and four to go,' Josh Nelson announced to his barracking audience.

There was no raise on ten thousand dollars. Lord Lister

231

bent solicitously over Kate. 'Kate?' he said gently. 'Kate? It's me, Perry.'

Dazedly she stared up at him, her face blank.

'It's me, Kate,' he said again, realising how deep her mental withdrawal had become. 'I love you, Kate. We're going to be married. We're going to be together for always.'

Her eyes opened wide, understanding beginning to dawn. 'Perry?' she said uncertainly, 'Perry? Is it really you? Have you really come to take me away?'

'Yes, my darling,' he said thickly, 'And you're never going to be on your own again, not for as long as I live.'

She gave a little cry, her hands fluttering from her lap, sliding up and around his neck. Tenderly he lifted her up in his arms and her head fell against his shoulder. Watching, tears glittering on her lashes, Lilli doubted if Kate would remember a single moment of the last hideous hours.

'Three cheers for the happy couple!' Josh Nelson exhorted and then, as the cheers willingly rang out, he stationed himself behind Edie's chair.

Even before he had opened his mouth The Pig was swaggering forward, thumbs tucked down the broad leather belt at his waist.

'Five hundred dollars,' he shouted aggressively.

'Six hundred,' someone else shouted.

'Seven hundred.'

It was The Pig again. He had walked forward from the crowd and there was now no way Edie could remain ignorant of his presence.

'Seven hundred and fifty,' a third voice chimed in.

Josh Nelson grinned. Simple looking girls were always popular and this one, in her childish, too-tight dress, had the advantage of being as pleasingly plump as a partridge.

'Eight hundred,' The Pig bellowed, clambering up on to the platform.

Edie clutched even tighter hold of Lilli's hand. 'Don't let him frighten me!' she begged. 'Oh, where is Marietta, Lilli? Where is Mr Saskatchewan Stan?

Lilli didn't know. What she did know, though, was that she wasn't going to allow the present obscenity to continue. Dragging her hand from Edie's she sprang to her feet.

'Stop this!' she said in raging tones to Josh Nelson. 'Miss Hobson is little more than a child and she isn't here willingly! She was sent here against her will!'

'Makes no difference,' Josh Nelson said, enjoying the interruption because he knew his audience were enjoying it. 'A little unwillingness can be right pleasing, can't it boys? Do I have any bids on eight hundred? No? Then the little lady here is going, going *gone* for eight hundred dollars!'

The money was peanuts but he didn't care. It covered the cost of her passage and left enough over to split nicely between himself and Mrs Peabody. And it brought crowds into the *Phoenix*. Crowds who would still be there, drinking and gambling, at five and six in the morning.

'*Lilli!*' Edie screamed as The Pig lunged towards her.

'*Nelson!*' Kitty shouted, men parting before her like the Red Sea.

'*Edie!*' Saskatchewan Stan bawled, his roly-poly figure hurtling across the sawdust-covered floor in front of the makeshift stage.

As dozens of pairs of willing hands lifted Kitty on to the right hand of the stage, Saskatchewan Stan scrambled up onto the left hand of it.

The din from the audience was deafening. Kitty was one of the most popular figures in Dawson and what the hell she was doing in a dance-hall rival to her own, no-one could begin to figure out.

'What the hell . . .' Josh Nelson began as Kitty marched to the centre of the stage and stood, facing the audience, her hands on her hips.

'I want you all to know what's going on!' she announced in a voice that still managed to remain throatily enticing. 'I want Miss Hobson as a personal maid and I'm prepared to stump up a handsome pay-off for her. If any of you gents make it difficult for me, none of you will ever step across

233

the threshold of the *Gold Nugget* or the *Mother-Lode* ever again!'

'I'll make it difficult for you!' The Pig roared, dragging a terrified Edie to her feet by her arm. 'A thousand dollars, Nelson! See if Coolidge's tart is willing to top that!'

'If she does you won't be able to outbid her!' Saskatchewan Stan roared, barrelling across the stage towards him.

'A thousand and five dollars,' Kitty said, reading Stan's intentions exactly.

'A thousand and . . .' The Pig began.

He didn't get any further. Saskatchewan Stan drew back his fist and then rocketed it at The Pig's jaw. The shouts and cheers and stamping feet, shook the walls.

'And now this little lady is coming with me,' Kitty said to an outraged Josh Nelson.

Hiding his fury with difficulty, Josh made a show of shrugging his shoulders and smiling. Kitty wasn't fooled. She'd made an enemy but she didn't care. She'd had enough of men to last her a lifetime. None of them were worth a cent. Not even Lucky Jack.

As The Pig's cohorts dragged him away by his heels she led Edie by the hand to where Marietta was waiting and where Saskatchewan Stan shortly joined them, Josh Nelson regained control of the proceedings yet again.

'We're having quite an evening, aren't we, boys? Two brides out of the running and only three to go!' Maliciously he strode towards Susan's chair. No-one would be fighting to put an end to the bidding for Miss Bumby, that was for sure! 'And now we have a lady who knows all about living in the Yukon! A lady so refined the man marrying her will find himself hob-nobbing with Commissioners and Governors! Now boys, who will start of the bidding? Have we to start it at a thousand dollars?'

'You'd do better starting it at five hundred and decreasing till you get a taker,' someone shouted coarsely occasioning a storm of laughter.

'Now, boys. Let's have a little gallantry please. A thousand dollars. Am I bid a thousand dollars?'

He was not. To his utter astonishment, and to the

disbelief of his audience, he was bid five thousand dollars. It was the entire wealth at the bidder's command and if he had had more, he would have bid more. Not because such a bid was necessary in order for him to be assured of gaining Miss Bumby as his bride, but because in his eyes she was a pearl without price; because it was his way of showing her how much he respected and honoured and loved her.

'Sweet saints' alive!' It's the new minister!' someone shouted.

As the Reverend Mr Jenkinson approached the stage, the laughter and cat-calling reached new heights. Lilli doubted if either he, or Susan, heard any of it.

With tears of happiness streaming down her face Susan had risen to her feet. With a dignity that wrung Lilli's heart the Reverend Mr Jenkinson mounted the stage and walked towards her.

'My dear Miss Bumby,' he said, taking both her hands in his, 'I would be so proud . . . so honoured . . . if you would agree to become my wife.'

The tears that had glittered on Lilli's lashes when Lord Lister had lifted Kate in his arms, now blurred her vision altogether. Part of the nightmare was over, thank God. Kate was safe and secure, loved by the man she loved with all her heart. As was Susan. Only she, herself, had not been claimed by the man she had believed loved her.

Her eyes no longer even roamed the sea of faces, looking for him. He wasn't going to come. She knew it just as surely as she knew she had never truly loved him; that she had merely been foolishly and girlishly infatuated with him, intoxicated by his surface glamour and Greek god good looks.

'And now for a little bit of real business!' Josh Nelson was announcing. 'This little lady,' he stood behind Lettie's chair, resting his hands on her shoulders, 'this little lady has come North to find herself a husband. She's darn pretty and worth her weight in gold. Now, belly up boys and let the best man win.'

Lilli looked across to Lettie in anguish. Lettie *did*

look pretty. Her dishwater-blonde hair was brushed until it shone, twisted high into an elegant chignon. Her raspberry-pink dress shimmered in the lamplight. Her composure was total. With her hands clasped in her lap, her knees and feet primly together, her back straight, she looked for all the world as if she were in a church, not a tawdry, sawdust-floored dance-hall.

As the bidding grew heated and frenzied Lilli reflected that at least Lettie wasn't being humiliated in quite the way Susan had been humiliated. Men aplenty wanted her as a wife. And Lettie wanted to be a wife. She wanted the respectability she believed it would bring; a home of her own; a new beginning in a raw, wild country she found healingly clean and pure.

'Fifteen thousand!'

'Sixteen thousand'

The clamour was a physical assault on the ear-drums. What would happen when it was her turn? Would Kitty Dufresne perhaps come to her rescue? Through the smoky haze she could see Kitty, one arm still protectively around Edie's shoulders, Marietta and Saskatchewan Stan standing close by. She wondered if Edie would eventually marry Saskatchewan Stan. She wondered how she could ever have been so romantically foolish, so idiotically unrealistic, to have ever believed that becoming a mail-order bride was a solution to the problem of making a home for Leo and Lottie.

The clamour had become a barrage of sound. A young man was striding towards Lettie's chair. An auburn-haired clean-shaven young man with broad shoulders and slim hips. As he stood a little awkwardly in front of Lettie, Lilli could see that his eyes were brown. Brown as pecans with blunt black lashes. His nose was straight as a knife. His mouth well-shaped.

Lilli felt relief almost swamp her. If he had ridden on stage on a white horse he couldn't have filled the bill as a rescuing knight more perfectly.

'Pleased to meet you, ma'am,' he was saying in a honey-dark voice to Lettie. 'My name's Will Bennett and

I'm a New Foundlander, heading out to Nome. I reckon I could provide real well for you, ma'am. I'm not much good with words, but I think you're pretty as a picture and I'd be right proud to have you as my wife.'

Cheers rang the rafters, hats were thrown into the air. Despite their rough-hewn appearance and manners it seemed that the audience possessed a strong, sentimental streak.

'And now boys!' Josh Nelson was hollering, 'Now we come to the last, but by no means the least, of the brides looking for husbands tonight.' He rested his sweaty palms on Lilli's shoulders and she wrenched herself out of his grasp. Fresh cheers went up. Smiling as though Lilli's reaction had been part of a pre-arranged joke, Josh Nelson continued, 'It isn't often we get such a beauty east of the Chilkoot and such an opportunity might never come again! She has a kid brother and sister in her care but that shouldn't be much of a disadvantage to all you men itching to get hitched. So come on, don't be shy, give me your bids!'

Dimly Lilli was aware that somewhere, someone had begun to cry. It wasn't herself. She was far, far beyond tears. Who was it then? Was it Susan? Kate? She thought how ironical it was that out of all her friends she, alone, was not going to have a happy ending. Perhaps, if it hadn't been for Lucky Jack, she might have had a happy ending. If it hadn't been for his promise to spare her from this debacle, her certainty that even if he hadn't succeeded in paying Josh Nelson off for her he would have been here, outbidding every man in Dawson for her, she would never have crossed the *Phoenix's* threshold. She would have tried to raise the money to pay Josh Nelson off. Even if it had taken her the rest of her life to pay off the debt it would have been worth it. She would have worked as a maid or a dance-hall girl. She would have done anything, anything at all . . .'

'Seventeen thousand dollars!'
'Eighteen thousand dollars!'
Nauseously she realised that she was bringing in the

highest bids of the evening. Who were the men making them? Was it the man clutching his poke of gold fiercely in his right hand, his cloth cap, a little too small for him, perched squarely across his bullet head? Was it the square-faced, sombre-eyed man, with a thickly knitted tie, heavy boots, and shapeless, high-waisted trousers?

'Going! Going! Go . . .'

'*Twenty-five thousand dollars*!'

Lilli gripped onto the hard seat of her chair. She knew that voice. She would have known it anywhere.

There were no topping bids and he began to shoulder his way through to the front of the audience, his thick red hair, springy as heather, gleaming copper-gold beneath the light of the *Phoenix's* oil-lamps.

Something very like hysteria bubbled up in her throat. Ringan wasn't a gold-rich prospector. How could he even begin to pay Josh Nelson twenty-five thousand dollars? And why should he even be prepared to? Unless . . . unless . . . The breath was tight in her chest as she thought of the reason Ringan Cameron might think twenty-five thousand dollars well spent.

With her emotions in tumult, dizzy with relief, she watched him vault on to the stage, his big body as limber as a cat's.

'I hope you dinna object to this arrangement,' he said seconds later, looking down at her his grey eyes dark with concern. 'But it would seem to be the only way of getting ye out of this hell-hole.'

To a storm of hurrahs he stretched a large hand out towards her. It was like being offered a lifeline. Her hand slid into his and as he drew her to her feet she swayed against him, so great was her relief.

'Hst, now,' he said comfortingly, his arm going round her waist to support her, 'It's all over now. Ye've nothing more to trouble yourself about.'

'And now we'll have a twenty minute break, boys, before the weddings!' Josh Nelson was announcing, giving the lie to Ringan's words. 'Just long enough for the ladies to prink themselves up and put on their bridal gowns.'

If Ringan's arm hadn't been very firmly around her waist, Lilli would have fallen. 'Surely the weddings aren't going to take place here, in a dance-hall?' she said incredulously.

'Sure are, ma'am,' a man busy clearing the stage of chairs said, 'That's what folks come here for. To see lots of purty brides gittin themselves hitched.'

Ringan sprang off the stage. 'Have ye got a bridal gown?' he asked, reaching up to her, circling her waist with his hands, lifting her down to the saw-dusted floor.

'No . . . I . . . Are we really going to get married?'

He stood very still, his hands still around her waist, his thumbs and fingers almost meeting. 'As I understand it, it's part of the contract,' he said at last. 'If we renege on what Mr Nelson chooses to term the "entertainment part of the agreement" he might well consider my bid null and void.'

At the thought of what would then happen to her, Lilli shuddered. She didn't want to stand on the stage behind her, ever again. And she didn't want Ringan to remove his hands from her waist. They were standing so close that her nose was a smidgeon's distance from fitting comfortably into the small hollow at the centre of his chest. If he had wanted, he could quite easily have rested his chin on the top of her head. She was a tall girl and it was an odd sensation to have someone tower over her in such a masterful way. Odd and profoundly pleasurable. 'I think,' she said, not trusting herself to meet his eyes, 'that I would prefer it if we didn't renege on the agreement.'

He was silent for several beats of time. What his expression was she didn't know. Her eyes were still fixed very firmly on his chest. People were milling all around them but all she was aware of was the opened buttons of his green plaid shirt, the strong tendons of his neck, the smell of his shaving soap.

'Then I think, if ye dinna mind, I'd like to spruce up for the event,' he said, the very timbre of his voice sending tingles down her spine. 'Will ye excuse me for a wee while?'

'Yes,' she said, still not lifting her face to his, not daring to in case he should read her emotions in her eyes. Sweet saints' alive! Was it happening to her all over again? Was she falling heedlessly, intoxicatedly in love with man she barely knew?

As he removed his hands from her waist and turned, once again shouldering his way through the mass of humanity crammed into the *Phoenix*, she felt as if a giant fist had slammed into her solar plexus. Yes, she *was* falling heedlessly and intoxicatedly in love, but it wasn't with a man she barely knew. She knew he was brave, for she had see him dive into the mid-Pacific to save Leo's life. She knew he was dependable because always, when he had been needed, he had been there. She knew he was compassionate, for she had witnessed his compassion in the Indian camp when he had brought Nana's mother's child into the world. And she knew he was tender, for she had seen it in his eyes, felt it in his hands.

She watched him disappear through the throng. 'How could I have been so blind? So unaware?' she asked herself, breathlessly.

'*Lilli*!' Marietta threw her arms around her, hugging her joyously. 'Wasn't Mr Cameron absolutely splendid? What will happen now? When Lucky Jack gets here will he reimburse him for the cost of his bid? I wonder what on earth is delaying him? Will . . .'

'Mr Jenkinson is going to perform our marriage ceremony,' Kate said radiantly, interrupting her. 'Perry asked him if he would do so because the minister due to perform the marriages is half-drunk, and Mr Jenkinson instantly agreed.'

'Am I getting married?' Edie suddenly asked. 'Am I getting married to Mr Saskatchewan Stan? I'd like to be married to Mr Saskatchewan Stan. He makes me laugh and he makes me feel safe.'

'Wasn't it wonderful when Lord Lister strode up on to the stage and swept Kate in his arms?' Marietta said, her voice fizzing with happiness at the way everything had worked out. 'And wasn't Mr Jenkinson brave? I'm sure merely coming into the *Phoenix* was the hardest thing he's ever done!'

'I have my bridal dress in my travel-bag,' Susan said, her heavy-featured face beautiful with happiness. 'Has anyone else got one? What are you all going to wear? Has . . .'

'Perry's rushed off to buy me a wedding gown,' Kate said, her eyes glowing. 'Apparently you can buy anything you want in Dawson, twenty-four hours a day, if you have the money.'

'I'm going to get married just as I am,' Lettie said, smoothing her hand over the skirt of her raspberry-pink gown. 'Ever since Kate gave me this gown, I've been lucky and happy. I'm going to keep it for always. I'm going to wear it when my children are christened and when it's my fiftieth wedding anniversary.'

'Land's sakes!' Kitty exclaimed, her voice thick with throaty laughter. If you can still get into it then you'll be the luckiest woman in Christendom!'

'Can I marry Mr Saskatchewan Stan?' Edie asked again, tugging on Marietta's arm to gain her attention. 'I really would like to, Marietta. Truly.'

'I'm not sure you're ready for marriage yet,' Marietta said gently, 'Not even to Saskatchewan Stan.'

'You may be wrong there,' Kitty said thoughtfully. 'I know Stan well. 'He wouldn't rush Edie's fences. He'd be just as patient and understanding as was necessarry.'

'Then I think we should talk to him,' Susan said, putting her seal of approval on the idea. 'I think we should find out what his feelings are.'

Lilli stood a little apart from them all. She knew what her feelings were. She knew she didn't want Lucky Jack finally remembering about her and re-paying Ringan the amount he had bid for her. She no longer wanted to marry Lucky Jack. She wanted to marry Ringan Cameron. She wanted to marry a man she could depend on. A man who would never let her down. A man who was honourable in every sense of the word.

'I'll talk to Stan,' Kitty said, more relieved than she

liked to admit at the thought of not having Edie as her personal maid. 'And I'll get Nelson to bring a little order to the proceedings. We don't want any barracking and cat-calling and we don't want any unsuitable music. If that organist of his refuses to play something dignified I'll play the darn thing myself!'

The minute they entered the parlour-like room with its tawdry drapes and tacky atmosphere Lottie rushed to greet them. 'What happened?' she demanded near hysterically, 'Did Ringan get there in time? Why are Susan and Kate looking so happy? *What's happened?*'

'What's happened,' Marietta said as Lottie threw her arms around Lilli, 'is that you're going to be a bridesmaid four times over, possibly five, so you'd better let me re-do your braids and find some ribbon for them.'

There was a knock at the door and a member of Nelson's bar staff handed over a gold beribboned dress-box.'

'For Miss Salway,' he said unnecessarily.

'I'll have the ribboning for Lottie's hair,' Marietta said, well-pleased at such unexpected bounty. 'There's yards of it! Enough for a sash as well!'

Ten minutes later there was another brief knock and Kitty entered, her arms full of a swirl of white satin and lace.

'Stan knows the situation perfectly,' she said to the room at large. 'He says he'd cut off his hands rather than fright Edie. And he wants to marry her.' A dancing smiled dimpled her cheeks. 'He says she's the only young woman he's ever met who doesn't make him feel jittery! He says she makes him feel safe and makes him laugh! Looks like it's a match made in heaven, doesn't it.'

'I'm going to be married?' Edie asked in breathless wonder. 'I'm going to marry Mr Saskatchewan Stan and live happy ever after?'

'You sure are, sweetie,' Kitty said, laying her billowing cargo down on a chair. 'And what's more, you're going to wear a London-made ball gown for a wedding-dress.'

'Land's sakes,' Rosalind Nettlesham's pale blue eyes

nearly popped out of her head. 'Is that lace *English* lace? Is it *Honiton* lace?'

Kitty eyed Rosalind Nettlesham with interest, 'It certainly is. How come you recognised it so easily?'

There was a moment's hesitation and then, deciding there was no further point in pretending to be what she wasn't, Rosalind Nettlesham said, 'I'm a dressmaker. A very *high-class* dressmaker.'

'Are you, indeed?' Kitty said, noting the exquisite tailoring of Rosalind Nettlesham's skirt and jacket, 'Then I think it's about time we had a long conversation together.'

Fifteen minutes later Lilli was looking at three of her friends in absolute disbelief. Susan looked scarcely recognisable. Her cream silk dress was ruched high at the neck, the sleeves peaked at the shoulders and narrow at the wrist, the bell-shaped skirt flouncing into a deep frill around her ankles. A small cream pancake hat sported pale feathers and was tipped at an almost rakish angle. Her gloves were pale kid, fastened at the wrist by pearl buttons. She looked exquisitely elegant; breathtakingly happy.

Kate's dress was a glorious confection of lemon tulle and chiffon. The high-necked bodice was decorated by a shoulderwide, bosom-deep frill, a yellow satin rose nestling in its centre. Satin ribbons held the sleeves tight at the elbows and then the sleeves fell full and gauzily, emphasising the delicate slenderness of her wrists and hands. With the cascading skirt falling into a demi-train she already looked every inch a member of the British aristocracy.

It was Edie, though, who had been truly transformed. The white satin and lace ball gown made a perfect bridal gown. She no longer looked dumpy. She no longer looked simple. Kitty had brushed her hair until it shone, restraining its heavy thickness in a delicately worked snood.

'There, sweetie,' she said, teasing a few ringletting

243

tendrils to frame Edie's face, tucking tiny sprays of white bud roses to rest gently against her temples, 'You look like a princess.'

'You surely do, Edie,' Marietta said, awed by the difference Kitty had effected. 'Saskatchewan Stan is one very lucky man.'

There was a sharp rap at the door and the bar man who had brought the dress box to the room said peremptorily, 'Everyone's ready and waitin. If you ain't primped by now, you'll have to do as you are.'

'I'm primped,' Edie said, her cheeks rosy with daring, 'I'm primped more than I've ever been primped in my life!'

Their descent down the stairs to the dance-floor was in stark contrast to their previous descent. This time they were no longer deathly pale and half senseless with apprehension. This time they were giggling and chattering, glowing-eyed and radiant-faced.

'The Reverend and his lady are going to be hitched first,' Josh Nelson said, striding to meet them, a cigar still clamped in his hand, 'the minister who so kindly officiates for us here at the *Phoenix* ain't a Methodist like the Reverend, or at least he don't think he is, but he's a Protestant of some sort and now he's part ways sobered up he'll do a fine job. Seeing as how the rest of you are partial to being married by the Reverend, the Reverend will conduct the other ceremonies. Now then, where's the lady who's put such a sparkle into the Reverend's eye?'

'I'm here,' Susan said, her cream-gloved hands clasping a white leather prayer book,

Josh Nelson stared at her and blinked. The ungainly, horsey, ravaged faced woman he had offered for auction such a little while ago was unrecognisable. She looked downright pretty now. Pretty and very, very elegant.

'Well now, Ma'am,' he said recovering from his surprise, 'As your Pa ain't here to give you away, I'm going to act as a stand-in. See that bower of flowers over there? You're goin' to be married beneath it. Up to a hundred Peabody

244

brides have been married beneath that bower and darn me, if I was to marry, *I'd* git married beneath it!'

Susan turned round to Lottie. 'Are you ready, Lottie?' she asked as Lottie positioned herself behind her, her braids decorated with gold ribbon; a gold ribbon sash around her waist.

As Kitty began to play a wedding march on the organ Lottie nodded, her eyes shining. She was going to be a bridesmaid. She was going to be a bridesmaid *five* times! And she was going to be a bridesmaid for Lilli and Ringan. Ringan would be her and Leo's brother-in-law. And he would be the best brother-in-law in the whole wide world. He would teach them about birds and animals and lots and lots of other wonderful things. He would teach them to fish and they would teach him to ride. They would be as happy together as a family as they had been when their pa had been alive. Their pa would have liked Ringan. Their pa would have thought she looked a cracker in her gold hair ribbons and sash.

The sawdust-covered floor was even more crowded than it had been earlier, for dance-hall girls and barmaids had piled into the *Phoenix* to witness the weddings. Amid loud cheering and clapping the crowd parted to allow Josh Nelson, with Susan on his arm, to lead a way through.

The bower was of artificial roses heavily laced with satin ribbons and a lavish sprinkling of small gold nuggets. Mr Jenkinson, looking agonisingly self-conscious, was standing one side of it. A white-whiskered, not very cleanly dressed clergyman was swaying unsteadily on the other side of it. Lord Lister, Will Bennett and Saskatchewan Stan were standing nearby. Lord Lister was wearing a cream linen suit with a cream silk gold-embroidered vest and looked even more out of place than Mr Jenkinson. Will Bennett's auburn hair had been slicked down until it gleamed. Saskatchewan Stan sported a wild briar rose in his button-hole. Only Ringan was absent.

'Dearly beloved . . .' the *Phoenix's* tame preacher began, 'we are gathered together here . . .'

Where was he? Panic suffused her. He wouldn't have

245

let her down, as Lucky Jack would have done, because he had become embroiled in a card game. Was he not here because Lucky Jack had detained him? Was Lucky Jack insisting that *he* be her bridegroom and was he trying to persuade Ringan to accept twenty-five thousand dollars as reimbursement?

'Wilt thou have this woman to be thy wedded wife . . .' the minister was saying, still swaying alarmingly.

And what would she do if that was the case? How did she know that Ringan had ever truly wanted to marry her? How did she know that he hadn't acted as he had simply out of compassion for her?

'I take thee, Susan Alison Victoria Mary, to my wedded wife . . .' Mr Jenkinson was saying, his voice unsteady with the passion of his feelings, 'to have and to hold . . .'

She turned her head, looking away from the bridal couple to the sea of faces behind her. There was no sign of Ringan. No sign of Lucky Jack and Leo.

'I now pronounce you . . .' the minister broke off to hiccup. 'I now pronounce you man and wife.'

The congregation of gold prospectors, gamblers, dance-hall girls and bar staff gave vent to their feelings with piercing whistles and shouts of good wishes.

'And now,' Josh Nelson announced, flapping his hands to signal a respective silence was again called for, 'The Reverend Mr Jenkinson will marry Miss Letitia Walker and Mr William Bennett.'

Lilli turned once more to face the rose-encrusted bower. She was learning new things about her friends with every minute; that Susan's other names were Alison Victoria Mary; that Lettie's surname was Walker.

With quiet dignity Mr Jenkinson was asking Lettie and Will if they would promise to love and honour each other, in sickness and in health. Will Bennett produced a spanking new wedding ring from his pocket and, at the due moment, slipped it onto the fourth finger of Lettie's left hand.

Once again Lilli turned around. Once again Ringan was conspicuous only by his absence.

When Kate and Lord Lister took Lettie and Will's place, Lilli couldn't help reflecting on what the groom's family would make of the marriage when they were told of it, and of the circumstances under which it had taken place. She wondered where Kate and Lord Lister would have married if they had married in London. Perhaps the wedding would have taken place at St Margaret's, Westminster, or perhaps St George's, Hanover Square.

'With this ring I thee wed,' Lord Lister was saying in his clipped, cut-glass accent, 'with my body I thee worship, and with all my worldly goods I thee endow.'

A dance-hall girl wearing a low-cut pink and black satin dress and a belt made up of twenty-dollar gold-pieces, was dabbing at her eyes with a handkerchief. Another dance-hall girl, sporting a diamond fastened between her two front teeth, was sniffing noisily in unashamedly sentimental enjoyment.

As Lord Lister kissed his bride Lilli wondered where on earth Ringan was; what it was that was delaying him.

'He'll be here,' Lottie said confidently in the slight pause between Kate's wedding and Edie's. 'Ringan will never let you down. Not ever.'

'And now if the bridesmaid will again take her place,' Josh Nelson requested as Kitty began to play a suitably decorous piece of music on the organ.

As Edie took Josh Nelson's arm and, followed by Lottie, walked the few steps to where Saskatchewan Stan and Mr Jenkinson were waiting for her, Lilli's throat tightened. Edie was a young woman transformed. Rosily and trustingly she smiled across at her proud, roly-poly bridegroom. From now on Saskatchewan Stan would love her and protect her. From now on she would never again be hurt or frightened in the ways she had been in the past.

As the wedding service began Lilli's thoughts returned to Ringan. She hadn't needed Lottie to assure her that Ringan would never let her down. She knew that already; she knew it in her blood and in her bones. But what if Lucky Jack was delaying him? What if Lucky Jack was convincing him that her happiness would be best served if he, not Ringan, strode into the *Phoenix* to marry her?

'Is Edie the name you were christened with?' Mr Jenkinson was asking Edie gently.

Edie stared at him blankly.

Lettie stepped forward and spoke quietly to Edie. A few seconds later she said to Mr Jenkinson, 'Edie's the diminutive of Edith.'

Lottie turned her head, her eyes meeting Lilli's, a grin splitting her face. Despite the fierceness of her anxieties Lilli grinned back, remembering the moment when, in explaining what a diminutive was, they had first made friends with Lettie.

'If you would take the bride's hand in yours,' Mr Jenkinson was saying to Saskatchewan Stan.

Lilli wondered if Stan was suffering from the 'jitters'. She wondered where Kitty Dufresne had learned to play Bach so faultlessly.

'Now say after me, Edith, 'I take thee Stanley . . .'

'I take thee Stanley,' Edie said uncertainly.

'To be my lawful wedded husband,' Mr Jenkinson prompted.

Edie was silent.

'To be my lawful wedded husband,' Mr Jenkinson prompted again.

Still Edie remained silent.

Susan's fingers tightened on her prayer-book.

Marietta took a nervous step forward, ready to reassure the bride if reassurance proved to be necessary.

'What is it, Edith?' Mr Jenkinson asked gently.

'It's Stanley,' Edie said bravely, 'I don't want to marry a Stanley. I want to marry Mr Saskatchewan Stan.'

In the packed dance-hall a pin could have been heard dropping. Not one of the hardened miners or world-weary gamblers laughed or cracked any jokes at the bride's expense.

'Then so you shall,' Mr Jenkinson said, an odd note in his voice as if his throat, too, was unnaturally tight. 'I take thee, Mr Saskatchewan Stan . . .'

Edie repeated the words after him faultlessly.

Miners, gamblers, dance-hall girls and bar staff breathed a hefty sigh of relief.

From the back of the jam-packed hall came the sound of movement, as if someone had just entered and their entry was causing a stir. As Edie and Saskatchewan Stan finished making their vows the stir became a commotion.

Edie and Saskatchewan Stan, Susan, Kate and Lord Lister, Lettie and Will, Marietta and Kitty, Lottie and Rosalind Nettlesham, all turned to see what the commotion was about.

Lilli turned, too. Was it Lucky Jack? Wherever Lucky Jack went he seemed to cause a commotion. Amid cheers and whistles and shouts the crowd massing the dance-hall parted to allow the last of the bridegrooms to stride through and take his place at his bride's side.

He looked magnificent. He looked more than magnificent. He looked breathtakingly resplendent. His thick red hair shone like burnished metal, sweeping the collar of a fine lawn shirt. The front of his shirt was tucked, the sleeves full, belling into lace-trimmed wrist-frills and at his throat was a lace jabot. Instead of breeches he wore a kilt in a plaid of singing reds with a yellow line, a sporran and knee-high woollen hose. The kilt swirled around his strong calves. A dirk gleamed from the top of one of his socks. Silver buckles gleamed on his black leather shoes.

'My, oh my,' Kitty said, her eyes glazing, 'Now I know why all those Highland girls fell in love with Bonnie Prince Charlie!'

'Lord a-mighty,' Marietta said devoutly, 'how can a man in a skirt look masculine enough to suicide oneself for?'

'Oh Ringan! I knew you'd come!' Lottie cried, running towards him and clasping tightly hold of his hand.

In his other hand he incongruously held a posy of flowers. 'They're the reason I'm a wee bit late,' he said apologetically as he came to a halt in front of Lilli. 'I wanted ye to have a wedding bouquet. I've picked them myself.'

She took the posy from him with trembling fingers.

'They're forget-me-nots,' he added as his fingers touched hers. 'To match your eyes.'

In that moment, as their flesh touched, Lilli knew she loved him with all her heart. That she would love him always and forever. Without a shadow of a doubt she knew that the love she had thought she felt for Lucky Jack had been nothing but a pale imitation of the real thing. This, the unutterably magnificent, strong and certain emotion now burning through her like liquid gold, was the real thing.

'Are ye ready?' he asked gently, his face carefully expressionless.

She nodded, quite unable to speak.

Lottie stationed herself behind them and together they faced Mr Jenkinson.

'Will you please take the bride's hand in yours, Mr Cameron,' Susan's husband was saying.

He reached for her hand and she saw that beneath the frill of his cuff his wrist was lightly haired with copper. As her fingers disappeared into his substantial grasp she found herself wondering what he looked like naked; if, before the night was over, she would see him naked.

'Wilt thou have this woman to thy wedded wife . . .'

As he made the responses her fingers tightened on his. He was marrying her but she still didn't know his reason for doing so. She could only hope and pray as to his reason.

'Wilt thou love her, comfort her, honour, and keep her in sickness and in health . . .'

When it came time for her to make her responses she felt herself tremble. Instantly his fingers tightened reassuringly on hers.

'I, Elizabeth, take thee Ringan, to my wedded husband, to have and to hold from this day forward . . .'

And now, Mr Jenkinson was saying, 'the ring . . .'

Ringan released her hand long enough to twist a signet ring from his finger. He slid it over the knuckle of her fourth finger.

'With this ring I thee wed, with my body I thee worship . . .'

The ring was so large it hung loose on her finger and would have slid off had Ringan not folded her fingers around it and enclosed her fist once more in his own.

At last it was over. Dizzily she heard Mr Jenkinson say, 'You may now kiss the bride.'

Even more dizzily she turned to face the man who was now her husband.

His eyes held hers and then, as she made no demur, his arm slid around her waist as he lowered his head to hers.

Chapter Fifteen

His lips were soft and warm on hers. Vaguely she was conscious of noises, whoops of enthusiasm and encouragement from the spectators, but all she was really aware of was the sweetness of his kiss and the sense of security and sanctuary his enfolding arms gave.

'Right folks!' Kitty was saying to all and sundry, 'The wedding breakfast is to be at *The Eldorado*! Champagne's compulsory, so I hope you've all got thirsts!'

Reluctantly Ringan released Lilli. With troubled eyes he said, 'We're going to have to go along with things a little longer. Ye dinna mind, do ye?'

'No.' The breath was tight in her chest, her disappointment so crushing she thought she might faint. So they were only 'going along with things' were they? He wasn't considering their marriage a real marriage. They wouldn't be living together, loving and laughing and having children.

'Champagne!' Edie was saying in childlike excitement, her arm tucked through Saskatchewan Stan's, 'I've never drunk champagne before!'

'Nathaniel and I are going to return to Whitehorse so that the Methodist minister there can marry us again,' Susan was saying to her friends as they all began to stream out into Front Street and the pale light of a Dawson midnight. 'Nathaniel isn't at all sure that Mr Nelson's minister is properly licensed.'

'Will and me are leaving on a boat for Nome first thing in the morning,' Lettie was saying to Lilli. 'But I'll write. I'll write care of Miss Dufresne.'

Even though it was the middle of the night, Dawson's

252

main street was as crowded as it had been at mid-day. Dogs still dashed madly up and down, saloon doors swung open and shut continually, male laughter merged with the tinkling of a score of pianos. On the side of a frame building an enormous magic lantern projected advertising messages. Newsboys ran spryly along the duckboards selling the *Nugget*. On an open-air stand a girl was selling dances at a dollar a dance.

'Welcome to *The Eldorado*,' Kitty announced, leading the way into a hotel which was at first sight as magnificently opulent as any in San Francisco.

Still clutching her posy of forget-me-nots, Lilli stood stockstill in the dust-beaten street, staring up at the giant lettering. *The Eldorado*. Hadn't Lucky Jack told her that Eldorado was the name of his home? He had said it was big, more than thirty rooms. Had he not been referring to a house after all, but to a hotel? And if so, why hadn't he said so?

Mistaking the reason for her hesitation Ringan cupped her elbow gently. It was the first physical contact there had been between them since their nuptial kiss.

'I dinna want ye worrying about anything,' he said as Lottie skipped on ahead of them, entering the *Eldorado* at Marietta's side. 'Ye can leave for wherever ye want in the morning. There's a boat at eight o'clock for Whitehorse. Your uncle canna take Leo and Lottie away from ye now you're a married woman. And I'll see ye alright for funds. I'll arrange a bank account for ye, wherever ye settle.'

'Yes,' she said tightly, feeling as if she were dying by inches. 'You're very kind. Thank you.'

She wanted to ask him about the twenty-five thousand dollars. She wanted to ask him how on earth he had been able to pay Josh Nelson such a huge sum. She needed to ask him if he was hoping she might one day be able to repay it. She tried to speak but no words would come. All her dreams had finally and irrevocably turned to ashes. She would never live in this wonderful wild country she already loved. She would never work with the Indians. She would never give birth to Ringan Cameron's babies.

'We need to go inside,' he prompted gently, 'or people will think it a mite odd.'

Crucified by a pain almost beyond bearing she allowed him to lead her up the steps into the *Eldorado's* plushly ornate lobby.

Leo rushed to meet her. 'Where've you been? What's been happening?' he demanded, hurling himself into her arms. 'Lucky Jack's here. He's leaving for Nome tomorrow and he's packing his bags. We're not leaving for Nome, are we? My magic lady isn't. She likes Dawson and I like Dawson too.'

Before she could even begin to answer his questions Lucky Jack strolled out of what appeared to be an enormous dining-room complete with dance-floor, into the lobby.

Ringan looked swiftly towards Lilli, the pain in her eyes and the tension in her face confirming all his worst fears. She looked like a woman barely holding herself together against an inner disintegration; a woman coping with an anguish of the deepest possible kind.

'Congratulations,' Lucky Jack was saying to them breezily. 'Kitty's just told me the happy news. Seems as how I did you both a good turn by not being able to get to the *Phoenix*.'

He shot Lilli his familiar down-slanting smile and then said to Ringan, 'I was going to pay Nelson off and engage Lilli as housekeeper, here, at the *Eldorado*. It would have given her and Leo and Lottie a roof over their heads.'

He gave a slight shrug of his shoulders, his grin widening, 'As it is, this is by far the better solution to her problem, isn't it? Would you like some champagne? I've a shrewd idea Kitty's trying to show me she doesn't give a darn about me leaving tomorrow for Nome, but whether that's the reason behind the extravagance of the wedding breakfast or not, she's certainly asked the staff here to go to town on it.'

Through the open doors of the dining-room they could see laden tables. Somewhere out of their field of vision a small orchestra was playing. Will and Lettie were circling the floor to a waltz, feasting their eyes on each other. They looked like two people who had been fiercely in love with each other for months and months and months. Kate and Lord Lister began to waltz together as gracefully as if they were in a London ballroom. Saskatchewan Stan began to propel Edie clumsily but enthusiastically around the floor.

The colours of her friends' dresses blurred and merged. Pink, lemon, white. Lucky Jack had never, ever, intended marrying her. He had been going to pay Josh Nelson off for no other reason than that he wanted her as a housekeeper for one of his hotels.

It was an incredible realization. A realization that, until a few short hours ago, would have totally destroyed her. Now, however, it caused her only a dazed wonderment. How could she have read so much into so little? How could she, from the moment she had entered the Peabody Marriage Bureau, have shown such bad judgment and lack of commonsense? No wonder Lottie had so often looked at her in anxiety and accused her of being unrealistic. Lottie had known the truth about Lucky Jack and Ringan right from the very beginning. She had known that Lucky Jack was a Greek god with feet of clay just as she had always known that Ringan was a big man in every sense of the word.

The waltz came to an end. The orchestra began playing another. Lucky Jack swirled Marietta out on to the dance-floor.

Even if she hadn't mis-read everything he had said to her so totally, by neglecting to make the arrangement he had promised her he would make with Josh Nelson, he had still let her down in a way which, if it hadn't been for Ringan, would have been grievous. Kitty, of course, had prophesied he would do so. She thought of him leaving for Nome in the morning and knew that he had let Kitty down; knew too, that he and Kitty had been lovers and that beneath Kitty's apparent gaiety was a savagely bruised heart.

'We dinna have to go in and dance,' Ringan said,

cursing Lucky Jack and the effect he had had on Lilli from the bottom of his soul. 'I've a room booked at *The Fairview*. Ye can take the bed and I'll take the couch.'

The despair emanating from her in waves, increased. On the *Eldorado's* dance floor Kate and Lettie and Edie were dancing with their new husbands. Susan was standing hand in hand with hers. All of them were blissfully happy. Wherever they were going to sleep tonight, none of them would be sleeping alone whilst their bridegroom slept on a couch.

Tiredness merged with her misery and despair, nearly swamping her. She was certainly too tired to dance and to pretend to a happiness she was so far from feeling. The lonely bed it would have to be. And in the morning? Had she really no other alternative but to return to Whitehorse and from there to San Francisco or Vancouver or Seattle? Her head ached. She was too tired to think straight. Too tired to feel anything but an overwhelming sense of loss. 'I'd like to go to *The Fairview*, please,' she said stiltedly.

As they turned to leave the lobby, Marietta left Lucky Jack alone on the dance floor and hurried after them. 'Don't worry about Leo and Lottie tonight,' she said breathlessly, catching hold of Lilli's arm. 'They can stay with me in the room Kitty has given me at the *Gold Nugget*.'

'Thank you, Marietta.' Incredibly, she had forgotten all about Lottie and Leo and the problem of where they would sleep that night.

Ringan had continued to walk towards the lobby's door and as Marietta saw Lilli's unnatural paleness and the deep, dark circles of strain which were beginning to appear below her eyes, she said urgently in a low voice, 'Sweet saints' alive! From what Lottie told me I thought you were happy with the way things have turned out! You're not still grieving over Lucky Jack, are you?'

'No.' There was no doubting the sincerity of the vehemence in her denial. 'No, it's just that . . .' She looked quickly over her shoulder but Ringan was now yards away

256

from them, his back still towards them. 'He doesn't love me,' she said, her voice cracking. 'He simply saved me from an intolerable situation as he might have saved Edie or Kate or even Rosalind Nettlesham. He's suggested I leave Dawson in the morning for Whitehorse and I think that's what I'm going to have to do, Marietta. I can't stay here now, can I? Not if he doesn't want me here.'

Ringan had turned, making what Lilli now thought of as his 'Scottish noise' in his throat, in order to gain her attention.

'Bye, Marietta. If I do leave I'll write to you at the *Gold Nugget*.' The thought of not being cheered daily by Marietta's friendship was almost too much for her to bear. Swiftly she turned away, walking rapidly towards Ringan and the door.

'Ye'll miss her I dinna doubt,' he said gently, reading the cause of her distress right for once.

'Yes.' Her voice was muffled, thick with tears.

'Hst,' he said, cupping her arm gently as they began to walk down the street, his heart hurting on account of her distress, 'Ye're over-tired. Things'll not seem so bad in the morning.'

She made an inarticulate sound that could have meant anything and his jaw tightened. This wasn't how he had wanted it to be. It was their wedding night and he wanted to be dancing with her as joyously as Perry and Will and Saskatchewan Stan were dancing with their brides. And when it came to walking to *The Fairview* he wanted to be doing so with his arm around her waist and her head nestling lovingly on his shoulder.

Dear God in heaven! There had been moments, in the *Phoenix*, when he had believed all his hopes were possible. The moment when their eyes had met as he swung her down from the obscenity of a stage she had sat on to be auctioned; the moment when he had given her the posy of forget-me-nots; the moment when he had kissed her. And then they had entered the *Eldorado* and he had seen the anguish in her eyes as Lucky Jack had strode towards them, and he had known that all his hopes were vain.

257

As they entered *The Fairview* a figure not unlike Kitty hurried to meet them. 'Congratulations!' she said, beaming at them, 'One-legged Pete gave me the news a half hour ago. It sure didn't take you long to make an impression on Dawson, Mr Cameron! First time anyone's married at the *Phoenix* in full Highland fig that's for sure!'

She turned her attention to Lilli. 'The name is Belinda Mulroney and I'm right pleased to meet you. I've been in Dawson ever since the spring of '97. I floated down the Yukon on a raft with two Indians in order to reach it and I've never regretted it once. I didn't know Mr Cameron would be honeymooning here when he booked in and so he wasn't given the honeymoon suite. However, I've rectified that omission and you'll find yourselves in the best room *The Fairview* can provide, and that's saying a lot.'

As she led the way upstairs to the bedrooms she continued inundating them with information almost non-stop. 'Despite all Lucky Jack's claims for the *Eldorado*, The *Fairview* is the finest and best-appointed hostelry in town. All my twenty-two rooms are steam-heated, my table silver is sterling and my china is bone. I brought the whole lot, cut-glass chandelier, brass bedsteads, everything, over the Chilkoot and then down the Yukon on fifteen flat-bottomed boats.'

On reaching the top of the stairs she began to lead the way down a crimson-carpeted corridor, silk skirts swishing around her ankles. 'I've had the girls fill your bath with hot water and put champagne on ice. Mrs Cameron's travelling-bag has been brought over from the *Phoenix*. I always have had a soft spot for Peabody brides but a Peabody bride who's a friend of Kitty Dufresne's is a Peabody bride worth pushing the boat out for. Now . . .' she flung a mahogany door open. 'Is there anything else you folks might be wanting?'

Ringan looked at Lilli's pale, strained face. 'A bite to eat would be verra welcome,' he said tentatively, 'A sandwich, perhaps?'

'A sandwich is the most uncomplicated request I've

258

ever received. If you're so easily pleased Mr Cameron, Mrs Cameron is one hell of a lucky lady!'

Mrs Cameron had already stepped inside the bridal suite and was looking around it in horror. The fittings were sumptuous. How they had all been manhandled over the Chilkoot she couldn't even begin to imagine. The brass-headed bed was vast, its pillows in their lace-trimmed pillow-cases, plump. The bedspread was virginally white, the sheets satin-edged. On a mahogany chest was an ice-bucket containing a bottle of champagne. On a marble-top wash-stand was a rose-painted jug and washing-bowl. There was a mahogany inlaid wardrobe on bracket feet, a matching tallboy, a dark green velvet upholstered chair with a buttoned tub back and through an open door leading off from the bedroom, a claw-footed bath, steam rising from its contents. What there was not, was a couch.

The door closed as Ringan entered the room and Belinda Mulroney departed. He stood, feet set wide apart, his kilt still swinging slightly, his hands on his hipbones as he looked around the room Belinda had well-intentionally moved him into.

He registered the absence of a couch and the smallness of the chair with a sinking heart. He could hardly demand they be moved back into his previous room with its single bed and couch. If he did, the news would be all over Dawson by the morning and Josh Nelson might well take the line that Lilli's marriage was null and void.

'Dinna fret, I'll sleep in the chair,' he said easily, not wanting to cause her more distress than she was already suffering on account of Lucky Jack.

'I wasn't fretting.' It was true. Her initial horror had been on his behalf. She hadn't wanted him to be embarrassed. She hadn't wanted their few hours together to be marred by even more awkwardness.

Carefully she set her wedding bouquet down on the bed. Wearily she sat down beside it. There was so much she wanted to ask him, so much she wanted to find out about him before she left on the steamer in the morning.

And she had no alternative but to leave. They were man and wife. She couldn't build a life for herself in Dawson separate from him. The consequent talk and speculation, added to speculation about his jail-bird past, would damn him utterly amongst his new neighbours.

'As we've been given champagne, it would be a shame to waste it,' Ringan said practically, walking across to the chest, his swinging kilt magnificently accentuating his strong, well-shaped calves.

It was a typically Scottish, typically thrifty remark and she wondered again about the ease with which he had paid Josh Nelson twentyfive thousand dollars.

'The money,' she said hesitantly as he eased the champagne cork from the bottle, 'at the *Phoenix*. How did you . . .? I'll never be able to repay . . .'

He poured champagne into a fluted glass and handed it to her. 'My grandfather was one of Britain's railway kings. My father invested the wealth he inherited wisely.' The tone of his voice altered as he added dryly, 'And for the last ten years I've had no opportunity at all of spending the even greater wealth he left to me.'

She was so startled she spilt some of her champagne on her skirt. 'You mean you're *rich*?' she said incredulously. 'You haven't come to the Klondike seeking a fortune? You already have one?'

He grinned, relieved that he had at least caught her attention and taken her thoughts away from Lucky Jack. 'Aye,' he said, filling his own glass to the brim, 'so no more mention of the money I bid. It isna necessary.'

There was a knock at the door and as he crossed the room to answer it she wondered what other surprises were in store for her. She still knew nothing about the supposed crime he had been convicted of. And she didn't know how he was going to occupy himself in Dawson. Everyone else was either a prospector or living off the backs of prospectors. By his own admission Ringan didn't fall into the first category and it was beyond imagination he would ever fall into the second.

An immaculately dressed member of one of Belinda

Mulroney's bar staff entered the room bearing a mammoth silver tray of sandwiches.

The anguish she had been feeling ever since the realisation that, unlike the other Peabody marriages, their marriage was not to be a proper marriage, surged through her with fresh vengeance. If only he felt for her a smidgeon of what she now felt for him, everything would have been so perfect.

The bar-man made a discreet, speedy exit. Ringan recrossed the room towards her, setting the silver salver down beside the ice-bucket. Not for the first time she noticed that all his movements betrayed athletic muscular co-ordination and grace.

'Tell me about your prison sentence,' she said quietly. 'Tell me how you came to be wrongfully convicted.'

His eyes darkened, something very like pain flaring through them. After a long moment he said tautly, 'I wasna totally wrongfully convicted.' Several beats of silence filled the room and then he said, 'I killed a man and, though I didna intend to kill him, when I had done so I felt no remorse.' His eyes held hers. 'And I still feel no remorse,' he said, a pulse throbbing at his jaw-line.

Her mouth was dry. The fizzing champagne in her glass suddenly seemed obscenely inappropriate. 'Why?' she asked, still absolutely certain he was morally innocent. 'Tell me.'

The pulse continued to beat. He had never spoken of Patti's death with anyone. He took off his jacket and his jabot and then, unbuttoning his shirt at the throat, he said, 'My mother died when I was a wee boy and my sister, Patti, was only a bairn. My father was a businessman and always busy with his own affairs. Patti and I were left in the care of nannies and governesses and a strong bond was forged between us.'

Her eyes held his in total empathy. When her own mother had died the bonds tying her to Leo and Lottie had been cast in hoops of steel.

'Eleven years ago, when she was seventeen and I was a newly qualified doctor in Edinburgh and far from home,

261

she fell in love with a man named Tad Rowntree, a man my father immediately discerned to be a blatant fortune-hunter.

He paused again, his pain agonisingly obvious.

'They ran away together and my father called Rowntree's bluff by refusing to give permission for their marriage and striking Patti out of his will.'

There was another long pause and then he said, 'Patty became pregnant and Rowntree took her to an abortionist. Afterwards, when she lay bleeding to death, he didna even call a doctor.'

He ran his hand through his gleamingly brushed helmet of hair making it thick and tumbled again. 'When I was told, I did what any man would have done. I sought Rowntree out to give him a beating.'

'And he died from it?'

Ringan gave a small, bitter laugh. 'I only hit him the once and that was on his jaw and yes, he died. And though I've tried and I've tried, I canna be sorry for it.'

The urge to cross the room to him and offer him physical comfort was so strong she had to hug her arms to prevent herself from doing so.

'She was a verra bonny lassie,' he said thickly, 'Like you, she had true Celtic skin, so white it was almost translucent, but her hair was red, not dark. So deep and rich a red ye felt your hand would burn if it touched it.'

This time the silence was deeper and longer than ever before. She wondered if he realised the compliment he had paid her. She wondered what on earth she could say that wouldn't sound hopelessly inadequate. He had served ten years for inadvertently killing the man who had destroyed his sister. Ten years locked in a prison cell. She thought of his passionate love of nature and the way he had tried to communicate that love to Leo and Lottie and shuddered. For a man who loved wild-life and the open air as much as Ringan did, it had been a savagely hard sentence. No wonder that after such an experience he hadn't mixed easily with the prospectors aboard the *Senator* but had stood alone, gazing out to sea for hour after hour.

262

'So perhaps, now ye know the truth of it, ye'll not want to be spending the night alone with me,' he said, his voice raw.

She shook her head, lights dancing in the soft upsweep of her hair. 'No. You're wrong. What you've just told me doesn't change anything about the way I feel about our . . . our friendship. I always knew you could never have killed anyone intentionally and I'm not shocked at your inability to feel remorse. I just think you're being very truthful. Far more truthful than most people would be.'

He made his Scottish noise again in his throat, so vastly relieved by her reaction he couldn't speak.

Neither could she. The room was thick again with their silence.

'About tomorrow . . .' he began awkwardly, wanting with every fibre of his being to somehow delay her departure, to perhaps deter her from leaving Dawson at all.

'I'll leave on the morning steamer,' she said swiftly, not wanting to cause him the embarrassment of being encumbered with a wife he had no desire to set up home with. She squeezed her hand into fists, her nails digging deep into her palms, not wanting to think of Leo and Lottie's reactions when she told them they were returning immediately to Whitehorse.

'Aye . . .' His despair was so deep he wondered if he was ever going to surface from it. It was understandable, of course, that she wanted to shake the dust of Dawson off her heels at the earliest opportunity. Hadn't he, knowing how she would feel, suggested she do so? And he had done so in order that she wouldn't have to suffer remaining in close proximity to the man who had so sorely let her down; the man she had believed was going to pay off Josh Nelson and marry her; the man who, by his own admision, had only wanted her as an employee.

His jaw tightened. How must she have felt when he, and not Lucky Jack, had made the bid that had saved her from marriage with a total stranger? How must she feel now, closeted in the intimacy of a bedroom with him? 'If ye dinna mind I'll think take advantage of the bath that's

263

waiting,' he said, unable to bear the fierce frustration of being so near to her and not being able to reach out and touch her; to take her in his arms; to make love to her with all his heart and all his soul.

She was relieved. He could tell. Savagely wishing the bath waiting for him was an ice-cold one he turned mutely on his heel and entered the bathroom, pushing the door closed behind him.

Lilli shut her eyes, squeezing them tight against the tears that threatened to fall. Dear Lord in heaven, how had she come to be in such an agonizing situation? An image of spilt milk flashed into her brain and she made a small sound, half hysterical laughter, half sob. It had been Lottie's spilt glass of milk that had triggered off the row with her uncle which had culminated in him demanding she leave his house for good. And then she had seen the newspaper article about Harriet Berton and her husband. And she had emulated Harriet Berton and stepped over the threshold of the Peabody Marriage Bureau.

She drew in a deep, shuddering breath. In many ways she didn't regret that step at all. It had led to her meeting Susan and Kate and Edie and Marietta and making friends she knew would be her friends for life. It had also led her to Alaska and the Yukon Valley and the scenery she had seen from the *Casca's* decks, blue hills rolling on towards the rim of the world and small creeks gurgling and bubbling down into the mighty river, were images that would stay with her forever.

If only she hadn't become so air-headedly besotted with Lucky Jack! If only Ringan had never seen her in such an intimate embrace with Lucky Jack! Then, perhaps, she would have realised the enormity of her feelings for Ringan much, much earlier. She would have sought out his company, as Lottie had done. And if she had done so perhaps he would have come to love her, instead of merely feeling compassion for her.

With heavy limbs she swung her legs from the bed. If she was to wash and clamber into her nightdress, then now was the time for her to do so.

The bathroom door hadn't quite shut and there were sounds of vigorous splashing. Presumably he was rinsing soap from his back. Trying hard not to think of how magnificent a sight his naked back would be she poured water from the washing jug into the bowl. Then, certain that he wouldn't re-enter the bedroom without first verifying she was decently clothed, she removed the cameo from the neck of her blouse and undid the tiny mother-of-pearl buttons at her wrists.

Once in her shift and bloomers she washed as adequately as she was able. The cold water revived her and her despair began to lift as her innate optimism re-asserted itself. She was *married* to Ringan. He had generously promised to open a bank account for her wherever she chose to settle. That meant that he would be remaining in touch with her. And that meant that there was at least hope that their relationship would change in character. They were, after all, already friends. That had been determined during the hours they had spent together at the Indian camp. And, given time and proper encouragement, friendship could lead to love.

As the sounds of splashing and wallowing continued she drew her nightdress from her travelling-bag and slid it over her head, then she removed her shift and bloomers. High-necked and long-sleeved and made of serviceable cambric, it wasn't the garment she would have chosen to wear on her wedding night. But then, she reminded herself, this wasn't her wedding night in the true sense of the word.

Bare-footed, she padded across to the bed and picked up her posy of forget-me-nots. He had picked them himself and he had chosen them because they matched the colour of her eyes. With hope coursing strongly though her veins she detached a tiny spray from the posy. She would press it in her New Testament. She would keep it for ever and ever.

The splashing abruptly ceased. There was a long moment's silence. His travel-bag was still near the door where the bell-boy had presumably deposited it. She wondered what he would be wearing when he emerged. Had he taken his night-shirt into the bathroom with him? And if not, would he dress again in full Highland regalia, even though it would mean his having to sleep in it?

The bathroom door opened a little hesitantly. 'Ye'll excuse me,' he said, a slow, fierce blush burning its way up from his throat, 'but I forgot to take my nightshirt with me.'

She was exceedingly glad he had done so. With only a white bath towel draped around his hips he looked even more wonderful than he had done in his kilt. His thick thatch of curly hair dripped water, the red transmuted a dark, rich mahogany. His powerful shoulders looked even broader naked than they had clothed. Gleaming wet, reddish-gold fuzz dusted his chest and his strong, well-shaped calves.

Grabbing his nightshirt from his bag he strode swiftly back into the privacy of the bathroom. She was aware of a quite shocking feeling of disappointment.

She climbed into the big, high bed. The chair looked very, very small and uncomfortable. Dare she suggest to him that he shared the bed with her? At the mere thought her cheeks burned even brighter than his had when he had emerged semi-naked from the bathroom. No, she could not. He would remember seeing her in Lucky Jack's embrace aboard the *Senator* and he would think her shameless. And if he thought her shameless he would never come to love her.

She pulled the bed-covers high above her cambric-covered breasts. How could she possibly have thought Lucky Jack was the be-all and the end-all of her world? He was a charmer, a likeable charmer, and that was all. And because of him she had probably lost all hope of Ringan ever regarding her with respect.

'I'll turn the lamps out,' he said, emerging from the bathroom once again, his nightshirt open at the throat to reveal the strong tendons in his neck, his hair still tumbled and damp.

She nodded assent. Even without the lamps a rosy light

still pervaded the room, for the Northern night sky was flushed with apricot.

He extinguished the lamps and through the window, against the deep, dark gold of the sky, the mountain that reared over Dawson could be seen, the gash in its flank showing a ghostly white.

Her stomach muscles tightened. It was going to be so hard to leave in the morning. Not only because she would be leaving Ringan behind and because she didn't know how she was going to persuade him to meet with her again, but because she would be leaving all the beauty of the Yukon Valley behind her also. She thought of the colourful Indian encampments and of caribou wading against the river's current and bears fishing with their giant paws, and her heart physically hurt her. All her life she had led a nomadic existence, moving first from Ireland to America and then, once in America, from Wyoming to Colorado to Montana to San Francisco. And now, when she had at last found the place where she felt truly at home, she was going to leave it, probably for ever.

'You need a blanket,' she said, her voice brusque as she fought to control her distress. Without waiting for him to say that he did, or did not, she swung her legs from the bed and stood up, gathering the top blanket in her arms and walking towards him with it.

'Thank ye.' He couldn't have said another word if he'd been paid a thousand dollars to do so. As she crossed the room to him the window was behind her and against the golden light the outline of her body showed with breathtaking clarity. He could see the high fullness of her breasts and the dark aureoles of her nipples; the narrowness of her waist, the soft, gentle roundness of her hips.

Blissfully unaware, Lilli handed him the blanket. She slowly made her way back to the lonely bed.

'Tell me,' she said when she was once again demurely beneath the covers, 'about your childhood. Where did you and Patti live? What games did you play? Where did you go to school?'

Deeply thankful of the blanket that so mercifully hid the physical effect she had had on him, he said in a strained voice, 'We were both born and brought up at Dalhaiveg House, a turreted monstrosity my grandfather built for himself in the 1860's.' With difficulty he forced his voice back to normality. 'It's buried away deep in the heart of Skye. It's a verra beautiful and verra lonely, which is perhaps why so much of the Yukon countryside reminds me of it.'

He told her of how his grandfather had taught both himself and Patti to fish for salmon in the Strath. How, as little more than toddlers, he had taken them high up the slopes of Sgurr Alasdair. And then he had realised that she was asleep, her arms curled around her pillow, her eyelashes soft against her cheek.

It wasn't surprising. It had been a long, long day. A day so emotionally charged and nervously exhausting it was a wonder she hadn't fallen asleep hours and hours ago. He wondered if he would be able to sleep and doubted it. He had too much to brood over; too much fierce disappointment to try and come to terms with.

Chapter Sixteen

When she woke a few hours later he was already dressed, not in his kilt and wonderful balloon-sleeved shirt, but in his serviceable green plaid shirt and breeches and boots.

'There's some coffee,' he said, indicating a silver breakfast tray. 'I thought I'd go and collect Leo and Lottie and then ye can have a bath if ye want to. The maids will fill it in two shakes of a lamb's tail.'

'Yes. Thank you.' She knew she sounded stilted but she couldn't help it. What else could she say to him? That she didn't want him to go for Leo and Lottie? That she didn't want to leave on the eight-o-clock boat? That she wanted him to have breakfast with her here, in their room?

Reluctantly she heaved herself from the bed and rang the service bell. She would have a bath. As long a bath and as hot a bath as possible, for there was no telling how long it might be before she would next be able to have one. And she wouldn't cry. Not until she was safely aboard the steamer. And then, she knew, she would cry as if her heart would break.

'Leaving?' Lottie stared at Ringan in incredulity. 'But why? I thought we were all going to live in Dawson together! I thought we were going to be a *family* together!'

'It's nae that easy, Lottie,' Ringan said, wondering if this moment wasn't going to prove to be the hardest moment of all. 'Your sister needs to get away from Dawson and she needs to do so as soon as possible.'

'But *why*' Lottie demanded wildly. 'I thought everything was going to be perfect now! I thought . . .'

269

'Because I've told her to,' he said gently, totally unable to explain to her that as Lilli wasn't in love with him she couldn't possibly live in the intimacy of marriage with him. Lottie was only ten years old, for the Lord's sake! She'd had enough to contend with already without his burdening her with facts of life she was too young to fully understand.

'Oh!' she stared at him, her world falling apart. If Lilli was leaving Dawson because Ringan had told her she must do so, it meant only one thing. It meant that though Ringan had rescued Lilli from marriage with a stranger, he didn't want her for a real wife. He didn't love Lilli as she had hoped and prayed he loved her. They weren't going to be a family together. They weren't all going to live together happily ever after.

'I think we'd better pack your gold ribbons and sash into your travel-bag,' Marietta said slowly, feeling almost as sledge-hammered as Lilli and just as bewildered.

Leo looked around at their shocked, distressed faces. 'Are we leaving? Really leaving? Won't I see my magic lady ever again?'

No-one could bear to answer him. All of them had thought that when they had left the *Phoenix* the worst was behind them. Now they all knew that the worst was yet to come.

She was dressed and waiting for him when he returned to their hotel room. The lace shirtwaist and blue skirt that had served as her bridal gown were carefully packed in her travel-bag. She would never think of them as being ordinary day wear ever again. 'Where are Leo and Lottie?' she asked, her voice sounding as if she were going down with a cold.

She was wearing her caramel coloured shirtwaist and a toffee coloured skirt, the rich warm colours emphasising the blue of her eyes and near-jet darkness of her upswept hair.

She was so beautiful, and Ringan's pain at the thought

of so soon saying goodbye to her was so intense, that when he answered her his voice sounded as odd as hers.

'With Marietta. They're . . . distressed. Marietta is going to bring them down to the wharf and meet us there.'

She was aware of a feeling of vast relief. They would at least have a little more time together alone. For a little longer she could pretend they were embarking on a life together just as Susan and Mr Jenkinson were, and Lettie and Will, and Kate and Perry.

He picked up her shabby carpet-bag, and opened the room door. They were going. And though he would be returning, she would not.

Outside the *Fairview*, Front Street was as busy and noisy as it had been the previous evening. Lilli wondered if it was ever quiet.

They began to walk in the direction of the river, their feet tom-tomming on the hollow boardwalk.

'What will you do?' she asked, wanting, when they were apart, to be able to imagine his daily routine. 'Will you practise medicine in Dawson?'

Beneath his bushy auburn moustache his lips twisted in a wry smile. 'Not quite.'

She waited, accustomed now to the little silences that peppered his speech, sensing they occurred only when he was speaking of things that mattered deeply to him.

'It would be difficult,' he said at last. 'Gossip about my conviction is soon going to spread and I don't see why anyone should trust a doctor who has been convicted of murder, do you?'

They were in sight of the river now. The morning sun glittered on the turbulent grey surface of the water and the purple-hazed hills beyond.

'But I am going to practise my profession,' he said, and the passionate intensity in his voice went through her like an electric charge. 'And I'm going to practise it where it is most needed. I'm going to practise it amongst the Indians.'

271

She stumbled and, if he hadn't shot out a hand to steady her, would have fallen.

'Do ye find that surprising?' he asked, knowing how different such a life would be from the life Lucky Jack and his kind led.

'Yes. No.' How could she say what was in her heart? That she, too, wanted to work with, and help, the Indians? That if he loved her they could do so together? As she thought of what might have been it was like seeing a glimpse of paradise. And she was being denied that paradise; she was being cast out into an outer darkness of loneliness and loss.

They were at the wharf now. Steam was rising from the *Casca's* funnels as, nearly empty of passengers, she prepared to make the journey up-river, back to Whitehorse. Other steamers and scows, crammed to the gunnels with men and supplies, were facing down-river, about to depart for the long haul to the Yukon's mouth and Nome.

As they stepped onto the dock Lettie hurried to greet them. 'Where on earth are you going?' she asked bewilderedly, the happiness that had been sparkling in her eyes vanishing at the sight of Lilli's pale, taut face and the familiar travel-bag Ringan was carrying.

'Whitehorse.' Lilli didn't trust herself to say anymore. If she did, she might lose her hard fought-for composure entirely.

Lettie stared at her in dismayed disbelief, her radiance ebbing entirely.

Will had joined them and as he saw the expression on her face he said in concern' 'What's the matter, sweetheart?'

Unable to tell him she put a hand reassuringly on his arm. The gesture was so loving and so intimate that Lilli's throat almost closed entirely. Twenty-four hours ago Lettie and Will hadn't even met. Now they were man and wife; as deeply bonded as if they had loved each other for years.

'Are you leaving for Nome now?' Lilli asked, striving for an appearance of normality.

Lettie nodded. 'But I'll write. Kitty is going to act as a letter drop for all of us. Saskatchewan Stan and Edie are leaving this afternoon for Stan's claim at Clinton Creek. Kate and Perry are staying on in Dawson until they decide whether or not to follow Will and me to Nome. Mr Jenkinson and Susan are . . .'

'We're sailing for Whitehorse this afternoon,' Susan finished for her as she strode up to them, a parasol held aloft in a net-gloved hand. 'We'd hoped to sail his morning but we've received a lunch invitation from Mr Tomlinson, the federal commissioner.'

She moved slightly, so that she was standing between Lilli and Ringan and so that, when she lowered he voice, Ringan wouldn't overhear her. 'I'm so sorry,' she said, choked with emotion. 'I'd thought you would be staying in Dawson. Mr Cameron is such a fine man . . . I'd hoped . . .'

'Yes,' Lilli said bleakly, knowing everything that Susan was trying to say and wondering for how much longer the torture could continue, 'So had I.'

The steamer whistle blew. Marietta hurried into view, Leo and Lottie trailing behind her. A buggy rattled to a halt and Kate and Lord Lister hastily stepped out of it.

'Where's Edie?' Lilli asked, an edge of panic entering her voice. 'I can't leave without saying goodbye to Edie!'

Ringan felt as if he were in the seventh circle of hell. He'd hoped to be able to say goodbye to her in relative privacy. Why hadn't he realised all her friends would be here to say goodbye to her? Why hadn't he realised how utterly and totally impossible the whole process of saying goodbye to her was going to be?

'Write to me care of The *Fairview*,' he said urgently, interrupting her goodbye to Marietta. 'Though I'll be spending nearly all my time on the river and with the Indians, The *Fairview* will be my base. There's money in your carpet-bag. I put it there last night when ye were sleeping. And the instant ye settle, give me the address of a local bank and I'll see money is regularly transferred.'

'Yes. Thankyou.' Hysteria bubbled in her throat. The

two trite words seemed to be the only words she was capable of saying to him.

'Are we sailing on the *Casca*?' Lottie asked, as pale-faced and as hunched as if she were a beaten child. 'What is Captain Stoddart going to say when he sees us again?'

Lilli didn't know and she didn't care. She only knew her heart was breaking and that if she didn't board the *Casca* immediately, the entire world would know it was doing so.

'Goodbye,' she said, the tears burning the backs of her eyes. 'Give my love to Edie. Tell her I'll write. I'll write to all of you.'

The *Casca's* whistle shrilled again. Leo began to cry. Harsh, tearing sobs that shuddered his entire body. No-one made a move to comfort him, knowing that all comfort would be vain.

In a sea of pain Lilli stretched out her hand and took her carpet-bag from Ringan's grasp. 'Goodbye,' she said, not able to look him in the eyes. Knowing that if she did so she would be totally lost. 'Thank you for . . . for everything,' and then, before he could even say goodbye in response, before the sound of his voice should unhinge her completely, she turned on her heel, walking quickly up the the steep incline of the *Casca's* gangplank.

'Lord in heaven,' Marietta said as Lottie, her little face bruised with grief, took hold of Leo's hand and began walking after Lilli with such unsteady steps she might have been blind.

Numbly they watched the children join Lilli at the deckrail; in stricken disbelief their eyes remained on them as the *Casca* began to pull away, heading out into the centre of the river.

'Lord in heaven,' Marietta said again, tears streaming down her face, 'How could you ask her to leave, Ringan? How could you send the three of them away?'

'She couldn't have stayed.' His voice was harsh, his eyes still fixed on the dark-haired figure in the caramel coloured shirtwaist and toffee coloured skirt as the *Casca* approached the first of the hundreds of bends that lay between Dawson and Whitehorse. 'It would have pained her too much.'

'Pained her?' The speaker wasn't Marietta, but Mr Jenkinson. 'But how? She wanted so much to make her life here. She asked me, if I were to open a school for Indian children, if she could work with me, teaching them. I feel badly that I told her there would be no such school, that I wouldn't be staying in Dawson, but that was, of course, when I thought Miss Bumby . . . when I thought Mrs Jenkinson . . . lost to me.'

The *Casca* steamed around the bend; was gone. All that remained was the white spume of her wake as it rippled the river's steel-grey surface.

'The Indians?' Ringan dragged his eyes away from the empty river, facing Mr Jenkinson. 'The Indians?' he said again dazedly, 'Lilli wanted to work with the Indians?'

'She most certainly did,' Mr Jenkinson said vehemently, wondering if his own statement, that there would be no school for Indian children at which she could teach, had been a contributing factor in Lilli's decision to leave and hoping very much that it hadn't.

Ringan felt as if the ground were shelving away at his feet. Dear God in heaven! Why hadn't she told him of her desire to work with Indian children when he had told her his own plans? Their mutual ambitions were, after all, wonderfully compatible. Or they would have been if only she could have remained in the Yukon Valley without being tormented by the thought of Lucky Jack's proximity.

'Are you really sailing with us this afternoon?' Lettie was asking Marietta.

With difficulty Marietta dragged her attention from Ringan's tortured face. What on earth had taken place between him and Lilli? Why were two people, so clearly destined for each other, making each other so very, very unhappy?

'Yes. Lucky Jack is supervising the loading of his supplies right now. He might have initially arrived in

Dawson with only the goods he could carry on his back, but he certainly isn't leaving that way!'

Ringan stared at her in stupified disbelief. 'Leaving? Coolidge is leaving for Nome? And taking you with him?'

Marietta nodded, returning her attention to him, wondering why on earth he found the news so staggering.

'For Christ's sake, woman! Why didna ye tell me sooner?' His face was sheet-white, every muscle he possessed clenched as tightly as a coiled spring.

Marietta's pekinese eyes widened. 'But why should I have? Why does it matter?'

'*Because if she'd known Coolidge was leaving Dawson, Lilli might have stayed!*'

Now not only Marietta was staring at him as if he had taken leave of his senses. So was everyone else.

'But Lilli did know,' Marietta said, a terrible suspicion forming in her mind. 'I told her here, on the wharf. She was pleased for me. She said Lucky Jack and I were so obviously suited and . . .'

Now it was Ringan's turn to stare in dumbfounded incomprehension. 'How could she have?' he protested, his grey eyes incredulous. 'She's in love with the man! It nearly killed her when he didna keep his promise to marry her! Did ye not see how distressed she was this morning? Her heart's been broken and it's Coolidge who's broken it!'

A ring of faces stared at him, Will Bennett's and Mr Jenkinson's bewildered. Marietta's face, and Kate's and Lettie's and Susan's and even Perry's, far from bewildered. There was a terrible look of stricken understanding in their eyes.

'No,' Marietta said to him slowly, 'It isn't Lucky Jack who has broken Lilli's heart. Lilli was never truly in love with Lucky Jack. She was girlishly infatuated with him for a time, but she had realised just how immature her infatuation was long before she stepped inside the *Phoenix*. The man who bid for her was the man she had come to truly love. And her hopes that he had bid for

276

her because he was as much in love with her as she was with him, were crushed utterly when he suggested she leave on this morning's steamer. The only reason Lilli has left Dawson is that she believes you wanted her to leave, Ringan. She believes that, if she had stayed, she would have been an embarrassment to you.'

'Dear Jesus Christ!' the words were a whisper. He was white to the lips. 'Are ye absolutely sure?'

She didn't even have to answer him. He could see the truth in her face. He could see it in Susan's face, and Kate's, and Lettie's.

'I need to hire a steamboat,' he said hoarsely, 'The *Casca* will be stopping at the Indian camp to take on cord wood. I can catch up with her there! For the Lord's sake, Perry! *Help me get my hands on a boat!*'

Lilli stood on deck, gripping hold of the deck rail so tightly her knuckles were white. There was no longer any sign of Dawson. A huge rocky bluff hid the town from sight. All the valiant optimism she had clung to earlier in the morning, her certainty that somehow she would make Ringan learn to love her, had vanished. How could she make him learn to love her when, no matter where she settled outside Alaska, thousands of miles would divide them?

The scenery that had filled her with such deep pleasure on her voyage down-river, now made no impact on her at all. Sightlessly she stared out across the swirling grey water at steep ravines and broad valleys and wooded creeks.

When she had settled somewhere and he had arranged for money to be paid into a bank account for her he would, no doubt, divorce her. He could, after all, do so with ease. Their marriage was unconsummated. She thought of the heat that had suffused her when she he had walked from the bathroom into the bedroom with only a bath-towel around his hips for covering. She hadn't wanted their marriage to remain unconsummated. She had wanted him with fierce hunger and, God help her, she still did so.

The *Casca* steamed around yet another bend. Soon they would be at the Indian encampment where they had stopped on their journey down-river for cord wood. She wondered if Lottie would want to visit it again; if she would want to see how Nana's baby brother was progressing.

Tears glittered on her eyelashes. Whether Lottie wanted to or not, *she* would visit it again. It was there where she had first realised just how special a person Ringan was. It was there, though she hadn't realised it at the time, that she had fallen in love with him.

'No, I don't want to go.' Lottie's eyes were red-rimmed from weeping. In the bunk above her Leo was exhaustedly asleep after crying until he could cry no more.

'Then I'll go by myself,' Lilli said, hoping that her relief at being able to do so didn't show. She wanted to be able to think about Ringan in privacy. She wanted to be able to remember so vividly, it would be like re-living those few precious hours all over again.

Very few people were travelling up-river to Whitehorse. The traffic was all the other way, to Dawson and then to the Yukon's mouth, and Nome. The only person in the boat leaving for the shore, apart from the member of the *Casca's* crew at the oars, was herself.

She stepped ashore to a tumult of barking and howling. 'Don't try and frighten me,' she said to the dogs, 'because you'll be wasting your time. I've been here before, remember?'

The dogs, it appeared, remembered. They swarmed around her but didn't snap at her.

'Missy! Missy!' a familiar voice cried joyously.

With Lottie's sailor-hat perched incongruously on her sleek-black hair, Nana ran to meet her, her eyes shining with welcome. 'You comum see papoose?' she asked breathlessly, sliding her hand in hers. 'You comum with more medicine? You comum to talket Nana?'

'Yes,' she said, as Nana danced along at her side and

278

they walked towards her family tepee, 'I've come to see your baby brother and talk with you.'

This time when Nana's grandmother rushed out of the tepee towards her, it was to greet her with toothless enthusiasm, not panic-stricken anxiety.

Within minutes she was being treated like a royal guest. Nana darted off to gather up her friends so that they, too, could make Lilli's acquaintance. Everyone wanted to know where the 'one with hair like the setting sun' was.

'He's in Dawson,' she said as Nana darted back inside the tepee.

'No,' Nana said vehemently, overhearing Lilli's last remark. 'The one with hair like the setting sun is comum. He comum now.'

Lilli stared at her. Was it possible Nana had misunderstood her or that she had misunderstood Nana?

'Mr Cameron is in Dawson,' she said again and then, through the open flap of the tepee, she saw down to the Yukon's banks; saw the smaller version of the *Casca* that had moored there; saw the tall, broad-shouldered, red-headed figure striding purposefully through a sea of dogs towards her.

Her heart began to slam in such heavy strokes she thought it was going to fail her. He had sailed after the *Casca*! Why? For what possible reason could he have done so?

Stumbling slightly, she walked to the open flap; stepped outside it. He was now only fifteen yards or so away from her and she could see the expression on his face clearly. It was one that left her in no doubt as to his motives for sailing after the *Casca*. He had come for her. He had come to take her with him back to Dawson.

'Ringan . . .?' His name was tentative on her lips and then he began to sprint towards her and all the misunderstandings that had ever existed between them were dust in the wind.

'Oh, God!' she sobbed, 'Oh Ringan! *Ringan!*'

She was running. Running as she had never run before in her life. Running as if she had wings on her heels.

Oblivious of children and dogs, oblivious of everything but the knowledge that he had come to take her back with him because he loved her, she raced towards him, entering his arms like an arrow entering the gold.

'Can ye ever forgive me?' he asked, his voice cracking with joy and thankfulness as his arms at last enfolded her. 'Can ye ever forgive me for being such a verra great fool?'

She could feel his heart hammering next to hers; feel the hard, powerful strength of his body, a body that would always love, honour and protect her.

'Oh, yes,' she said, raising her radiant face to his, 'as long as you promise me you'll never be so foolish ever again!'

'I promise.' There was deep, sweet laughter in his voice and then, as the children and dogs surged around them, he said thickly, 'I love ye, Lilli. I shall love ye for always.'

'And I shall love you for always,' she said passionately, tears of joy shimmering on her cheeks. 'Forever and throughout all eternity!'

His mouth came down hard and sweet on hers. Far out in the river the *Casca*'s whistle began to shrill insistently. Both of them ignored it. They ignored it for for a very, very long time.

Epilogue

The log cabin was sturdily built, set beside a gurgling creek in a valley thick with lupins and forget-me-nots. Red gingham-check curtains fluttered at its open windows, white briar roses surged around its door. A little distance away were two larger log buildings. One had the word CLINIC carved above its doorway, the other proudly displayed the word SCHOOL.

Children were playing on the intervening grassy ground. The majority of them were Siwashes, their hair night-black, their cheekbones high. Two of them, however, a boy and a girl, were red-haired. The boy was six years old and sturdy-limbed with a scattering of freckles across his nose. The girl was three years his junior, chubby-legged and with a mop of curly hair not carrot-red, but a rich, warm Titian.

As their laughter drifted in through the cabin's open windows, Lilli continued with her task of kneading pastry for a last batch of tarts and smiled to herself. It was a glorious day. The anniversary of her, and her friends' arrival in Dawson, always was.

Eight years. She paused in her task, looking out at the school-house and the clinic. The school-house was her domain, only closed today because it was such a special day. And the clinic was closed because Ringan was down-river, dealing with a medical emergency at a Tagish Indian camp. She resumed her task, rolling the pastry out on a floured board, hoping he would be back before their guests began to arrive.

Susan and Nathanial would, of course, be the first to put in an appearance. They always were. Kate and Perry would be hard on their heels, bringing their five year old daughter with them. Lettie and Will would have their seven year old son with them. A son who, to judge by his birthday, had been conceived on Lettie and Will's wedding night. Kitty would arrive with the federal commissioner, a gentleman she had married three years ago. They would bring Rosalind Nettlesham, now Dawson's dressmaker *extraordinaire*, with them. Stan and Edie would arrive noisily and in happy chaos, their three little girls whooping and shouting in the back of their battered buggy. And Marietta and Lucky Jack who, after several gold-rich years at Nome, had finally settled at Fairbanks, would arrive last and in great style.

Using an up-turned enamel mug Lilli skewered out tart-sized rounds of pastry. Lottie and Nana were gathering flowers with which to decorate the mammoth dining-table set up in the school-room, where Lottie also, now taught. Leo was up on the hill-side behind the cabin, avidly bird-watching and making notes. The minute he saw the first of their visitors arriving he would be down to greet them.

She began spooning raspberry jam she had made last autumn into the tart cases. As she did so the baby within her womb stirred, its movements as light as butterfly wings. A smile of happiness curved her lips. Lettie, too, was pregnant again. And perhaps Edie would be, or even Kate or Susan or, now that she and Lucky Jack were married, Marietta. At the thought of Lucky Jack as a father her smile deepened and then she looked through the window and dropped her spoon with a clatter.

Ringan was back! He was back and, as always when she caught unexpected sight of him, tall and broad-shouldered, his hair as fiery as a burning brand, excitement spiralled through her.

Hastily she took off her apron. Hurriedly she made for the door. He waved when he saw her and, her heart singing with joy, she wiped a smudge of flour from her cheek and began to make her way over the forget-me-not starred grass to meet the man who was the centre of her world; the man she loved with all her heart.